Reconciling With the Rival

Emily Tudor

For anyone who has ever been told that they're too much. You'll never be too much of anything for the people who are just right for you. Sing louder. Shine brighter. Never stop being authentically yourself.

And for Lexi—this book was always going to be for you.

Content Warnings

This book features on-page descriptions of childhood trauma, parental abandonment, depression, parental health struggles, and explicit sexual content and language. Please proceed cautiously.

Dicktionary

For those who want to skip the spicy parts, or those who want to skip straight to them. Whatever you prefer!

Playlist

After Hours by The Weeknd
Bad for Business by Sabrina Carpenter
Bed Chem by Sabrina Carpenter
Calling After Me by Wallows
Casual by Chappell Roan
Cinderella (feat. Ty Dolla $ign) by Mac Miller
Don't Blame Me (Taylor's Version) by Taylor Swift
English Love Affair by 5 Seconds of Summer
Floating in the Night by Judah & The Lion
Full machine by Gracie Abrams
gold rush by Taylor Swift
THE GREATEST by Billie Eilish
HER by Chase Atlantic
ICU by Phoebe Bridgers
Love by Lana Del Rey
LOVE IS (NOT) EASY by Chase Atlantic
The Man by Taylor Swift
needy by Ariana Grande
Power Couple by Labrinth

Ruin My Life by Zara Larsson
so american by Olivia Rodrigo
Somebody Else by the 1975
Streets by Doja Cat
Summer Child by Conan Gray
Talk by Hozier
Tell Me How by Paramore
Temporary Fix by One Direction
Tonight (I Wish I Was Your Boy) by the 1975
True Blue by boygenius
us. (feat. Taylor Swift) by Gracie Abrams

"It is literally impossible to be a woman. Like, we have to always be extraordinary, but somehow, we're always doing it wrong. You have to be a boss, but you can't be mean. You have to lead, but you can't squash other people's ideas. You have to be a career woman, but also always be looking out for other people. You have to answer for men's bad behavior, which is insane, but if you point that out, you're accused of complaining. You have to never get old, never be rude, never show off, never be selfish, never fall down, never fail, never show fear, never get out of line. It's too hard! It's too contradictory, and nobody gives you a medal or says thank you! And it turns out in fact that not only are you doing everything wrong, but also everything is your fault. I'm just so tired of watching myself and every single other woman tie herself into knots so that people will like us."

— AMERICA FERRARA, *Barbie*

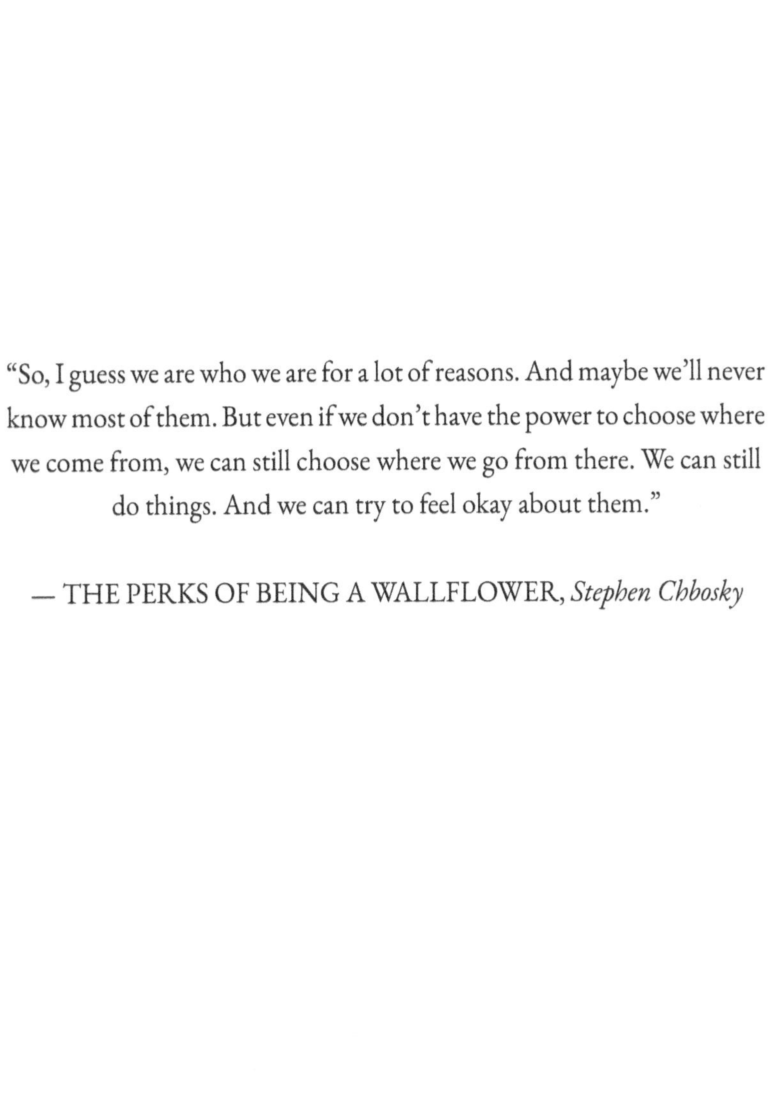

"So, I guess we are who we are for a lot of reasons. And maybe we'll never know most of them. But even if we don't have the power to choose where we come from, we can still choose where we go from there. We can still do things. And we can try to feel okay about them."

— THE PERKS OF BEING A WALLFLOWER, *Stephen Chbosky*

Prologue

Little Bitch Drink

September 2021

"Four tequila shots, please!" I shout to the bartender on duty tonight. The Hidden Bear is *packed* with people, since the semester just started. I look around the bar and see a few hockey players, some people I know from classes I've taken, and a few *really* cute girls dancing. When I look at the booth I came from, I see my beautiful friends, who I've once again dragged here for a night out.

My girls.

Hads, Paige, and Amelia are having a heated conversation that probably has something to do with the book we just finished. For once, the four of us were split down the middle in how we felt about it. Amelia and I have made it our new obsession, Paige thought it was just good, and Hads hated it. For me, it was the perfect literary equivalent to the show *Gossip Girl*, and it was everything I didn't know I needed. It focused on high society, fashion, and there was so much drama, it made me want to start a rewatch.

I think Paige will come around when we read the second book, but part of me knew Hads wasn't going to like it. It wasn't her cup of tea, but our conversations about it have spread out of the tiny classroom we meet in every Wednesday and into the bar we're at.

The bartender places a single shot in front of me, and I go to open my mouth when he points to some guy at the end of the bar. The mystery man looking in my direction looks like a deer caught in headlights, but damn, he's kind of cute.

He seems too shy for someone who just sent me a tequila shot.

Whatever. I down the shot in one go and look back at the bartender. "Can I get four more of those, please?" I throw him a smile, and he pours them out for me. The girls are going to hate me for these, since they all hate tequila, but I don't care.

Oh shit, Paige is technically our designated driver, even though we walked here. Paige doesn't drink much, so I'll have to take two of these.

I'm leaning against the bar when someone taps me on the shoulder. I turn around, thinking it's one of the girls, but it's the guy who sent me the shot a few moments ago. "Can I help you?"

"You never sent anything back." He's yelling since the music is so loud, but I can hear him clearly enough because of how close he is.

Is that an accent I'm detecting? "What?"

"I sent a shot to you, although you're not who I was *trying* to send it to—the bartender must've misheard me—but you still didn't have the decency to return one." He smiles and puts his drink to his lips, and damn, he was cute until he opened his mouth. What a shame. I follow his eyes to the girl he *meant* to send a shot to—a cute blonde at the end of the bar.

"I'm sorry, that shot *wasn't* for me? How sad for you that the girl it was meant for seems to be going for someone else now." We both look over at the girl at the end of the bar—cute—but she's leaving hand in hand with some hockey player. "Better luck next time, *loverboy*."

He smirks at me. "You have that drink on me, darling. The only drink someone buys you, and it wasn't even meant for you. How sad."

Who the hell does this guy think he is? "I'm trying to have a nice night, and you're ruining it. Run along and send tequila to someone who will tolerate your attitude."

"Oh, I don't know," he looks me up and down, "I've always quite liked playing with fire..." He takes another sip of his little bitch drink and then walks away. *What the fuck?* I've never seen him before, and I find myself wondering if he goes to school at Grand Mountain.

Whatever. I shake off the conversation, grab the four shots on the bar, and head back to my friends.

"I don't condone murder, but when it's fictional and he does it to protect his girl, I don't care!" Paige is shouting at Hads and Amelia, and weirdly enough, this isn't the oddest thing I've heard her say.

"Easy, girl," I say as I place the drinks in front of them.

"Ells, please tell me this isn't tequila," Amelia says as she picks up the shot, smells it, and gags.

"I know you usually like prosecco, but we're celebrating tonight. It's mandatory you guys do a shot with me."

"What are we celebrating?" Hads asks the table. "Amelia's birthday isn't for a few weeks, and school just started."

"Are we celebrating the fact that I finally got out of my reading slump?" Paige asks, her eyes all bright like usual.

"No. We're celebrating my senior year and that the four of us are much closer to real life." I hold my shot up, signaling a toast. "To the beginning of the end!"

I hear Paige sniffle a little bit as she raises her water. "Ella, I don't want you to leave, but I know you'll have to go eventually. So, to Ella!"

"To Ella!" Hads and Amelia join as we all tip our shots back. I take Paige's with no problem. After a few moans and groans and dragging Paige to the dance floor, I tell them I'm getting another round, and before I can hear them complain, I walk to the bar.

I notice a cute girl sitting at one of the stools when I'm up there, so I make eyes with her for a few seconds before she gets up and comes over to me. "Do you wanna dance?"

"Absolutely, I do. Let me bring these to my friends." I head back, down another shot of tequila, and head off to dance.

After some dancing, I end up leaving with her, and Paige promises me she'll get Hads and Amelia home safe. I make her swear she'll text me pictures of them in bed so I know they're actually home, but she tells me to go have fun and to stop worrying about them.

I don't know if that will ever happen, but I definitely need to let loose a little, and some fun sex with this smoke show is the best way to do that.

Senior year is off to a good start.

1

Subpar Dick

June 2024

"So, DID YOU FUCK him or not?" I ask my roommate and best friend as she sips on her Aperol spritz with lemonade.

"Babes, it was the first date, so no. I usually wait until the third, but most of them are so boring. Their chat is so dry."

I laugh before taking a drink of my lavender martini. Alissa is far tamer than I am in the dating department, but the two of us have been in the same boat for a while—we haven't had much luck dating-wise.

Not that we're trying to find partners, but even our one night stands have been shitty.

Regardless of what Paige says, I don't mind being single. In fact, I love it. It's way easier, and based on the way my last relationship ended, I don't want to be tied up again. If she would stop texting me begging to get back together, the two of us could move on. God knows I've moved on already after a year, and I'm close to blocking her number so she takes a fucking hint. "Subpar dick is better than none if it means avoiding a drought, Liss. Just saying."

"Ells, I barely have time as it is. If I'm going to fuck, it needs to be good."

Alissa Zimmerman is too busy girlbossing in the private sector as some sort of hacker or something to have a long-term relationship. I don't really know what she does, because when she explained it, none of what she said made any sense. Something with analysis, or data...I think? Either way, she's a badass. That's all that matters.

Alissa flips her long brown hair as she takes another sip of her drink. I don't know how she manages to just sit and look as beautiful as she does, but once she opens her mouth, her spunky personality shines through. My best friend is the perfect match for me—we both crave chaos in different ways, and I love it. She doesn't take shit from anyone, and that's why we get along so well. Despite her being shorter than I am, she has as much fire in her body as I do.

"If you're not looking for anyone tonight, then maybe I can. This bar is trendy and new, which means there must be someone here looking for a fun night." Alissa and I are out for drinks at this new place by our apartment. It only opened last week, but it's cute. She and I are sitting at a table in the corner, away from all the loud shit but good enough for us to scope out the people in here.

"At least this place is nicer than the Hidden Bear. I remember it always being sticky when Leo dragged me out against my will." The Hidden Bear was the bar near our alma mater, Grand Mountain College. Alissa graduated a year before I did, which means we never got to go out together while we were both still in school. I met her my senior year, and we became fast friends. I also might have flirted with her before I knew who she was, but instead of going that route, we became friends, and now, roommates.

My entire body tenses at the mention of her brother. While Alissa Zimmerman is one of my favorite people on the planet, Leo is not.

In fact, he's quite literally the worst.

"Liss, I thought I told you—"

"Yeah, yeah, don't mention my brother around you or else. Whatever." She rolls her eyes, not understanding my intense dislike of her brother. They're Irish twins—born less than a year apart—so they're very close. She loves her brother a lot, and she also deals with me talking shit about him all the time. It's far tamer than what it used to be when we had our internship together—where I may or may not have threatened to kill him a few times. "He's moving back here, you know."

"You've got to be fucking kidding me. To Virginia? Is he even allowed back in this country?"

"Yup. I'm sorry to say, you'll have to deal with him again." I internally groan as Alissa downs the rest of her drink, smirking at me.

"Why is he coming back, and should we let customs know to look out for him?"

"He got some sort of job offer he couldn't pass up. That's all I know."

"Wow. I can't believe that company would hire the worst person on the planet. I hope they know who they're dealing with." I down my drink as well, suddenly wanting to be as drunk as possible.

"Ells, it's going to be fine. You'll only have to deal with him when he comes to bother me, and I'll tell you when he's coming so you can avoid him. I'm sick of you two fighting all the time, but I deal with it because I love you both."

"Ugh. I'm getting another drink. Do you want one?"

"No, babes. I'm okay. I'm gonna head to pee." I nod at her before getting up and heading to the bar. My phone buzzes as I reach it, but I order before I check it.

"Lavender martini, please."

"Coming right up." I pull my phone out as it keeps buzzing, and I laugh when I see who's texting me. Since we've all graduated and now live further apart, my friends love a good group message. And of course, Oliver and Amelia keep their bickering going, even an ocean apart.

> **Oliver:** Amelia, did you get a flight yet or what? Paige's birthday is in two weeks, and no matter how much your face annoys me, she'll be excited you're here.

> **Amelia:** Oh yeah, I've had one for weeks. Did I forget to tell you? Must've slipped my mind...

> **Oliver:** Yeah, I'm sure it did, Medusa.

> **Amelia:** Can it, Jack Frost.

> **Grant:** That's not very nice.

> **Ella:** Ames, I can't wait to see you! We miss you so much.

> **Hads:** I second that, Ells.

> **Grant:** I third that! Talking shit isn't as fun without you, Amelia.

Amelia: It's nice to know some people miss me.

Oliver: Paige misses you, and therefore, I miss you by osmosis.

Grant: That's all you get out of him, but trust me, he misses you.

Oliver: Shut the fuck up, Grant.

Grant: See? He has nobody to make fun of, so he takes it out on us.

Hads: Oliver, chill. You can survive one week of Amelia staying with you. Think about how happy Paige will be.

Oliver: The only reason I'm doing this is for her. If it was up to me, Amelia would be as far away from me as possible.

Ella: Well, you almost were far from us. You know, because of the whole jail thing...

Amelia: Ella, you beat me by one second! But yeah, she's right. You could've been celebrating P's birthday from a cell.

Oliver: I'm not having this conversation again.

Grant: Guys, it was a holding cell, but regardless, it was a cell, so…

Oliver: I'm going to cancel this whole thing if you guys don't stop.

Amelia: Fine, fine.

Ella: Ames, let us know when your flight leaves and such. I want updates at all times!

Hads: And don't forget your book or kindle for your flight. It's a long one.

Amelia: I will, I promise.

Grant: Can you bring me some Flake's?

Amelia: Yes. Now, I have to go to work. See you guys soon.

Ella: Don't work too hard!

Hads: Love you! Go kick some National Geographic ass!

Grant: Have fun, old sport.

Oliver: Good God, not this again.

I laugh as I pick up my drink in front of me. I love my friends and all the chaos they bring, this conversation being no different. It's weird to think about how long I've known Hads, Paige, and Amelia for. They're some of those relationships that feel like we've known each other for a lifetime, but we all became friends in our time at Grand Mountain, so it has only been a few years.

Those days are long behind us, though. Hads and Grant just graduated, and Amelia, Paige, and Oliver have been out of school for a year. I've been out for two, and I need time to slow the hell down.

Us girls met through books. I sat down with Paige in the library and started chatting about the book she was reading. I had just finished it, and we must've talked for hours. That led to us creating a book club on campus, to which only she and Amelia showed up to. A year later, Hads joined, and the rest is history.

Books brought us together, but the bond we created over them will last a lifetime.

When I turn around and head to my table, I make eye contact with a really cute woman sitting at the end of the bar. *Damn, she's fucking hot.* I check her out before I go back to my seat, and Alissa joins me a few moments later. "I forgot to ask how your freelance stuff is going. Didn't you have a project or something the other day?"

My main job is working for the top marketing firm in Virginia—Loft Media. I love my job there, the atmosphere and the people. This is all I've wanted to do since I started my degree. I've been at this job for around two years, but I do some freelance work on the side. I've taken my love for books and transformed that into marketing for independently published authors on social media platforms. It's another good source of income, and I love doing it.

"It's going really well, actually. I created an entire campaign for this author surrounding her new release next month, and she loved it. I swear, I thought she was going to cry when I showed it all to her."

"That's amazing, Ells. I know how hard you work, and I'm glad it's being appreciated." Alissa smiles at me as she grabs my hand and squeezes it. Emotions fill my chest, but I shove those down before they become anything.

"Fuck, Liss. Now is not the time to get sentimental."

"I know. Oh, and there's a girl at the end of the bar who's been staring at you since I sat down." I look over, and sure enough, the girl from earlier pushes off the bar and starts walking over. Alissa slowly rises out of her chair and points toward a guy at the bar. "I'll be over talking to that beautiful man if you need me."

"Have fun," I say as I sip my drink. *Fuck, this girl is gorgeous.*

"Is this seat taken?"

"Yes—by you."

We start talking—Aubrey and I—and just as I think this is about to go somewhere, my phone buzzes. "Sorry, one second." When I pull my phone out, my face falls a bit.

> **Lizzie: Can you take me to dance on Thursday? Dad's car is in the shop, and I can't get a ride with Sabrina.**

> **Lizzie: Don't tell Dad I told you about his car either. He said he's taking care of it, but he won't have it by Thursday, and he's working late.**

> **Ella: Of course I can. What time?**

> **Lizzie: Six thirty.**

> **Ella: Okay, I can leave work early.**

> **Lizzie: Are you sure? I'm sure I can figure something out.**

> **Ella: Anything for you, sis. Don't worry about it. I'll be there.**

> **Lizzie: Okay. Thank you.**

> **Ella: See you Thursday.**

> **Lizzie: Love you.**

> **Ella: Love you more!**

"Is everything okay?"

"Yeah, but I have an early day tomorrow. So, here's my number," I say as I lock eyes with her. "You should use it."

Aubrey takes the business card I hand her, smiles, and pockets it in her handbag. I smile, suddenly not feeling in the mood anymore, before I look over at Alissa. She smiles at the guy she's talking to before I see her hand turn into a thumbs down. *That one's a no-go.*

I clear my throat before I go over there and give the guy an Oscar worthy performance of some fake scenario. Whenever one of us gives the help signal, it's the other person's job to get them out, and my favorite part is coming up with a reason to get her out of here. Putting on my best panic face, I go up to them. "Alissa, we have to go! Your brother is stuck in a mouse trap and he can't get out!"

Her eyes widen as she tries not to laugh.

"I'm serious! We have to go, or he'll never get out! You know how stupid he is!"

"I'm so sorry, but I have to go deal with this emergency." Alissa pats the guy on the arm before grabbing her purse.

"I totally get it. Younger siblings can be interesting sometimes." He pulls a pen out of his jacket before writing down his phone number on a napkin. "Call me."

Alissa pockets the napkin before I forcibly drag her from the bar, and when we get down the street, we burst out laughing. "I'm telling Leo about what you said."

"Good. Maybe one day, he'll actually get stuck in a mouse trap and cut off his toes."

"Whatever you say, Ells. I'm positive he'll love hearing that you talk about him."

I roll my eyes. "I'm sure that'll boost his already gigantic ego."

"Let's go home and watch *Love Island*," Alissa says as she shoves me in the side.

"You really know the way to my heart, Liss. This is why we don't need anybody else."

Alissa laughs as we head back to our apartment, and I smile as the warm June wind hits my face. *Why would I need anybody else when I have Alissa and the girls?*

Oh yeah, sex. That's why.

Well, there's always next time.

2

I Don't Need To Be Handled

"Ella!"

I jump as I hear a loud clap.

"What! What?" I look up at Rae—my work bestie—as she makes a face at me.

"I've been talking to you for five minutes, and you haven't been listening. What's up? Long night?" she asks as she takes a seat across from me.

"I don't know what's up with me today. I can't seem to get anything done."

"Were you up late fucking someone? I had this guy in bed last week, and he—"

I cut her off. "Rae, as much as I love our chats, I know you're about to say something that will have HR up our asses again. What were you talking to me about before?"

Her face lights up as she remembers. "Right! Brody got the promotion! Can you believe they promoted him?"

"He's a project manager now?" There's no fucking way *Brody* got promoted. He's the worst employee. I steal a glance of his office directly across from mine, and sure enough, it's empty. *Shit.* "How did he manage to get that? Did he suck someone's dick?"

Rae just laughs. *Thank God my office door is closed.* "You never know..."

"Does that mean Imogen is hiring someone new?" I ask, and she nods her head.

"Apparently, she already did. They start Monday."

As I start to respond, there's a knock at my office door. "Come in."

Adam, another colleague, peeks his head in. "Did you guys hear about Brody?"

"Yup. We were just talking about it." Rae takes a sip of coffee from her mug.

"Weren't you up for that promotion? How did he get it over you?" Adam asks me.

"It is what it is, I guess. He has been here longer than I have."

"Yeah, but he sucks. You're at least a good and reliable human with more than an ounce of work ethic. Fuck, he's gonna be even more insufferable than before." Rae sighs before getting up, her long, black hair swinging behind her as she opens my tudor. "Who wants to get drinks after work?"

Adam shakes his head, and that's all I'll get from him. He's a pretty private person and tends not to give up too much.

"I can't either. I have to take Lizzie to dance tonight."

"Family time sounds nice," Adam states. "I originally came in here to tell you Imogen wanted to talk to you."

"Did she say why?" I ask, wanting to ease my nerves a bit.

"No, but don't worry. It's Imogen. You'll be fine." He taps on my desk before leaving my office, keeping the door slightly ajar. I take a deep breath before collecting myself. *Why am I so distracted today?* Not wanting to dive into that scenario right now, I head out of my office and to Imogen's at the front of our floor. I pass by the bullpen, a collection of cubicles for some of the entry-level employees, and beeline for her office.

I knock twice on her door before I hear her tell me to come in. "Hi, Imogen. Adam said you wanted to see me?"

She smiles at me. "Yes. Have a seat, Ella."

I sit in one of the chairs across from her desk, and I almost forgot how comfy these were. It has been a while since I've been in here. Imogen tends to hover around the office. She doesn't sit still very well and prefers to be on her feet when taking calls and such. I'm also surprised her desk isn't in the standing position. All our desks can be changed to standing ones, and I use mine sometimes when I'm tired of sitting all day.

"You know I hate doing this, but I need you to work some overtime this Sunday."

"I don't mind. Is it to finish up the campaign for the new hotel chain?"

She nods at me. "Yes. I've also asked Rae, Brody, and Brad to help. I'm sure the four of you can push us over the finish line."

I internally cringe at having to deal with Brody and Brad on Sunday, but at least I can see my friends after. That makes it all worth it. *Fuck, I still have to get Paige a birthday present.* I'll add it to the never-ending list of shit I have to do this week.

One day at a time.

"That sounds great. What time do you need me here?"

"How about ten? I don't think it'll take all day, and I can have some catering sent for lunch as a thank you. I'll be here, showing the new person around, but I'll be out of your way so you four can focus."

"You're the best, Imogen. Is that all?" She smiles at me before nodding.

"That's all, Ella." I get up, and as I exit her office, I run into someone who seemed to be eavesdropping in the hallway. When I look up, Brody's stupid fucking face is in front of me.

"Ella! I'm sure you've heard the news by now…" He trails off, as if he's waiting for me to congratulate him.

"Yes! I heard your STD screening came back negative. Such great news!" I pat his shoulder as I try to move, only for him to block my path.

"That's cute, but I know you're going to miss having me across from your office. I know you enjoyed the view…"

Absolutely the fuck not. "Aw, Brody, you and I both know I wouldn't touch you with a twenty-foot pole. I *will* miss catching you using artificial intelligence to draft your proposals and your two hour lunch breaks! Such a shame the front offices will have to deal with that. Best of luck to them!" I say before rushing past him and back to my office. Brody is the kind of guy who thinks he's the shit when, in reality, he peaked in high school and is now a lazy, selfish human being.

I guess now that he's technically my superior, I should be nicer to him. I just can't find it in me to care. As I sit back down at my desk, I look at the time—1:13 p.m.

Great. Only two more hours. I'm leaving at three so I have time in case traffic is bad on the hour drive to my dad's house. Before I leave, I have a meeting with our design team to finalize a new campaign I've been working on with Rae.

My life always feels on-the-go, and one of these days, I crave some down time so I can take a much-needed breather. But until then, at least I don't have to think about all the shit that's gone wrong in my life.

Nothing keeps the bad thoughts away like constantly having something to do, right?

THE LONG DRIVE IS worth it to see my sister's face as she dances.

She got all the graceful genes. I might be the organized, type A sister, but she's more go-with-the-flow than I will ever be. Today, they're practicing some sort of ballet routine or something. I don't have a clue about any of this. Lizzie was more interested in sports and stuff like this. She's been dancing at this same studio since she was young.

Well, since I could drive her, because our dad was always too busy working. It was a good bonding experience, and he never missed any of her recitals, despite working so much.

The three of us used to have this tradition where after every recital—I think they had two a year—we would go to a diner and have milkshakes. Mine was dairy-free, of course, but those nights are some of my favorite memories of us as a family.

Now, as I sit and watch her in her last year of dancing for this company, I can't help but smile. I'm still in denial that she's graduating high school next year. It feels like just yesterday, I was sitting on her bed, reading her stories.

I shake my thoughts out of those memories. It's not like I don't enjoy thinking about them, but they remind me of a time I would rather not think about.

I don't have many fond memories of my childhood. All I remember is the feeling of being left by my mother and how I had to grow up quickly to help take care of my sister. I was a kid myself when she left, but my sister was younger, which meant the burden fell on my shoulders.

I didn't mind it, I guess. I just hate that I missed out on a few extra years of being a kid that most other people got to have.

I'm not bitter about it, but I do yearn for the stress-free time before my mom left. I often wonder how different I would've turned out if not for her absence. Maybe I would be more carefree like my sister. Maybe people would stop thinking I'm too much when they get to know me. Maybe I would worry less and not be the mom friend in every friend group.

Maybe I would be better at talking about my struggles with the people who care about me.

Maybe, maybe, maybe.

Too bad that isn't me. I like who I am, but some days, I wonder what would have been different if she was still around.

Regardless, I've found some pretty fucking awesome people to live my life with. Not only did Grand Mountain bring me my forever friends, it also made me realize I have to live my life without worrying about my family needing me.

Still, I worry. It's impossible not to. It feels like all I'm wired to do is make sure my family's okay even though I'm an hour away from them.

And as I watch my sister traipse across the floor, I'm glad she got to experience a different childhood than I did. She has grown up to be such an authentic, soft, gentle person.

The direct opposite of me. I can be cold sometimes, most people think I'm a bitch when they first meet me, and I have a way of saying anything that comes to mind with absolutely no filter. Most people can't handle me, and that's fine. I don't need to be handled.

I need to be *heard* amidst all the dumbass people who exist nowadays.

My phone rings in my purse, and I pull it out. Seeing it's my Dad, I answer. "Hey. What's wrong?"

He only laughs. "Why do you always answer the phone like that?"

"Because you never know!" I tell him. "What's up?"

"I wanted to see how you were. Did Liz get to dance okay?"

"She did, and by the looks of it, she's having a good time." I smile, noting how different my sister looks when she dances. It's like there's this whole other side of her.

"I'm sorry you had to leave work—"

"Dad, you know I don't mind doing this. Whatever you need, I can make it work."

"I know, but I worry I'm asking too much of you."

"Nothing is ever too much for you guys. You're my family, remember?"

He sighs across the line. "I know, Ella. I wish I could meet you guys for dinner, but maybe you can come over one of these nights if you're not too busy?"

I hate how little I see my family nowadays. Back in college, I was always around to help, but since I have my own life happening away from them, I don't see them as often as I would like. It feels like every time I go over, my dad looks more tired than he did before. He might be a little over fifty, but his brown skin has more wrinkles and exhaustion lines every time I see him.

Though his eyes never look too tired. Whenever he looks at Lizzie and me, I swear, I see them sparkle. I always joke that he's where we get our good looks from, but he denies it every time.

"I'd love that," I say as applause ensues. "I have to go, Dad. Practice is over. Do you want me to stay with her until you get home? I don't mind."

"No, it's okay. I'll only be an hour or two. I know your drive is long and it's a work night, so you don't have to."

"Well, I want to. I'll see you when you get home. Do you need me to do laundry for you or anything?" I always offer. If I'm going to be home, I might as well keep my hands busy and help out if they need it.

"There's some things in the laundry room if you have time." I can feel his apprehension over the line. "Thank you, Ella."

"Anything for you, Dad. I love you."

"Love you too, bug."

I smile as my sister walks out of the studio, a twin expression on her face when she sees I stayed to watch the whole time. Most of the parents don't, but with the little time I do see my sister these days, I'd rather wait here and watch than leave and come back.

"You looked so graceful in there, Lizzie," I say as I throw my arm around her. "I wish I had as good of balance as you do."

She shakes her head. "No, my arabesque wasn't fully stretched like it should have been, and—"

"Liz, it's just practice. Don't beat yourself up about it."

"We have a recital at the end of the year, Ells. I want a solo in the group dance," she says as she leans into me to take her pointe shoes off. "I won't get it by looking like shit in class."

My mouth drops open. "First of all, language, Liz. Second, you'll be fine. You're a Williams, and we never give up, remember?"

She nods her head. "I know." She removes the tape from her toes before she throws her stuff in her bag.

"So, what do you want for dinner? I'm hanging with you at the house until Dad gets home, so it's your choice."

Her face lights up. "Can you make pasta? And can we watch a movie after?"

"Is your homework done?" I ask her, knowing it probably already is. My sister is good at staying on top of things. After all, she learned from the best—me.

"Yes, it is," she says as I open the door.

"Then we can."

She smiles, and I'm glad I can still have these moments with her before she grows up, heads to college, and leaves me for good. I don't know what her plan is, but I know it's going to be somewhere out of state.

Which is fine, but I'm going to miss my sister like hell when she leaves, so these small, stolen moments are ones I will cherish forever.

3

Just Like Old Times

THE FIT AS FUCK waitress from this restaurant keeps staring at my mouth.

If it wasn't early in the afternoon and I didn't have somewhere to be, I'd probably take her back to my flat and show her all the things I could do with it.

"Ahem!"

My eyes snap back to my sister across from me, an annoyed look on her face. "What?"

"I've been talking for five minutes, and all you've been doing is drooling over the waitress. Don't make her another one of your conquests, Leo. I like this place. Ella and I come here all the time."

At the mention of *her*, I can feel my shoulders tense. "Anything for you, dear sister," I say, omitting the fact that I've been in a dry spell for a while—two weeks. I'd been too busy packing and barely had time for anything else. Moving countries is hard fucking work, and I wanted it to go smoothly—which it has, for the most part.

But now, I think I've forgotten how to use my dick.

"Did Mum and Dad seem okay when you left?" she asks, and I know she's really asking about Dad.

"Yeah, everything was okay. I told them we'd video call once a week when you got settled." I see her nervousness about a possible emergency with both of us here. When I told my parents about the job offer, they were practically begging me to leave, but I was the apprehensive one. I knew Alissa worried about being in the States, but I always told her I was close by in case something happened. Now that we're both over here, we're more on edge.

"Good. Now, where is this new job? You've been surprisingly hush-hush about it when normally, you'd be rubbing your paycheck in my face," my sister asks as she takes a bite of her salad.

"Says you. You probably make more than I will in one day. It's at this marketing firm in the city. My commute from the rental isn't too bad, but when I move into my new place, it'll be even closer."

"What's it called? Maybe I can visit for lunch when you get settled."

"I'd love that." Most older brothers would probably hate that, but Alissa and I have always been close. Being less than a year apart will do that. She may be my older sister, but I've always been fiercely protective over her, and she'd probably say the same for me. She's my built-in best friend. "It's called Loft Media."

My sister suddenly drops her fork into her bowl and laughs.

"I'm sorry, did I tell a joke I wasn't aware of, or am I really *that* funny?"

Alissa continues laughing, waving her hand in front of her face. "Oh no, it's nothing really. I was just remembering something funny from work."

Suddenly not feeling very hungry anymore, I flag our waitress down and ask her for a box. "Has someone caught your eye at work, Liss, or are you lying to me?"

Her face is always unreadable, which pisses me off, but I guess that means she went into the right line of work doing...whatever she does. "Oh no, nothing like that. You know I don't have time to date, Leo. Work is too busy."

"Good. I'd hate to have to scare them all off if I saw someone trying it on with you. Dad's not here, so I have to fill the role of the scary protective guy in your life."

"Whatever you say, but you should know I'm not scared of you. I never have been." She smiles at me, and I roll my eyes. "Or do you keep forgetting I was born first?"

"How can I forget when you remind me about it a thousand times a day?" I joke with her as the waitress drops the check off. When I snatch it before Liss can, she glares at me. "Too slow. This one's on me."

"Fine." She pouts, and when I take a look at the check, a smile glosses over my face. "What's that look for?"

"She left her number on the bottom of the receipt." I wave it up so she can see, and she groans.

"If you fuck her and ruin this place for Ella and me, I'm not responsible for what wrath she imposes."

"I'm sure I can take on whatever she throws my way. I've never had a problem before. And how do you know this waitress isn't the one?" I say while pressing a hand to my heart, but Alissa knows I'm bullshitting her.

"Oh, please. The day you settle down is the day I can relax. Do you even remember her name?"

Shit. I think it started with an M. "Melissa?" I question, and Alissa waves her hand off.

"What time is your tour?"

I look down at my watch—Van Cleef Perlée, 18K yellow gold, with a brown band that my dad bought me for Christmas last year. "About an hour and a half. It shouldn't take long to get there, though. I'll be fine."

When the waitress comes back with my card, I shoot her a wink before she blushes and walks away. I know what I look like, so that happens a bit too often. She was cute, but I can't bring myself to ever use her number, so I throw it in the bin before Alissa and I leave. It's a fairly nice day out, the warm breeze flowing through my curly brown hair.

"Are you headed home for the day?"

"Yeah. I'm having a self-care day while Ella is stuck at the office." She smirks at me, and I'm not sure why.

"What was that look for?"

"What look?" And she does it again.

"That. The stupid smirk."

"Oh, nothing. I hope your tour goes well." And I swear, I hear her mumble something else before she gets into her car parked right next to my rental. I don't have an official license yet, but I have three months to get one, according to what Alissa told me. That's fine, but I'm stuck in this small car until then. I miss my Range Rover back in England so much when I get into this small car.

"Thanks, sis," I mumble as I try to get the odd feeling out of my stomach that she knows something I don't. Turning my car on, I speed away from the curb and head to my new place of employment.

As I PULL INTO a spot in the parking garage, I look down to make sure my clothes aren't wrinkled before getting out of my car. I'm excited to start tomorrow, and this tour I'm taking is making this seem more real—the fact that I've moved to the States and I'm working in a field I love.

I'm glad I'm closer to my sister, but leaving my parents behind—especially my dad—was difficult. *He'll be fine*, I remind myself for the twentieth time. They're only a phone call away. Thinking of them, I grab my phone as I get into the lift and press the thirteenth floor.

> **Leo: Heading in for the tour now. Hope you guys are well.**

> **Alissa: Good luck! Be on the lookout; you never know what new jobs can hold...**

> **Mum: Have fun, sweet boy!**

> **Leo: Liss, what does that mean?**

> **Alissa: Nothing! Have fun!**

> **Dad: Can't wait to hear about it.**

> **Leo: Talk soon.**

I pocket my phone again, suddenly feeling a bit on edge with whatever the fuck my sister is telling me to look out for. *She's probably just pushing my buttons.* Alissa was always one for doing that on purpose, especially when we were kids. She was a goddamn menace.

A few seconds later, I'm thrust into a reception area where nobody is sitting. It's Sunday, so that makes sense, but I can faintly make out a few voices. Imogen—my boss—told me a few people are working overtime today, and I might see them when she gives me the tour. As I sit in the reception area like she instructed, I take a quick look around. It's a nice office, with warm tones all over it. The walls are an off-white, and the pictures framing this area are quite nice. I assume some of them are campaigns they've done for other companies, and they look great.

A knock startles me out of my analysis, and when I look up, I see my new boss. She gives me a smile before holding out her hand, and I shake it. "Hello, ma'am. It's nice to finally meet you in person and not over a screen."

"Please, call me Imogen. Formalities make my skin crawl." When I nod, she smiles again. Imogen is only a bit older than me, probably mid-to-late thirties or early forties. She's got short brown hair, thick black glasses, and a sweet smile. "Shall we get started? It's not a big office, but I wanted you to have a lay of the land before you officially started."

"I appreciate that. It'll be nice to walk in tomorrow and know exactly where I'm going rather than looking like a lost puppy."

"Follow me. I'll keep it short and sweet, I promise." She waves her hand out, and I step into the full office area, liking what I'm seeing so far.

"So, to the left is our copy room, where you can see we have different computers, printers, and anything else you might need if you're printing something for any of the campaigns we do. It's very helpful having them in-office. When we were a much smaller company, we had to send things out to get printed, and it was a nightmare."

"Sounds like it would be. That's what we did at my last job in London. It was an absolute pain."

She nods at me before walking toward some cubicles. "This is where John and Adam work, along with a few other people you'll meet tomorrow. They handle client relations. Over there is the conference room. You'll notice the frosted glass is on right now because everyone is working on our latest deadline. That's the only room with the feature, and it's used most often when we have big meetings and the like."

"That's cool."

"I'll show you that room tomorrow so as to not disturb them."

"Of course." She continues to show me the small kitchen and dining area in the corner of the office, and then we get to a few smaller offices in the corner.

"Your office is right next to Brad's, so if you have any questions, you can ask him."

"Is he the one I'm shadowing for the first thirty days?" One of my first tasks is to shadow someone who has worked here for a while. I learn best on my feet and by watching what others do, so Imogen suggested this when I agreed to take the job. She seems like a great boss already, and I'm excited to work under her and Brody—the guy whose job I'm filling, since he got a promotion.

"No. I picked one of our best employees for that. You'll meet her later." Imogen smiles before she opens a door to an empty office. "This is where you'll be. Your shadow's office is straight across from yours for easy access." *Great.*

"Is decor allowed? Don't get me wrong, this office is wonderful, but the emptiness gives me the creeps."

She just laughs. "Of course. Feel free to make it your own. Now, let's head to my office so I can go over what your first month will look like." I close the door—*my* door—behind me as we head to her office at the front. She pushes her door open and signals for me to sit. "I'm going to let them know we're in here. Just give me one second."

"Of course, ma'am." I shake my head and laugh, noting the slip-up. "Imogen."

"Great. I'll be right back."

This office feels like the perfect fit for me, and I'm really excited to start working here so soon. I've been sick with worry I was never going to find something over here. I hate relying on my parents for money and shit like that, so getting the job came at the perfect time.

I have a lot of it—money—but I've always prided myself on being self-sufficient, even with a massive trust fund hanging over my head. If I wanted to, I wouldn't have to work a day in my life, but I love what I do, and I'd get bored sitting around all day doing nothing.

Imogen comes back a few moments later, and the two of us get to talking about what a typical day looks like and all the other boring shit that happens during these kinds of chats. By the time we're done, I'm even more excited. I don't think anything could dull my spirits.

"Do you have anything else for me?" Imogen asks, and as I'm about to say no, I hear the door open, and a voice I know all too well speaks.

"You wanted to see me?"

"Yes, Ella. Come sit and meet our newest employee, your shadow for his first thirty days." *Ella. No fucking way.* I paste my best asshole smile on and turn around. Sure enough, her face falls when she notices it's me. *Fuck, that shouldn't feel good, but it does.*

Ella sits in the chair next to mine, her face still in shock and partly pissed off. I can tell she's angry—she has her fake smile on, but her eyes are glaring at me as if lasers are about to shoot out of them. *Just the way I like it.* "Nice to see you again, Ella."

She keeps glaring at me, clearly blindsided, and Imogen speaks up. "Oh, do you two know each other? That's perfect!"

"We went to university together! Isn't that right, Williams?" I turn and throw a smile at her.

"It's college," she grits through her teeth.

I smile at her. "I'm from England."

"Yes, but we're in America." *She's so easy to piss off.* Fuck, I'm going to love every second of this.

"What a small world! Well, I guess we can skip the formalities. Ella, Leo is your trainee for thirty days. Go easy on him so he understands the basics, and don't be afraid to let him try some things on his own. He starts tomorrow, so I'll have Brody show him the ropes for then, but on Tuesday, he's all yours."

"Wonderful. I can't wait." Ella's tone indicates otherwise, but Imogen doesn't seem to catch on. "I'll see you then. If you'll excuse me, I have a party to get to."

"See you on Tuesday. Thank you for your help today! I can't wait to see what you guys have done with the campaign." Imogen smiles as Ella leaves, and after giving me a folder filled with entrance documents, I shuffle out of her office as well. As I look around, not seeing a trace of the woman who makes my blood boil, I head for the lift, stopping it before it shuts.

My lips curve into a smirk as I see Ella in it already. The tension is thick as I step in and press the button for the parking garage.

"I already pressed it." I don't even have to look to know she's rolling her eyes at me. *Just like old times.*

"Forgive me if I don't trust you not to crash this thing now that I'm in here."

"Oh please. Don't give me any great ideas, asshole." As I'm about to speak, she beats me to it. "What the fuck are you doing here?"

"Heading to my car. What does it look like I'm doing?"

She sighs heavily. "What are you doing at my job, Zimmerman? Is this some sort of sick joke?"

"I got a job here, Williams. It looks like we'll be working together. Remember how much fun last time was? It's like college all over again." Ella surprises me by stopping the lift as soon as I say that. The lights go dark, and she comes face to face with me; well, more like face to chest, but I think she's about to stab my eyes out with those sharp nails of hers.

"Stop being a smug prick. College was horrid, and having to spend time with your condescending ass back then was bad enough. I love this place, and now you've tainted it with your fucking presence. Don't talk about our past, and don't fucking test me. I have seniority, and Imogen will listen to me no matter how much charm you apparently have. This isn't our internship office filled with testosterone anymore."

"Darling, I have no problem keeping things professional. It's you we have to worry about." Ella is a firecracker, and for as long as I've known her, we've hated each other. I don't quite know why she dislikes me, but she has always been a lot. Every time I tried to talk to her in college ended with her yelling at me or threatening me, and I got tired of it. Her attitude is awful, and I think the two of us are destined to never get along.

"What the fuck does that mean?"

I step closer to her, and she doesn't move. "Well, considering you're the one yelling at me in a stopped lift, that should give you your answer. Now, can we get this over with? I have somewhere to be."

Ella scoffs, keeping eye contact. "Oh, I'm sorry, am I keeping you from a hot date? Maybe I'll lock us both in here and save the poor woman some mediocre sex and your fuck boy personality."

I lean down, getting in her face because I know how much she hates it, especially when it's me crowding her. "Let's not lie, Williams. You of all people know sex with me is anything but mediocre. After all, you were the one who listened like such a good girl when I bossed you around that night." I reach behind her and start the lift again, suddenly wanting to get the fuck out of here so I can get home and call my parents. Ella turns around and faces the front as we move. I know I got under her skin because she's gone quiet—that's about the only time she shuts up and stops making judgements about me. To secure my win in today's squabble, I add something else that will piss her off. "I have to say, I forgot how much I prefer you with your mouth full."

The doors open, and she doesn't say a word as she heads to her car. I smile, knowing she's going to come at me full force on Tuesday. I'm capable of being a normal human being, but Ella having the power to tell me what to do is a dynamic we've never experienced together.

Bring it on, Williams.

4

Tequila, I'm Guessing?

Fuck my motherfucking life.

As I drive toward Paige and Oliver's place, I look around and try to discern if I entered an alternate reality in the past hour.

Leo fucking Zimmerman. The person I hate most in the world is going to be working with me. He's going to be in the office right across from mine, and I have to look at his stupid fucking face every day, starting Tuesday.

What the hell am I going to do? I could barely stand being around his annoying ass during our internship senior year, and now, I have to *work* with him.

I need alcohol. Lots of alcohol.

I take a calming breath before realizing where I'm headed. There's no way I'm going to be able to hold this in all night, so maybe I'll ask them what I should do.

Quitting sounds nice.

Just as I think about the girls, Hads calls me, and I pick it up through my car's Bluetooth. "Hey! We just got to my brother's place. Are you on your way?"

"Yup. I'll be there in fifteen."

"Woah, Ells. Are you okay? You sound like you're five seconds away from murdering someone," Grant asks me.

"It's nothing. I got stuck dealing with an imbecile at work." I clench my jaw hard remembering I have to see him in two days, and I take another deep breath.

"Want to talk about it?" Hads asks, compassion lacing her voice.

"I can always tell Paige and Oliver to take care of it." Hads must've hit Grant, because I hear him say *ow* in the background.

"I'll see you guys soon. Is Amelia there yet?"

"I think so. A cab just left their complex, so I assume that was her," Hads tells me.

"See you soon, Ells. Don't crash into anyone on the way here. I'd hate to lose my favorite karaoke partner," Grant adds, making me smile for the first time tonight.

"Yeah, I'll see you guys soon." I hang up and try to calm myself down, because if there's one thing I don't want to do, it's ruin Paige's birthday with my anger.

But God, I'm angry. I'm angry I had just found my footing at a job I love, and now, he's going to ruin everything with his big ass ego. The girls don't—and wouldn't—understand my hatred for the fucker, the most annoying thing he does is walking into every room as if he owns the place. People hand him things without him even doing anything just because he has a penis.

It's not fucking fair that I, as a woman, have to work four times as hard to get the same things a man could. I've been dealing with it my whole life. At our internship, I was sent to get coffee, bagels, and menial tasks a receptionist could do while Leo got to sit in on important meetings and briefings because all the male executives loved him.

I can't help but compare my internship experience with everything happening in the office with Brody. It gets fucking tiring after a while, and Leo didn't make it any easier. He used his stupid fucking charm to his advantage and purposely left me out of the loop.

So yeah, I hate the guy, and now, he's going to be my shadow for thirty days so he can learn about our company.

Fuck. My. Life.

I should just quit. The idea pops into my head again, and I let that sit in my mind before I bring up my voice-to-text in my car and text the group chat.

> **Ella: Someone better have a bottle of wine for me, because I'm gonna need it.**

If I have the day off tomorrow, I'm getting drunk. Maybe then, I'll forget about the worst person in the world crashing my place of work. A few messages come through as I'm pulling into the lot.

> **Hads: A whole bottle?**

> **Amelia: I have mine ready, but I'll tell Oliver to get one for you.**

> **Oliver: Amelia, I'm in this group chat, and I can read.**

> **Amelia: Oh, I thought this was the book club one.**

> **Grant: Nope. Although I'm in that one too!**

As I park, I shoot off one last text, grab my purse with Paige's present in it, and stalk up the stairs. I read Paige's text from my phone as I rip open her apartment door.

"No, everything is *not* okay!" I see Oliver rush to get me a bottle of wine as I drop my purse on the floor, and all my anger comes rushing in again. I slump down on the empty loveseat as I take a deep breath. "I have to quit my job."

"What?" Hads questions, probably confused as to how our conversation from earlier got to this conclusion.

"Wait, why?" Amelia asks. *God, it's good to see her.*

"But you love your job!" Paige exclaims. *Fuck, she's right. But I'm going to hate it if he's there now.*

"What do you do again?" Grant asks me, and Oliver simply says nothing as he hands me a bottle of red wine. *Thank fuck.*

"Thank you," I say as I take a long sip from the bottle, silently hoping I'll wake up from this nightmare soon. "Everything was *fine* until I got called into my boss' office. I'll admit, I was slightly nervous; I thought she was going to fire me or something."

"Did she have a reason to fire you?" Hads asks.

"No, but you never know in this economy. Anyways, she calls me in, and when I get to her office, a guy is sitting in the chair across from her desk. She tells me he was just hired, and I was picked for him to shadow me for thirty days while he learns the ropes. I was fine with that because

I had trained other people before. But then, he turned around." I stop to take a long sip of wine, not wanting his stupid fucking name to be the taste on my lips.

"That was a terrible cutoff point! Just tell us who it was!" I know as soon as Paige hears this, she's going to go feral or something. She has been shipping me and Leo together ever since she found out we hated each other. The Halloween party her senior year didn't help matters either, especially since Leo couldn't keep his fucking mouth shut.

"I'm on the edge of my seat," Oliver says in the most monotone voice ever, and Paige smacks him. "Ow, what the fuck? I was being serious!"

"Shh! Let her tell it!" Amelia snaps at Oliver.

"It was Leo—pain in my ass—Zimmerman. He's going to be fucking working with me, at my dream job, the one place I love. He's going to ruin *everything!*"

"Oh my God." Hads grabs my hand. Out of all the people in this room, she gets it. During my senior year, the two of us were in a similar situation. The only difference is, Hads ended up in love with Grant. I want to throw up just thinking about being near Leo for the rest of my life. I can hear Amelia laughing, and even though I missed her, I didn't miss her love of poking fun at everyone's misery. I see Grant and Paige lock eyes, probably already mentally designing the t-shirts they're going to make. *Fuck.* I love my friends, but they just don't get it.

"Is Leo the British guy? Alissa's brother?" Oliver asks me.

"Yes. Seeing him around my apartment when he comes over to visit Alissa will be bad enough, but now, I'm going to have to interact with him five days a week! This is my worst nightmare."

"But wait, why were you working on a Sunday?" Grant asks.

"Our company has a major deadline soon, so a few of us worked overtime to get shit done. But now, I have to quit!" I take a sip and suddenly wish this was tequila. "Do you guys have anything stronger? Wine is not cutting it right now."

"Tequila, I'm guessing?" Oliver asks as he gets up.

"I knew I liked you." We trade, and he hands me a huge bottle of tequila he just opened. I love how they keep our favorite drinks here; I know the two of them don't like tequila. Oliver doesn't drink, and Paige is more of a vodka girl when she does—which is a rare occurrence.

"Ells, you don't have to quit. Just avoid him—or fuck him, whichever works best to make him less annoying," Grant says. I've never been one for violence, but I could punch him for saying that.

"I'm only going to say this once, but I'm *never* going to get naked with that man." *Again.* "I'm avoiding him at all costs."

"Don't you have to train him?" Amelia asks.

"Fuck!" I need this alcohol to kick in so I can forget about this until I have to actually deal with it on Tuesday.

"Ells, look on the bright side. You two *have* to be professional at work, so how annoying can he be?" Paige smiles at me. I love her optimism, but I could barely stomach a short conversation with him at the office earlier.

I sigh heavily. "I'm not actually going to quit, but I hate this so much. Since I worked today, I took tomorrow off. Are you good if I crash on your couch tonight? I need to get insanely hammered to try and forget I'll be working with the fucker for an undetermined amount of time."

"Ells, you can crash in the spare room with me. They have a pullout couch, but I don't mind sharing the bed. It'll be like old times." Amelia smiles at me.

"I can blow up the air mattress if you two want to stay over too!" Paige's eyes light up, looking at Hads, at the thought of us all having a sleepover again.

"I'm only agreeing to that if you sleep on it with me, P."

"Of course I can! A birthday sleepover! This is the best day of my life!" I see Oliver smile an actual smile before Paige leans over and kisses him. My heart lurches for some reason, so to combat it, I take another sip of tequila. *Much better.*

"Does this mean I'm rooming with Oliver tonight? What's a little light cuddling between two almost-brothers?" Grant smiles at him.

"You're on the couch tonight, pretty boy. Don't worry. It's memory foam, so your back will be fine." Oliver slaps him on the shoulder.

"Okay, now that sleeping arrangements are all set for tonight, can we get to the movies? I want to get them over with as soon as possible," Hads asks.

"I'm pressing play, Hads," Oliver tells his sister.

"Not fast enough, Oliver!" she quips while sipping her wine glass.

Amelia raises her bottle. "To the best year ahead for all of us, and to Paige. Happy birthday, my girl." The rest of us raise our glasses.

"To Paige," Hads says.

"Happy birthday, P!" I say, already feeling a buzz. *Thank fuck.* Oliver turns all the lights off as the movie starts to play, and I find myself not being able to pay attention to it. My mind keeps going back to the face Leo made when he saw me walk in. *Did he know I worked there? Did he take the job knowing it would drive me nuts?* I wouldn't put it past him. He practically gets off on pushing my buttons—he always has.

"Down in front!" Amelia softly kicks Oliver, and he crouches back down next to Grant.

A few hours later, us girls are camped out in Paige's guest room as we sit on the floor, drinking and catching up.

"So, besides Ella's big revelation tonight, what has everyone else been up to?" Paige asks as she smiles around at us. *I'm so glad she's smiling again.* The past few years have been tough for her, and I'm glad she found her shine again.

"Well, I have a boyfriend," Amelia slurs as her eyes pop and she realizes what she said.

"A what?" Hads asks, shock in her tone.

"Amelia, how did you keep this from us?" Paige points at her. "What's the lucky guy's name?" I know she's secretly hoping Amelia says a different name than the one she's going to say.

"His name is Harvey."

"Harvey?" I question.

"That sounds eerily close to Hen—"

Hads cuts Paige off before she can finish speaking. "Where did you meet him?"

Amelia's eyes look sad before she masks her expression. She tells us she met him at some bar and originally only planned for it to be a one night stand, but she kept running into him at the weirdest places—the grocery store, bookstore, her commute to work.

"He sounds like a stalker," Paige says.

"Or it's fate." I practically choke on my drink as Hads says that. "What?"

"Grant's made you soft," Amelia laughs as she looks at Paige. "And you've made Oliver semi-likeable. This is why we need to Facetime more. The world is going to spin off its axis if I see Oliver smile one more time. It's upsetting the timeline."

"Well, if one of us could get used to the time difference and stop accidentally missing calls, we'd be set," Hads says before Ames throws a pillow at her.

The four of us laugh before a calm silence envelops the room.

"Guys, what am I going to do? Just the thought of being near that British fucker is driving me insane." I'm not usually one to *ask* for help, but the alcohol is loosening my entire body. It also helps that I trust the girls. I know they can understand my pain, even if only a little.

"I think that's a question we can answer when we're sober," Paige says as she slumps onto the air mattress.

"Good idea," Hads says as she looks at the clock. "It is two in the morning, after all."

After we all agree to go to sleep, Paige's voice filters through the room. "This was one of my favorite days ever. Thank you all for coming. I love you guys so much." I hear her sniffle and Hads roll into her, probably smothering her in a hug. Those two have become much closer since Paige started dating her brother, and it makes my heart ache, especially since they were strained after everything that happened during Paige and Amelia's senior year. It's good to know time can heal most things.

I turn my head to Ames and notice she's still awake. "Are you doing okay?"

She nods her head. "Yeah, I'm okay." I notice a tear fall from her eye, and I wipe it away. "I missed you guys a lot. I'm glad I'm here."

"Is your sleep schedule still fucked?" I ask, knowing she'll probably be like me tonight: tossing and turning.

"Yeah, I haven't slept well in London. I haven't slept well since..." She trails off, and I know it's because she's thinking about Henry. Paige always told me she slept more when he was around, and after everything that happened, I bet it's hard to go back to how she was before.

"Ames, you don't have to feel guilty about doing what you thought was best for you." Even if her leaving was sudden, if it's what she had to do, it makes sense. She does need to work better on her communication, though. It has been difficult to get in touch with her, and sometimes, I worry it's not just the time difference.

She smiles, but again, it's sad. It's like she's trying to convince herself she made the right call, even though it has been two years. "Thanks, Ells. We should head to bed." She turns away from me, and I know she's not going to sleep; Amelia has never liked talking about Henry after it all went to shit. I know not to press, but I hate not being there for my friends if they're struggling. It kills me to see them like that, but Ames will talk about it when she's ready. I think this Harvey guy is a step in the right direction for her, but I know she still thinks about Henry.

I sigh as I try to get comfortable, knowing damn well I'm not going to be able to sleep since my heart is still racing.

Just try not to think about the fucker, and you'll be fine. Unfortunately, his stupid fucking smirk is the only thing I see when I close my eyes, but eventually, sleep consumes me.

A LOUD BANG WAKES me up.

Fuck, my head hurts. I haven't been that drunk in a while, and when I look around and see us girls clutching our heads, I know we're in the same boat. I gather my bearings before I get out of bed and head for the kitchen. "I'll grab water and some painkillers. Nobody move for at least an hour."

"I feel like I'm being repeatedly punched in the face," Paige groans with a smile on her face. Only she could be this happy hungover, and somehow, she ended up on the floor and not on the air mattress. *Typical Paige.*

"Ells, I can help," Hads says as she stumbles to get up.

"No. Everyone stay here, I'll be right back." As I open the door to the kitchen, the bright ass lights hit my face, and I flinch. When my vision clears, I see Oliver and Grant in the kitchen, and they freeze when they see me.

"Oh good, you guys are awake," Grant says as he hands me a water bottle and some painkillers. "Here, take these, and drink lots of water." He smiles at me as I feel the girls file out of the bedroom behind me.

Oliver seems to be making breakfast for us as he stands at the stove, and he only turns around when Paige wraps her arms around him. He presses a quick kiss to her forehead before opening her water for her and handing her the pills they set out for us.

"Baby, here. You better down that whole thing. That goes for all of you ladies. Water only today, or you'll hate yourselves." Grant waves his spatula in the air as if his word is the law, and I hear us girls laugh—we've noticed what he's wearing. "What?"

"My love, what is Grant wearing, and how do I get one for you?" Paige asks Oliver, and he rolls his eyes.

"Hey, if I'm cooking, I'm going to do it with style. Thank you very much." Grant presses a kiss to Hads' cheek, and she laughs again. Grant is wearing a bright pink apron that says, 'Kiss the Cook,' and I hate that pink looks so good on him.

"You're not even the one cooking, pretty boy. I am," Oliver says.

"Grant, where did you get that from?" I ask while trying not to laugh. He's shirtless underneath it, and I guarantee the bang that woke us was Oliver throwing something at his head.

"It was in my car. It was originally a present for Paige, since I bought it for Oliver, but now that I'm wearing it, he doesn't want it." Grant side-eyes Oliver, and he ignores him as he continues making eggs. "Now, you girls sit and enjoy the show." Grant picks Hads up and places her on one of Paige's counter stools.

"I'd rather watch paint dry than enjoy the show that is Oliver cooking," Amelia says as she sits down.

"I could get used to seeing this," Paige says as she hands Oliver fresh coffee before sitting down.

"Do any of you have work today?" I ask.

"We all took a long weekend for Paige's birthday. Plus, Amelia is staying with Paige and me until Thursday, so Paige took off for that too," Oliver tells me as he throws a bagel onto my plate just how I like it.

"Yes, it's such a shame you have to work," Amelia deadpans.

"Does that mean we can have book club fully in person on Wednesday before you leave? I'm so excited!" Hads says as she takes a bite of her waffle.

"Do you guys want any help with breakfast? My painkillers have kicked in, and—"

"Ells, if you move a muscle, I'm going to hit you with this spatula," Grant threatens, and I raise my eyebrows at him.

"Kinky. That ruler's done a number on you, pretty boy," I say as I sit back down.

"Yeah, well, my hand isn't the only thing that gets smacked—"

"Grant, if you say another word, I'm going to burn your fingerprints off on my stove. It's hard enough I know you two have sex." Oliver pauses to shiver. "I don't need or want to hear about it."

"Understood, old sport." Grant salutes him, and I hear Paige laughing as Oliver rolls his eyes again.

"Oliver, you're such a prude. I know for a fact you and Paige—"

"Hads, don't. Just don't. This is not an appropriate breakfast conversation." Oliver palms his forehead, and we all laugh while eating.

"Oliver, you do know what kind of books we like to read, right?" I ask him, especially since the one we're reading right now is a reverse-harem romance with three bodyguards. This was one of my picks, and I can't wait to discuss it on Wednesday.

"Oh, trust me, he knows. He peeked at our book club pick the other day and was suddenly *very* interested. It was hilarious." Paige smiles as she looks over at Oliver.

"Gross," Amelia says.

"I also took a look, and Hads has agreed to let me borrow her copy as long as I don't ruin her tabs. I feel like I need to see what the hype is about." Grant smiles as he throws more pepper on his eggs.

We talk about anything and everything before my mind focuses on the fact that, in twenty four hours, I'm going to have to see Leo again.

There's no way I can get out of him shadowing me. I'm going to have to be as civil as possible and try to refrain from snapping his neck whenever he makes a snide comment.

I can do that, right? I can be the bigger person in this scenario, especially since I know he's going to do everything in his power to make this situation horrible for me.

"Guys, what the fuck do I do about tomorrow? I'm not going to let Leo force me to quit my dream job, but he's not going to make this easy on me."

"Because you both hate each other?" Oliver asks, and I nod.

"More like they want to hate-fuck each other," Hads mumbles into her coffee.

"God, not you too. I thought Paige and Grant were the only ones on Team Ella and Leo." All I hear as I slump my head is the sound of Paige and Grant high-fiving.

Amelia silently rubs my back as she speaks. "Ells, I know we don't know what happened between you two, but I think you both know you have to be civil. This is the real world. It's not a college internship anymore. I hope he's not too much of a stubborn jackass to realize that."

She's right. We might get off to a rocky start, but I can be the bigger person. I'm fully capable of being civil. It's his stupid cocky attitude that I'll have to rein in the first few days. *I do get to boss him around for thirty days...* "You're right. I can do this."

"I believe in you, Ells." Paige smiles at me before she gets up. "I need a shower. I smell like alcohol." Oliver goes to press a kiss to her mouth, but she leans away before she heads into their room.

"I second that. I'll see you guys soon, though." Amelia whisks herself away to the guest bedroom, leaving Grant, Oliver, Hads, and I in the kitchen.

"What was that about? Trouble in paradise already?" Grant asks Oliver.

"I told you not to fuck this up, Ol," Hads scolds him.

"Can you guys calm the fuck down? Whenever Paige drinks, she doesn't like to kiss me until the alcohol is off her breath because I don't drink. I told her a million times it's fine, but she still does it." Oliver blushes. *Blushes.* I never thought I'd see the fucking day.

"I should probably head home for a shower too." I lean over to hug Hads and Grant and give Oliver a wave as I collect my purse. "Unless you guys need help cleaning up?"

Hads waves her arms towards the door. "Go enjoy your last day of peace before you have to deal with Zimmerman."

"Thank you." I smile at her. "I'll text you guys when I'm home."

"Thanks, Ells!" Grant shouts from behind me.

I pull out my phone as I walk down the stairs of their complex toward my car, wanting to talk to another Zimmerman about how she forgot to mention her brother's new place of work.

I get into my car and fire off a message to Alissa, letting her know I'll be waiting for her when she gets home from work tonight.

> **Ella:** Care to explain why your brother showed up at my office yesterday?

> **Ella:** His new job is at my firm... I'm going to kill you if you knew about it and didn't tell me. How are you related to him? It truly boggles my mind sometimes.

> **Alissa:** I have no comment.

> **Ella:** I'll see you at home.

> **Alissa:** Sounds good. I hope Paigey's birthday was awesome!

Damn, she's really hard to be mad at.

5

Enjoy Today While It Lasts

July 2024

MY ALARM WAKES ME up at the usual time—four in the morning—and I immediately get up and throw my gym gear on. As I grab my already-made protein shake from the fridge, I relish in the fact that I have the same morning routine I did back home. Amidst all the change, at least I still have a slice of home.

Having a set routine has helped me stay sane over the past few years. I wake up early, head to the gym for a workout, head back home, shower, prepare for the workday, and then I go to work. I do weights every other day, but I always make sure to hit cardio.

My night routine is usually different, depending on what I have going on. Sometimes, I go out and get a few pints with the lads. Occasionally, I'll meet a beautiful woman, and sometimes, my night ends with her coming back to mine, which is my ideal conclusion.

Lately, that hasn't happened, but I'm blaming that on the move and the adjustment period that comes with it. Now that I'm back in the States, I should call Holt—Liam Holt, my best friend and former hockey captain at Grand Mountain—and see if he wants to grab a drink or something.

As I get into my car, I ring my parents, hoping to catch them at a good time. "Darling! How are you this morning? Is it your first day?"

My mum's shining voice comes through my car. "It is. I'm up bright and early for a workout, and then I'll head straight there." I pause, afraid to ask my next question. "How's Dad?"

"He's fine. You both need to stop worrying about him."

"I'm afraid Alissa and I will never stop, so you'll have to deal with us asking about him twenty-four seven, at least while we're over here."

"I know, my love. Now, go enjoy your day and stop worrying. You need to be focused for your first day. You've got this."

"Thanks. We'll chat soon." I smile as I end the call. The past few years have been tough for Alissa and me; our father has a heart condition and had a really bad heart attack about a year ago. He was in the hospital for a while and had to have major surgery. It was tough at the start. When I got the call he was in the hospital, I thought he was going to die. When I arrived and he was already in surgery, I panicked. I had no clue what happened because nobody would tell me anything, so I had to grin and bear it through fifteen hours of surgery.

Hypertrophic cardiomyopathy—HCM. It's a genetic condition that makes the walls of the heart thick and stiff so it's difficult to pump blood throughout his body.

It was horrible—the heart attack. Alissa had to get back to the States for work, so I stayed in England to help my parents out and take a bit of pressure off Mum. It was fine, of course. I was happy to do it, but leaving was one of the hardest decisions I'd ever made.

I was scared that if I left and he had another heart attack, I'd miss my chance to say goodbye. Or what if my parents needed something and I was an ocean away? I had endless concerns, lots of feelings about how terrible of a son I would be if I left. Both of them told me to take this job; now, I call them a thousand times a week to check in—as does Alissa—and it helps alleviate the pain of being so far away. *Sort of.*

Ever since Dad had his scare, I've started to up my cardio workouts to make sure my heart stays healthy. I've made it part of my morning routine, and I find I feel a little calmer after—all those endorphins or whatever the fuck they're called.

Today, I have lots of pent up stress to work out, thanks to a fiery fucking girl who pushes all my bloody buttons. Seeing her yesterday made all the muscles in my body tense, and even though I worked out for three hours last night, it's still there. I'm glad I won't see her today; I can't start my first day already pissed off as hell.

That's tomorrow's problem.

Two hours and a few miles on the treadmill later, I step out of the shower and change into my work clothes—a cream-colored polo, brown trousers, and loafers, with my usual watch. My curly brown hair falls just before my eyebrows, and it looks as it usually does—fucking fantastic. I grab my bag with my lunch and all the papers Imogen needed me to sign and return and head for the office.

My short term rental is a bit of a commute at half an hour, so I make sure to leave early enough to beat the Richmond traffic I've heard about from my sister. My actual apartment will be ready in a few months. It's in a brand new building, so they're working on plumbing, electrical, and all that shit before I can officially move in. It's a beautiful spot, a lot closer to work than this place. I'm itching for it to be done so I can finally settle in, but until then, I'm stuck in this place, with all my crap mostly in boxes.

I take a deep breath before I drive off to my first official day at work.

When I finally get in, I'm a bit nervous. I assume it's going to be pretty chill since Ella isn't here, and I'm glad I at least have one day before she comes and annoys the hell out of me.

I get into my office, flip the light on, and a weird sense of something washes over me. It's a feeling I don't recognize, like I'm finally meant to be here after all the shit that has happened.

For once, I feel like I belong.

But this won't last long. As soon as Ella shows up, it'll fade, but for today, I'm going to embrace it.

This isn't just another job to get me by in life. This is all I've been looking forward to since I left university. Now that I'm here, it feels good. It feels right.

I head over to my desk and set down the small box I brought in. This office is so dull and bland, and Imogen told me I could spruce it up a bit—make it my own and such. So, I grab the picture of my parents I recently framed and set it on my desk next to my screen.

Then, I take out the massive plant my sister got me and set it in the corner against the wall. Alissa fucking loves plants. I swear, she used to have a hundred different ones back home. Sometimes, I could barely see her actual room for the sheer number of plants. In her place with Ella, she has a few too. Not as many as she did at home, but still enough to make her place mostly green.

As I'm taking my favorite pens out of my bag to shove into a drawer, someone knocks on my door.

"Happy first day, new guy," a tall blond man says to me. "I see you're already making my old office your own. That's good." He sits down in one of the chairs in front of my desk.

This must be Brody—the guy whose job I took because he got promoted.

"Leo Zimmerman," I say to him, holding my hand out. "Nice to meet you."

"Brody, but I think you already knew that." He smirks before he leans back in his chair. "Since Ella isn't here today, you'll be with me. I think you'll like me better than her, so enjoy today while it lasts."

"Isn't that the truth?" I smile back at him. I'm really not excited to be working so closely with Ella over the next month. I throw my pens into the drawer and close it, sitting in my chair so I can chat with this guy. I think I like him already.

"So, today is pretty chill. We have one meeting later about a contract renewal coming up, but other than that, it's a pretty standard day."

"Sounds good to me."

"So, did Ella scare you off already? I heard you met with her and Imogen the other day. She can be pretty edgy when you first meet her."

"Ella Williams has always been a pain in my arse," I tell him. I'm unsure of why he keeps bringing her up, but I don't mind finding out about how she operates here. I know Imogen is fond of her, but I don't know about everyone else.

"You two know each other?"

"Quite well, unfortunately," I tell him. He feels like someone I can trust, especially since he just got promoted. I wondered why Imogen didn't put him as my shadow, but his workload is probably heftier since the promotion. It makes sense that Ella—whose office is across from mine—is going to be teaching me everything I need to know for my first month here.

"Oh, I cannot wait to hear about all those stories. Look," he leans closer to me, "she's not my favorite person here, but Imogen likes her. She does fine work, but wow, she can be a lot to handle sometimes. Lots of fucking opinions."

He's right. Ella might be the most opinionated person I've ever met. She always has something to say about anyone and everything.

"Well, enough about her," Brody says. "I already sent you an email of some stuff I want you to look over."

I turn to my desktop, shake the mouse so the screen turns on, and open my email. "What do you want me to look for?"

"I sent a few things, some contracts I want you to review for me before I send them out. Every time we have a new client acquired, we send them contracts, but I'm sure you knew that."

I nod. That's simple business procedure.

"And the other attachment is a list of companies we're thinking of pitching to, ranging from small chains here to bigger and wider known ones across the East Coast."

"You want me to pick a few from the list I think would be good for us?"

"Yes, exactly. That way, you can go over our current client list and familiarize yourself with the kind of work we like to take on."

"Thanks, Brody. I'll get right on that. When do you need this all by?"

"End of the day?"

"Sounds good," I tell him.

"Wonderful." He stands. "If you have any questions or need my help, my extension number is 277."

"Appreciate it, man."

He's about to leave my office before he stops in the doorway. "I like you already, Leo. I think you'll fit perfectly here with us."

I think I will too.

6

An Oscar Worthy Performance

Monday Night

"Lizzie, I already told you, I'm fine."

"No offense, Ells, but I can tell you're stressed out just from hearing your voice over the phone. What's going on?" My little sister sounds genuinely concerned and, not wanting to worry her with my problems, I change the subject.

"I should be asking you that. What happened to that cute guy you mentioned? Did he ask you out or what?" I smile at the thought of my little sister dating, but part of me is also terrified for some reason. Getting your heart shattered into a thousand pieces sucks, and knowing something like that could happen to her makes me want to lock her in her room at my dad's house for the rest of her fucking life.

"Nothing has happened. I'm a thousand percent sure he doesn't even know I exist." I can hear her smile from over the phone, but I don't press.

"Well, if he ever comes to his senses, make sure to tell me so I can have a talk with him."

"Ella! That's disgusting."

"Lizzie, I wasn't talking about *that*, but now I'm thinking I should..." I trail off, mentally noting to do that if she ever introduces anyone to me.

"You're worse than dad. Why are you guys so embarrassing?"

"It comes with the territory. We care about you, that's all. And I've been in enough relationships to know all about them, so listen to me over Dad."

"Yeah, yeah. Whatever. What are you up to?"

"Well, troublemaker, I'm currently working on a campaign for an author that goes live on their social media tomorrow." I smile, loving what I do as a freelancer. I'm glad that, even though my office job might be making me feel like shit lately, I still have *something* that brings me joy.

"Can you tell me who it is? I know I prefer movies to books, but I always love hearing your voice when you talk about this. You're always so ecstatic, and I like hearing you like that." My heart drops a little bit, because no matter how hard I try to keep my shit together, it kills me to know people, especially my sister, worry about me.

"Lizzie, I'm okay. I promise. But yes, I do love doing this. It's fun combining my love for books and my degree. I'm working on a series of snippets for this one mafia author Paige and I both love. She's the sweetest human ever, and I'd do this for free if she'd let me."

"I think she knows how valuable you are, sis. She knows your worth."

A smile overtakes my face at my sister knowing me a bit too well. "Thanks, Lizzie. Now, it's late. You need to go to sleep. Get some rest."

"Ella, it's summer! You worry too much."

"Forgive me for being a bit overprotective. I was a teenager once," I say, knowing I didn't have the same experiences a normal teenager would. Part of me is melancholic for missing out, but I'm glad Lizzie is able to enjoy these years. After all, everything I did, I did to make sure she and my dad were okay—even if that meant sacrificing my entire childhood. I tell myself it's fine, but my throat feels a bit heavy as I try to swallow. "Just be careful, especially if you go out at night with friends. The buddy system is important!"

"I know, sis. Have a good day tomorrow, and tell Alissa and the girls I say hi."

"I will. I love you." I smile, loving how close my sister is with my friends despite having only met them a few times.

"I love you, Ella."

I end the call and stare at my laptop for a few seconds to decompress before I get to work. I have a bunch of content to make for an author I had a call with a few days ago. She hired me to make some videos and stagnant posts for her next release—a queer romance novel, to which I screamed at her how excited I was to read it.

I've been trying to get myself out there more with authors online, and my goal is to one day do this full-time, but for now, I have my day job *and* this side hustle.

I'm fucking exhausted, but if there's one thing I've learned over the years, it's that it takes a lot for me to quit something. I want this future for myself. I want it badly. And if it means working myself to death, then so be it.

Tuesday Morning

"I FORGOT THE HOT new hire started yesterday." Rae storms into my office before I've even sat down. "I'm so excited for some new eye candy. I didn't get to see him Sunday and scope him out."

Don't make a face. Do not make an annoyed face at the fact that she called your worst nightmare hot. "Where did you hear that?"

"Adam told me, and I hear you're the lucky bitch Imogen selected to train him."

I roll my eyes. It's an automated response every time I think, hear, or breathe near Leo Zimmerman. "I don't know if lucky is the correct word," I tell her as I slump in my chair. Today is the beginning of the worst time of my life. I'm sure I can't get lower than this—having to work with him again. It was bad enough during our internship, but I've already promised myself I'm going to *try* to be professional with him.

But I know when I see him, all my professionalism is going to fly out the window.

Rae raises both of her eyebrows as she leans forward in her chair. "Is this an open or closed door conversation?"

"Closed."

"On it," she says as she kicks my door closed with her foot. "I assume this isn't a good story based on the look on your face."

I smooth down my cream-colored pantsuit before I try to be as nice as possible. "We went to college together, and he is my worst nightmare."

Well, I tried.

"There is absolutely more to this story, and I'm so excited." Rae takes a sip of her coffee before coaxing me into telling her the rest.

I tell her all about our shared internship our senior year of college, and by the time I'm done, she has a mischievous look on her face.

"So, you two have fucked, then?"

"What? No! Why the hell would you say that?" I say defensively.

"I don't know. It just seems like you two would have really hot hate sex if he dislikes you as much as you do him."

"I'm never having sex with that man ever again." The words come out before I can stop them. *Shit.*

"Ever again? Oh, babe, I *need* this story more than air. Was it good? How big is his—"

She stops talking, on account of Adam joining us in my office. "Holy shit. The new guy is here, and he has an accent."

"Ella fucked him!" Rae all but shouts.

"*What?*" Adam looks at me, and I swear there's pride in his eyes. *Seriously?*

"Not recently! Fuck! I knew I shouldn't have said anything. Stop bringing it up, please. I don't need to be reminded of the worst mistake I've ever made."

"But—"

"Rae, no. This is teetering on another HR conversation, and that would only give Leo something to hold over my head. I have to start training him today, and I'm already on the brink of quitting because of it."

"Quitting? But you love it here!" Adam says—a bit too enthusiastically, I might add.

"Yeah, I do. But if *he* is here, it's only a matter of time before I hate it. That's what he does; he's like an infectious disease that poisons everything he touches with his accent, his greasy hair—"

"Don't forget my beautiful eyes, Ella. I'd hate for you to leave out one of my better qualities in whatever list of yours this is."

The fucker just let himself in. *Or Adam didn't close my door.* No, Leo is the type to let himself into rooms because he can. Because he has a penis attached to his body, doors will always be open and unlocked for him.

Meanwhile, some of us have to knock, apologize profusely, and make our tone of voice eight octaves higher so we don't come across as wasting someone's time.

I paste on my fakest smile possible as Rae and Adam turn their heads between the two of us like they're watching a tennis match. "Leo. How nice to see you this morning. Have you been finding your way around the office?"

A smirk takes over his face as he leans against my doorway. "Please stop with the fake niceties, Ella. I heard your conversation from my office. I came over here to wave my white flag, on account of this being a professional environment. I want this transition to be as easy as possible for everyone involved. I'll play nice if you do."

Oh, how nice of him to wave his flag first. How nice of him, truly. This is an Oscar-worthy performance from Leo Zimmerman. I think I should call the Academy. Maybe they'll create an entire new category for him—Biggest Asshole in a Drama.

"I always play nice, Leo. I was explaining to my friends our history. Forgive me for forgetting to close my door. You weren't supposed to hear it."

He and I are staring at one another, an annoying smirk still on his face, my fake smile trying its best not to slip into a scowl.

"Ah. Well, when you're ready to begin with training, I'll be in my office," he points straight across from where we are, "over there."

He looks at Adam and Rae before he offers them both his hand. "Leo Zimmerman. Please don't take Ella's account of me as complete truth. I promise I'm not the twat she says I am."

Adam takes his hand and shakes it. "Nice to meet you, dude. If you have any questions, you can find me in my cubicle."

Traitor.

He flashes his blinding smile at Rae, and I swear, her cheeks change color. There it is: the Leo fucking Zimmerman effect. Thank God it has never worked on me.

Except that one time you were drunk and—

Nope. My mind is *not* going there. Not today. Not ever again.

"It's nice to meet you, Leo. And don't worry, I won't let Ella's stories cloud my judgment of you. That's not who I am."

I shoot her a glare, knowing that's exactly how we operate here. If I hate someone, so does she. If Rae declares someone is an asshole, then they go on my mental list of people to avoid. But Leo doesn't need to know that.

"Wonderful," he says as his eyes meet mine again. "I'll be in my office."

And then he walks out of mine and closes the door behind him.

"Wow. Talk about tension," Adam says. "I wish I had the confidence he has. God, I think he's my hero. Did you see how he walked in here?"

"They totally want to fuck each other again," Rae quips, and I have to hesitate before I throw my stapler at her.

"I've never been less horny in my life," I say as I look at my watch. "And we have a meeting to get to, so let's go."

"I have to grab my laptop, so I'll meet you guys in the conference room," Adam says before he leaves.

Rae stands and follows, heading back to her office, and I remember I have to grab the devil's spawn for this meeting. He is my shadow, after all.

I knock twice on his door and hear him mumble through it. I let myself in, and I hate that I can see directly into my office from inside of his. He's able to see me when I'm sitting at my desk because of how our offices are set up.

"Ella, I'm aware we have a meeting. You didn't need to come get me. I'm a big boy; I can handle myself."

Before I roll my eyes again, I stop myself. "You're my shadow, Leo. I'm supposed to teach you how the office runs, so that's what I'm doing."

"And I appreciate that, but I'm capable of walking a few steps to get to a meeting."

"You know what, Leo—"

Before I can finish my sentence, he shuts his door and corners me in front of it.

"What, Ella? What insult is going to come out of your mouth this time? Something about my outfit? Or are you going to go right for how annoying you find me?"

Well, it is pretty annoying you're in my personal space right now. "Careful, Zimmerman. You're so close to me, I could spit on you and ruin your perfectly styled hair."

He tilts his head at me, a smirk crossing his face. "Ah, so the hair this time. Got it."

"It's not my fault it looks like you smeared gallons of gel on your head. Maybe you *should* try using spit next time. I think it would look better, less crunchy."

"Help me out then," he says, a challenge in his gaze. *He's not serious?*

I hold his stare for a few seconds, his chocolate brown eyes staring through my soul as I reach out and grab his tie hanging between us.

And I yank it.

"Let's go, Zimmerman. We can't be late."

And I swear, I hear him laugh under his breath as he grabs his laptop and follows me to the conference room.

7

Dior Sauvage and Pretentiousness

College

I AM SO FUCKING exhausted.

Not only did I stay up all night working on my homework, but as I walk into my internship, it starts raining, and the asshole in front of me doesn't bother to hold the door.

Now, I'm soaked, looking very unprofessional as I get into the building.

It's fine, I say to myself. *Put your fucking game face on, Williams, and you'll be fine.*

I get into the office and set all my stuff down, but the files I was working on the other day aren't here. They should've been right in my desk drawer where I left them, but I can't find them. *Shit. Fuck. Fuck!*

Where could they have gone? They're for a long-time client, and if I really did lose them, they're not going to trust me to do anything else for them.

God, can't something go right for me today?

"Ella, there you are. Do you have the marketing plan I asked you to prepare for today?" Tim—the head of the firm—asks me, and I swallow hard before I answer.

"I do, but I seem to have misplaced them."

"You what?" he asks me, raising his voice ever so slightly.

I scramble around my desk, searching for the blue folder I'm positive I left here on Tuesday. "I'm sure they're around here somewhere, and if they're not, I have another copy on my computer that I can—"

"You lost it? I gave you one simple task, and you can't even manage that?"

"No, I can. I—"

He cut me off for the second time, and I knew when I first met him in my interview, I was going to dislike working for him. I clocked his holier-than-thou attitude when he called me sweetheart in my interview.

"Is this what you're looking for?" Leo asks as he waltzes over, my blue file folder in his hand, a shit-eating grin on his face.

He stole my fucking folder, I'm sure of it. He has been sabotaging me since we got here, and I wouldn't be surprised if he came over to my desk before I arrived today and took it to make me look incompetent. For some reason, Leo Zimmerman was put on this planet to push every fucking button of mine, and he knows just how to do it.

Tim grabs the folder from him and flips through it for about two seconds before he smiles at Leo. "Yes it is. Thank you, son. Will you sit in with me during the meeting with the client?"

He looks over at me, smiles, and nods his head. "I'd be honored, sir."

I shake my head at both of them. "But that's my work! Leo has no idea about any of the proposals, or what the client even does! How can he sit in on something he knows nothing about?"

"He clearly knows how to keep track of things better than you, Miss Williams. Let this be a lesson. Make sure this doesn't happen again," Tim says. "Ten minutes, Leo. Meet me in the conference room."

"Of course, sir."

Tim then leaves, and as I slump down in my cubicle, Leo lingers behind me. I'm assuming his huge ego takes up most of the space around him, because that's how I can tell when he's near.

His ego smells like Dior Sauvage and pretentiousness.

"You stole my folder," I say as I open my laptop.

"Maybe, but you should stop leaving things on your desk. It's fair game when it's out in the open."

I shove my chair out from behind me and spin around to face him, my finger pointed at his chest. "If you're going to play dirty, I can too. All you've done by being a snake is get on my bad side, and once that happens, you never get off my shit list."

"How sad," is all he says, a triumphant smirk on his face. "Maybe if you weren't late, I wouldn't have had to steal that folder. Tim was all up in arms about it this morning. You would know that if you were here on time."

My confidence falters. I was only five minutes late, and I'm usually punctual, but today hasn't been my day. My dad's car broke down on his way to take my little sister to school. He normally drops her off and then goes to work, and this was a hitch in his morning. So, when he called me as I was walking out the door, I dropped what I was doing to help.

It took me an extra half an hour to drop my sister at school and my dad at work. Yet, I was *only* five minutes late. Fucking impressive, if you ask me.

I try so hard to act like I have it all together, that I'm put together and can handle anything and everything life throws at me, but some days, it all falls apart.

Today was one of those days, and it has barely started. I'd hate to see what the rest of the fucking day has in store for me.

"Go away, Zimmerman," I say as I turn around and sit at my desk.

Huh. I never thought I would see the day Ella Williams backed down from one of our quips. I enjoy pushing her buttons a bit too much, but the girl has to lighten up.

Despite her thinking I'm a selfish arsehole who only cares about himself and his looks, I'm actually a decent guy. She would know that if she didn't judge me based on a few interactions.

I *did* steal her folder, but only because Tim was going ballistic looking for her this morning and I didn't want her to get yelled at.

I thought she enjoyed these games we played, but maybe I'm misreading the situation.

Whatever, I think to myself as I sit down in the conference room.

Ella Williams might love to read, but in reality, she judges books by their covers. We met once before this internship, and when I introduced myself on our first day, she refused to shake my hand and rolled her eyes at me.

And that fucking pissed me off. She doesn't know a single thing about me. Sure, she probably heard the whispers about me around campus. Grand Mountain is small, and shit spreads like wildfire because nobody can keep their mouth shut.

I like to fuck. I don't date because I don't have the time or energy for a relationship with everything on my plate, and the girls who get with me know that.

Assuming Ella knew all of this when we first met, she didn't even bother to get to know me, and that's how our mutual hatred started. She hates me for some stupid bullshit reason, I'm sure, and I hate her because she judged me without knowing me.

On top of all that, it's way too easy to push her buttons. She wears every expression on her face, and I can always tell what she's thinking. It's almost *too* easy.

As if she knows I'm thinking about her, she walks into the conference room moments before our meeting and begins to fill the coffee, bagels, and donuts.

She doesn't meet my stare, and since I'm the only one in here, the silence is deafening.

"Do you have decaf over there?"

She doesn't turn around as she answers. "Yes, but you have two legs and can get it yourself. I'm not your fucking servant, Leo."

God, the way she spits my name with all that jest, you think I'd done something unforgivable to her. "I didn't ask you to. It was only a question."

"Nothing is ever that simple with you," she says, turning around to walk out of the room. "Enjoy your meeting, asshole."

8

Be Ella's Bitch

July 2024

I've been training under Ella for one week, and it has already been a nightmare.

Thank fucking God it's Friday.

All I've done this entire week is be Ella's bitch. I'm not even kidding. I know I have thirty days shadowing her, but I thought for sure I'd be doing more than just shit she doesn't want to do.

It started small. At first, she asked me to make copies and showed me how to use the machines—which I thought was helpful, until she made me copy random sheets of paper. Did she assume I wasn't going to read the things she gave me? Is this some sort of test? Initiation? Or is it because she can't stand me?

Probably all of the above...

And that's exactly what I'm doing now. I'm making copies of some important documents Ella said she needs for a client, but all that's on the paper is a singular sentence.

My name is Leo Zimmerman, and I think I'm hotter than I am.

Bitch work, like I said.

And the papers keep fucking jamming in this bloody machine. I go to kick it, but someone stops me.

"Need some help?" Brody asks, his hand on my shoulder.

"Yeah, that'd be nice."

He steps where I was standing in front of the machine and surprises me when he raises his hand and smacks the copier on the side.

I could've done that...

"Sometimes, all you have to do is hit it, and it seems to work again. It's the weirdest thing," he tells me, a smile on his face.

"Thanks. I appreciate it."

"No problem, man. We have to stick together around here, you know?" I'm puzzled by what he means, and it must show on my face, because he speaks again. "Us men have to stick together."

"Oh, of course," I tell him. This is the most I've talked to Brody since I took over his position, and I feel like we could be good friends.

"If you need anything, let me know. I know Ella can be a pain to work with sometimes. At least she was when I sat across the hall from her." He smirks, and I can only imagine what he had to deal with before I got here.

"You must be happy to be in another office now."

"Very happy." He winks at me before someone calls his name. "Duty calls. Good luck with the copier, man."

"Thanks for your help," I say again, and after a few more minutes, I finish this task. Having to go give these to Ella is somehow the worst part. I guarantee, she's going to give me another useless task to do.

I knock on her office door, and she tells me to come in, so I do. Her face turns annoyed as soon as I walk inside. I haven't even said anything, but apparently, the way I breathe isn't up to her standards.

"Here are those copies," I say as I hand them to her. "What else do you want me to do so you can waste more of my time?"

She gives me a pointed look. "Excuse me?"

I lean my palms against her desk. "I don't mind being bossed around, but you're not giving me any actual work."

"Leo, you're shadowing for the first thirty days. It's only been a week, and you need to learn how to stay organized, make copies, and—"

"And get your coffee for you?"

Her eyes move down and then back up. "It doesn't feel good, does it?"

"Not really," I tell her. I knew she was aware of what she was doing.

"Now you understand what it feels like not being equal to someone you work with on the same level. Good; that took less time than I thought." She smiles and motions for me to sit. What the fuck is going on?

"What the heck are you doing, Ella?"

"Teaching you a lesson. We're all on the same playing field here. We all work together on contracts and shit for our clients. Sure, there are team leaders and promotions to be had, but at the end of the day, we all have the same goal—to make our clients happy."

"So this was a test?"

"Yes, and you actually did alright," she says before she types a few things on her computer. "I sent you an email with a fake proposal for a client's brand. Look it over, make some mockups, and by the end of next week, I expect it to be in my inbox."

"Really?"

"Unless you think you can't handle it. Then you can—"

"No, I can." I meet her eyes again. "I didn't think this conversation would end like this."

"I'm not going to fail you on purpose, Zimmerman. I just needed to test you a little bit, especially with everything that happened at our internship. You played dirty, and just because you're a man, you got more than I did." She shakes her head. "That's not how it works here."

"I understand."

"Now, get out. I have shit to do." I stand from my chair and head for the door.

"There's the girl I knew you were. I was starting to think all your talk meant you were going soft on me, Williams."

"Soft has never been used to describe me, and you know that." She rolls her eyes at me. "Close my door behind you and have those mockups done by next week."

"Got it."

And as I sit down at my desk to prepare to do *actual* work, I realize it might not be as bad as I thought it would be working under Ella.

But I'd never say that out loud. I wouldn't want to jinx myself.

9

Sunday Linens

"Alissa, can you grab the orange juice out of the fridge for me?" I ask as I grab the plates. I place them around our table, along with the silverware and napkins I folded into bow ties this morning.

I swear, nothing makes me feel better than seeing my friends, hosting a party, and brunch.

That's a recipe for a good time, and since I've been stuck in the pits of hell lately, I've needed a day to forget all my worries and spend time with the people I love.

"You got it, babe. I can turn the music on too," Alissa says as she glides through the room.

"It's the least you could do, considering you didn't warn me Leo was joining my firm." I still haven't let it go. When I got home and found

Alissa waiting for me with a bottle of wine, ice cream, and our favorite reality show queued up, I knew it was an apology.

"Ells, whatever arguing you do with my brother is between you two. I've never understood why you can't just get along."

Before I start a long-winded conversation about how much I hate her brother, someone knocks on my door. Based on what time it is, I know it's Paige and Oliver. The girl is always early to everything. It's probably for the best; I'd hate to ruin today by talking about him.

"Are you sure I can't invite him?" Alissa asks me again. "He has no friends, Ella. He just moved back here, you know."

"I'm sure whoever slept on his dick last night is keeping him company this morning!" I say as I finish setting the table. "It's bad enough I have to see him at work every day. He's not infecting my weekends too."

"Fine."

I head to my door, swing it open, and am immediately met with Paige's smiling face.

She barrels into me with a hug, and I can almost feel the sunlight radiating off of her.

I'm not a sunny person like she is. I'm a bit rough around the edges, way too honest to the point that some people think I'm mean, and I'm often told I'm too much for people.

But with Paige, she doesn't give a shit. She balances me out in a way. The two of us understand one another, especially with our family situations. Her dad is a piece of shit, and my mom walked out on me and my family when I was younger.

We both know what it feels like to be a second choice to someone who's supposed to love you unconditionally. But neither of us has let that stop us; we somehow found one another amidst all the people in the world. We love one another unconditionally to make up for all we missed out on, and I couldn't be more grateful for her presence.

I lock eyes with Oliver over Paige's shoulder, a slight smile on his face. I don't know if I'll ever get used to that, but I'm glad Paige has found someone who makes her happy.

And I'm glad Oliver is happy too, I guess. As long as he treats Paige right, that's all that matters. If he doesn't, he knows Hads, Grant, and I will be first in line to kick his ass.

And Amelia, if she was here.

"Ella, I've missed you so much! God, it's been way too long."

"Babe, I saw you on Wednesday at book club."

Oliver pushes past the two of us and comes inside. "She's been dressed since six this morning."

I tilt my head at Paige, confused but glad she's so excited. I've missed hosting things at our apartment. Today's theme was coastal, so Paige is on theme in her flowing white dress and large hat. Oliver is wearing color for once, so he's on theme too. This outfit screams Paige. I bet she laid it out for him this morning. I made a bet with Grant he would be on theme, and it looks like I was right.

"Alissa! You look wonderful!" Paige says as she hugs her. Alissa's big headpiece almost knocks her in the head, but she dodges it.

Those two continue talking as I look over at Oliver. "Why was she up so early this morning?"

"She hasn't been sleeping a lot lately," he says, a somber expression on his face. Or, well, that's just his face. "Amelia hasn't been calling her like she usually does."

That's not what I was expecting him to say, but it tracks. "She didn't join us Wednesday either. She told us she had a late meeting and wasn't able to get out of it, but she didn't even let us know until days later."

Oliver only rolls his eyes. "I bet."

He's only saying what I'm thinking. Ever since Amelia went back to England, she has been worse at answering our messages. I understand the time difference is a bitch and a half, but no matter what, we always promised that book club would still be the one night a week we made time for one another.

Amelia hasn't been very good at doing that lately, and I'm not impressed.

"Paige misses her. A lot."

"We all do," I tell him, lying to myself. I wasn't happy with Amelia and how she left. She's still one of my best friends, but some of the decisions she made this past year have made me think differently of her. For one, she broke up with Henry at the airport right before she boarded her flight—literally ripped his heart out in front of all of us and then left.

How fucking cracked do you have to be to do that? I'll never forget the look on his face when he turned around to face us after Ames walked away. If heartbroken had a picture in the dictionary, his face would be on the page.

She's pulling away from us. It started slow. At first, she just stopped answering our messages. Now, she doesn't answer our calls and is missing book club.

And according to what Oliver said, she's even cutting Paige off. Those two were as close as you could get in college. Amelia promised her before she left that they would still do morning debriefs like they did in their apartment, but now, she stopped doing those too.

I would text her and ask if she wants to talk, but I don't bother. Why should I continue to reach out only to get nothing in return? Amelia tends to be like this, but she always comes back to us after a week or two.

It has been almost a month since she was here, and we haven't heard a thing from her.

Another few knocks at my door, and I hear Grant and Hads come in.

"We're not late, are we?" Hads asks.

"No, you're not," I say as she comes into view. She smirks before I grab a dish from her hands.

"Banana bread, courtesy of Grant's mom's recipe."

I wrap her in a hug, her long skirt flowing since Alissa and I opened the sliding doors to our balcony. It's a really nice day out, and the warm Virginia air is setting the vibe perfectly.

"Where's Grant?" Paige asks as she hugs Hads.

"Probably tip-toeing over here so as to not wrinkle his Sunday linens," she jokes, but as Grant comes into view, that's exactly what he's doing.

In his fully white and linen outfit, he's shuffling over to us. "Sorry, no hugs. I am *not* ruining this outfit if we're taking pictures."

"What the hell are you wearing?" Oliver asks him.

Grant looks Oliver up and down before meeting my eyes. "Dammit, Ells," Grant says as he fishes twenty dollars out of his pocket and hands it to me. "You won, congrats."

"Did you guys bet on something again?" Paige asks, probably already knowing we did.

"Yes, and I won fair and square." I smirk as I head over to the counter, wanting a mimosa. "So, who wants a drink?"

As I LOOK AT my friends around the table, I soak up the moment. As laughs are traded and smiles are given, I hope this isn't as good as it will ever get. We've all come so far from that small classroom on campus, and I wish time would slow the fuck down for a second. I know we have more time, but as the oldest in the group—besides Alissa—I worry one day, I'm going to look back and wish we were back in college.

Everyone always talks about how college is the best time of your life, but I think life starts after you leave. Sure, college is great, and it brought me the friends I'll have forever, but I've never been more excited to experience life with my family still around me.

"So wait, you're telling me they want you to run some sort of hockey camp? You?" Alissa asks Grant, as confused as to how hockey works as I am.

"Yes! It's a summer camp the school I work for is running. I'm excited. We've had a bunch of sign-ups so far, and I'm looking forward to teaching young kids to skate and play."

"Good for you, Grant." Paige smiles at him as they fist bump. "Alissa, you know he won a championship, don't you?"

"Oh, really?" Alissa says as she sips her mimosa.

"Paige, please, there's no need to brag... Yeah, Jacks and I had a final assist for the winning goal. It's no big deal, really," Grant says, downplaying that championship game. All of us were there supporting him, and it was one of the most exhilarating games I've ever watched. That could be because I was buzzed, but let's pretend it was because of the game.

"It was amazing, babe. Truly one of the best games you've played," Hads says as she grabs his hand. It's nice to see her all soft. Grant has truly weakened her defenses. I'm glad my girls are happy with their partners.

Most people would be uncomfortable being single and surrounded by all these couples, but I love being on the market. I'm having fun; well, I was before work and life got in the way.

I enjoy casual sex with people, but lately, I've been in a weird limbo. I can't even remember the last time I fucked someone, and I've been all out of sorts since I found out Leo was going to be working with me. Yet another thing he ruined. Most nights, I come home way too tired to deal with anything but a hot shower and reality television.

It's exhausting being around someone you despise with every molecule in your body all day.

"So, Ella, how has work been? Have you killed Leo yet?" Hads asks me before turning to Alissa. "Sorry, Liss."

"Don't be. I asked her the same thing when she came home on their first day working together."

"I haven't killed him yet, but it's only been a few days, so that could change."

"Listen, if you need help burying his body, you know who to call," Oliver says as he throws his napkin down.

The rest of us look at him like he's crazy, considering what happened last year.

"Really, bro?" Hads says, a disinterested expression on her face.

"What? It was a joke!" he says, but nobody's laughing. "How is it still too soon for those jokes? It's been an entire year, for fuck's sake."

"I thought it was funny, babe," Paige says as she rests her head on his shoulder.

"I'll divert the subject," Grant says. "So, does anyone else have any fun things happening lately?"

We all shake our heads, not being able to think of anything remotely fun that happened in the past few weeks.

"Nothing? God, are we officially boring adults?" Grant asks.

"Not yet," I say as I collect some plates.

"Ella, let me help," Paige says, and before I try to stop her, Hads starts to help too.

"Guys, go sit down and relax. I can do this," I say as I place some stuff in the sink.

"Ells, you put this entire day together. The least you can let us do is help clean up," Paige tells me as she starts to clean the plates I put in the sink.

Before I can grab the rag to start drying, Hads gets it first. "Too slow."

"Guys, come on, I'm the host. I should be—"

"Relax, Ella. You've had a long week dealing with Leo. Let us do something for you for once. Okay?"

Hads always knows just what to say to get me to listen. "Fine."

"So, has it been okay working with him? I know you were worried about it."

I sigh heavily as I try to make my thoughts coherent. For some reason, when it comes to describing Leo Zimmerman and his presence, I have a hard time. I think it's because he pisses me off so much that all my thoughts get jumbled.

"It's been fine, I guess. He's constantly in my bubble, and it gets annoying, but we have a truce, and he's stuck to it."

"Huh, that's good," Paige says, and I know she still thinks we're going to get together, but she couldn't be farther from the truth. I would *never* date Leo fucking Zimmerman. If he was the last person on Earth, I'd lock myself in a room and figure out how to procreate with my dildo.

"Paige, don't get any ideas, babe."

"Oh, come on! We're literally reading a workplace romance novel next month! How am I not supposed to draw connections between that and your situation?" She hands Hads a plate and she dries it, putting it into the rack Alissa and I keep on our counter.

"I told you guys I wanted to read another book! Workplace romance and I are not friends at the moment." *No matter how much I love that trope.* I wish Amelia joined us Wednesday, because I know she would've picked the other book like I did. But Hads and Paige outnumbered me, and they chose our read for next month.

"Whoops!" Hads says, and I know she understands how I feel about Leo—it's similar to how she felt about Grant at first—but I think her boyfriend is slowly turning her to their side. Paige and Grant are relationship cheerleaders. The two of them want all of us to be happy and in love like they are, but I've told them countless times I'm okay how I am.

I have too much going on to have a relationship anyway. My dad and sister still rely on me a lot, and work keeps me busy. I like my life, and I don't need anything else putting a hitch in my routine.

"Ella, look—" Paige says, but as she's talking, the faucet slips and starts to spray her. "Ah! Oh my God!"

The three of us are yelling, trying to turn it off, but Paige only points it at me and Hads, spraying us too.

"Hey!"

"Paige! This is not the time for a water fight!"

She only continues to laugh as Grant comes in, and she points the detachable faucet at him.

"Not my linens, Paigey! What are you guys doing?" Grant says as he gets soaked. I cannot stop laughing, even though my kitchen is a mess.

Hads turns the faucet off as Oliver and Alissa join us, eyes wide as they see the water all over the place.

"Well, now we can't say we're boring adults." Paige smiles, and after a few seconds of silence, we all start to laugh. "I'll clean it up, don't worry."

"I'll go grab some towels," Alissa says, headed for our bathroom.

"Just so you all know, we're not boring. We're growing up," Paige tells us. "Never use that word ever again when describing us, deal?"

"Deal."

And for the rest of the afternoon, we clean the water out of my kitchen and laugh like idiots as we reminisce.

As far as I know, the good old days are whenever I'm with these people.

10

Mommy Issues

August 8th, 2024

I THINK THIS IS the first year my birthday won't end in sex.

A fucking shame, that is.

I started my day the same way I always do: by going to the gym. My birthday has never been my favorite thing to celebrate. To me, it's just another day of the year. It's nice to go out when I'm in the mood, but lately, there hasn't been a single reason to celebrate.

Well, maybe getting a job is a reason, but even that doesn't bring me much of anything, since I'm too worried about my dad back home. This past year has been tough as hell, and turning another year older isn't a big deal.

Now, I'm sitting at my desk at work, going through a portfolio Ella gave me to familiarize myself with the company's typical campaigns.

My body shivers when it hears her name in my head. It hasn't been horrible working alongside her here, but I'm starting to get sick of all the fucking attitude she throws my way. Not only is there no reason for it, but I'm trying my best not to cause any commotion while I'm here. All I want to do is come in, do my job to the best of my ability, and leave. Work-life balance is important to me, and if something happens to my dad again, I'm probably going to end up moving back to London. This job is a means to an end, no matter what way I look at it. It would be nice if Ella did the same and not cause any more squabbles between us.

I do start shit sometimes. I'm not completely innocent in anything between us, but Ella Williams pushes my bloody buttons more than anyone else on the fucking planet. She gets under my skin, and somehow, she always knows which ones to press.

It's exactly how we were back in college, and even then, I didn't understand it.

The only time we ever got along was when we had sex that one night, and even then, she fought me.

Stop thinking about sex with Ella while you're at work, I remind myself. It has been popping up in my mind recently, and that's only because we're back in such close proximity. On top of that, add my dry spell, and it's a recipe for disaster.

It was only one time, and it will never happen again.

God, I need to get fucking laid.

I grab my phone from where it sits on my desk and dial the one person I know who can help. He answers on the third ring.

"I was about to call you, Birthday Boy," Liam says over the line.

"Well, we always did have some sort of sixth sense with one another."

"Happy birthday, dude. Got any fun plans for tonight?"

A smirk catches in my mouth. "Actually, that's why I called."

"Are you finally letting me plan a night out for you? Leo Zimmerman is letting *me* have control of a night out? This seems too good to be true."

"And I'll even pay for it," I offer.

I hear him sigh. "God, I've missed you, you rich prick."

"Shut the hell up, Holt. But you better exceed my expectations."

He only laughs. "Let me worry about that, Leo. I'm sure you'll be impressed."

"Good," I say as Ella comes back to her office. *Damn, where was she for twenty minutes?* "Listen, I have to go. I'll see you later?"

"I'll text you an address in a few."

"Perfect," I say as I hang up and continue to check out the portfolios. This company has done some great work. A few things have caught my eye, and I wonder how many of these Ella has worked on. The girl might be a pain in my ass, but she does good work. That has never been up for debate.

I watch as Ella swiftly moves around her office, grabbing a few folders and things before she takes a big deep breath and starts to walk toward my office.

"Is coming over here really so bad you have to take a deeper breath than a blowfish?"

She rolls her eyes at me. "When you greet me like that, then yes, it does."

"Can I help you with something?"

She sticks her leg out as if she's balancing herself. Today, she's wearing long, pleated pants, black to match her heels, with a white blouse. It's simpler than most of her outfits that seem to be monochrome.

Why are you paying attention to her outfits?

Christ, I need to get fucking laid. If Holt fails me tonight, he's never in charge of anything ever again.

"Get a notepad. We have a meeting."

"You sound excited," I say as I get out of my chair, grabbing a pen and a large notebook. Ella has been making me take notes during meetings. I never have to take too many, since I can remember what most of them are about, but if I don't, Ella will shout at me. She *thinks* she's the boss of me, but once these thirty days of shadowing are over, we'll be on the same level.

"Overjoyed, especially since it's not with Imogen." And then, she walks away from me. It doesn't take me too long to catch up to her—my legs are as long as half her body.

We walk through the office, and instead of going into the conference room, we instead head for Brody's office.

I quite like Brody. He seems like a good guy, but Ella has a problem with him. Well, Ella seems to have a problem with every man in this office besides Adam. They seem closer than she is to most of the men here.

Kind of pisses me the fuck off, but I decide not to dwell on that.

"Leo, Ella, come sit," Brody says as soon as we get into his office. He's a project manager now, and maybe one day, if everything works out, I can take his job when he moves up again.

If everything doesn't go to shit, that is. Meaning my dad stays healthy and I can stop worrying about him.

But in my gut, I know the worry will never go away.

"So, what do you need from us?" Ella asks, her tone more clipped than usual.

"Well, we have a potential new client I think you both could be interested in. We have a meeting with them soon, and I want you two to put together a design portfolio to showcase what we could do for them."

I scratch down what he's saying as I let Ella take the lead in all the questions.

"What's the client?"

"A publishing house."

I can feel Ella freeze in her chair. I guess her love of reading hasn't wavered in the past few years. I remember in college that she was in some sort of book club with Grant's girlfriend. I heard him talking about it one night when I was out with the hockey team. There's four of them—I'm pretty sure I met them all when I celebrated Halloween with them last year.

"Which one?" I ask. I'm not too familiar with the literary world, but I'm good at my job. With a little research, it shouldn't be that big of an issue. Plus, having Ella working on it with me will be a big help.

"Literary Nook Publishing House."

"The one who published Henry Hayes' new novel?" Ella asks.

"That's the one," Brody says with a weird look on his face.

"Okay, well, Leo and I can start coming up with a—"

"Actually, that's not going to work," Brody tells us, and I'm starting to get a feeling he called us in here with an ulterior motive. "You two are going to be...competing for this account, in a way."

"What does that mean?" Ella asks him, her fists bunched at her sides.

"Leo's shadowing period is almost over, and I think this could be a good opportunity for him to prove himself. Ella, I know how much you've been begging Imogen to let you know when any account relating to books popped up." He turns to look at me. "And Leo, this could be a great first grab for you."

"So, what do you want us to do then?" I ask, confused as to why he's pitting me and Ella against one another on an account she has clearly been waiting for.

"Well, you two have to work together to create the portfolio. Then, if we land the client, one of you can lead the campaigns we run for them."

Oh, so we're not competing to land the client. First, we have to work together and come up with a plan. If we get the publishing house, then we're competing, or whatever. This all seems kind of fucked up, but I would love to lead a big client when I've only just started here.

"How long do we get to prepare everything?" Ella asks.

"The meeting is in three weeks. We will find out if they want to contract us at the end of September."

"Wonderful," Ella says as she gets up from her chair. "If that's all, we'll go get started."

"That's all. Thank you for coming in," Brody says as he turns back to his computer.

I follow Ella out of his office, neither of us saying a word, and when she turns left to go into her office, I do the same. She heads to her desk, not noticing I'm still standing in the doorway.

I start to roll up my sleeves as I sit in the chair across from her. When she notices me, she jumps.

"What are you doing in here?"

"Well, we have to work together on this thing. I thought we should brainstorm or something."

She sighs heavily. "Look, I'm not thrilled about working on this with you either, but if you want to take the weekend to think of some things, we can come back on Monday and coordinate then."

"And there you go again." Ella constantly jumps to fucking conclusions about everything. Yeah, it's a little weird that Brody is making us do this together when Ella is perfectly capable of doing it herself, but I never said I was pissed off about it.

"What?" she asks as she slams her laptop closed.

"I never said I wasn't thrilled about this. In fact, I'm excited to learn how you do things around here. Shadowing has been fine, but this is a real client. So, stop assuming the worst, and we'll figure out a way we can land this account."

"Fine."

"Am I dismissed?" I ask her, purposefully pushing her buttons this time.

"I'm not your mother, Leo. You can move your own feet and go back to your office if you want to."

I tilt my head at her. "If I remember correctly, you're the one with mommy issues, not me, Williams." I stand up from my spot. "I'll send you an email this weekend with my thoughts on this client."

"Shut the door when you leave," she whispers.

"I'll even let it hit me in the ass on the way out."

"Whatever, Leo."

And then, I leave her office. But when I sit down in my chair, I notice Ella has drawn the curtains over the glass so I can't see in.

My phone buzzes when I sit down, and I see my best friend from back home's name on my screen.

Wyatt: Happy birthday, wanker.

Leo: Thanks, idiot.

Wyatt: Plans for tonight?

Leo: Holt is in charge.

Wyatt: Yikes, good luck to you then.

Leo: How's everything back home? Is your sister doing okay?

Wyatt: She's fine. Thanks for asking. I saw your folks in the hospital the other day. Had a chat with them for a few minutes.

What? My parents neglected to mention that to me.

Leo: Oh. How did my dad look?

Wyatt: Better. Stronger.

Leo: Good. Thanks, man.

Wyatt: Have a good birthday, mate. You deserve it.

11

All Mouth & No Pants

September 20th, 2024

"Paige, can you drive any faster than this?" Hads asks her, only to be met with a stare Paige probably thinks is scary but isn't. The girl couldn't be scary no matter how hard she tries.

"Fine. But I'm almost at five over."

"Holy fuck, Paige. *Almost* five over? We're not going to get pulled over; just drive like a normal person," I tell her as I lean over the center console, trying to confirm she's actually driving as slow as she is.

"I am driving like a normal person!"

I look back at Hads, and the two of us burst into laughter. I don't know why we always let Paige drive, but tonight, we had to make sure of it, since Oliver needed us out of their apartment. It kind of made no sense, since he's also not there.

Oliver demanded we distract Paige tonight while he and Grant go pick out an engagement ring. One of my best friends is getting engaged to the love of her life, and even if that's Oliver, I'm overjoyed for her. Paige deserves love and happiness after all she has been through.

As if he knew we were talking about him, the group chat Hads and I have with him and Grant buzzes.

> **Grant: You guys should see how nervous Oliver is. I've never seen him so flustered. It's hilarious.**

> **Hads: Send a picture. I'd like to catalog this moment for the future.**

> **Ella: Stonehenge is nervous? He's only picking the ring out!**

> **Grant: I know. Imagine what he's going to look like proposing...**

> **Oliver: I want it to be perfect. Fucking sue me.**

> **Ella: Well, if the ring isn't perfect, I might.**

"Have you guys gotten ahold of Ames yet?" Paige asks us, and when I look back at Hads, she shakes her head.

"No. She hasn't even read my text messages."

Goddammit, Amelia. It's easy to tell what's going on. She's been pulling away from us—like usual—but this time, it doesn't feel like she wants to come back.

Her birthday was this month, and all our well wishes for her went unanswered.

Even Paige is discouraged. They usually talk a few times a week to debrief. Paige likes to keep her in the loop even though she's so far away, but she can't be kept in the loop if she doesn't want to answer any of our messages.

"Oh, that's okay. Maybe she had another late meeting," Paige says, trying to keep her spirits up, even though I can tell by her smile that she's disappointed. Paige always looks on the bright side for most situations, but I can tell my friend is hurting.

We all miss Ames, but besides going to England and making sure her phone isn't broken, all we can do is wait for her to respond—which could be in a day, a week, or never.

"Yeah, probably," Hads says, an edge to her voice.

Wanting to change the subject, I start talking about why I recommended a night drive in the first place.

"Leo and I finished our pitch, and we find out if we get the account next week."

"Oh, I forgot about that. Are you nervous? I'm sure you got the publishing house. You worked so hard on it."

Paige's compliment makes me smile, so I reach over and grab her hand resting on the stick shift and squeeze it. I know she's down, yet she's still trying to make sure I feel okay.

"How was it working with him so closely for a few weeks?"

"I don't know. It was fine, I guess. He's good at the job, and he wasn't the biggest pain in my ass..." I stop to gather my words. "The only problem is, if we land the account, we're going to be fighting to lead the project. I know he's not going to let me have it—he wants to prove himself. I've been waiting forever for a publishing house to contact us, and now that it's here, I have to fight and claw to prove I'm the best person for the job."

"I bet that gets tiring, Ells," Hads says.

I slump down in the passenger seat. "Yeah, it does. I'm always fighting for something. It's bad enough I worked my ass off to get this job, but every day I walk into the office, I have to prove myself. And just when I felt like I was getting somewhere, Leo comes in and knocks all my progress down."

"And that one asshole got promoted over you," Hads adds.

"Yeah, that too. I don't even know how he got the promotion over me, but that's how it always fucking works. I do twice the amount of work he does. I'm constantly staying late to make sure everything I turn in is perfect, yet he leaves early to go golfing a few times a week and still gets a promotion. It fucking sucks."

"You're positive Leo is going to go after the account?" Paige asks me. "Maybe if you asked him to lay off, he would."

"You don't know him like I do, P."

"Huh," Paige says as she skips the song. "I guess I always assumed he was all mouth and no pants."

Hads snickers in the back seat as I try to stop the laugh from coming out.

"What?" Paige asks as she looks between Hads and me.

"Never change, P," I say, a real smile making my lips turn up for the first time today.

"Wait, Paige, can you throw on the playlist I made for tonight? It's a special one for night drives since we've been doing this a lot more lately."

Paige hands Hads her phone, and while Hads configures the playlist, I roll my window down and feel the breeze across my face.

I'm the reason we've been doing night drives more lately, though the girls don't know why I keep suggesting them. They never question it either. Whenever I text an SOS and tell them I need to go on a drive, they always hop right in the car and come pick me up. These girls always have my back, even though I'm not as open with them as I should be.

Being in the passenger seat of a car while we drive through the night has always calmed me down. When I was little and my mom was still around, sometimes she would take my sister and I on drives to help tire us out. She would play this special music—classical, I think—and according to my dad, it worked like a charm. We would come back exhausted, and the two of them would put us right to bed.

Drives like this remind me of what my life was like as an actual kid, not a girl who had to grow into an adult when her mom walked out on her family and never came back. It reminds me of what it was like when everything felt good and easy, not hard and exhausting.

Ever since my mom left, I've had to keep my family afloat. My dad was working two jobs to support us, so I kept the house going. I raised my sister and helped her with her homework every night while I was also doing school work at the same time. Along with cooking, cleaning, and trying to figure out if we had enough money to be able to pay our bills.

I've been clawing my way back from the hole my mom threw me in when she left. I fight to be heard, to be taken seriously, and I'm exhausted.

I just want something to go my way for once—no fighting required. All my hard work has to pay off at some point, right? But I don't know how much longer I can keep doing this—making sure my family is okay while still living my life for me, not them.

I hear Paige and Hads singing along to a song as loud as they can, and I join in, wanting to forget.

I'm here with my best friends, and for once, I want to live in this moment and forget about all the things troubling me. That's what I love about the girls—they make me forget about all the shit I've been dealing with since before I met them and get me out of my own head. I've always needed people to do that for me.

I worry I'm too much sometimes. I'm always asking questions, always wondering how I can help in any situation or trouble they find themselves in. Sometimes, people hate that. There have been many friends who have left my side because they thought I was too overbearing, but not these girls around me now.

I used to think it was me—that I was the problem. It was hard for me to keep friends, and my own mother left when I was young, so why would anyone else stay? It always felt like my fault. I thought I drove everyone away because I internalized all my fears and always assume I'm the issue.

But now I know the people who are meant to be around me will stay no matter what. Hads and Paige fit that bill perfectly. And Amelia did too, when she was around.

It's moments like these, when the windows are down, the music is up, and you're surrounded by your favorite people in the world, that you feel like you can do anything, like you can be whoever you want with no judgment. I suddenly have forgotten about my work problems, my family struggles, and Leo being around me five days a week. It all seems insignificant when I'm here in this car with my friends. Being able to hear Paige, Hads, and I sing until our lungs give out makes everything I've been worried about so pointless.

This is what life should be. This is how I want to feel every single day.

All the pain, all the long days... They all start to mean something in moments like these. I feel freer than I have in a long time, and maybe ,what lies ahead isn't so bad.

No, it won't be bad. And if it is, I know these girls will be around to help me pick up all the pieces when I eventually shatter.

One Week Later

As I STALK INTO the conference room to find out if we landed the publishing house, I notice I'm the first one in here. *The meeting does start in five minutes, right?*

I grab my phone to make sure I have the right time, but Leo's presence makes me pause. I can always tell it's him because he wears the same cologne every fucking day. The worst part is, I don't hate the smell. He smells like whiskey and bad decisions—decisions I'm all too familiar with.

Thankfully, before Leo can engage, Rae walks in. *Thank God.* She meets my eyes and immediately hurries to sit next to me. Leo continues to look at me as he finds a spot.

"Hey, are you nervous? Brody seems to be in a good mood today, so you probably got the account."

"Brody is always in a good mood. He was five under par yesterday while we were all here, working our asses off."

She only smiles at me. "Well, at least we didn't have to deal with him."

I nod my head in agreement. I don't know what's worse: Brody being here in the office, or being out of the office when he should be here.

People continue to filter into the conference room as Rae and I talk amongst ourselves. Brody steps in and goes to the front of the room, Imogen to the right of him as the meeting starts.

"So, before we get into all the normal stuff, Imogen and I have an announcement to make. Imogen?" Brody hands the floor over to her.

"We have officially landed Literary Nook Publishing House as a client." Imogen looks at Leo and I. "Congratulations, you two. The proposal was perfect, and they were very impressed."

I smile to myself, glad it all worked out. But now, the hard part.

"So, who is interested in leading this project?" Brody asks, knowing what's about to happen.

"I am," Leo and I say at the same time. I'm glaring at him, but he's only smiling at me, that same rich-boy smile he has always had.

"Well, you can both prepare separate proposals, and Brody and I will see which one suits us best," Imogen says. "The contract begins in November, so you have until then. One month to put your best foot forward."

"Got it," I say before I sit back. For some reason, that conversation had me on the edge of my seat.

I look over at Leo, his eyes pinned straight onto me, and return his stare. He should know I'm not going down easily. If he wants to compete for this contract, a competition is what he'll get. I don't think I have anything to worry about. This is Leo's first contract. I've done this a million times. I could manage this project in my fucking sleep.

I can tell he wants this; maybe he even needs this.

Too fucking bad I want it more. This contract is mine.

12

Smells Like Sex

As I WALK INTO the office this morning, I can already tell something is off.

Maybe it's not the office; maybe it's me. My workout this morning was mediocre at best, and thanks to Holt failing his promise on my birthday, I still haven't gotten laid. Now, it has been a few months since I've had sex, and that needs to change soon, or else my dick is going to fall off from how much I've been wanking.

I feel like a stupid fucking teenager again, and I hate it. I'm an attractive man; I should be able to go out and pick somebody up with no problem.

I'm off my game lately, and if I'm not careful, I'm going to start smoking again. I quit when I found out about my dad's heart issues, but every now and again, when I'm stressed, I crawl right back to cigarettes.

I greet a few people as I head back to my office. I don't stop in Ella's office to say good morning—the last thing I want to do is make this already weird day worse.

But when I flick the light on in my office, I notice an array of colors around the room.

My entire office is covered in sticky notes.

What the fuck?

I hear a click form behind me, and when I spin around, Ella is taking a picture of me standing in my office.

"Do you like it? I thought it could use a pop of color, so I redecorated for you."

I sigh heavily. Of course, this was her doing. "Is this amusing to you?"

She nods her head at me. "Yeah, actually, it is. Have you seen your face?" She tries to turn her phone around to show me, but I grab her wrist and shove her against my wall, pissed off and annoyed she took the time to do this.

"What happened to being civil in the workplace?" I ask her, noting what she said the first time we worked together here.

"What is with you and shoving me against things? First your door, and now a wall." She tries to shake out of my hold, but I have a decent grip on her.

"Answer the fucking question, Ella."

"It's just a stupid prank. I'll even help you take them all down if you're going to be a little bitch about it." Her words come out breathless, as if there's not enough air in my tiny office for her.

"I don't need your help. I need you to leave me the fuck alone so I can work."

Her eyes drill into mine, almost murderous. I'd think she'd be able to kill me if I didn't have her caged against my wall. "Did you wake up on the wrong side of the bed this morning? What's wrong with you? I thought you'd get a kick out of this because of how competitive we are."

"My problem is you." *You're always around, always pushing me to my limits. Today started out terribly, and you're making it fucking worse.* And as the cherry on top, Ella smells like sex. She smells like she has been fucked recently, and it's invading my senses and driving me crazy.

Only because I'm not having any.

An image flashes through my mind of her coming undone beneath me all those years ago, and I feel an urge to smear her maroon lipstick all over her face while she chokes on my cock.

I can feel my dick jerk in my pants. *Jesus, I need to calm the fuck down.* But I can't do that around her. She makes every molecule of my body pissed off with her cold stares, snide comments, and now, her stupid fucking pranks.

"You're a fucking jerk," Ella says. "Let me go, Zimmerman. Now."

I tilt my head at her, a challenge in my features.

"Why don't you make me, Williams?"

And then, she spits on me.

Pride laces her features as she looks up at me, thinking she won this round.

"Open that mouth, darling. It's my turn."

I feel her pulse start to quicken, and just when I think she's going to back down, she does the last thing I expect and opens her mouth. My eyes won't leave hers, her pupils so dilated, I can barely see her brown eyes underneath them. It's like we're locked in some sort of trance as we stand here, chest to chest.

I wonder what she's thinking about as she stares at my mouth, waiting with bated breath to see if I'm actually going to follow through with what I said.

If I was, I don't know if anything could make me stop. I don't know if I could simply touch her lips without needing more from her.

Woah. Absolutely the fuck not.

Needing to get the fuck out of this room that suddenly feels too small, I leg it to the kitchen to get some breakfast, and I manage to avoid Ella for the rest of the day.

The Next Day

I'M IN THE OFFICE early today so I can see the look on Ella's face when she walks in. Yesterday, she beat me. She got the best of me, and I can admit that.

It only took me a half an hour to get all the sticky notes off, but today's prank might take Ella slightly longer than that.

She started this, after all. I'm playing into her hands if this is how she wants to do shit around here. Ella normally gets here before I do, but today, I arrived extra early, even skipping my workout so I could pull this off. About an hour passes before I hear her and Rae talking in her office. I can tell Ella is here because it just got a few degrees colder.

I hear her shut Rae's door, and I see her body float across my window before the light goes on in her office.

Show time.

I can hear her gasp before I fully open my door.

"What? Is there something wrong with your present?" I ask as I lean against my door frame, a smile bursting from my face. I have to admit, it's way better being on this side of things.

"What the hell did you do?" Ella asks as she lifts her stapler—which is wrapped in Holiday paper. Her entire office is gift wrapped.

It took me all fucking morning, but seeing the look on her face made it worth it.

"You gave me a present, so I thought I'd return the favor. Merry fucking Christmas, Ella." I smile at her again, and by the look on her face, I can tell she's thinking about how many ways she can slap it right off my face.

"It's September. You're a few months early, jackass."

"Oh, come on. It's just a prank, and I can help you unwrap it all," I give her the same words she said to me yesterday morning.

Ella only continues to glare at me before she looks back at her stapler. I bet she's thinking about throwing it at me, but that wouldn't work out in her favor, and she knows it.

Plus, we're at work, and both of us have done stupid shit like this. If either of us went to HR, it would only cause a bunch of mindless paperwork.

"Ready to concede?" I ask her, and all she does is shake her head at me.

"No. Are you?" she asks as she walks toward me, her chin jutting out in front of her. Ella Williams, always the confident and self-assured woman—in public.

"Nope," I say, my jaw tensing.

She leans closer to me, her hands flat on the lapels of my jacket as she smooths them out, even though I ironed this last night.

"Can I help you with something, Miss Williams?"

"No, Mr. Zimmerman. I just want you to watch your back," she leans in closer to me, "because I'm coming for you. Consider this your only warning."

"Don't worry." I lean down to her ear. "I've seen you come for me before, and the sight was astonishing, so I'm not worried, darling."

And then I head back into my office and close my door.

A few hours into working on my proposal, I step out of my office to grab some lunch from the kitchen, and my phone buzzes.

Grant: Hey man, you up for drinks tonight?

Leo: Yeah, that sounds good. Just us?

Grant: Oliver might come too. Is that okay?

Leo: Birthday boy?

Grant: Yup.

Leo: That's fine. Just let me know where to be and when.

Grant: Will do. See you later.

Leo liked a message.

I guess my night just got a lot more interesting. Hopefully, tonight, I can pick someone up, because between this thing with Ella, the contract for the publishing house, and everything else, I need to relieve some stress.

And I might as well have some fun while doing so.

"Dude, don't embarrass me in front of—" Grant stops what he was saying as he notices me. "Leo! Hey! What's up, man?"

I sit down next to him at the small table with Oliver, and Grant slides a drink over to me.

"I remembered what you preferred," he tells me.

"Thanks. This is so needed after the crappy week I've had."

"Too much time spent with Ella, huh?" Oliver asks me.

I forgot these two run in the same social circle. I wonder what she told them about me. I doubt it's anything good. "You could say that."

"Yeah, she's scary until you get to know her. She's a good person to have around. If you're on her good side, at least."

I look at Grant as if he's speaking a different language. "I'm pretty sure I'm the only person on her bad side, then."

I take a long sip of my drink, the alcohol hopefully loosening some of the tension I've felt the past few weeks.

"It can't be *that* bad at work. Ella thought about quitting before, and she hasn't yet, so you two must be getting along, right?"

"Grant, stop asking about her. I told you he wouldn't answer any of your questions," Oliver says to him rather sharply.

"I want to hear both sides of the story!" Grant pauses to take a sip. "I've tried talking to her, and she's as closed off about you as you are about her."

"Because they have a history, asshole," Oliver tells him, and he's right. Damn, does Ella talk about me that much, or are these two just smart?

Grant and I have slowly become friends. I knew about him from Liam, since they were both on the hockey team together, and when we were formally introduced at Oliver's party last year, I liked him. He's fun, and he's got a good energy, which is exactly the opposite of Oliver.

I don't know him that well, but I'm pretty sure they're connected through their girlfriends, who are members of Ella's book club.

"So, how did you two become so close?" I ask, changing the subject off Ella fucking Williams. It's bad enough she pushes all my buttons at work; I'd rather not talk about her after hours.

"I'm dating his sister," Grant says as Oliver grunts.

"I'm dating my sister's best friend," Oliver tells me as he sips his water bottle. "Well, one of them."

"How many of them are there?" I ask. Ella makes three, but I thought there were a few more. My sister used to talk about this book club a lot, and I always assumed there were more people.

"Four," Oliver tells me. "There's your girl, the other is overseas, so she's not around as much."

Oliver looks happy about that fact, but I don't miss the look that crosses Grant's face. There's a history there, but I'm not going to ask about it. "Ella isn't my girl."

"Keep lying to yourself, buddy."

"Grant, stop." Oliver smacks him on the arm. "Leo, how are you enjoying the States?"

"It's fine, I guess. I miss my family a lot, but having my sister here helps a little bit."

"Do you still wanna hit the gym tomorrow morning?" Grant asks me, and I forgot we were going to work out together tomorrow.

"Yeah, that's fine," I tell him. "Oliver, do you want to join us?'

"No thanks," he says.

Grant smacks him on the shoulder. "This guy? In a gym?"

He shrugs. "I prefer the pavement."

"Ah, that's understandable," I say as I sip the last of my drink. "I'm gonna get another. Either of you fancy one?"

"I'm good," Oliver says.

"Yeah, I'll take one."

"Cool," I say as I head up to the bar. It's not too loud in here, but music is playing that I don't recognize, and that makes me feel old as fuck. I shift my gaze around the space, hoping someone catches my eye. A few girls are already staring at me, and I try to think of something I can say to any of them, but my mind draws a blank.

Am I never going to be able to flirt with anyone ever again? What the hell is wrong with me?

I know what I look like, and I used to be able to smooth talk my way into anything. I don't know if all this shit with my family has fucked with my head more than I thought, or what. I don't know what my issue is, and it's pissing me off.

The only time my dick has been hard over a woman lately is when I've been fighting with Ella in our stupid prank war. Maybe I'm ill. Maybe that's why my dick seems attracted to the person who pushes my fucking buttons more than anyone on the planet.

That has got to be why.

I somehow need to get out of my own head enough to be able to talk to normal women again. I tilt my head from side to side, feeling my neck crack, and some of the tension loosens as I grab the drinks and head back to the table.

"Do you guys ever have a hard time flirting?"

"Well, not really. It's easy to flirt with my girlfriend. I just—"

Oliver almost shoves Grant out of his chair. "If you talk about what you and my sister do in your free time, I'm going to have to kill you." Oliver turns to me. "I was terrible at it. Are you out of practice or something?"

"I don't even think you have to flirt. Have you looked in a mirror lately?"

"Yes, Grant. This morning, and I looked fucking fantastic, as usual." I run a hand through my hair. "But that's not enough."

"Maybe you need practice," Oliver says, and Grant and I look at him like he's crazy. "Or maybe you have to get your confidence back. When was the last time you talked to someone one-on-one?"

This morning, with Ella. "I can't remember."

"Flirting is like riding a bike: you remember how to do it, but sometimes, you get a little rusty. It's okay to ease back into it if you need to."

I stop myself from saying it has been months since I've been able to pick someone up; these two don't need to know that. I don't even know why I'm confiding in them about this.

"Hey, can we keep this between us?"

"We won't tell her anything," Oliver says. "Unless she asks me, then I'm not lying. Ella still scares the shit out of me."

"More than Amelia does?" Grant asks him. Amelia... That name sounds familiar. I bet she's the fourth member of the book club.

"Did. She's not around anymore, Grant. She's officially past tense in my eyes."

"Thanks, guys. I appreciate it."

Both of their phones buzz on the table, and when they pick them up, they both smile.

Jesus, is that what being in love is like? Any time my phone buzzes, I assume it's bad news about my dad coming through. I've never looked that happy about anything before.

"Sorry, Leo, we have to cut tonight a bit short. The girls might have set Oliver's apartment on fire."

"Go," I say as I finish off my drink. "We'll catch up another time soon, I'm sure."

"Nice to see you again, Zimmerman." Grant smacks my shoulder. "I'll text our group chat to make plans next time."

"When did you have time to make a group chat?" Oliver asks him.

"When Leo was at the bar, duh."

"That sounds good to me. I'm gonna head out too. I have an early morning tomorrow. I'm sure Ella has been up all night planning her next prank."

"Prank?" Grant asks me.

And as the three of us walk out the door, I wave my hand at them. "That's a story for next time."

13

From Bad To Worse

"Guys, this book was everything to me," I say as I wave my Kindle around.

"I knew you were going to say that, Ells. It had literally all your favorite things," Paige tells me, and I can't even argue because she's right.

Not only did our book club pick this month have a slightly tortured main male character, but it was also a reverse harem that featured double penetration. "I just really like characters I can fix."

"You *could* fix him, Ella. I believe it," Hads tells me, and I put my hand to my chest.

"Thank you so much."

"I thought it was really fun!" Paige says, her eyes lighting up as I know what she's about to say. "My favorite part was when they killed that one guy. He was an asshole."

"Paige, when is your favorite part of these books we read not the murder?"

She thinks for a second. "You're right."

You would think finding a dead body and almost getting killed by a serial killer—correction, two—would deter this girl from liking stuff like this, but it doesn't. I guess therapy really does help in the long run. I'm proud of Paige and Hads. They've both seemed to go in the right direction after some bad shit happened in college. I can't see myself ever going to talk to someone about my problems.

As the oldest daughter, I don't need therapy. I'm way too self-aware with what's wrong with me; it probably wouldn't help. So, I deal with it all on my own, and for now, I'm doing an amazing job at it. And yes, I'm aware that's my toxic trait, and no, I don't want to talk about it.

"Before we move out of book discussion, I'm going to try calling Ames again," Paige says as she gets off her couch and heads to a different room.

Hads and I look at one another, the silence all too deafening as we sit. Both of us know Amelia isn't going to answer, but neither of us wants to burst Paige's bubble.

"She's not coming back, is she?" Hads says under her breath.

"I don't know." I really don't. Normally, it takes Ames about a week to answer us, but the longer it gets with her blowing us off all the time, the more I think she's actually ghosting us from across the globe.

Paige pads back into the room, her eyes drooping. "Voicemail."

"Leo and I have been having a prank war at work for the last week."

Paige's eyes light up, and when she looks at me from her floor, I know she wants to know more.

"You guys have been doing what for a week?" Hads asks as I shift the topic off of our friend and onto a better one. Well, better for them, not me, but I'll do anything to get the vibe in here back up. Plus, I'm done talking about someone who clearly doesn't want to talk to me. I've put in effort. I've tried calling, and if the unanswered messages have taught me one thing, it's that I'm not going to beg someone to be my friend—even if I thought the four of us were forever.

"A prank war."

"Oh, I need more details right now." Paige smiles at me.

"I kind of started it, but only because this fucker and I are competing. I wanted to lessen the stress we're both under. He's always tense and brooding across from me in his office, and his mood was dampening mine." That's only partly true. If fucking with Leo Zimmerman was a full-time job, I'd sign up immediately. It's way too fun watching him get pissed off.

"I forgot you guys are competing for the contract," Hads says. "So, how did you start it?"

"I put sticky notes up all around his office. I covered *everything*. It was funny and harmless, but he got pissed. The next morning, I came in, and my office was gift wrapped."

"Wait, your entire office?"

"Yes, P. He wrapped every little thing, including my staple remover." And the worst part was, it looked gorgeous. I might hate Leo, but I can appreciate his gift-wrapping, from one pro to another—even if it pissed me off.

Again, another thing the fucker doesn't have to work for or practice at. He's just good at it.

"Damn."

"Then, I changed his Microsoft Word to be British English rather than American English. Some of his reports were turned in with some spelling errors. And what did he do? He covered my entire office in glitter."

"Was it red glitter, by chance?" Paige asks me.

"Please don't tell me it's on this outfit too." I thought I had finally gotten rid of it all.

"It's on your left sleeve," Hads tells me, and when I look down, I see it taunting me on my arm.

"Of course, it is." I shake my sleeve. It's not that I hate glitter, but how the fuck does it get into every crevice? He only smeared the loose glitter all over my work area, but somehow, I keep finding it in my closet.

"What did you do in retaliation for the glitter?" Hads asks me.

"I covered his office in googly eyes."

Paige and Hads laugh, and I metaphorically pat myself on the back. Leo might think he bested me, but he has no idea how far I'm willing to go—well, to a certain extent. I'm not about to get fired from my job over a stupid prank war.

"So, what have you guys been up to?" I see these girls once a week, sometimes more, but it never really feels like enough. I hate the feeling I'm missing out on some piece of their life or worse, I hate missing the parts where they need me. Not being there for one of them if they're going through something is quite literally my worst nightmare.

Honestly, the subject of me and Leo has taken over most conversations lately. The same thing happened before Hads and Grant were dating—book club became a weekly rant session about how much he annoyed her, and now, they're dating.

The same thing happened with Paige and Oliver, though it was a bit more on the down low. Those two were attempting to solve a whole ass murder—which they did, so props to those psychos—but we always checked on Paige every week. And now, she and Oliver are dating, soon to be engaged. The fact that Leo and I are the main focus... I'm determined to break this pattern. Leo Zimmerman and I will never be anything more than coworkers.

"Oliver and I have started watching a new show! Other than that, nothing has been going on besides work. Same old, same old."

"Grant recently came up with a plan for his birthday in October. He really wants to go to a trampoline park." Hads sounds so unimpressed right now, but I know she loves that man. If he wants to go to a trampoline park for his birthday, she'll make it happen. "He asked if we could get a small trampoline so he can start practicing his backflips."

"Where are you going to fit a trampoline?" I ask, knowing their place could never fit one.

"In the imaginary backyard we don't have." Hads rolls her eyes. "I don't know. I think he was joking, but sometimes, I can't tell."

"Or he's buying you a house!" Paige says, and the rest of us laugh.

For the rest of the night, we chat about books, and I smile more than I have in the past few weeks. If there's one thing I always know for sure, it's that my friends can always recharge my batteries when they're starting to drain.

THIS WEEK HAS OFFICIALLY gone from bad to worse. As I knock on the door of my sister's apartment, I hope and pray to anything I can that the one person I don't want to see right now doesn't open the door. That would be the fucking cherry on top of this fucking week.

"Leo? What are you doing here?"

"Is Ella here?"

My sister looks at me like I've grown four heads. "No, she's at Paige's flat for book club."

"Thank God," I say as I step into their place.

"What are you doing here? And why do you look so," my sister does a once over of me, "disheveled?"

"I need your help," I say as I sink onto her couch. I can't remember the last time I said that to someone. It feels odd coming from my lips.

"Please tell me you didn't get a girl pregnant, Leo. The last thing I want is to become an Aunty from some one night stand you had."

"Well…"

"Leo Zimmerman, you did not get—"

I put my hands up in defense as she grabs one of her sandals from by the door. *Is she about to throw that at me?* "I'm joking! Fucking hell, sis, you should see your face right now."

Then, she smacks me in the face with her shoe.

"For God's sake, Liss, not the fucking face!"

"Never do that again, Leo. I mean it." My sister throws her shoe back to where she got it. "God, you're the reason my heart rate is so high."

Me getting a girl pregnant is quite literally the last thing that could happen. In order to get someone pregnant, you would have to have sex—unprotected, might I add. Not only do I always wrap my dick, but I haven't had sex in months.

Maybe that wasn't the best road to go down, considering what I came over here for. Whatever. I'm sure it'll be fine.

"Okay, can we talk for real?"

"Spit it out, Leo. I know you don't need money, so what is it?" she asks me as she takes a sip of her drink. I'm not sure if there's alcohol in it, but that could work in my favor. I'm also glad Ella isn't over here, because I know she would turn down what I'm about to ask my sister.

"I need somewhere to live."

Her face pinches together. "You have a place to live."

"No, I don't. I got a call earlier. The flat I planned on moving into soon got delayed for a few more months. There's some sort of leak that set the construction back. My contract is up at my rental, and I can't extend it, since someone else is moving in right after me."

"Shit," my sister says, knowing what I'm asking her.

"I'll pay a third of your rent. That's still cheaper than what I'm paying now, and it will help you guys out a little bit while I'm invading your space."

"You do realize Ella also lives here, right?"

Yes, I do. And if I end up moving in, Ella and I are going to be around one another every single fucking day—at work and at home. "Yes, but I'll be nice if she is."

"I don't believe you."

"Please, Liss. I'll do anything. I'm going to be homeless next week if you don't say yes. I'll clean, I'll cook, I'll pay for food, whatever you want." I sound like I'm begging because I am. This is quite literally my last resort. The last thing I wanted was to live with Ella and my sister, but hotels are too expensive per night, and there are no other places to rent around here that have stays long enough to last me until my flat is ready.

My sister and my worst nightmare are my only choice.

Alissa sighs heavily at me. "Fine."

"Thank you so much. Seriously, sis, I appreciate it."

She shakes her head at me. "Don't thank me yet, Leo. I have to talk to Ella first."

For fuck's sake. I was afraid she would say that. "Got it."

"But if you did to her what you did to me, I'm sure she would come around."

"What?"

"Beg. It was quite funny, actually. I'm totally going to tell our parents about that when they ring."

Another thing that helps with me moving in here for a few months is my parents can talk to Alissa and I more frequently. I haven't spoken to them in a few days, and I regret that. I try to check in once a day, but with all the work and the new client Ella and I are fighting over, I haven't had much time to carve out my day for them.

"Have you talked to them lately?"

She nods her head at me. "Yesterday. Only for a bit, though. Dad had a doctor's appointment."

"How did it go?"

"They haven't told me how it went, but they seem alright. Healthy."

I sigh. I shouldn't be forgetting about them, no matter how much work I have.

"Stop stressing, Leo. You'll have a place to live, even if Ella hates it. She's not mean enough to throw you out onto the street."

That's what you think. I have no doubt that Ella would rather not have me invading her personal space all day, every day. "Yeah, sure."

"Actually, I think this could be good for you two. Maybe you'll work out whatever differences you have. If not, at least I'll get some good in-person reality television."

I only roll my eyes at her. Of course, my sister would like watching Ella and I bicker.

"Don't get your knickers in a twist, Leo. I wouldn't want you smoking because of how stressed you look right now. Oh, also, none of that if you live here."

"I know, sis."

"Good," she says as she turns the television on and gets comfortable. "Now, get out. Ella is coming home soon, and we have a self-care night planned before she kills me for asking if you can move in."

"Got it. Well, thanks. I appreciate it, Liss."

"I know, I'm the best sister ever. You don't have to tell me."

I stifle a laugh before I walk out of her apartment—soon to be *our* apartment if Ella says yes.

I know just how to persuade her, and as I head back to my rental, I'm sure my plan will work.

14

So, You Agree? You're Beneath Me?

I OFFICIALLY HAVE A fucking leech who goes by the name of Leo Zimmerman.

Not only has this fucker invaded my job, but now, he wants to move into my home—the area I take pride in, the place where I go to decompress after a long day of dealing with Leo at work.

Now, he's going to live there. With me.

When I got home last night and Alissa immediately handed me a pint of my favorite dairy-free ice cream, I knew something was up.

And then the bomb was dropped—literally and figuratively. I felt like my anger was about to explode from my feet to my ears. I couldn't believe what Alissa was telling me, and at first, I didn't care about his stupid apartment being pushed back.

But when Alissa told me if the roles were reversed, he would do it for us, I conceded. I'm sure he would only let us since it involved Alissa and not me, but she was right.

As I get out of my car and head to the elevator to go into work, I know he's probably going to talk to me about it today. I doubt he'll appreciate my graciousness, and I'm sure he'll figure out some way to piss me off.

I press the button to go to the thirteenth floor, and as the doors are about to close, a hand stops them.

In comes the man of the fucking hour.

How come I can't seem to get the fuck away from him? Why does he have to be everywhere?

"Ella."

I scoff at him as the doors finally close, the two of us the only ones in this small fucking elevator.

"So...did my sister talk to you at all last night?"

"Yes, Leo, we live together, so we tend to have conversations..." This might be the last time I'm able to fuck with him, so I continue playing coy, since soon, we're going to have to be more civil.

"Did she talk to you about me?"

"Hmm, I don't recall you coming up in our conversation."

He surprises me by stopping the elevator. "Ella, please. Just take me seriously for one second. I'm trying to have a simple conversation, and you always have to make things difficult."

"Oh, I'm the one making this complicated? You're the one invading my entire life! If I didn't know any better, I'd say you were obsessed with me or something." I know it's not true. It's just really fun to piss him off, and nothing pisses him off more than me.

"In your fucking dreams, sweetheart."

"If you want to move in so badly, you'll have to prove it."

He tilts his head at me, knowing what's coming. "What do I have to do?"

"Beg, Leo. Get down on those knees of yours and ask me nicely."

He only looks at me with a stupid smirk on his face before he drops to both of his knees, his briefcase discarded next to him. He looks up at me, his eyes hooded, and suddenly, I'm remembering a time when—

Ella, get your fucking head out of the gutter.

I reach down and cup his chin. "Now ask me nicely, Leo."

"Ella, will you please allow me to move into your apartment for a few months? I have nowhere else to go, and you are my only hope."

He's talking slowly, in a tone I've only heard once before. I have to stop my body from shivering in remembrance of the last time I heard him speak like this. He must be really fucking desperate if he's going through all this trouble.

"Fine."

"Seriously?"

I sigh heavily. "Yes," I say as I flick the switch so the elevator starts working again. "Now, get up before someone sees you and assumes we were doing something in here."

"Would that be the worst thing in the world?" he asks, throwing his arms out and still not getting up.

"Leo, we *work* here. Get the fuck up."

"Oh, but it seems like you enjoy seeing me on my knees for—"

The elevator dings on the tenth floor, and before I can register what I'm doing, I grab him by his tie and yank him up so he's standing. Well, the best I can. The fucker is way taller than me, and those muscles of his don't fucking help either.

Not that I noticed them or anything.

A few people enter as Leo and I move to the back of the elevator. We're standing side by side for three more floors, and it's already way too fucking cramped in here.

"Since we're going to be living and working together, we need to be civil," I say, almost under my breath, since I don't want these random fucking people to hear my conversation.

I can feel his shoulders tense. "I can be civil if you can. That means no more pranks."

"And when you move in, you're not allowed to talk to me about anything work related. And don't ask me about the project we're competing over."

"Fine. But the same goes for you."

"I know. That's why I mentioned it."

"Good; you're listening already." The elevator dings, and the doors open to our office as Leo grabs his briefcase and steps out in front of me.

I rush to get out, the doors almost closing on me, but as I get into the reception area, he's smiling at me.

"That wasn't very civil of you."

"You're a strong and independent woman, Ella. You don't need men beneath you to hold doors open for you."

I cock my head at him. "So you agree? You're beneath me?"

"Not yet, but I do remember what it felt like, as I'm sure you do." *Is he ever going to stop bringing that up?* He grabs the door to our office and holds it open. "Ladies first."

"Fuck off," is all I say as I walk into the office, my heels clicking as I feel him trail behind me.

15

Forgiveness, Not Permission

Two Days Later

"You can put those right over there," I say to the movers I hired to do all the heavy lifting. My sister offered to help pack up all my shit, but since she's already doing me a favor by letting me move in, I didn't want to impose anything else on her.

Tonight is officially my very first night here. I thought about getting some sort of alarm in case Ella tries to smother me in my sleep but decided against it. If she comes into my room and tries anything, she'll have to bear the consequences.

Even though this isn't ideal, and I definitely could've asked my parents for help, I didn't want to impose. I'm a grown man, and with all the medical shit my dad has been going through, I didn't want to ask.

It's bad enough he has barely been working, but I feel weird asking my parents for anything with all we've had going on.

I should call them later.

Maybe Alissa and I can ring them after dinner. That's the one thing I'm going to like being around here—Alissa and I can talk to our parents at the same time. I feel so out of the loop lately, since I've been adjusting to the job, my living situation, and dealing with a certain pain in my arse at work, that I barely know anything about the appointments they've been at. Is my dad healing okay? Is he on the right track, or could this happen again and end worse?

I feel like I've been nothing but a huge letdown lately, and that stops now. Since I finally have a place to call home for now, I'm going to be better about being in the loop on things.

I'm okay with being a lot of things to different people, but the one thing I hope I never am is a terrible son. Not after all my parents have done for me. Not after what happened.

My dad's health issues have certainly been a wakeup call for me; it allowed me to slow the fuck down and remember what really matters in life. But nothing helps the guilt that creeps in when I feel like I could be doing more.

My spiral is broken when one of the movers talks to me. "That was the last box."

"Thank you for the help." I paid them beforehand, but I take a hundred out and tip them.

"No problem, man. Have a good day."

I watch as they walk out of the open door before I see my sister's face pop in. "Are you done yet? Ella and I want to watch a movie."

"Yes, I'm done. I have to unpack, but what do you say I make dinner?"

My sister's eyebrows go up. "I would say that's a great idea, and the bare minimum, since I let you move in here."

"I don't know, Liss. He might try to give me food poisoning," Ella says as she walks past me, a bag in her hand.

"Well, since we share a bathroom now, that wouldn't be wise of me, would it?"

She stops in her tracks. "Liss, I thought you said you were switching rooms."

"Ella, I—"

I cut Alissa off. "I wasn't going to make my sister switch rooms in her own place. This is easier."

Ella only sighs heavily as she looks past me to my sister. "So that's why you offered to pay for my books."

"I was asking forgiveness, not permission. Now, Leo, go make us dinner while we watch this sad movie Ella likes."

"It's not sad; it's my comfort movie!" Ella says as she heads toward her room—the one right across from mine.

"This should be fun," my sister says as she smacks me in the chest. "I give you guys a week until you're at each other's throats."

"Is that a bet you're willing to make, sis?"

She nods her head. "Yes, actually, it is. Fifty bucks."

I reach out and take her hand. "Deal."

I MADE DINNER—PASTA ALLA vodka—and Ella only complained once. It's a new bloody record, and it was only because I refused to pass the butter.

Now, I'm cleaning up. And as I sit in the kitchen and listen to the movie they're watching, I find myself stealing glances at the screen. My sister has ice cream in the living room for her and Ella—to be honest, that's all I'm *actually* interested in.

As I set the final plate in the dishwasher and run it, I notice they're watching *Little Women*. How in the world is this a comfort movie? Doesn't Beth die? In what way is that comforting?

"Seriously? This is your idea of comfort?"

"Leo..." my sister warns.

"Yes, actually. It's a story of a beautiful family and sisters who love each other." Ella rolls her eyes as she takes a bite of her ice cream. "I know you're only used to movies with naked people, but for some of us, we like an actual story."

I can only laugh.

"Now, move," Ella says. "This is my favorite part."

"Actually, I would love to take part in movie night. After all, I'll be here for a few months. Might as well spend some much needed time with you guys."

Ella only rolls her eyes as my sister scooches over on the couch.

"Thanks."

"Leo, stop talking during the movie."

I only ignore Ella as the movie plays, and for the rest of it, I shut my mouth. At the end, Ella and my sister are tearing up, and I can't understand why.

"So the girl who didn't want to get married ended up getting married anyway? I'm so fucking confused."

"Leo, you don't get it," my sister tells me.

"No, I don't. The entire movie, she refuses to get with Laurie, even after he confesses his love to her on the hill, but then as soon as she figures out she could love him, he gets with her sister!" This movie makes no sense, and I know Ella is going to tell me I didn't understand it, but it can't be that deep.

"You just don't understand certain characters, Leo. One day, if I have enough time, I can explain it in terms you'll understand."

"Small words?" I ask.

"Exactly!" she says as she gets up. "See? You get it!" Ella only walks to her room and shuts her door.

"No goodnight for us?"

"Nope. She's probably going to talk to her sister." Alissa goes to put the ice cream away. "Do you want to ring our parents?"

"Do you think they're still awake?"

"Shit. I always forget about the time difference." She runs a hand down her face. "We'll talk to them tomorrow before we both go to work?"

"Sounds good."

She pats me on the shoulder before she leaves. "Enjoy your first night here, Leo. I hope you sleep well."

"Thanks, sis. For everything, I mean."

She locks eyes with me. "You're my baby brother, Leo. You know I'd do anything for you."

Even if our parents are an ocean away, I'm glad I still have my sister here. She was my very first friend in life, and I'm thankful that, no matter where I end up, I know I'll always have her.

16

Stockholm Syndrome

"Leo, if you don't get your ass out of the shower, I'm going to pour a bucket of ice water on you!" I say as I knock on the door, knowing it's no use.

Every single fucking morning, Leo takes hour long showers after he gets home from his workout. It's fucking annoying, and it derails my entire morning. I even woke up early to get in before he got back home, but he supposedly cut his workout short.

It has been forty-five minutes, and if he uses all the hot water, I might kill him.

What does he even do in there any way? Jerk off? There's no way it takes *that* long, and he probably doesn't even need to. Some girl probably sucked him off last night when he went out with some of the guys after work.

I've been trying to avoid Leo at work, since it's the only time I don't have to actually talk to him. When I'm at home, he's always around, and I literally have nowhere to run. I can avoid him a bit easier at the office. Since he's all buddy-buddy with Brody and the other assholes, he hasn't been in his office a lot lately.

Which means I don't have to stare at his stupid fucking face through my window all day, and that is the best present anyone could have given me.

It has only been a week, and I already have a countdown for when he's hopefully leaving. His place is supposed to be ready in November, which means I only have two months of him living here.

It has been one week, and it already feels like a fucking eternity.

I hear the shower turn off after I bang on the door a few more times. When the door finally opens and Leo walks out wearing just a towel, staring down at me with that stupid smirk on his face, I have to fight the urge to knee him in the balls.

"All yours, darling."

"Fuck. You. If I'm late, I'm blaming you." And then I slam the door and turn the shower to the hottest setting, only to discover it's lukewarm when I step into it.

Today better not get any worse. If it does, I'm going to have to call Paige and Oliver to help me bury Leo's body when I eventually murder him.

WORK HAS BEEN OKAY so far.

I've been slowly putting together some things for the publishing account, and I have this other account—a coffee brand—that Imogen assigned me. It has been fun configuring an entire new Instagram feed for them. I sent them some test photos, and they loved what I was doing, so they booked Loft Media for the rest of the year.

After all the losses I've been taking, it feels nice to have some positive energy back in my life. Lately, all it seems like I'm doing is trying and failing.

Fuck, I forgot to call Lizzie last night.

Dammit, I guess I spoke too soon. My sister texted me the other day saying she wanted to talk to me about something, and I was in the middle of a meeting with an author when she did. I had to decline; I told her I'd call her after, but I was so exhausted, I fell asleep at my desk.

Shit. I should know better. I should be doing better, but life feels way too overwhelming lately, and I can't get it to stop. I'm normally so good about juggling multiple things at once, so I don't know what's throwing me off my game.

I take my phone out to text her.

> **Ella:** Hey! Sorry I forgot to call you last night. I'm available after work if you want to chat. Was it something important? Is it about Dad? Is he okay? Are you okay?

She answers me a few minutes later.

> **Lizzie:** Dad and I are both fine, Ella. Stop worrying. It wasn't a big deal.

> **Ella:** If it matters to you, it matters to me.

> **Lizzie:** It's more of an in-person conversation. Can you come to Dad's for dinner sometime this week?

I don't know why her choice of words has my stomach dropping. My mind races through all the possible things it could be, and none of them are good.

> **Ella:** Anything for you. How does tomorrow night sound?

> **Lizzie:** That works. Can you pick me up from school too? Dad's car is in the shop.

> **Ella:** Again? What for this time, and why didn't you tell me about it?

> **Lizzie:** Something with the engine. But it's fine; my friend has been driving me to school.

> **Ella:** But I could've helped, Liz.

> **Lizzie:** Ells, it's okay. I'll see you tomorrow? I have to go to class.

> **Ella:** Okay. See you then. I love you!

> **Lizzie liked a message.**

I try not to think about the conversation too much, especially since she didn't say she loved me back. I hope this is some sort of phase, but maybe it's what she has to talk to me about that's making things so weird.

Have I not been there enough? Has there been something going on at home I don't know about? Does she resent me for leaving? Does she think I don't check in enough anymore, and now she hates me?

God, I can't deal with this. I knew I should have been there more for her and my dad, but it slipped my mind the past few weeks. I'm a terrible sister. That's probably what she wants to talk to me about.

Fuck my life.

My phone rings a few seconds after I put it down, and I immediately pick it up.

"Lizzie?"

"Nope. It's your other sister."

Hads. "Hey. Sorry, it's been a long ass morning."

"Want to talk about it?"

"Not really. It's nothing, actually. What's up?"

I hear her sigh heavily from across the line. "This is your formal invitation to Grant's birthday party. Check your email. I sent an e-invite."

"Okay," I say as I open my email and click on the one from Hads. Grant is officially having his birthday at a trampoline park, and he invited us all to come. "Why did you call me for this?"

"Grant wanted me to. He also wanted me to tell you he made his own invites."

"Okay...?" I question.

"Look, Ella, you're the queen of hosting things. I think he really wanted your approval of how he did. This is all him, not me. So if you can call or text him and hype up his party-planning skills, I'm sure he would love it."

I can only laugh. That might be the sweetest thing I've ever heard. Not only do I pride myself on the events and parties I host, but it feels good someone else thinks I do okay at it. Grant never fails to make me feel better, and truth be told, he isn't bad at designing invitations at all. This one looks good. "I'll call him later and let him know I love it."

"Thank God," Hads says. "He was nervous to send these out this morning. It's all he talked about at breakfast. I love the man, don't get me wrong, but he is taking this way too seriously."

"Hads, not all of us hate our birthday like you and Oliver do," I point out.

"Yeah, yeah. Whatever. I have to go. I'll see you at book club?"

"I'll be there. I love you."

"I love you too, Ells," she says as she hangs up, and I hear my stomach growl. I didn't have time to grab something for breakfast this morning since Leo took so fucking long in the shower.

I get up from my desk and head to the kitchen, but not before I stop in Rae's office. I knock twice on her already-open door, and she looks up from her desktop.

"Do you want coffee or a snack? I'm grabbing something from the kitchen."

"How nice of you." She smiles at me. "I'll take a coffee, please."

"Coming right up."

"Two—"

I cut her off. "Two sugars and a cream. I know, babe."

"I knew I loved you."

I only smile as I head over to the kitchen. I was going to ask Adam if he wanted something when I passed his cubicle, but I forgot he's out of the office with a client today.

I'm almost to the kitchen when I hear a bunch of voices drifting out of it. I recognize them—Brody, Leo, and all the other assholes in the office. They're all standing around in the kitchen, talking about something. I'm not sure what, but when I hear my name brought up, I pause.

I stop just out of sight as I listen to what they're saying. Normally, I'd walk in and say something, but I want to know what they're talking about.

"You're competing with her on that one project, right?"

"Uh, yeah," Leo answers.

"You've got it in the bag, then," Brody says to him. "Why do you think I got promoted over her? She's been turning in mediocre work for months."

"Yeah, I saw one of the campaigns she did for this one small business. It was average at best," another asshole says.

Are you fucking kidding me? This cannot be happening. First of all, to be talking shit about me in the office we currently work at is highly unprofessional. Secondly, I only create what the brand wants from me, and they loved the campaign.

"Don't even get me started on her side hustle," some guy says.

"What?" Leo asks.

"You haven't seen her online profile? She does a bunch of marketing on the side for authors or whatever. It explains why she wants this project so bad. Though, with the shit she makes online, I doubt she'll get it," Brody says, and I think he smacks Leo or something. Maybe he's giving him a pat on the back; you know, that thing assholes do to one another when they think they're funny but aren't.

"Listen, mate, we work with her. Show some respect to your coworkers occasionally. Ella works hard—harder than you, even. If there's one thing I admire about her, it's her work ethic. I've never seen you stay later than three in the afternoon, Brody."

Leo said that. Leo Zimmerman just stood up for me in front of a bunch of assholes trying to degrade me and my work.

He stood up for me not knowing I'm listening in around the corner.

Did I just walk into the twilight zone? An alternate universe? Why is he sticking up for me in front of our asshole coworkers?

What the hell is going on? I must be asleep. There's absolutely no way, in no universe, that Leo would stick up for me. He hates me as much as I hate him. So, what's his angle? What's his fucking play in doing this?

I try not to think about it as I raise my chin and walk into the kitchen. I keep my expression neutral so they don't know I heard everything they said as I grab a banana and turn the coffee machine on for Rae.

"Morning, boys," I say as I turn and lean against the counter. "How's it going today? Any more mediocre work going on?"

I smile as Leo locks eyes with me, a knowing look on his face.

"Just taking a small break, Ella."

"How nice," I say as I take a bite of my snack. "You know, Brody, I almost forgot you worked here and not at the golf course. How over par were you this week or should I not bring that up?"

He only stares at me in disbelief that I would ever say such a thing to him, and to be honest, I probably shouldn't have, since he is technically my boss.

But then again, if he can talk shit about me behind my back, then I should be able to do the same right to his face. At least my way, he's hearing it from me. I may be a bitch in some people's eyes, but at least I'm a bitch enough to say it right to your face.

"Ella, you better—"

"What? Watch my tone?"

"Yes."

I cross my arms in front of me. "Well, maybe you should be careful about how loud you speak. People could hear who you really are if you're not too careful. And we wouldn't want that happening, would we?"

"Ella—"

"Brody, get the fuck out," Leo snaps. "You guys too. I need to speak with Ella in private."

"Dude, what the—"

"Go do some actual work for once, Brody. Just because you got promoted doesn't mean you can slack off. We have a huge deadline coming up, and we're not even halfway done," Leo tells him, and for some reason, Brody listens. Typical man. They only listen to other guys on the same level as them. If I had said that to Brody, he would've yelled at me and told Imogen. Hell, he might still tell Imogen about what happened, but she'll only tell him to get back to work.

Brody can get away with a lot of shit here, but Imogen knows what he's like. She doesn't take any shit from him, and that's why I love having her as my boss. Even if Brody is above me, I can always count on her.

The guys leave, and Leo and I are now in here by ourselves. He's still sitting at the table, and I'm still against the counter.

"How much did you hear?" he asks me.

"Enough," I say as I turn around and grab Rae's mug.

"Look, I'm—"

"I also heard you stick up for me, so don't apologize for them, Leo. Even though I don't need you fighting my battles for me, I appreciate you saying what you did."

"No need to thank me."

"There is, though. You could have chosen to say something about me and be as mean as they were, but you didn't. And that tells me a lot about who you are, Zimmerman." Maybe I've been wrong about him all this time, but one incident of him doing the bare minimum for me isn't going to suddenly change how I feel. "I'll see you at home."

I start to walk out of the kitchen, my banana and Rae's coffee both in my left hand, and when I walk by where Leo sits, he reaches out and grabs my free hand.

"They're wrong, Ella. You do great work. Competing with you has been a challenge, but one I'm not backing down from."

"Careful, Leo. If you keep being this nice to me, I'll think you have Stockholm syndrome or something."

"Wouldn't be the worst thing I've had."

"Oh, right." I nod my head. "I forgot about your recent STI diagnosis. That must be a bitch to deal with." I separate from his hand and pat him on the shoulder. "I hear antibiotics help chlamydia. Do you want me to look into that for you, or—"

He only starts to laugh. "Just get back to work before I piss you off again, Williams."

"It's only a matter of time, Zimmerman," I say as I leave the kitchen and head to Rae's office. "It's only a matter of time."

A Slip Up?

I'm in the car with my sister—who's being uncharacteristically quiet—and I have to stifle the side of myself that wants to ask her what's wrong. After our conversation yesterday, it's clear something is bugging her, but I'm not sure what.

She's getting older, so maybe she thinks I'm too overbearing and I need to pull back.

Or maybe I'm not doing enough for her and our dad.

It could be any number of things, but until she talks to me about it, I don't want to ask. If I ask and the problem is with me, then I'm only proving her point.

After the past few days I've had, I need something good. After Leo stood up for me at work yesterday, he went back to being an ass. I knew it wasn't going to last, but I didn't think I'd get home and see half of the hockey team from Grand Mountain in my living room. It would have been nice if Grant was over, but he wasn't. It was only Liam, Leo, and a few other people.

But it would've been nice to know about it before I walked in looking disheveled after staying late to finish something. I was really looking forward to watching reality television with Alissa tonight, but she's going out with some guy she has been seeing and is sleeping over at his place.

Which means she's getting fucked. I'm happy for her, really, I am, but not only am I not getting fucked, but I have to deal with Leo for the entire night without Liss being there to buffer.

It's the first time Leo and I have been completely alone at the apartment, and it could go one of two ways. We could either be civil and not speak to each other all night, or we're going to fight.

"Mom called me the other day," my sister says, effectively breaking my mind off all thoughts of Leo.

"Our mother called you? On the phone?" Shock doesn't even begin to cover all of what I'm feeling. "What did she say?"

"She wanted to talk and catch up."

I try to stop the laugh that comes out, but I can't. "She wants to catch up after walking out on us? You're telling me *now* she wants to talk? What did you say to her?"

Lizzie looks away, and I can't tell what she's thinking. She was so young when our mom left. I didn't even think she remembered much about her.

But I remember. I remember what it was like watching her walk out the door and never seeing her again. I remember what it felt like when I realized I had to be the one to step up, to keep the family afloat because it was too hard for my mother to stay.

It was really fucking easy for her to leave, and now that we're older, she suddenly wants to be part of our lives? No. Not only is it not fucking fair, but if she left once, she would absolutely do it again.

"We talked for a bit, and it was nice, Ells. She asked about me and what has been going on, and she even asked me about you—"

I laugh again. "Lizzie, you realize she walked out on us over a decade ago, right? She can't waltz back in here and act like she cares when she clearly didn't care enough to stay when we were younger."

"Ella, people can change. She sounded genuinely interested in what—"

I park the car in my dad's driveway before I turn to my sister. "This is what happens, Lizzie. She'll get your hopes up, and when you think everything is okay again, she'll leave."

"But sis—"

I cut her off again, and I know I shouldn't, but she needs to understand our mother is nothing but a runner. She bolts when she realizes she needs to be responsible. It's what she has always done, and I'll be damned if she tries to come crawling back, only to break my sister's heart.

She doesn't get to break mine again, not after I practically raised my sister. She doesn't get to take credit for everything I've done to keep us afloat while she left and didn't spare a single fucking glance back.

"Lizzie, she's not a good person. If you want to keep your heart intact, you'll stop talking to her."

"You might be my older sister, but you can't tell me what to do."

"Sis, I'm trying to protect you from her." I grab her hand. "She'll only leave you with empty promises and a broken heart. Trust me, I know what it feels like to want to believe she's changed." *But she never will.* I don't add that, because I can tell my sister truly believes our mother is capable of becoming a good person.

She only thinks that because of how I've shielded her from our mother her entire life. For good reason, too. I can handle the broken heart from not having a mother figure my entire life, but Lizzie is softer than I am. She wants to believe people can change, that people are capable of doing and being better.

But our mother isn't one of those people.

"I don't need you to keep protecting me, Ella. I need you to live your life and stop worrying about me all the time. I'm a big girl. I can make my own decisions."

That kind of hits me in the chest. I know she's older now, and I know she's capable of doing things herself, but to me, she'll always be the sister who used to crawl into bed with me in the middle of the night. She'll always be the kid who cried when one of her stuffed animals fell off her bed and got left out during the night.

"I know, Lizzie, but—"

My sister gets out of my car as if it's on fire, slamming the door behind her. I flinch, feeling like I got punched in the face. I get that she's mad at me, but she would thank me if she knew what our mother was really like. I don't want her to find out. I don't think she could handle the heartbreak.

As I watch her go inside, I slump against my seat. All I want to do is protect her. That's all I've done since our mom left the first time.

It fucking hurts hearing she wants a relationship with Lizzie now, and me, I guess. But I know better than to believe in her. It makes me mad she picks now, of all times, to come back.

It's bad enough she's around again, but now, my sister is mad at me.

Today has officially been the worst, and all I need when I get home is a bottle of tequila and some shitty movie to distract me from the weirdness I'm feeling.

IT TURNS OUT, THE only thing I have at home is wine and an annoyed roommate.

It seems like Leo and I have both had days from hell, and being mad in the same space is a recipe for disaster.

The disaster starts now, because Leo is cooking around me in the kitchen as I try to find the corkscrew, and there's nothing that pisses me off more than someone being in the kitchen at the same time as me. I don't know why it angers me, but him being in my space is always an annoyance, and today is no different.

I sigh heavily as I search another drawer and can't find it. I swear, we always keep it in the drawer next to where we store the alcohol, but it's not in there.

"Do you need some help or something?" Leo asks, a pinch of attitude in his voice.

"No. Go back to huffing by the stove," I tell him as I open another cabinet. *Where the fuck is this corkscrew?*

"Only you could make this day worse," he whispers under his breath, though not very well, because I heard every word.

"How is it possible your day was bad? You went to work and came home. It's no different than any other day for you, and Brody was even in today— Oh! That's it then." I stand from the hunched over position I was in.

"What?"

"You're probably pissed off because you spent the entire day up Brody's ass."

His eyes narrow at me, and he looks more pissed than before. *Good.* His mere presence in my safe space angers me every time I come home to find he's here.

I open another drawer, and as I see the corkscrew and try to grab it, Leo shuts it and almost breaks my fucking hands.

"What the fuck is your problem? You could have broken my fingers, you fucking psychopath!"

He cages me into the kitchen island, both of his arms on either side of me. "You. You are my fucking problem, Williams."

"Give me a fucking break, Zimmerman. You're the one slamming shit with a pissed off expression on your face."

"It's been a long day, and I wanted to come home, make a nice meal, and enjoy my night."

I point my finger at him. "Then do that! Nobody's fucking stopping you!" I press my finger into his chest and try to shove him away, but he doesn't budge.

"You are! You're stopping me from having a good night!"

"I've barely talked to you since I got home!" I say as I push off the island. I'm sick of this. I didn't come home just to get into a yelling match with Leo. All I want is to get drunk and try to forget about the bomb my sister dropped on me this afternoon, but I can't, because he's here. He's always fucking around no matter where I go, and it pisses me off.

I hate looking at his stupid face all day, and I hate seeing his annoying ass when I come home and try to unwind.

Alissa owes me big time for letting him stay here.

I open the drawer and grab the corkscrew before I stab it into the cork. If I was a better person, I wouldn't be seeing Leo's face in the cork as I stab it, but I'm not.

Fuck, what I would give to stab Leo for real. I'm sure he'd be fine. I'm sure he'd have some hot nurse come and look after him.

Stop, Ella.

"You imagined that was me, didn't you?"

"No comment." I smile sweetly at him as I abandon the glass and drink straight from the bottle. As I walk by him, I turn the stove off. If he wants to play these stupid fucking games, I will too.

I get into my room and place my wine bottle on my side table, but I notice I don't hear my door shut. When I turn around, Leo is in my room.

"Why did you turn the stove off? I was using it."

"Because you tried to cut my hands off when you shut the drawer."

He runs a hand through his already messy hair. "God, Williams, you act so high and mighty for someone who plays games like a bloody child."

"Coming from you," I poke his chest again, "that's fucking rich."

He steps closer to me, officially invading my personal space. "I only fight with you because you piss me off unlike anyone else."

"Then I deserve a medal. It's way too fucking easy."

"A medal? Oh, you want a trophy for pushing every goddamn button and getting under my skin? Is that what you want? A fucking prize?" he asks me, his face close to mine.

"Yes, actually—"

And before I can register what's happening, his lips smash into mine.

I MIGHT HATE MOST things about Ella, but when my lips connect with hers and she shuts her mouth, I like her.

I don't know why I'm kissing her, if I'm being honest. All I know is that today was fucking terrible, and for some reason, when she was yelling and pointing her finger at me, I was turned on.

There's something so devilish about Ella when she's angry. I've always liked playing with fire, but her fire is more explosive, more intense.

That's what makes her such a good fuck. She's just as explosive in the bedroom as she is with her mouth.

But she's kissing me back, just like last time we did this.

Fuck, I've missed how good this feels. Not because it's with Ella, but in general. Normally, I'm not much of a kisser, but it was the only way I could shut Ella up, other than shoving her down onto her knees and shoving my dick in her mouth.

On second thought...

I snake one of my hands to her chest and shove her back on her bed. She bounces on the mattress before I grab her by the neck and hoist her up onto her knees.

"What the fuck, Zimmerman?"

"Oh, back to surnames, are we?" I ask as I tighten my hold on her neck. "I like you much better when you're not talking back like a little fucking brat."

Her pupils dilate, and I know her pussy is pulsing between her legs. Ella might hate me, but she loves my mouth. She loved when I talked dirty in her ear while I thrusted into her. Well, her pussy loved it. The last and only time we fucked, it was practically strangling my cock when I told her how good she looked taking my dick.

My hand was around her throat, so she couldn't say something snippy back to me, but I know she liked it. She came all over my cock and then bolted, but nothing could ever erase that memory from my head.

"S-Shut the fuck u-up," she stammers, my hand still wrapped around her throat.

"Not until you stop acting like a brat, or do I need to take you over my knee and teach you a lesson?"

"We're not doing this again, Leo." I loosen my hold on her neck before I turn her around so she's on her stomach.

And then, I smack her arse—hard. And I swear, I hear her moan into her bed.

"You're telling me one thing, but your pussy says another. How badly is it aching to be filled by the person you hate the most right now? Tell me the truth, Ella, or your arse is getting smacked even harder."

She squirms underneath me, her thighs rubbing together tells me all I need to know.

"It won't mean anything if we do, Ella. It's just sex, just like it was last time we slipped up."

She laughs. "Is that what we're calling it now? A slip up?"

"Seems fitting, doesn't it?"

"Whatever."

"Oh, so you don't want me to take care of your needy fucking pussy? You don't want me to fuck you how I know you liked to be fucked?"

She turns her head to look at me, her gaze tormented, as if she can't figure out what's worse: having sex with me or not.

At least if she has sex, she'll get an orgasm.

"It's me or your vibrator, darling."

"Why do you want to fuck me, Leo? Can't you go find someone else?"

No, apparently, I can't. "Because you piss me off and my dick is hard. And since we both had a shit day, we could use something good, like an orgasm."

She doesn't say a word as I stare at her from where she lies on her bed.

"Take it or fucking leave it, Williams."

I see the moment she gives in. Her eyes narrow at me, and she turns her head back around. "If you try and kiss me again, I'll bite your lip off. We're fucking, and that's it."

"God, I liked you so much better when you couldn't talk back," I say as I shove her head into her bed. "Now, sit there and take my dick like the bad girl you are."

I unzip my pants, my underwear coming off with them as I toss them aside. My dick is hard and ready, practically throbbing. It hasn't felt anything but my fist the past few months.

"Condom, Leo. I don't want you anywhere near me without one on."

"I'm not a fucking idiot, Ella."

"I didn't say you were—"

"On second thought, maybe your mouth should be full," I say as I grab her legs and drag her to the edge of the bed. She sits up, and her face is perfectly in line with my cock. "Suck."

"I would rather die—"

I grab her chin and lift it up. "Suck my fucking cock, darling."

"Are you sure you want me to? I could bite it off." My dick jerks in front of her. "Seriously?"

"Ella, you better start listening—" Before I can finish my sentence, her mouth is around my dick, and she starts to suck.

Holy fuck.

Her mouth is warm, wet, and takes my cock so well. What she can't fit in her mouth, she uses her hand to jerk as she sucks, and I swear, I could come right down her throat. It has been way too long since I've had someone else do this for me, and it feels way too damn good, even if it *is* Ella making me feel like this.

She might be the biggest pain in my fucking backside, but she sucks cock like a fucking champ. Good to know her mouth is useful for something other than giving me attitude.

She releases my dick with a pop and then looks up at me with that signature Ella pissed off face.

"Are you going to fuck me or what? I don't have all night."

I grab the condom I got from her drawer and bring it up to my mouth, ripping the foil with my teeth as I keep my eyes on her.

Then, I shove her back on her bed like I did before.

"Take your clothes off."

"No."

I kind of like this game we play. The last time we fucked, she did the same thing—fought me at every turn—and I can't remember a time my dick was as hard as it was then and now.

It seems arguing with Ella Williams gets my cock hard.

"Take your clothes off, Ella. Now."

She keeps her eyes on mine as she drags her pants down her body as slow as she possibly can. Can't she ever make this easy?

I roll the condom on, and as she gets her pants off, I flip her over. She's lying on her stomach, her perky arse in the air as her legs hang off the side of her bed.

Before she can talk back to me again, I thrust into her.

And my God, it feels like coming home after a long day away.

Her pussy is tight, wet, and the best thing I've felt after months of fisting my cock to make myself come.

I can't help the moan that slips from my mouth.

"Are you going to just sit there, or are you going to fuck me?" she asks as she pushes her ass into me, my dick going even deeper.

Then, I start moving, her ass bouncing against me as I slam into her over and over again.

She's holding back, I can fucking tell, and it's pissing me off.

"Scream, Ella. You know you want to."

"I would rather die," she tells me, her face twisted in pleasure.

Is death really better in her eyes than getting fucked how I know she wants to be? "Fine. We're doing this the hard way then."

"What does—"

She doesn't have time to finish her thought before I spank her again. *Hard*. And before she has time to throw another quip back at me, I flip her over, and my hand finds her neck.

"If you want to hold back your noises from me, then I'll make it easier for you."

Her eyes bulge out of her head, her pussy tightening as I look her in the eye while I fuck her. And what a sight it is, seeing her writhe underneath me.

Ella likes being choked more than anyone else I've been with, but actually feeling her get more aroused with my hand around her neck is spinning me out of control.

As I continue thrusting into her tight pussy, I see her hand slide down to her clit as she starts to play with herself.

"That's it, darling. Help me get you off. Help me make you come while I choke you until you can't breathe."

I feel her throat move as she takes small breaths, obviously wanting to say something, but with all the back talk she gave me, she doesn't deserve it.

I grab her legs and hoist them onto my shoulders before I throw her hand off her clit and take control. She doesn't deserve to get herself off. That's my fucking job.

I'm in control here, not her. And God, it feels good finally having her submit to me after all the times she stood her ground. Don't get me wrong, I love making her face red and arguing with her. It feels good knowing I get under her skin as much as she does mine.

But seeing her like this? Overwhelmed with pleasure because of me? Nothing will ever beat that. *Nothing*.

"Let go, Ella. Stop fighting it and fucking come on my cock," I tell her, and as her eyes roll to the back of her head, I feel her pussy spasm around me as she coats my dick.

A few seconds later, I follow her, unable to hold back my release any longer. It feels so fucking good, and it's so much stronger than it has been in months.

Fuck my dry spell. *This* is what pleasure feels like, and fuck, I've missed it.

I roll off her, and we lay beside one another in stunned silence for way too long. When I finally turn to talk to her, I notice she's fast asleep.

I'm jolted back to the last time we did this in college—the same thing happened. I wonder if she's always like this after sex, or if it only happens when she has sex with me.

After I get my bearings, I grab a washcloth and clean her up. I don't bother showering because I'm too fucking exhausted from the emotional whiplash of today. I've gone from pissed off to feeling like I'm on top of the world.

All because of her.

And just like last time, I fall asleep with her in bed next to me.

Maybe this time, she won't be gone when I wake up, but knowing Ella and how our relationship works, when we wake up tomorrow, it'll be back to normal.

Just how it's supposed to be.

18

A Date With My Dildo

College

"Alissa, I swear to all that is holy, if you leave me here with your brother of all people, one of us might end up dead." *And it's probably going to be him.*

"Look, Ells, all I need is the car. Leo can drive you home since he's not drinking tonight." Alissa is pleading with me to get the car since there's a guy she wants to go home with at the Hidden Bear. I'm not about to let her get into this guy's car, so the only option is for her to take the car we drove over in. Who knows what kind of people come to this place? Even though it is a college bar, men are fucking weird and creepy. Any one of these people could be a serial killer.

And according to Paige, you never know if someone walking by you could have killed someone. Apparently, one in seven people you pass in your life could have potentially killed someone and gotten away with it.

"If I give you the car, I'll take an Uber home. Leo can drive home by himself or with whatever girl he picks up tonight." I'm not about to third wheel on the way home if Leo takes me. I'm sure some girl is going to suck his face or dick while driving, and that's not a show I want to be privy to.

"Thank you, Ells!" Alissa hugs me, and I hand her the keys. "I'll tell you all about it tomorrow, and maybe you'll have your own story for me..." She trails off as she looks over my shoulder. When I turn to see what she's looking at, a *very* cute girl looks me up and down before winking at me.

Damn, maybe tonight isn't a total loss.

I lean against the bar and order another drink. If I'm stuck in the same vicinity as Leo Zimmerman, I'm going to need it to drown out his stare against my body—not in a sexual way, but a pissed off one. I'm sure Leo isn't happy being left here with me either.

Alissa and I came out and, of course, her stupid brother had to tag along. As if I don't see him enough already at our internship twice a week. I hate how he's always hanging around with us, but part of me understands it.

My sister and I are as close as Alissa and Leo are. If she was a bit closer to my age, I'd probably spend as much time with her as those two do with one another.

It only annoys me because Leo is a pain in my ass at our internship and a pain in my ass whenever he's around.

I grab my drink from the bar and head back to my table, seeing Leo sit there with some blonde on his arm. I can't tell what they're talking about, but when I slide into the booth across from them, she takes one look at me and leaves.

That was easy.

"Seriously?"

"What?" I ask him, a smile on my face.

He shakes his head at me. "Nothing."

"Oh, come on. I know you've got something better in that tiny brain of yours. We don't have to be civil now that your sister is gone."

He raises his eyebrow at me. "Well, for starters, you're dressed like it isn't fucking freezing outside."

I look down at my outfit—a black mini skirt with stockings, a red, lacy corset top, and my black leather jacket—and I think I look great. "You act like I care what you think about me."

"I think you secretly do, underneath all those layers of hatred and murderous glares."

"Stop flattering yourself. I think I look nice, and so do half the people in this bar who have been giving me eyes all night." He can't say the same, since the girl who was over here is the first person to make contact with him all night.

He prides himself on his looks, but he should know you have to have an actual personality to make people want to go home with you, and he doesn't have one.

Well, besides being a man and an asshole.

"Well, if you did, I'd tell you I think you look like a slag in that outfit, Ella." He takes a sip of his water while I glare at him. "But you don't care, so who am I to say anything?"

"Fuck off," I say as I down the rest of my drink, slam the empty glass on the table, and leave.

I grab my phone from my purse as I storm out of the bar, unwilling to listen to Leo give me his stupid and unsolicited opinions that don't matter. I pull my phone out to text...nobody. Dammit. Paige is busy with Ames doing who knows what, and Hads is studying. Plus, I wouldn't want either of them coming to pick me up and seeing Leo here with me.

Uber it is.

I pull out the app and see how far away one is, but nothing is showing up. I know Grand Mountain is a decently small college town, but there's usually a few running every night. Why aren't any showing up?

"Ella, let me take you home. It's the least I can do for my sister."

Of course it's for Alissa. Leo Zimmerman would never do anything out of the kindness of his heart for me. "That's okay. I wouldn't want my slutty outfit to get all over your car."

"Look, I'm sorry. I didn't mean it like that. Just get in the fucking car and let me drive you home."

I shove him back a bit. He's way too in my personal space for my liking. "No." I sway on my feet, a little tipsy.

"I'm waving a white flag here, okay? I'll be nice. We don't even have to speak—"

"Ideal for you, isn't it?"

"Just let me take you home safely."

I look down at my phone again, still not seeing any Uber's available, so I concede. "Fine. But if you piss me off, I'm tucking and rolling out of your car."

He only smirks at me. "I'll make sure to drive fast, then."

LEO PULLS UP TO my apartment building, and I have to say, that was the most civil the two of us have ever been. Granted, neither of us said a word, but I would still call it a win.

"Safe and sound. Would you look at that?"

I know he wants me to thank him, but I'm not going to. "Whatever. Do you want to come up for a drink or something?" My eyes bulge, as if

I didn't know I was going to say that. I don't know why I did it. The last thing I want to do is continue being in his presence, but I couldn't stop the words as they flowed out of my mouth. *Shit.*

"Are you continuing our truce, or are you trying to stab me or something?"

"Well, you never know. I guess it's a gamble."

He doesn't answer, only turning his car off and getting out of it. He doesn't wait for me as he walks to the door to my building and waits. I have the passkey to get in, and when I scan my badge, the two of us walk up the stairs and head to my apartment.

This feels weird.

If someone asked me how I imagined tonight going, I would have told them I assumed I'd be going home with somebody and having hot sex.

But now, as I climb the stairs with Leo Zimmerman next to me, I wonder where I've gone wrong to end up in this situation. Though, if we're being technical, I got myself into this situation by asking him if he wanted to come up for a drink.

Why the fuck did I do that again?

I open the door to my apartment and throw my purse on the hook before I head to the beverage cart and grab two glasses.

"Is tequila okay?"

He took his jacket off, and now he's rolling up his sleeves. It is a bit warm in here, but for some reason, seeing Leo's forearms is making my body feel weird. "Yeah, that's fine."

I pour him a shot before I hand it to him, and the two of us congregate on the couch. I grab my glass and take a sip, needing to feel something besides weird that Leo is currently sitting in my apartment.

"Why do you look so glum, Ella?"

"What?"

"You look like you're about to burst into tears."

I sigh before I roll my shoulders back, trying to appear more confident. "Well, I was hoping to go home with someone tonight, but things don't always work out how we want them to." I take another sip. "And don't pretend like you know my emotions. It's weird as fuck."

"You did go home with someone." I raise my eyebrows at him, confused. "Me."

I shake my head. "I didn't go home with you."

"Well, what do you call what we're doing now?"

"Having a drink. Nothing more and nothing less," I say as I finish mine off. "Now, drink yours so you can leave."

"Are you trying to get rid of me?"

"Yes. I have a date with my dildo, and I'd rather you not be here for that." I get up and place my empty glass in the sink. I'll wash it out tomorrow. I'm too exhausted to deal with any of the dishes right now.

"Oh, do you?"

"Yes," I say as I turn around, but he's way closer to me than I thought. He stares at me while he takes one long sip of his tequila, and I see his throat move as he swallows.

I must be really horny, because that was the hottest thing I've ever seen. Or maybe I'm drunk. Let's go with that.

He sets his glass next to mine in the sink before he backs up and leans against my counter. I didn't bother turning the light on, and for some reason, that makes me all more aware of his body in my kitchen. "Can I ask you a question?"

"You just did."

"Stop being a smart arse, Ella."

"Fine," I say. "But if you get one, then I get one."

"Go ahead then. Ask me whatever it is that's on your mind."

I step toward him. "What is it about you that makes girls lose their panties? I've been racking my brain about it all semester, and I don't get it."

He smiles at me. "Well, besides my dick and my willingness to eat pussy, I'm not quite sure."

"Ah, makes sense, I guess." I roll my eyes at him, hoping he can't see me, though I wouldn't care if he did. He sees me do it all day long at our internship while he's sitting in on meetings and I'm running to get coffee and bagels. "What did you want to ask me? Where do I get my slutty outfits from?"

He steps closer to me, invading my personal space more than he usually does. "Did you like it when I called you that earlier?" His voice is lower than normal, and if I was clinically insane, I'd think it's because he's turned on.

I let out a breathy laugh. "What? No."

He steps closer to me, and I can feel his breath on my face. "See, I think you're lying to me."

"I'm not lying." I don't even believe what I'm saying. I can't control my voice right now for some reason, and it's pissing me off. My guard is down, and I don't know how it got to be that way. Normally, it's always up, always three layers thick, but something shifted tonight, and now, all my defenses are down.

He reaches an arm behind my head, and before I can register what's happening, he takes my ponytail around his fist and pulls. A moan slips out of my mouth before I can stop it.

"See?" His lips meet the sensitive skin on my neck as he lightly bites. "I think you liked it, Ella. I think your panties got wet while you were sitting across from me, slamming your drink to stop feeling whatever it is you were."

"I—"

He bites my neck again. "Correction, what you *are* feeling, right here and right now."

"Leo," I say as I hold onto him for dear life.

"Tell me what you need, Ella. Tell me what you want from me. You're always willing to say something when you argue with me, so don't get all shy on me now."

Fuck him and his stupid fucking mouth.

I want to say no. I want to say no so badly. It's on the tip of my tongue, but for some reason, it won't come out.

"Ella, darling, tell me what you need," he coaxes as he puts his hands around my thighs and lifts me onto the counter. His face is in line with mine, the two of us breathing heavily as he waits for me to answer.

All I can see is him in front of me, and it's making my thoughts messy. I can't think. I can't breathe. I can't do anything but focus on the color of his eyes. They're brown, but not the normal chocolate color most people have. They remind me of cinnamon, and in the darkness of the kitchen, it reminds me of coming home after a cold winter day and wrapping myself up in a blanket.

"You, Leo. I want you." I never thought I'd utter those words in my life, but it's how I feel at this moment, and I knew if I let him walk out the door, it would piss me off even more.

That's all it takes for his lips to meet mine. This isn't a gentle kiss. Leo knows what he wants, and what he wants right now is me. He's devouring me, and I'd never say this out loud, but it's one of the best kisses I've had in my life.

The guy fucking knows what he's doing.

"Spread your legs, Ella," he says between kisses.

I keep them closed. If there's one thing I know about us—not that there's an us—is that we will always fight with one another. Even though we're probably about to have sex, he still has to earn it.

"Spread. Your. Fucking. Legs," he says as his hand comes around my throat.

I can't breathe, but I try my best to make sense when I reply. "Make me."

He only smirks as he runs a hand through his hair. "If that's what you want, then so be it."

I hear a rip, and the stockings I was wearing are now partially in Leo's hand before he leans me back on the counter, his hand still on my throat.

"Don't move."

I think about saying something snippy back, but I'm caught off guard when two of his fingers enter me. I can't think. He's going way too fucking slow, and he knows he's teasing me.

"Leo, I—"

"Just let me take my fucking time, Ella. Be patient for once in your life."

Then, he gets on his knees, and I feel his mouth start to circle my clit as his fingers keep pumping. This feels way too fucking good, and the fact that Leo Zimmerman is making me feel like this is something my brain can't process.

"Oh, fuck."

"It feels good finally giving in, doesn't it?" His voice is low, turned on, and I've never heard a sexier sound. Normally, that would scare me, but I don't have the brain power to think about that right now.

Then, he starts pumping faster, licking faster, but what sends me over the edge is how he bites my clit—not too hard, not too soft. Perfectly.

I should smack him for that or something.

I'm so fucking close. I'm teetering on the edge of my orgasm, and—

He stops.

"Leo, what the fuck?"

I see him stand up, a smile on his face as he looks at me. His sleeves somehow got rolled down, so as I sit and stare at him on the counter, edged way more than I can handle, he leans back across from me. He starts rolling up his sleeves again, his forearms bulging, and my gaze trails down his arms, all the way to the fingers that were just inside me.

"I'll tell you when you can come, Ella. And you don't deserve it yet."

"You are so fucking infuriating—"

"Go to your room, take off your clothes, and wait for me," he says as he starts to wash his hands and the dishes in my sink.

"What?"

"You fucking heard me, Ella. If you're a good girl and you do what you're told, I'll fuck you, make you scream my name, and you'll get to come." His eyes meet mine. "Go."

My brain wants to deny every order he's given me, but my legs move of their own volition toward my room. *You'll regret this tomorrow, Ella.*

I know I will, but right now, I don't give a fuck.

So, I take off all my clothes and lay down in bed, and a few minutes later, Leo comes into my room. The lights are off still, but I can feel his gaze brush my entire body.

"Fucking exquisite," he says as he grabs my ass. I'm lying on my stomach because he didn't tell me how to lay, so I chose a position comfortable for me. "You're such a good girl, Ella. Look at you, listening to me for once."

"Don't get used to it."

"Oh, I won't, darling." I hear the tear of foil, and my body is humming with excitement as I look back and watch him roll the condom onto his dick.

His *huge* dick. I've never taken one that big before, and of course, with a personality like his, he has the dick to back it up.

I don't know if it being small would've been better or worse in this situation.

"Don't worry, it'll fit."

I try to brush it off with a smile. "I wasn't worried."

"Good," he says, his voice tight as he thrusts into me in one go. "Fuck, you're tight, baby."

"Just keep moving, Leo," I tell him, not wanting him to know how much he's affecting me. I can barely fucking breathe as it is.

And so, he does. Leo fucks me hard, the only sounds I can hear is my ass slapping against him and our pants and moans as we fuck.

God, it feels so good. So fucking good.

"Do you hear us together, Ella? Do you hear how much your pussy loves me?"

"Y-Yes," I say as he keeps thrusting. I'm surprised he never wavers; most guys can't handle more than a few pumps. I've had some shitty hookups, and this one is blowing all of those out of the water.

My orgasm has been building since he stopped fingering me in the kitchen, and I'm so goddamn close to just letting go.

But I can't.

"Can I come?" I whisper, breathless from all the things I'm feeling.

Leo keeps thrusting, and just as I think he didn't hear me, he answers, "Yes, Ella, you can."

And that's all it takes for me to finally let go.

"Scream my name, Ella. Let everyone know who's doing this to you."

"Leo, fuck!" It just slips out.

"Ella. God, Ella," he says, his dick pulsing in my pussy as he comes.

And as the two of us come down from our highs, I can barely register what happens before I fall asleep.

I WAKE UP WITH legs tangled in mine.

And when I see Leo Zimmerman sleeping next to me, the memories of last night hitting me like a train, all I want to do is cry.

I can't believe we did what we did.

What the hell is wrong with me? Did I really have to stoop so low and have sex with the one person on this planet I can't stand? The one person who gets under my skin and pushes every button because he knows how much it annoys me?

Oh, what the fuck have I done?

I'm such a fucking idiot.

My phone starts to buzz, and I reach for it where it's plugged in.

Hads: Are we still on for coffee this morning?

Fuck. Hads and I always have coffee every Sunday. It's this tradition we started this semester because of everything going on with her and Grant. I thought she could use it to talk through her feelings, since I know she struggles with that. I go to answer her, but Leo moves, and I'm jolted back into what we did last night.

This didn't mean anything. I'm just another girl Leo fucked. I'm no different than the other girls he takes home for one night, and I don't know why it's throwing me off so much.

Because you let your guard down last night.

I did, didn't I? And what good did that do for me? All it ended up getting me was fucked by the one person I hate the most. I feel like a fucking idiot, like a fool.

I let Leo Zimmerman sweet talk his way up to my apartment, and I let my guard down. Nothing is going to change between us. When he wakes up, he'll still despise me, and I still hate him, no matter if we had sex and said all those things we did.

None of it meant anything, just like it means nothing with everyone else we fuck.

Checking the time, I realize I don't have long before I have to meet Hads, so I slide out of bed, take the quickest shower of my life, and make myself look decently presentable.

The look of embarrassment on my face is the shining star of my outfit today, and I hope I can hide it from Hads so she doesn't ask me about it.

Leo still isn't awake when I'm ready to leave, so I write him a note to let himself out and hope by the time I'm back from coffee, he's not here.

I don't want to talk about last night. I don't want to acknowledge what we did. I just want things to go back to normal.

I know one thing for sure: I'll never allow anything like that to happen between us again.

19

A Mistake

As I WAKE UP with an arm draped across my torso, I smile to myself.

God, it's just like old times, and I couldn't be happier about ending my fucking dry spell—

Wait.

No, this isn't right.

Because when I look down and see Ella cuddled against my chest, I must still be asleep. *What the hell happened?*

I see her eyes slowly flutter open as all the memories of what we did filter back into my brain. Her gaze focuses on me, and it takes all of two seconds for her to revert to her old self.

"Get the fuck off of me." She pushes me away from her.

"Darling, you were the one sprawled on top of me," I say as she puts her clothes back on.

"Great. Now I'm going to have to burn my sheets. They smell like you."

I shrug. "Is that the worst thing in the world? If there's any reason to burn them, it should be because the thread count is terrible." I swing my body off her bed and grab my clothes, and the two of us face one another as we get dressed.

"Not all of us are rich and can afford shit like that," she bites back at me.

"If I could afford shit like that," I make fun of her, "then I wouldn't be living here with you."

"Dear God, don't fucking remind me you're across the hall."

I'm about to bicker back with her, but the door to the apartment opens and closes, and I hear my sister come in.

"You guys didn't kill each other last night, did you?"

No. Definitely not.

"Get the fuck out of my room," Ella snaps, practically pushing me across the hall before my sister can see me walk out of her room half-naked.

I'm standing in my doorway, staring at Ella, who's crossing her arms at me in her doorway.

"This was a mistake," she tells me.

"Agreed."

"Don't tell anyone about this. Got it?"

I nod. "Don't tell your friends, then."

She rolls her eyes at me. "Trust me, they would be more excited about this than I am."

"I'll never bring it up again, Ella." Before she can say anything else, I slam my door on her.

What the fuck is going on?

I cannot believe I had sex with Ella Williams, the girl who pushes my fucking buttons and pisses me off to no end.

It had to have been the dry spell. That's the only reason I fucked her last night, not because when she was yelling at me, I couldn't stop staring at her lips.

All she ever does is yell at me, and after the shitty day I had, I had enough of her pissing me off. So, I kissed her. And it shut her up real quick.

I don't like Ella, but we both needed a distraction. Sex is good like that. It's a good distraction in the moment, but then you wake up with regrets like I'm having now, and it doesn't seem like a good idea.

My parents called me on my way home yesterday, and said my dad's recovery was moving slower than they would like. I asked if that meant anything bad, but they danced around an answer.

The doctors also told them he might have to have another surgery soon, but they'll cross that bridge when they get to it.

Which means my Dad refused to do it. My mom told me he doesn't want to go through surgery again, and I understand. Heart surgery is grueling, and I can't imagine how much stress it puts on his body.

But I don't want him to have another heart attack—or something worse—in order for him to have the surgery. I don't want to wait until that happens.

Which caused my mood to drop. Not only am I helpless over here in the States, but he won't even listen to what I have to say over the phone.

Then, I came home, wanting to make myself dinner and lock myself in my room until my mood got better, and then Ella started slamming anything she could, which pissed me off more.

All I wanted to do was forget about the shit going on with my family and how helpless I felt. Sex with her did help, but I somehow feel shittier than I did yesterday.

I'd promise not to do it again, but if my dry spell continues after this, I might find solace and release with the girl who hates me. She sure looked like she was enjoying herself last night, so maybe she would take me up on that offer.

It would work out, because neither of us has feelings for one another—not like that, anyway. The only feelings Ella and I have for one another are hatred and annoyance.

And it will forever stay that way, no matter how good the sex was.

Ella and I will never get along. Not only can I not stand her, but all she has done since I met her was judge me before she knew me. She'll never know who I really am because she refuses to see that side of me.

Fine by me.

20

We're All Friends Here

As I SIT IN front of my vanity and swipe mascara on my eyelashes, my phone buzzes.

> **Grant: I can't wait to give my speech tonight and tell everyone I saw Oliver cry.**

> **Ella: I didn't know he was capable.**

> **Hads: I'm surprised his tear ducts haven't stopped working from improper use.**

I start to laugh as another text comes through.

Oliver: You guys know I'm in this group chat, right?

Grant: Shit. I thought this was the book club one I'm in.

Oliver: Grant, you realize you're not actually part of book club?

Hads: With Ames gone, he basically is.

Ella: I agree. He's an honorary member.

Grant: Yeah, Ol. Honorary! Put some respect on my name, please.

Oliver: Fuck off. This is my engagement celebration. You guys are supposed to be nice to me.

Ella: "Supposed to."

Hads: I'm your sister. I'm never nice to you.

I keep laughing as I swipe black liner on and finish off my makeup. It doesn't take too long, and by then, I'm stepping into my dress. It's a black, skin-tight dress with lace sleeves. Hads told me she's wearing something green, and since it's Paige's engagement celebration, she's wearing a white dress.

I'm so excited to celebrate my best friend finding love, and Alissa is even tagging along too. It's going to be a great night.

But part of me wishes Amelia was around for this. Her and Paige were close, and I know us girls are upset our messages are still unanswered.

With every passing day of silence, I feel my patience with the situation wearing thinner.

If she was really our friend, she would be here for these moments, even if just over the phone. The radio silence is not only rude, but it's getting old.

Whatever, I say to myself. Tonight is about Paige and the love she and Oliver will share for the rest of their lives. I'm happy for her. After all that girl has been through, she deserves this.

Her and I have some similarities with how we were raised. Paige basically raised herself since her dad left and her mom wasn't around, and I had to raise my sister and myself, and take care of my house while my dad worked two jobs to sustain us.

I haven't told any of them about what's been going on with my mom, but if I was to say something, it would be to Paige. People who have happy parents don't really understand what it's like to have one or both parents be absent your entire life.

My dad did the best he could with the hand he was dealt—hell, his fucking wife and mother of his kids left—but he still wasn't there. I don't resent him for it, but it does fucking suck when I look back on that part of my life.

"Hey, Ells," Alissa says as she pokes her head into my room. "Wow, you look hot."

"Thanks. You look wonderful as well." Liss opted for a red dress that falls to her knees. The long sleeves are tight, and she looks fabulous with her black red-bottom heels. Sometimes, I forget Alissa has a fuck ton of money.

"Oh, by the way, Leo is coming."

My face falls. "Alissa, why? He doesn't even know Paige!"

"Oliver said it was fine! I'm trying to get him out of the house." Alissa comes further into my room and shuts the door. "Our dad had a scare the other day, and it really rattled him. He needs to get out of the house and mingle."

I nod in understanding. "How's your dad? And how are you doing with all of this?" Alissa is a strong girl—mentally and physically—but I know all this stuff with her family has shaken her up, and it has been a minute since I checked in on her.

"I'm okay. It's shit being over here sometimes, but I know if I went back to England, my parents would shout at me to go follow my dreams."

"You know I'm always here if you need anything, and—"

"Ella, I know that. Anyone who knows you knows that about you." She grabs my hand in hers. "What I need from you tonight is to make Leo feel included. I can only do so much."

"Well, he knows Grant." I know they've gone out a few times. Grant always asks me if it's okay they hang out. It makes me laugh that he feels like he has to ask permission, but I always tell him it's fine. "But I'll be nice. For you."

"That's all I ask, Ells." She gets up from my bed and leaves my room. *The bed you fucked her brother on...*

That is *not* what I want to think about right now, so I grab my purse and head out, only to run into Leo exiting his bedroom as well. He does a quick once-over, and my body becomes all too aware of his eyes on me, which pisses me off.

"You look..." I struggle to find a word nice enough to say what I want to say. "Clean."

He cocks his head at me, a stupid expression on his face. "You too."

And I'm not lying. He's wearing black dress pants, a white button up, a tie, and his sleeves are rolled up. Why the fuck does he always do that?

I head into the living room to find Alissa standing by the door, typing something on her phone. She looks up when she hears my heels click toward her.

"Ready?"

"Let's go," I say as we leave the apartment.

AS THE THREE OF us walk into the restaurant and I see Grant and Hads at the table, my mood is immediately lifted.

It's not that I'm upset about all the happiness floating in the air for Paige and Oliver; I just feel weird and off for some reason.

I don't hate being alone—that I don't have a date to bring to things like these. I prefer it, actually. I think I'm worried the older I get, the more likely it is I'll end up alone for the rest of my life.

I know I have time—realistically—but these feelings won't go away. I haven't tried to date since I broke up with my ex-girlfriend, and I have no urge to put myself back out there. It all seems...exhausting, if I'm being honest. I'm tired of doing the whole get to know me thing, only for it to peter out at month three or four. It's a vicious cycle that always ends with me being by myself.

Plus, nobody can match my energy. Some people have broken up with me because I'm too loud in public, because I like to sing at random times. Some people just can't handle how much I am.

I can't help it if I'm an extroverted person who likes karaoke. And more often than not, the person on the other side of the table bores me to death. I need someone interesting, someone who challenges me, and I have yet to find someone like that. I don't have time to date either. If this shit with my mom blows up, I need to put all my focus on protecting my sister from her claws.

I go over to Hads as I shake myself out of those bad thoughts I don't need to be having. Tonight is a night for celebrating my friends and an engagement—not for feeling shitty about the current state of my life.

"Hey, girl," I say as I hug her. "Missed you."

"I missed you too, babe." Hads moves her gaze to Alissa. "Hi, Liss!"

Those two start to talk, and Grant and I lock eyes.

"Ells, did you know this place has karaoke tonight?" Grant asks me as he crushes me in a hug.

"I didn't." I smile at him.

"Are you up for a duet?"

"A what?" Leo asks as he slides in next to Grant.

"Ella and I are karaoke partners." Grant lifts his hand, and I high-five him.

"You guys do this often?" Leo asks as we all start to sit down. Paige and Oliver still aren't here yet, and I'm shocked. Normally, they're first everywhere.

"As often as we can," Grant tells him. "It's hard to get us all together without a few weeks' notice."

"And all of us aren't even here..." Hads says under her breath. I don't blame her. I was thinking the exact same thing.

"So, where the heck are Paige and Oliver?" Alissa asks as she sits next to her brother. "Those two are late to their own celebration."

As if she summoned them, I hear Paige squeal behind us.

"I'm sorry we're late!" Paige tells us as she comes over, her arms spread out wide, as if she's going to try to hug all of us at once.

"It's okay, P. It's your celebration; you can be late," Grant tells her. "Plus, it was probably Oliver's fault."

Oliver just glares at Grant. "Wow. Okay."

"Well, it was, actually," Paige confirms, her cheeks going all flushed.

Oh, they absolutely had sex before coming here. I feel like a proud mom right now. Paigey was finally late to something, and that's about the only reason I'm okay with it.

"Ew, ew, ew," Hads says, her hand on her forehead.

"Hey, if I have to hear about you and Grant, you can deal with it too," Oliver tells his sister as he sits down next to her.

"Oh, come on, we're all friends here." Grant smiles.

"If friends can't talk about sex, then what are we even doing here?" I ask them, which gets a few laughs around the table.

"Agreed," Leo says, much to my surprise. When I look over at him, he's smirking. "Don't get used to hearing that from me when it comes to you."

"I won't, but I do wish I got to record it or something."

He leans closer, dropping his voice to a whisper. "Going to use it to get off? You could always ask me, darling. I am right across the hall."

I hate that my body gets hot. "I'd rather listen to screeching than hear your voice."

"That's not the impression I got the other night."

Grant's voice cuts into my ears. "Ells, we're up next. Are you ready?"

I detach from Leo's gaze as I turn to my friend. "Yes, I'm ready."

AFTER GRANT AND I sang the best duet of *Smooth Criminal*, we returned to the table, and the group of us ate dinner, chatted, laughed, and overall had a great night. We're still here—Paige ordered dessert for the table.

I'm in no rush to leave. Tonight has been fun, and I haven't even thought about my sister and impending family troubles.

Shit. Until now.

My phone buzzes in my pocket, and I grab it.

> **Lizzie: Mom has a permanent place here. She's going to be around more.**

> **Lizzie: We've been talking on the phone. She sounds genuine, Ells. I want to give her a chance.**

> **Lizzie: Please just think about it. That's all I ask.**

"I'm going to the ladies room," I say to the table.

"We'll join you," Alissa says as Hads and Paige get up.

"Love, where are you going?" Oliver asks as he grabs her hand.

"To the bathroom."

Oliver looks confused as Grant pats his shoulder. "Dude, you know they do this."

"I just don't get it."

"Me neither, mate. It feels like they're leaving to talk shit about us all," Leo says. It's strange how well he fits in with the boys, and that causes me a ton of unease. I know in a couple of months, he'll be out of the apartment and in his own space, but if he gets close with the guys, he'll probably still be around.

I don't know how I feel about that.

"Not all of you," I tell them as I lock eyes with Leo. "Just you."

I all but drag the girls to the restroom, and when we get in there and all three stalls are empty, I let out a breath.

I hear Hads lock the door, and they all turn to face me.

"What's going on, Ells? You've looked weird all night," Alissa asks me. Oh, fuck. There's no way she knows what happened between me and Leo when she was gone, right?

"Yeah, and you didn't look as excited as you normally do when you sing with Grant," Hads tells me. "It was still a great performance, but it was missing something."

I dart my eyes to Paige where she leans against the counter.

"Ells, stop worrying about ruining the night if you say something."

"I'm not. I—"

"If something is troubling you, we want to know, regardless of what we're all doing here. You're not stealing my thunder or whatever." Paige grabs my hand, squeezing it once. "What's going on?"

I didn't realize they noticed I wasn't fully myself tonight. I guess this shit is affecting me more than I thought. They must've seen my face when those texts came through.

No more hiding, I guess.

"My mom is back."

All their faces drop. I'm not one to highlight all my shit, and none of them really know much about my childhood, other than the fact that my mom wasn't there.

Nobody knows how bad it actually was, how much I wish I could have had different cards dealt to me. I realized quickly as a kid I had to keep my family afloat, but that doesn't mean I liked it.

I *had* to do it. It only could've been me to fix everything, and I thought I did an okay job. But now that my mom is back and my sister wants to give her a chance, it feels unfair.

"For how long?" Hads asks.

"My sister told me last week that she contacted her." I shake my head, trying to will the emotions I'm having to go the fuck away. This is Paige's night. I can't be crying about my own shit when we're here to celebrate her.

But I need my girls. I need their comfort to try and navigate this, because I'm not doing a great job of it. For the first time ever, I *need* my friends to help, and it feels good finally talking about this thing hanging over my head the past week.

"She texted me tonight that she wants to give her a chance." I look down at my hands. "Am I a horrible person for not wanting to let my mom even try with me?"

"No, you're not," Paige says as she hugs me.

I let her arms drape around me as a few tears start to fall. Never have I felt so conflicted. I know in my heart who my mom really is, but I can't stop my sister from wanting something from her. I wish I could because I know in the end, both of our hearts are going to be broken again.

Hers will be because of my mom, and mine will be because I couldn't protect my sister from the feelings I know come from trusting our mother.

Paige pulls back from me, and I can only look between the three of them, unsure of what the hell I'm going to do.

"I don't know what to do." For the first time ever, I can't decide if I should grin and bear it for my sister's sake, or if I should tell her how I really feel about our mother.

Either way crushes me.

"Maybe talk to Lizzie about it more, Ells. See what she wants to do, and maybe one dinner won't kill you?" Hads says, and I know she's trying to be helpful, but I don't think she understands.

"Can you guys give Ella and I a minute?" Paige says to them.

"Take your time," Hads tells us, shooting me a smile.

"I'll get you a drink, Ells," Alissa says, and I love her for it. She truly knows exactly what I need. I guess that's what happens when you live with someone as long as we have.

The two of them leave the bathroom, and I'm glad there's not a line forming outside of it. We did have the door locked, but most of the other tables have cleared out by now. The restaurant is still open for a few more hours, and the group of us are going to milk it as long as we can.

"Are you okay?" Paige asks me.

I'm not sure what to say. "Kind of."

She takes a deep breath before speaking again. "You know, I started talking to my mom again."

Her saying that shocks me. I knew eventually, Paige wanted to try again with her mom, but I didn't think it would be so soon. "Wow."

"I was scared to give her another shot. When I reached out, I felt like a kid again, begging for attention from someone who didn't want to give me any."

I understand that, in a way.

"But then she responded to me, told me she was willing to try."

"Did you believe her?"

She nods her head. "I was weary at first. But she's been texting me a lot and actually calling me first."

Wow. "Did you tell her about your engagement?"

"I did. After you guys and Sadie, she was the person I called." She smiles to herself. "She was really happy for me, and for the first time, it felt like I had a parent."

A tear falls from my eyes. I know the feeling she's describing. I never felt like I had any parents either. It all fell onto my shoulders since my dad was working so hard. I'm proud of him, but I still needed him. "I'm scared, Paige. What if she ends up walking away again? What if I get my hopes up, and it's all for nothing?"

"You're smart, Ella. You know her better than your sister does, but I think you're nervous because you spent your entire life protecting her from the pain you felt."

I know she's right. That's what's getting me so worked up. I'm mad at Lizzie for wanting to give her a chance, but of course she would want to, considering she never saw the bad stuff. She never knew what it was like because she was so young. I shielded her, protected her because I didn't want to tell a young kid her mom left with no reason to give.

"Actions are better than words, Ells. Your mom can say she's changed all she wants, but if there's no action to back that up, you're right to not give her a chance. Just think about it, and if anything, do it for Lizzie. Not for you, but for her."

"Thanks, P."

"If you need anything, Ella, and I mean that, call me. I'm always here for you."

"I know."

She smiles at me, and suddenly, it feels like the sun is coming out after a rainy afternoon. I don't know how she does it—remain positive and steady despite all she has been through.

"Now, can we go have dessert? I think we deserve a lot of ice cream and brownies tonight."

Paige interlinks her arm with mine as I nod, and I feel a little lighter knowing I was able to talk it through with someone who understands how complicated families can get.

Even our own little found family is complicated, but I'm grateful for those still around me who can lift me up when I feel down.

Grant: Wait, guys, we forgot to talk about game night.

Paige: Whose number is that?

Unknown: Is this another group chat? How many of these do you have?

Unknown: It's Leo.

Paige: Oh, hi!

Oliver: Grant, are you fucking serious?

Ella: -_-

Hads: Babe, I told you to text everyone separately.

Grant: This is easier.

Grant: So, game night is at our place this week. Whoever wins gets to pick the activity we do for Halloween. We're doing it on November 1st since Halloween is on a Thursday this year.

Paige: YAY! Girls against guys this time?

Ella: Oh, I'm so down for that.

Leo: Do you guys do this often?

Oliver: Unfortunately, yes.

Grant: Sold. See you all at game night!

21

Punish Me

November 1st

"Seriously?" is all I hear when I step out of my room.

When I look over at Ella, she folds her arms—clearly not impressed with my Halloween costume I spent forever thinking about. The girls got to pick what we did tonight since they won game night, and they chose to go to a club in costumes.

At least we're not matching this year.

Ella made sure of it by matching costumes with my sister—as if she wouldn't be caught dead matching with me again. She did try to swing a bat at me last time, and she would have succeeded if I didn't stop her.

Fiery little fucking thing. I know she would've actually hurt me if that thing had hit me. There were nails on the end of it too.

"Is there a problem, Ella?"

"You can't smoke in here." She points to the vintage cigarette holder I bought.

I walk past where she stands and poke her in the face with it. "Good thing it's not lit, then."

I can practically feel her eyes roll as I head into the living room and see my sister pouring shots. Twelve of them, to be exact.

"Alissa, are you trying to blackout before we even leave the house?" I say as I sit down at the table.

"No. I'm pre-drinking, Leo. And so is everyone else when they get here."

"Except Paige and Oliver. Neither of them are drinking," Ella tells her as she grabs water from the fridge and downs it in one go.

Oh, right. Grant told me Oliver avoids alcohol, and so does Paige sometimes. Those two are usually the designated drivers, which is fine by me. I need a night to let loose. That's the reason I picked being a gangster for my costume. Not only will it allow me to smoke for one night only to combat my stress, but I look fucking fantastic dressed like this. I look like I walked right out of *Peaky Blinders*, and that's exactly what I was going for.

"Dehydrated, Ells?" my sister asks her.

"Yes."

These two look kind of ridiculous in their costumes. "Who are you guys again?"

Alissa just smacks me over the head.

"Daphne and Velma, dumbass," Ella tells me. Ah, I see it now.

Ella seems to be Velma, with an orange cropped shirt, a red skirt that's way too short—not that I mind—orange socks that go to her knees, and fake glasses on her face. My sister has a red wig on, a purple dress, and pink tights or whatever.

"Cute," I say as someone knocks on their door.

I hear Ella mutter something under her breath as she goes to answer it.

"Oh, wow," is all she says as I hear Paige's voice fill the room.

"You look so cute! Where's Alissa?"

"In here, girl!" my sister yells at her.

When they come into view, I almost laugh. Oliver is wearing a bowler hat, and I wonder what Paige had to do to convince him to wear it. She's wearing a top hat and some sort of knit coat. I know exactly who they are without asking.

"Sherlock and Watson?"

"What gave us away?" Oliver deadpans, and I laugh. "Paige, I told you the accent was stupid."

"You have to practice! Look how good I am!"

I shrug my shoulders. She's not that bad, but Oliver's could use some work.

"I'm not doing it, especially in front of Leo and Alissa." Oliver sits next to me.

"Yeah, probably for the best, dude." I slap him on the shoulder and he smirks back at me. Though, I'm not sure if I can even call that a smirk.

"Where are Hads and Grant?" Alissa asks them.

"They should be right behind me. Oliver is driving their car with the boys and I've got us girls!"

"P, can you at least drive above the speed limit?" Ella asks her, taking a shot. "God, I've missed tequila."

"I will drive how I best see fit." She pinches Ella's cheeks as I hear the door open.

"We're here! Let the actual party begin!" Grant says from the entrance.

"Babe, don't say that."

"What? I was joking. Ella's already here, you know." Grant comes into view dressed like Jay Gatsby and when I see Hads walk in with a flapper dress on, it's all but confirmed they're the characters from *The Great Gatsby*.

"Oh, that's fitting." Oliver says.

"This was totally worth the wait!" Paige says as she grabs her phone and starts snapping pictures of the two of them, well, everyone else too.

"Sorry, why is it fitting?" I ask the room.

"Well, old sport, this book is the reason Hads and I are together." Grant tells me, holding his hand out.

"Is it now?" I ask as I shake his hand.

"Why yes, Leo, it is." Hadleigh tells me. "You see, this guy over here had no idea what the book was about and I had to tutor him."

"Don't forget the metaphors." He tells her.

"And the fact that you didn't know the main character's last name." Ella laughs as she takes another shot.

"Shit, I forgot you guys knew about that," Grant leans on his walking stick. "Well, who cares. Now, I'm an honorary book club member, so I feel good."

"Ella, are you really making us do shots before we go out? You know how much I hate tequila..." Hads trails off as she looks at them all laid out on the counter.

For some reason, I feel like I'm part of something with all these people here. I know Ella probably hates it, but me living in her flat has made me a lot closer with her friends. I know Grant and Oliver like me; at least, I think Oliver does. He hasn't said otherwise, but sometimes, I think he's giving me a weird face.

I'm starting to understand that's just his face unless he's looking at Paige.

It's odd—becoming close to a group of people I know won't speak to me after I move out. Or maybe they will. I don't know how to feel. I don't have *many* friends over here, or even at home, I guess. I know many people, but I wouldn't consider all of them friends. Only a few people really know me to my core, and that's just my sister and parents.

"Okay, everyone but Paige and Oliver, take one shot and let's go," Alissa says and I hear a few moans and groans as I grab two shots and down them immediately.

I will not go home alone tonight, I say to myself. And maybe that'll be true, because I need all the distractions I can get right now.

Especially from the girl dressed in orange who hates my fucking guts.

Oh, how I've missed leaving the house to go to some sweaty pub with shitty lighting and terrible dancing.

At least there's alcohol—and the guys, too. I haven't known Grant and Oliver for long, but I find myself enjoying their company. I much prefer them over Ella—who's currently in the middle of the dance floor with my sister and the other two.

"So, Leo, how is everything going at work with Ella?" Grant practically screams at me.

"It's fine, I guess. Why? What has she told you?"

"Nothing, and it's driving Grant crazy," Oliver tells me, sipping his water.

"No! It's driving *everyone* crazy. Not only do you two live together, but you also work together." Grant looks at me. "There's been nothing going on with you guys?"

I could tell them we had sex the other night, but I don't think that's something I want to bring up. Plus, I'd be a hypocrite if I told them. We swore not to tell anyone it happened, and that was fine with me. If other people knew about it, they would think there's something going on between us.

It was just sex. That's all it ever is with me. Every girl I take to bed wants one thing and one thing only. It was fine at first, but now, it feels...unfulfilling, and I don't know what to do to counter that feeling.

I don't see myself in a relationship, but I somehow want something more than a fling.

That's why I'm in no mood to pick up someone tonight. I thought I would be when I got here, but it's the furthest thing on my mind now.

Due to her proximity, Ella has been flashing through my mind, and not just because we had sex. No. Her in that skimpy fucking outfit is all I see—except in my mind, those orange socks are wrapped around my head as I get her off.

Jesus. I need to calm down.

"Leo, do you want another?" Grant asks me, and I nod.

"And a shot or two." I hand him my card. "Or a few more." I need to stop thinking about Ella fucking Williams immediately.

When it's Oliver and I at the table, it gets a bit awkward, but I'm surprised when he starts a conversation. "I'm sorry if all the Ella talk makes you uncomfortable. I know you two hate each other."

"It's fine, mate."

"Why do you hate one another? I've never gotten a full story."

I lift my brow at him. "Too afraid to ask?"

"Yup," he tells me as he takes another sip, his eyes drifting to the girls behind me. I can tell when he notices Paige, because his eyes soften the tiniest bit.

Disgusting.

"She judged me before she knew me," I tell him.

"Really?" He looks surprised. "That's not like her. Usually, she judges you after she knows you."

I laugh at that, because I've seen it happen in real time. Ella had one conversation with this new coordinator at work and put him on her shit-list immediately. According to Adam, he made some sort of sexist comment.

That got him on *my* shit-list too.

"Yeah. Day one of our internship, she hated me as soon as I walked in the door. I have no explanation about it either." And I don't want one. If she made her decision in a split-second about who I was, then I don't care to change her fucking mind.

"Huh," is all Oliver says.

Grant returns as he says that, and as soon as he puts the drinks on our small table, Ella and my sister slide in, take one of the shots from him, and head back to the dance floor.

Typical fucking Ella.

"I can go get some more," Grant offers as he looks at my face—clearly being able to sense my annoyance.

I take one, loving the burn that coats my throat before I turn and look at where Ella's dancing. "It's fine, Grant."

"So, did Oliver tell you about the time he was arrested?"

I spin around. "What?"

"I'm going to the bathroom," Oliver says as he downs his water. "Make sure no creepy guys touch Paige. You're dead if someone does, Grant."

"On it! Although, you should really stop saying things like that be-cause of your record— And he's walking away." He turns to me. "It's a great story."

The song changes to *The Walls* by Chase Atlantic as Grant starts telling me the story of how Paige and Oliver ended up in the middle of an active murder investigation during their senior year.

But I'm not paying attention to him—a really fit guy is dancing with Ella, and as if she can sense me staring, she turns her head ever so slightly so my eyes now lock with hers.

It just got a thousand degrees hotter here. She may be dancing with some prick, their bodies pressed together, but her eyes are on *me*.

And that's all that fucking matters.

Is she doing this to get my attention? There's no fucking way. She's trying to mess with my fucking head or something, and I hate to say that it's working. If I had less self-control, I'd be on that dance floor, picking her up, spanking her in front of everybody, and taking her somewhere where I could fuck her out of my system one more time.

The guitar solo starts to play, and suddenly, all I can think about is Ella underneath me. She looked fucking fantastic with my cock in her mouth, and I wouldn't say no to it happening again.

No. I need to get it together.

But our eye contact isn't helping, and I won't look away first. God knows Ella would hold that over my head too.

I take another shot as Grant finishes his story and Oliver gets back to the table.

"Excuse me, gentlemen." I don't bother waiting to hear what they say as I head toward Ella. She split off from the other girls, so it's her and this prick in the corner of the floor.

"Leave," I say as I reach them.

"Leo—" Ella's voice is laced with annoyance.

"Now," is all I say as I stare at the guy. He looks between the two of us, shakes his head, and walks away.

"That was rude. I was getting somewhere with him." She looks up at me as if she didn't want me to come over here. Her eyes were practically fucking me, and I know she wants me to dance with her, even if she would never outright ask.

There's always a game to be played with her, and I somehow always fall for her fucking tricks that I know aren't tricks.

"You owe me a dance for that."

"Do I?" I question. "Do I also owe you for the sex you won't be having tonight?" She shrugs her shoulders. "Too bad all you're getting from me tonight is a dance, Williams."

That earns me an eye roll. "Whatever. I guess if you're here, you'll do."

Then, the girl turns around and starts to dance against my front. Jesus Christ, I've never seen someone move as sexy as she does. Normally, I hate dancing in situations like this. Only Ella fucking Williams could get me out here and actually force me to do this.

"You took my tequila shot earlier." I lean down to her ear so she can hear me.

She leans her head back into me. "Did I?"

She's acting all coy, but suddenly, I'm having a flashback to when I first met her back in college. We were in a similar situation. I had bought a drink for a hot girl, and the bartender gave it to the wrong person—Ella. She stared at me while she downed it.

I went over to her, we talked, she pissed me off, and I went home alone.

Nothing has really changed after all these years.

"You have a nasty habit of taking drinks I pay for."

She spins around to face me, puts her hands on my shoulders, and I feel her lips near my ear. "Punish me then."

I shake my head forward, and my forehead somehow ends up against hers. "You'd like that, wouldn't you?"

She says nothing, but her pupils are *huge*, her eyes practically filled with lust.

"I bet you want me to shove your panties to the side right here on this dance floor. Is that right?"

Her hands go limp against my body as we keep dancing against one another. There's not a single inch between us, and I can barely see anyone else on this packed floor besides Ella.

This girl is driving me mad, and I don't hate it.

"Leo," is all she says before Paige cuts in.

"I'm sorry to interrupt." Her face is all red. "But we're heading out soon. Hads and Alissa are halfway to trashed."

"Hads?" Ella asks her, and Paige nods. "Where is she now?"

"With Grant outside. She needed some fresh air."

Ella grabs Paige's hand. "Take me to her."

"Okay. Leo, you can follow us. Oliver is by the door with all our stuff from the table."

I nod, knowing she won't be able to hear me over the music that somehow got louder.

The three of us make our way to the exit, and when we get outside, I breathe in the fresh air, and it puts my head back on straight.

Oliver hands me my cigarettes I left at the table, along with my hat.

"You smoke?" Oliver asks me. "Or is it just with the outfit?"

"Both, but I only smoke when I'm really stressed out, and it's always just one," I tell him. I don't know why I felt the need to explain, but I couldn't stop it coming from my mouth.

"Hads, are you okay?" Ella says as she heads to Paige's car. "Here's some water. Grant, give her a glass when you get home and put some aspirin on her side table for the morning. It's what I'll be doing for Alissa."

"Where is my sister?" I ask, a bit worried about her. She usually knows how to handle her alcohol.

"Right here!" she says as she pops her head out from the back seat. "Paigey, drive slow. You know I get travel sickness."

"I know, Liss," Paige laughs. "There's water in the back for you."

"You good?" I say as I ruffle her hair. "God, I should send our parents a picture."

"Oh my God, you should! Better yet, send them a video of me doing the national anthem. Ready?" she asks me, and Ella tucks her head back into the car.

"Maybe another time, Liss."

"Okay, you're right," she says as she slumps against the seat.

"Is everyone ready to go?" Oliver asks, and I hear a murmur of different answers.

"Old sport, your chariot awaits," Grant says as he ushers me over to Oliver's car.

I turn around to where Ella stands, about to get into the front seat of Paige's car. "Am I an old sport?"

She only laughs and nods.

I turn to Grant. "You know, I may be older than you, but I'm not old."

Oliver cracks a smile when I say that. "Oh, Leo, you have so much to learn."

22

Got Myself Off

I WOKE UP TO my pussy throbbing after I had a sex dream about Leo Zimmerman. I got myself off, took a shower, and started my day.

Worst start to the day ever.

23

The Rift Between Us

November 3rd

"Knock, knock," I say as I open the door to my childhood home.

"Sweetie, is that you?" my dad asks as he rounds the corner. I barely have time to answer before he wraps his arms around me and squeezes. "Missed you, bug."

Hearing that nickname always makes me emotional. My dad used to call me and my sister his lovebugs when we were little. I hated it when I was younger, but now, I think it's beautiful that someone can love you so much, they want to give you your own special name.

"I missed you guys too." I look around, seeing no sign of my sister. "Where's Lizzie?"

"In her room. Her door is closed, so she probably didn't hear you come in."

Or she's avoiding me. She knew I was coming over today, and normally, she hangs out in the living room so she can meet me right at the door, but she's not down here.

She's most likely still upset about our conversation. I even answered the messages she sent me a week ago, and she only read them and didn't respond.

Lizzie and I have always been close, and I'd be a fucking liar if I said that this rift between us isn't stabbing me in the chest.

"Do you want help making dinner? I brought shit to make a salad, but I can multitask."

My dad presses a kiss to my head. "You know I love sharing a kitchen with you, Ells."

"Great. I'll turn some music on and we can get started. What's on the menu tonight?" I never know what my dad has in stock, so as I search the fridge and pantry, I find a few options. "What about burgers and some pasta salad?"

"That sounds good. I'll boil some water and get started on the sauce."

"Wonderful." I smile as my dad and I start shuffling around one another as we cook. I think he's the only person who doesn't piss me off while in the kitchen with me. We've been doing this since I was a teenager—cooking alongside one another—and it's like we have our own unspoken dance when we're in here. I love it.

After a few minutes of working quietly together, he speaks up. "Lizzie told me your mother is back."

I should have known this was going to come up. "I heard."

"I know how she feels, but how do you feel, El?"

"Jury's still out." I was fully prepared to say no, but what Paige and I talked about in the bathroom changed my view. I don't know if I could do something in-person with her yet, but maybe a phone call or something.

When I say that in my head, it reminds me of all the times she could have called and didn't. I'm not going to blame myself for not reaching out, because I physically couldn't—she didn't leave her phone number when she walked out.

The phone works both ways. I'm sure if she wanted to, she could have found it somewhere. She sure as hell was able to remember our address after all these years, so she probably could remember a fucking phone number.

"You don't have to make a decision right now, Ella."

But I do—to an extent. My sister is pissed it wasn't as easy for me to say yes to her offer of seeing our mother again. I don't know how much longer I can handle the silent treatment.

"I don't know, Dad," I say as I flip a burger.

"I get it, bug. You were older than Lizzie. You understood what was happening at that age more than most."

I've heard that all my life. How mature I was for my age. How I always take care of others before myself. It was practically on every report card I got in school. And in every friend group, I'm the mom friend.

I don't mind being that for everyone else, but sometimes, I want to be able to need someone without the guilt pouring into my lungs. I don't know how to *need* other people. I've always relied on myself first and foremost in any situation. I'm independent as fuck, and even just the thought of settling down and being with someone for the rest of my life terrifies the fuck out of me.

But it sounds nice—loving someone forever, creating new memories and being able to reminisce on them decades in the future. All of my friends have found that kind of love, all except Amelia and me.

But Ames isn't around anymore, so it's only me who's alone.

Well, not alone, just not in love. As long as the girls and Grant exist, I won't be alone. But it's different now—the group dynamic. It has changed and shifted in so many ways over the years.

"Ella?"

I shake out of my haze. "Sorry, what?"

"Can you go get your sister? Everything's almost ready."

I nod before I turn the burner off and head down the hall. I hear music playing softly as I knock.

"Come in," she says. When she notices it's me, her face drops. *Wonderful.*

"Dinner is almost ready."

"Okay. I'll be down in a second."

I start to leave, but I stop myself. "Look, I don't want dinner to be uncomfortable." I lean against her door frame, needing support to keep me upright. "With Mom coming back, I've been worried about the three of us."

"Sure, Ella."

"I'm serious, Lizzie."

"Why are you always so worried about everything? We're humans too. We can make our own decisions."

I know that, but it doesn't stop the instinct to worry at the slightest change. Our mother coming back feels like we're the ocean floor and she's the anchor slamming down on us. "I know, sis, but I can't just turn it off. It's how I'm wired. It's how I've been since she left the first time. I can't help but try and protect you from things I think might hurt you."

Her eyes soften, and I think she's starting to understand my point of view, even if only a little. "But why can't you be a little more open to it? For me?"

"I'm worried if she comes back and makes empty promises, it'll leave us worse off than when we were younger. You didn't see Dad back then, Lizzie. He was working himself to the bone trying to support us. He's in a good place now, and so are we. I don't want her coming in and bursting the bubble we created."

She takes a few seconds to think about what I said. "I understand, Ella. But I want to at least give her a chance. She's been calling more and more, and I think she means what she's saying."

I still don't believe that, but I don't think there's any way I can change her mind without making her get madder at me. "One phone call."

Her eyes light up. "Really?"

"Yes, but you have to be there with me," I tell her. I have a sinking feeling I'm going to regret this in a few weeks.

"Deal," she says as she gives me a hug. "Thank you."

"Anything for you, sis."

24

A Bloody Miracle

THIS PROPOSAL IS GOING to drive me to insanity.

But I want to get it. I want it more than I've ever wanted any contract here, but I've been burning the candle at both ends to make this the best pitch ever.

I had a call with the design team the other day, and they sent me the mockups for the campaign. I'm so glad they turned out exactly how I imagined. I really think the publishing company is going to like mine. Not only do I have an advantage over Leo, since I work with authors all the time, but I have a little more experience. I'm not saying he's bad at his job—he does good work—but I'm way more passionate about this contract than he is. I'm an avid reader, and the only thing Leo reads is the laundry label on his fancy fucking sheets.

Since I approved my mockups today, I'm ahead of the schedule I set for myself. Leo and I don't have long before we have to turn our proposals in, and being ahead of the game bodes well for me.

Leaving early today might throw a hitch in my plans, but I'm not going to ditch Alissa on the one night a week we spend together. I've been working late a lot, and if I keep this up, I'm going to burn myself out.

Tuesday and Wednesday nights are my designated early days, but every other day of the week is fair game.

My phone rings, and I pick it up, already knowing who's on the other side.

"Scott, how are you doing on this fine Tuesday?" I ask him.

"I'm doing wonderful, Ella. You sound ecstatic for this call," he jokes. Financial planning is boring as hell to me, but you have to do it. Marketing costs a lot of money, and I have to figure out where to allocate specific funds for the campaign.

A lot of publishing companies run ads on different sites—mostly retailers that stock books. Social media ads are also a huge part of my campaign. With the explosion of new readers on all these different sites, independently published authors have had to step up on marketing. The same goes for publishing houses.

"I'm always excited to talk numbers with you." I truly mean that. Scott is one of my favorite people to work with. He's a cut and dry kind of guy, and he makes this part of my job easy.

"I saw your projected estimates, and honestly, I think this is doable, especially with the proposed budget they gave you. You'd end up being under by a little bit, and most places enjoy saving money in any way they can."

"Plus, it would work well, since it would be evenly split through a few different places." And then, judging off how those do, whichever site or retailer has the best click and purchase rate, we could always spend more there over an app that's not doing so well.

Some sites don't do well with certain books of certain genres. It's all a guessing game. So, if one site doesn't perform as well, we can take some money we would use there and spend it where clicks are higher and more effective. It's foolproof.

"Do you think it's okay then? Did you have enough time to look? Because we can always chat tomorrow if—"

"Ella, stop. I ran your projections three different times, and they all came up the same. It's perfect. I'd approve this immediately."

"I knew I liked you," I tell him, a smile on my face.

"Flattery will get you everywhere, Ella. You know I like working with you. You're more organized than anyone else I know."

"Well, I have to be."

"I know," Scott sighs on the other side of the line. "Is that all? Or did you need anything else?"

"Nothing right now, Scott. Thank you for all your help." I look at the time and notice it's almost four. "I'll talk to you soon."

I hang up the phone with him and start to gather all my shit, but movement across the hallway catches my eye.

Why is Imogen in Leo's office? My alarm bells are ringing, but when she closes the door and sits across from Leo, it doesn't seem like work talk, but maybe it is?

I don't care. It doesn't concern me.

I *really* hope I don't get caught in traffic when I leave, but we'll see. I stop by Rae's office before I leave.

"I'm headed out for the day," I tell her.

"How's the proposal going? I feel like we've barely talked lately. The two of us have been so busy."

I decide I can spare five minutes for her as I sit down in her very colorful office. "What's been up with you?"

"Well, I heard Brad and John talking about Leo in the kitchen. Brody was there too. The three of them are so far up Leo's ass. I think they're going to recruit him to golf together."

Oh, fuck. Of course Leo would get along with those fuckers. But I can't imagine him playing golf. That seems more up Grant's alley than his. "Is that right?"

"Yeah. They *love* Leo, and I know you don't, so maybe be careful about what you say around him at home. It could come back to bite you."

"Well, that won't be a problem. All Leo and I do is bicker at home, but he'll be out of my hair soon enough."

Rae smiles at me. "Good. Now, get home and enjoy your night. I'll see you tomorrow."

"I'll bring you a coffee tomorrow." I say as I stand. "I think the both of us could use a nice drink to start our morning, don't you?"

"And this is why I love you."

"I'll see you tomorrow, babe."

And as I leave the office and head to my car, I notice I'm smiling for real the first time all day. Maybe life is looking up after all the shit thrown my way.

I can only hope.

"I AM SO READY for tonight," I say as I get home. Alissa's already there, and when she meets me in our entryway with a glass of wine, I take a breath. "Have I told you lately how much I love you?"

"Yes, but it never hurts to hear it again."

"I love you," I say as I hang my coat up and take a big sip.

One of my favorite things Alissa and I do once a week is Tuesday nights. Wednesday nights are for book club, but Tuesdays are for Alissa and me to unwind. We have dinner together, and usually, the night ends with rewatching reality television shows we've seen a million times.

We've been doing this tradition for the entire time we've lived together. The both of us leave work early every single Tuesday, unless we have a deadline, and whoever gets home first decides what we're eating.

"What's on the plate for tonight?"

"Sushi I grabbed on the way home."

I could cry where I'm standing. Sushi, wine, and *Vanderpump Rules* is my ideal way of spending my night. It's like Alissa read my fucking mind.

I watch her put our food on plates, the spread making my mouth water as I queue up the episode we left off on. We've started our rewatch and finally reached the part where one of our favorite cast members has come back to the restaurant the cast works in.

"It just wasn't the same without her," Alissa says.

"Ugh, I couldn't agree more. Hands down, the most quotable cast member in the history of the show. Oh turn it up," I say, hitting Liss' side, "This line is perfection."

Alissa scrambles for the remote, turning it up, and we say the lines in perfect unison with our fave: "I'm not sure what I've done to you, but I'll take a Pinot Grigio."

We laugh into our wine glasses and continue catching up over dinner and our show. About halfway into our third episode, the front door opens, and in walks the third member of this household.

He had to stay late tonight because he was working on his pitch for the publishing house contract, and when I walked by his office when I left, he was talking to Imogen about something. He looked...different. I couldn't really tell what the nature of the conversation was, but it's not my business anyway.

"Hey, you two."

"Hi, Leo," Alissa says. I don't bother saying anything as I look over at him.

He gives the two of us a weird look. "What the hell is on your face?"

"A face mask," I tell him as I pause the show.

"Of seaweed?"

I can only laugh when he says that and immediately cover my mouth; there's no way I voluntarily laughed at something Leo said.

"Actually, yes. Your skin would look great if you tried it, Leo. I swear, it makes for a smoother face. Cleans your pores too," Alissa tells her brother as she gets up for a refill of wine.

He only tilts his head at us as he heads to his room.

"Liss, can you grab me another California roll?"

"Ditto," Leo says as he comes back out in checkered pajama pants and no shirt. *What is he doing out here?*

"It's girls night, Leo."

He plops next to me on the couch. "Consider me one of the girls then. Where is this face mask that makes my pores clear?"

"Ella's bathroom," Alissa tells him.

"Cool," he says as he goes over to our now shared space. He's in there for all of a minute before he comes back out. "Can I put this over my beard?"

"Yes," I tell him.

He looks at me with a pinched expression. "Alissa?"

"She's right, Leo."

I raise my eyebrows at him. "Just checking."

Yeah, I bet. "I don't fuck around when it comes to skin care, Leo. You should know that by the dozens of products on my side of the counter."

Alissa comes back into the living room with a small plate, a few different things on it, and I grab a California roll before Leo steals it from me.

"Can we start the show now?" I ask.

"Go ahead," Leo says as he comes back to the couch, his face also green. "How long do I have to leave this on?"

"Thirty minutes," I say as the episode keeps playing.

Not even five minutes later, Leo starts asking us questions.

"Wait, so did he cheat on her or not? And what on Earth is 'motorboating a dick'?" Leo asks. Alissa is giggling, probably shocked this man is paying this much attention. I'll admit, I am too.

"Leo, it's exactly what it sounds like," I respond.

"And just watch the show. It all comes out eventually." Alissa adds.

"I don't understand why he thought buying her a puppy would get him out of this mess if he's legitimately going around kissing other women. He must be mad," Leo says.

As Alissa clears our dishes before I can, I look to Leo.

"You know, for someone who claims to hate reality shows, you sure seemed invested."

He shakes his head. "I wasn't."

"Oh, really? Denying it?"

He nods.

"Then how come you looked shocked and distraught when another cheating rumor came out? I could tell you're into it. I think there's more to you than meets the eye."

His voice drops when he responds. "You couldn't be more right about that, Ella."

I have a feeling there's some sort of double meaning to that, but I disregard it for now as he gets up and heads to his room. He doesn't look back at me before he closes the door.

"Wow, I'm impressed," Alissa says to me when I drop my wine glass in the sink and start to clean it.

"Why?"

"You two didn't argue all night. At least, not how you usually do." She throws her hands in the air. "It's a bloody miracle."

As she heads to her room, I can't help but notice she was right. We didn't fight at all tonight. Actually, I had fun just being in his presence. He didn't push my buttons or try to get under my skin. The two of us simply existed around one another, and if I'm not careful, I'll get used to it.

I can't afford to get used to anything, because Leo will sweep the rug out from underneath me soon—just like he always does.

25

A Sex Pact

Wednesday, November 6th

I woke up stressed.

Correction, I woke up at four this morning sweating and thinking my heart was going to explode after some sort of dream. The worst part being, I don't remember the dream at all. All I know is I woke up, thought I was going to die, and couldn't get back to sleep.

Now, I'm at the gym, trying to work out my anxiety.

I fucking hate everything.

Fuck this. Fuck all the guilt I feel, fuck how helpless I am over here. I hate it, and nothing I do will make it go away. It lingers in my body, always sitting and waiting to attack. It hides and bides its time before I'm at a low point, and it makes me go even lower.

What if my dad dies while I'm over here? What if it's sudden like last time, and I never get to say goodbye to him? What if he dies while both of his kids are an ocean away?

I don't think I'd be able to live with that. It doesn't feel possible. If I had to go back to England knowing my dad was no longer a living entity in the country, I don't know if I could do it.

I take the speed of the treadmill up a few beats and start sprinting, hoping the intensity of my workout will drown out the thoughts flooding my head. It's not going to work. I know it's not going to work, but I do it anyway.

After the most intense two-hour workout of my life, I get home, and I'm still on edge. Thankfully, I have a half-day today. I talked to Imogen about it yesterday. My dad has a consultation today with a new heart surgeon who's going to show him an alternative way to do the surgery he needs.

My mum thought Alissa and I being on the phone for the appointment would help convince him this route is what's best. I know we all don't want to wait for him to have another heart attack or stroke, but he's stubborn.

I can't imagine having my body go through something as difficult as heart surgery, but I wish he knew we don't want to lose him way too soon. I'm nervous he's going to hold off like he did last time. But this is a new surgeon, and maybe he can get my father to bite the bullet if we can't.

As I slump against my door and grab my towel, I open the door, about to head to shower, when Ella opens hers.

Her bathrobe is in her hand, and she pins me with the same glare she does every morning when I beat her in here. I can't find it in myself to care.

"Do you want to arm wrestle or something?" she asks me, dead serious.

"Just shower, Ella. I can wait."

She pinches her brows at me. "Is this a trick? Did you do something to my shampoo?"

I shake my head, not having much fight left in me. She doesn't say a word as she walks into the bathroom, the same skeptical look on her face that's always there when we don't fight.

Right before she shuts the door fully, her eyes stare into mine, so many questions in her gaze. She settles on an easy one. "Are you okay?"

I don't bother answering her before I head back into my room, shut my door, and sigh.

Today is going to suck. I can already feel it in the air. There's a heavy weight around me, and as the day progresses, it's only going to get worse.

As my sister and I sit down to order our lunch, a heaviness settles across my chest. I don't know if Alissa and I are going to be able to help.

"Are you as worried about this as I am?" I ask her.

"Yes. Our father is the most stubborn man I've ever met." She looks over at me. "That must be where you get it from."

"Hilarious, sis." But I'm not laughing.

"Leo, come on. Dad will be fine. We just have to ease him into having the surgery. He might be scared. We don't know what he's feeling."

She reaches over and grabs my hand. "It doesn't make sense, Liss." God, I need a fucking cigarette.

"What?"

"Why doesn't he want the surgery? Doesn't he know how scared we all were last time, thinking he wasn't going to make it?"

My sister only sighs. "I don't know, Leo. But we have to make sure he understands this surgery is a good thing."

I don't know if she and I can do that. If none of us can convince him to stay a little longer on Earth, then what can? What is it going to take to convince our father we want him to have a longer life than he will if he keeps pushing this off?

Our salads come, and I'm thankful we're in the corner of this place, because I don't know how this conversation is going to go. The two of us start to eat, and about twenty minutes into our meals, the phone rings.

"Are you guys there?"

"We're here," I tell her.

"Okay. We just got to the office. The doctor should be in soon. Say hi, William."

"I still don't understand why they need to be here for this," I hear him say. My dad isn't a soft guy. He's pretty rough around the edges, but he loves us. I think he's sick of being carted around to appointments when he wants to live his life and go back to work.

He works for a huge business in England. He's actually why I wanted to get my degree in marketing. My original plan was to work for his company in that department, but I quickly realized working for my father was not something I wanted to do.

And I didn't want to be stuck in England my entire life. It's a beautiful place, but I wanted to see more, discover more.

My parents are the greatest in the world, and not only have they let Alissa and I forge our own paths in the world, but they've been nothing but supportive. Even after my dad had his first heart attack, he still pushed me to come back to the States despite my worries about him.

Truth be told, he hates when people dote on him. He's stubborn, independent, and usually pretty level-headed. All this medical stuff has thrown him off his axis.

Well, not the stubbornness.

"Dad, how do you feel today?"

"Tired, but I'm fine."

That's all you'll get out of him. Before either of us can say anything, the doctor comes in and starts to talk about the options. This surgery he's proposing is less invasive, at least that's what it sounds like. I used to be terrible with all this medical jargon, but I can follow pretty decently after all this time.

Especially after all the research I've done on the nights I can't sleep. The guilt always seems to creep in late at night when I miss them. And that's when I spiral down the rabbit hole of research to try and see if I can find something to bring to the doctors—to see if I can find something to keep my dad alive.

"How does that sound, William?"

"It still sounds like a surgery, Lorraine."

"Well, it is," the doctor says. "But compared to most of the other options you've explored, it not only has a higher rate of survival, it has better longevity. Which means at this point, you would only have to do it once, and you would be set for the rest of your life."

"No," is all my father says.

I look at my sister, who seems calm. We both figured this would happen, but I know both of our stomachs just dropped. I don't know why I thought he wouldn't need our persuading to say yes to this. I guess I had a little too much hope.

I guess that's why hope is such a dangerous emotion. When you have it and it doesn't work out, it punches you in the gut.

"Dad, why not go home with all the information and think about it?" my sister offers, shrugging her shoulders.

"Darling, I don't want to think about it." I hear some shuffling across the line. "I've heard enough. Thank you, but no."

"Dad, come on."

"Son, don't. I've made my decision, and you need to accept I won't have another surgery. One was plenty."

"But it wasn't—"

He cuts me off. "We'll talk tomorrow." And then, the line goes dead.

"Well, that went about how I expected it to," Alissa says as she finishes her meal. "Just give Mum a few days to talk to him about it. If anyone can get him to come around, it's her."

Suddenly, my food feels like rubber, and I swear, I can feel my heart practically beating out of my chest. My father is going to die without this surgery, and yet he still refuses to do it. Nothing any of us do or say can make him reconsider, so the next time he has a heart attack, he's probably going to die.

It could happen any time, any minute, any fucking day.

"Fuck this," I say as I get up, throw some bills down, and walk out. My sister doesn't even bother to stop me as I leave her at the table.

I get in my car and speed to the office, pissed off and angry my dad could be so reckless with his life.

I need to *do* something. I need a cigarette or a woman in my bed to get out all the weird fucking emotions swirling around in my head. If only I wasn't so broken, maybe I could remember how to flirt or pick up a woman somewhere.

But then an idea forms in my mind, and before I'm smart enough to push it away, it grows legs and sticks inside my brain. It won't leave, and by the time I pull into work and head up, I know for sure I'm about to do this. I might get kicked in the balls for even proposing it, but even that would feel better than remembering my dad is about to die.

I head off the lift, greeting the receptionist like I always do, and as I pass through the office, I don't stop for anyone.

I've only got one person here on my mind.

And when I turn into her office and her eyes meet mine at the sudden interruption, I set my bag down, sit in her chair, and lean forward on her desk.

"Can I help you?"

"Actually, I think we can help one another." I smile at her.

She tilts her head at me. "How is that possible?"

I turn around and make sure I closed her door. "With a sex pact."

"I'm sorry, what?" I must have misheard him. There's no way he actually said the words I think he did out loud, in our office.

"A sex pact," he repeats.

"Are you trying to get fired? Your psychotic break is sounding a lot like an HR nightmare."

"As long as nobody finds out, and it's not like we're in a relationship. We wouldn't be. We would just be two people having sex for a certain amount of time."

I stare at him in disbelief. "You came to me with this proposition because?"

He leans forward, so much so that he reaches out and grabs a piece of my curly hair. "Because we had our slip up the other day."

"And?" I ask, my voice a whisper compared to what it was.

"And I know you needed it as much as I did. Well, I need a distraction from some shit that's going on, and since you're right across the hall, it would work perfectly."

Oh, fuck, he's being serious. "Leo, it wouldn't work. How would we even go about this?" I hate that I'm even entertaining his idea, but I have to admit, I'm intrigued. "We hate each other."

"All the more reason to do it. We have no strings attached, Ella. It would be easy to only do it a few times."

"I think I'd rather—"

He scoffs at me. "Don't fucking lie, Ella. You *loved* fucking me."

"Don't flatter yourself. It was fine. I barely even remember it." I roll my eyes at him. The fucking audacity on this man is astounding.

He shakes his head, his curly brown hair unstyled today, so it waves around as his head moves. I hate that I can't stop staring at it.

"You're a terrible liar, darling."

I get up out of my desk and start to pace. "I'm not a liar. You're the most infuriating man I've ever met."

"Keep going, Ella."

"And you chew way too fucking loudly. You were eating granola the other day, and it sounded like you were chewing on rocks."

He stands from the chair he was sitting in. "What else?"

"You wear way too much cologne. It always smells like you showered in it."

"And?"

"And you assume everyone is attracted to you because of how you look."

He steps closer to me, and suddenly, the list of things that pissed me off about Leo Zimmerman vanishes from my mind.

"Please keep going, Ella. You're turning me on."

"And I hate you."

He smiles softly at me. "I hate you too, darling." His mouth comes to my ear. "But that's why this would work so well."

I can't move. I can't breathe. All that's flashing through my mind is the night I saw him naked in my bedroom for the first time in years. God, he's fucking with my mind, and I can't stand it.

His breath on my ear makes my body shiver. "Think about it tonight while you're alone in your room, trying to get yourself off, Ella." He steps back from me, grabs his bag, and opens the door. "Let me know by tomorrow."

"What?" The door slams behind him. "Tomorrow?"

I have no idea what to do, and there's only a few people who can help me figure it out.

I'm going to have to tell them tonight at book club. The only problem is, I'm going to have to tell them *everything*, every part of our history, so they understand why I can't fucking figure out what to tell him.

Paige and Grant are going to freak the fuck out, and I don't feel ready to air all our dirty laundry to my favorite people on the planet.

But I am considering it. I just need to know how much it's going to fuck my life up before I agree.

"So, that's it." When I turn around and face my friends, Paige's mouth is wide open, Hads is in disbelief, Grant is smiling wider than I've ever seen, and Oliver looks confused. "Please say something. I'm going fucking crazy."

"I knew it! I knew there was a history between you two! Ever since last Halloween, it was basically confirmed." Paige is ecstatic right now, and rightfully so. She has always been the biggest cheerleader for us—same with Grant. I'm sure those two are already thinking this is going to lead into some sort of relationship between us.

That's exactly what's *not* going to happen, because Leo and I barely tolerate each other. But a little hate sex and orgasms never hurt, did they?

"Oh, I'm so making sex pact shirts," Grant says, and I know he's one hundred percent serious about it.

"Grant, I swear—"

"Ella, I don't know if this is the best idea," Hads tells me. "He sounds like he's using you."

"That's the point, Hads. No strings attached, just sex. And no feelings, since we hate one another. It's almost the perfect plan."

"Are you complimenting him?" Paige asks, a smile on her face.

"No. I would never."

"Well, you did that one time..." Hads tells me. "When we came over for your birthday a few years ago."

Wow, it has been so long, I forgot about that. He did one nice thing for me at our internship, and that was it. It was a very confusing time back then—even more so than now. Not only had we had sex once, but he was still being the same old Leo he had always been. And then, he did something nice for me, and I thought maybe one day, we could be civil.

Then, he always did something that backfired. It was the weirdest case of whiplash ever.

"That was one time. He's been horrible about five hundred times since," I say as I slump onto the couch next to my girls. "Guys, what the hell do I do? He gave me until tomorrow, so I need to make a decision tonight."

"Well, you guys have had sex all of two times. I say go for it and get some dick," Grant says, and Paige and Hads start to laugh. "What?"

"You sound like us," Hads tells him.

"Look, I'm all for supporting Ella, and she gets orgasms out of this. That's a win-win."

Oliver speaks up for the first time. "Yes, but she would be getting those with her roommate's brother, the guy she hates more than anyone."

I was about to bring that up, but he beat me to it. "Thank you, Oliver. Great point."

"No, this is not how we're doing this." Hads goes into the spare bedroom and comes back with a giant whiteboard. Is that where Oliver put it?

"Is that my whiteboard?" Paige asks.

"Yes," Hads says. "My brother put it in there because you kept staying up late listening to true crime podcasts and making link charts."

"Oliver!"

"Love, we are past that chapter of our lives, okay? And you needed to sleep at night instead of listening to those fucking things," he tells her while running a hand down his face.

She only slumps further into the couch. "Fine."

"Can we please get back to the matter at hand? I need help, you guys," I beg.

"We're making a pros and cons list," Hads says as Grant grabs her a chair for the whiteboard to sit on. She draws a line down the middle and writes pros on one side and cons on the other. One is in red marker, one in green. "This is the best way to figure out what to do, Ells. I swear, we'll figure this out."

Leave it to Hads to make some sort of chart to help me figure this out. I truly don't deserve my friends.

"Okay, who has something for either side?" she asks as she turns to four of us.

"I feel like it being Leo is a con," Oliver tells her, and I nod in agreement.

"It's definitely not a pro," I say to the room.

"The sex is a pro, right?" Paige asks, and I nod.

"Unfortunately," I say. I'm not going to ever admit out loud that Leo Zimmerman is the best sex I've ever had, but he is. It's why I'm even considering this. He not only knows what drives me crazy, but since we hate each other, the sex is fucking phenomenal.

"Orgasms are always a pro," Grant says, and I see Oliver gag.

"If someone at work finds out, we could get fired," I tell them. "That's a con."

"But you're not in a relationship, so why does it matter?" Hads asks me.

"We still work together, and any one of the assholes at my job would love to hold that above my head." I wouldn't put it past any of them, especially Brody and Brad. They'll probably sell me out to Imogen and pat Leo on the back.

Oh, the infamous double standards.

"Would him being Alissa's brother be a pro or a con?" Paige asks the room.

"Con," Hads says, and I agree.

"Lying to Alissa is not a pro. I already feel bad about lying to her now."

"Yeah, and she almost caught you," Grant says. "That would've been hilarious."

I shake my head. "The word you're looking for is horrifying."

"Actually, I think Alissa would be okay with it," Oliver says. "She said you two needed to hook up at the Halloween party while you two were fighting."

"Yes, but she doesn't know we would be fucking. Therefore, I'd be lying to her."

"Well, she would probably take it better than Hads did when she found out about Paige and Oliver," Grant says, and Hads throws a marker at him. "What?"

"To be fair, I found out after Oliver had been arrested in front of me and I couldn't get ahold of my parents. I think I reacted well based on what the hell happened that day."

"Agreed," Paige says. "I was shocked you didn't smack me or something."

Hads writes down another con on the board. "Well, I can't say I didn't think about it."

"At least it's all good now," Grant says.

"Agreed. Let's never have anything like that happen again," I say. That was a tough day for all of us. Not only was Oliver arrested and Hads pissed, but Paige almost got herself killed that night. My friends are certifiably fucking insane.

"Okay, so how many of each do we have?" I ask, wondering if this will help make my decision for me.

"Three cons and one pro."

I throw my arms up in the air. "Well, there we go! I'm saying no tomorrow." I only hear moans and groans come from my friends. "What?"

"Is that really the right answer?" Grant asks me.

"According to the board, yes," I tell him.

Hads throws another marker at him. "Don't question the chart, babe."

"But why not sleep on it and then figure it out? Maybe a good night's sleep will help you firmly decide," Paige says. I know she's hoping I change my mind about this so Leo and I will somehow fall in love, which will never happen.

No matter how many times I dream about him, his stupid face, and dreamy eyes, it will *never* happen.

My heart is under a lock and key, and if I do end up saying yes to this ridiculous plan, Leo will never be granted access.

No matter how much I think about him every single fucking day. It's only because he's everywhere—work and home. And now, he's even around my friends, since Oliver and Grant have taken a liking to him.

My feelings for Leo—however minute they are—are only because he's fucking everywhere I turn. As soon as he moves out and I only have to deal with him at work, the sex dreams will stop, and the weird feelings I have when I see him every morning will too.

Leo Zimmerman and I will never be anything more than two people who work together.

26

Some Aches A Dildo Can't Fix

November 7th

NOTHING IN MY LIFE the past day has made any fucking sense.

Not only did the person I despise the most proposition me with a sex pact, but I'm actually considering it.

Tonight, we're stuck in the office doing overtime because of this huge presentation. It landed on Imogen's desk this morning, and the meeting is *tomorrow*. She left ten minutes ago, needing to get some rest, but the rest of us—Leo, Adam, Rae, Brody, and I—are here until we finish. If it takes all night, it takes all night.

And the only reason she saw it so late was because it got lost in the shuffle of other paperwork, all thanks to Brad. Needless to say, he got sent home for the rest of the week, and his employment is under review because of how much he pissed off the board and Imogen.

"Ella, can you figure out a color palette for their new brand? The rest of us can configure the slides and figure out an order," Brody tells me, and I nod, immediately opening their social media accounts and seeing what they have going for them already.

It's fine, I guess. It's definitely doing...something for them.

This contract is for a local grocery store chain expanding to a few more locations across Virginia. In order for them to do it, they need to ramp up their marketing, so they approached us. We just didn't find out about it until earlier today.

All through their social media accounts, there's a mix of fonts and colors, and nothing is cohesive at all. Most of the time, companies assume bright colors will pop on their ads and social media pages, but this looks like a color nightmare. For a chain like theirs, I think more muted colors would work best—like earth tones. I think some browns, greens, and beiges will look better. I'm also thinking of creating a custom serif font for them. Serif fonts usually look better online, and they're easy enough to manipulate so it's still readable.

"So, we have twenty slides that outline a rough draft of the campaign we would run for them," Rae tells us. "Ella, what color scheme are you thinking?"

"Muted earth tones. They're a grocery store, and if we make them their own serif font they can use for every post, it might draw more people in." I swipe on their feed. "Their accounts are all connected, so if we do a complete overhaul and start fresh, it might help to attract more people to their stores."

"Good." She smiles at me. "I'll head home and work on the slide designs and match it to the projected feed we want to create for them. I've seen way too much of this office today, and I need a change." Rae starts to pack her stuff up, gathering her laptop and everything spread across the table.

"Yeah, I hear you," Brody says, also packing his things up.

"I'll work on Imogen's pitch," Adam says, also grabbing his laptop. "I'll write it out at home so she's not reading from the presentation and send it over to you guys to proofread before I give it to her."

I look at my phone, noting the time—seven p.m.—before I decide if I want to leave with Rae and work from home tonight, or if I should keep chugging along here.

"I can read it for you, Adam. Just send it to me whenever you have a chance." I can't go home. If I go home, I'm going to fall asleep, and that's something I can't do, at least not until we have a solid foundation and this is done.

"You're not headed home?" Rae says as she notices I'm not moving to pack anything up.

"No. I'll focus better here. Plus, the conference room has a bigger screen for me to see if their new social media feed will look okay."

"Ah, well, whatever works best for you, Ella," Brody says, his tone condescending as fuck. Sometimes, I wish I could deck him in the face for the way he speaks to the women in this office, but I always refrain. "Leo, do you wanna come grab a drink with me and talk some stuff out?"

Leo—who has been unusually quiet tonight—only looks up at him from where he's typing. I actually don't know what he's working on.

"No, I think I'll stay here. I'm the new guy, right? I should stay and learn how a last-minute presentation goes."

I feel two pairs of eyes on me—Adam and Rae.

"Are you sure? I feel bad leaving you two here to do all this." Adam is looking at me, knowing how I feel about Leo.

"It'll be fine," I say to the room. "We'll get it done. Won't we, Zimmerman?"

He smirks at me from across the conference room table. "We will."

"Suit yourself," Brody says as he opens the conference room door. "See you guys tomorrow."

As soon as he leaves, I swear, the air in the room is much cleaner. I can suddenly breathe better.

"Ella?" Rae questions me.

"It's fine, Rae." I look at Adam. "Send me the pitch, and I'll proofread it as soon as I can, okay? You'll have it back by tonight." I still have so much shit to do, and being stuck here with Leo could end horribly—especially since I still have no idea what to do about his proposal.

"Got it. We'll leave you guys to it," Rae says as she leaves, pulling out her phone. Mine buzzes after she leaves.

> **Rae: If you end up murdering him tonight, call me. I'll be back in record time.**

> **Ella: It's fine, babe. We're civil, remember?**

> **Rae: Doubt it, but have fun. I'll see you in like ten hours.**

> **Ella: Don't remind me.**

I laugh to myself as I feel Leo's gaze on me.

"Do you need an instruction manual or something?"

"No. Believe it or not, I'm capable of doing my job correctly."

I look at him, eyes widened in shock. "It's a miracle."

I print some stock photos and go to grab them, wanting to see how they would fit together on their social media accounts, and when I come back, Leo's laptop connected to the screen is on some sort of food place.

"What's this?" I say as I drop the stack of photos I have in my hand.

"I figured if we're going to be here all night, we might as well order some food." He looks at me. "When was the last time you ate?"

I'm about to argue back at him, but I actually don't remember. It might have been this morning, and all I had was a banana and coffee. It has been all hands on deck all day since Brad fucked up, and I skipped lunch to work.

"Exactly. I'll order us some sushi from the place around the corner."

My stomach decides to rumble at the worst time. "Fine."

"Do you want your usual?"

"How do you know my order?" I ask him.

"You and my sister get sushi at least once a week. It's not hard to memorize it."

I roll my eyes. "Thanks."

"Wow, did I really just hear that?"

"Don't get used to it."

For the next hour, the two of us work in a quiet, simple rhythm. I'm organizing their feed for the days leading up to their new launch, and Leo is working on getting in contact with some vendors for the day they open. A launch party for their new stores would be the perfect way to draw people in, and including free shit like coupons and other goodies could also help.

The two of us work well together when we're not at each other's throats.

Leo grabs the food from the delivery guy downstairs and puts it in the fridge, since we're still working diligently. I can't stop when I'm in my zone. It only takes another hour and a half to bring their feed together and finish it.

Adam also sent me the pitch he drew up, and with minimal spelling and grammar errors, I sent it back to him in half an hour.

Tonight was a success. We just have to hope tomorrow goes smoothly for Imogen with all the work we've done today. I'm leaning over the conference room table, admiring my work, when I feel Leo's hand on my shoulder.

"Sit down and eat, Ella. You're going to pass out if you don't."

I turn to meet his gaze. "As if you care. Then you could take credit for all the shit I did tonight."

He rolls his eyes at me. "I'd never do that."

You have before. I stop myself from saying that, because I really don't have much energy left to fight with him. "Fine," I say as I grab the sushi from his hand. When I open it, my mouth immediately starts to water. I guess I didn't realize how hungry I was.

He sits next to me instead of across from me, and I hate how close he is. It was nice having an entire table between us, but now, we don't. And there's no way he forgot about the sex proposal he made. He did tell me I had one day to think about it, and that day is almost up.

"Alissa told me you talked to your parents the other day. How are they doing?" I ask, trying to break the weird tension in the room. I don't know if it's because we've been alone all night or if it's the pact that looms over us, but I need it to go the fuck away.

"My dad is still recovering, but he's the same stubborn bastard who raised me, so he's okay."

"That's good." I know Alissa has been struggling with everything going on, and I assume he is too. Their family is close—like most are. I'm not used to that. Sure, I'm close with my dad and my sister, but it's not the same. There's been a missing piece my entire life, and now she's back, and I have no idea what to do about it.

I can't think about this right now.

"How about you? How's your family?"

"They're fine."

"And it's just you, your dad, and your sister, right?"

I nod. "My younger sister has been giving me a run for my money lately, but I think it's just the burdens of being a teenager."

"Well, it happens to everyone, right?"

"I guess," I tell him, and as we keep eating, the tension skyrockets. I'm way too focused on his mouth, and I can't seem to pull my gaze away.

Nobody should look like that while eating sushi. If you told me Leo was modeling for this fucking delivery place, I'd believe you.

He sits in his chair, sleeves rolled up, arm veins bulging, his chopsticks in his hand. The guy works out excessively—every fucking morning—and he has the muscles to prove it.

Stop fucking staring, Ella.

I bet he's used to it by now. In college, girls used to look at him, and their panties would fall off. Everyone on campus wanted to either be him or fuck him. It was no goddamn secret.

"Have you given much thought to my indecent proposal?"

His question startles me out of my haze. "No, actually. I've been trying not to think about it." I stand to throw out the remains of my dinner, and when I turn around, he's walking toward me—*so fucking slowly*.

By the time he gets to me, he reaches around and throws his shit out too. But when he's done, he doesn't move out of my personal space.

"Don't lie to me, Ella."

Ella. For some reason, when he uses my actual name, I get weak in the knees. The way it rolls off his tongue with that damn accent should be considered criminal.

"I'm not," I whisper.

He looks down at me, his brow cocked at my obvious lie. "So if I bent you over this table right now, you would hate that?" He reaches for where my hair sits in a bun and releases the clip. That light touch drives me more insane than I care to admit.

His hand trails behind my neck and reaches my cheek, his eyes still attached to mine.

"Zimmerman, I swear—"

"Oh, the surname now? God, you want me so bad, Ella. How do you not see it?"

"Just because we had sex one time—"

"Twice. Or did you forget about our college slip-up?" He smirks as he grabs my hair in his fist and pulls it. "We do that a lot, don't we?"

"It's only happened twice, and it never will again."

He pulls my head in close to his, and suddenly, I have the urge to kiss him, and I don't know why.

"I can see you, Ella. I see you more clearly than you see yourself." His fingers trail across my neck, down my chest, toward my center. "You may not like me, but you like how I fuck you." He softly bites my neck. "You love when I make you scream, when I fuck you how I know you like it—hard, rough, and dirty."

"Leo..." His hand wraps around my throat, cutting off my sentence. *I'm fucking aching.*

"Let me give you what you need, Ella. This pact will help the both of us, and you know it. I haven't seen you take someone home since I moved in."

Prick. *But he does have a point...*

"Okay," I whisper through his hold.

He releases me and takes one step back, staring into my fucking soul as he looks across my face. It's like he's making sure he actually heard me say that before he shakes out of his haze. "Thank fucking God," is all I hear before he smashes his lips to mine and takes control. Good God, this man knows how to fucking kiss.

"I need you right now, Ella."

"Then take me," I tell him as I start to unbuckle his belt.

"Bend over like a good girl and let me," he says between my lips. His plea sounds like music to my fucking ears, and all I can think about is how wrong this is as he rips my shirt off my body, buttons flying everywhere. My bra comes off next, and Leo stares at my tits for a solid minute.

My mind may hate him, but my pussy has never been happier.

There are some aches a dildo can't fix.

I comply with his directions and bend over the conference table, the glass cold against my body. "You owe me a shirt."

"I'll buy you whatever you want, but let me focus on giving you what you need first, okay?"

I'm about to argue with him as he unwraps a condom, and thrusts right into me.

"Keep that quip to yourself, Ella. I've learned a few good ways to shut you up, and this is one of them," he says as he starts to move in and out of my pussy.

Christ, I don't know if I could ever get used to his size.

"God, you feel like a fucking dream, Ella. See how good it is when we both give in?" His voice comes out strangled.

"It's fine, Leo. Truly."

Then he grabs my ass and lifts me higher, his dick hitting an even deeper spot.

"Oh, fuck," I say before I can stop it. "Don't fucking stop."

"Stop fighting me, Ella, and enjoy yourself."

Then, he speeds up, the only sounds I hear our pants, moans, and his body slapping against my ass. The conference room table is shaking with each thrust, and I would worry about it breaking, but Leo's dick is holding me hostage.

It feels way too fucking good. I should be scared, but all I can focus on is how hard he's fucking me. He knows what I need every single time—hard and rough—but I need more right now.

"Leo!" I say as he goes even deeper. He's hitting spots nobody has hit in years—including myself. "More."

"I know, darling." He reaches for my hair and pulls, my neck exposed for his hand to take over and choke me like he did before. "Tell me how much you hate me."

I can barely speak, but I utter the words. "I fucking hate you."

"Again." He loosens his hold ever so slightly.

"I despise you, Leo. You drive me crazy."

"God, I love how you clench around me when you say that. Does it happen every time, or only while my dick is filling you?"

He squeezes my neck harder, and I can't respond.

"You might hate me, but your pussy drips for me, Ella." A moan overtakes his sentence, and I can feel myself teetering on the edge. He leans down to my ear, moving some strands of my hair out of the way. "I hate you too, Ella. I hate you so much, it's all I can think about sometimes."

"Glad the feeling is mutual, Leo."

"Come for me if you hate me so much," he whispers in my ear.

"Don't fucking stop," is all I tell him as I feel myself fly over the edge, his stupid voice driving me insane.

By the time I come down, he is too, and there's smile on my face from the orgasm he gave me before I notice the blinking red light. "We have to erase the fucking tape or we're fucked."

"Shit, I didn't even think about the security cameras." He starts to laugh. "Oops?"

God, we cannot do this. Neither of us is ever this reckless, and I hate that this spur of the moment sex has clouded my judgment. "That didn't count. We didn't even set rules for however this arrangement is going to work."

"Rules sound good," he agrees as he pulls his clothes back on. "Here."

His shirt is in one hand as I put my bra back on. "Well, it's the least you could do since you ripped mine."

"You liked it."

Yeah, I did. "For starters, this is never happening at work again."

"Agreed," he says as he sits next to me.

"And this is our little secret. I'm not losing my job over this."

"It's not against the rules, technically, but I get it."

"Good." The last thing I need is someone here finding out and me getting fired. Of course, Leo would probably be fine since he's a man, but neither of us wants to risk it. I look at him, his face twisted with a few different emotions I can't place. "Something to add?"

"Are you going to be fucking other men?" His voice is tight as he coughs. "Or women?"

Why the fuck would he care about that? "No. At least not while we're in this arrangement."

"Good," he says, a sigh of relief. "I won't be either, just so you know."

"Fine by me, Leo. And the pact is for what? Three times?"

"Sure. And whenever our three times are up is when it's done."

"Perfect." I smile at him. Sex with Leo. Three times. I can do that.

"Oh, and one more thing."

"What?"

He stares at me, looking ever so serious when he utters a sentence I never thought I'd hear. "Don't fall in love with me."

I burst out laughing. I can't help it. "Good joke," I say as I pass by him, patting his chest. "Lucky for you, I'm not looking for anything serious."

His lips thin into a line. "Yeah, no one ever is when it comes to me."

I'm about to ask him about the tone of voice he used, but he gets up and beats me to the door.

"I'll erase the tape. You get home and get some rest."

"Sounds good." I head for the elevator. "I want video evidence it's gone, Leo!"

He turns back around and looks at me. "You don't trust me?"

I shrug my shoulders. "I trust you with orgasms, and that's it," I say as I push the button.

I hear him laugh under his breath as he walks away from me, his middle finger up when I turn around in the elevator.

What the hell did I get myself into?

27

Nothing More Than Just A Fuck

THIS MORNING, I FINALLY got the call my apartment is going to be ready in two weeks.

Part of me is elated I can finally have my own space separate from my sister, but another part of me started to feel like this place wasn't so bad. I got comfortable, even though I knew I would be leaving at some point.

Well, that point has arrived, and I should be ecstatic, but I feel odd.

I *knew* I shouldn't have gotten used to living here. I think part of me is going to miss seeing my sister this much. It has been nice to be around her; it reminds me of home and when we were kids. I miss that—us when we were younger. Life felt so much more manageable when we were children.

Now, it feels like our family has slowly been falling apart for the past year. Not in the traditional sense, but since I've been over here and not constantly checking in, it feels like they have no idea of anything going on in my life. That used to be so different, but growing up has that effect on you, I guess.

Your parents' job is to raise you and send you out into the world, and hopefully, they do a good job so you feel prepared for all the shit life can throw your way. But nowhere was I taught what to do when the people you've looked up to your whole life suddenly have problems you can't fix. No matter how much one is prepared, nothing punches you in the gut like seeing your parents hurt or in harm's way.

And nothing can prepare me for what might happen in the future since my dad chose not to have the surgery.

"Leo?" My sister shakes me out of my thoughts. "Are you okay?" she asks me, sitting on the couch next to me. I was watching a film, but I lost track of what was going on when I got the call about my place.

"I'm alright," I lie.

She cocks her head at me. "Are you thinking about Dad?"

God, Alissa always knows how to read every one of my emotions. It must be an Irish twin thing.

"Yeah, I was," I say as I pause the film.

"I know you're worried, but there's not much we can do from over here."

"What if we—"

She smacks my arm. "I want to go back as much as you do, but they would kill us if we showed up out of the blue. Dad would think we came home just for him, and that would be worse. He hates when we worry about him."

"He has to know we can't *not* worry about him. He's our father, for fuck's sake."

"I know, Leo. But maybe Mum can get him to come around? She told me this morning she's going to try and convince him at his next physical therapy appointment."

That's good, I guess, but it still doesn't help the fear coursing through my veins. "Yeah, if anyone can do it, it's her." My mother is a force of nature. Not only is she inspiring through her work ethic, but she's the best person I know. I am who I am today because of her.

"So, what else is new? I feel like we've barely had time to chat these past few weeks," my sister says, getting more comfortable on the couch.

"Yeah, we've both been working a lot. It's a good thing we like our jobs, right?" I smirk at her, and she rolls her eyes at me.

"I bet you *love* seeing Ella every single day. I wish I was a fly on the wall at your office. I wonder how your coworkers deal with the bickering between you two all day."

"We don't bicker that much," I tell her.

She shakes her head at me. "I don't believe you. You guys have argued over the dumbest shit for years."

"Well, if she would actually get to know me before assuming things, maybe we could have been friends." It comes out before I can stop it.

"Is that why you hate her so much?"

"Yeah, it is." But I'm not sure how much I hate her anymore. The lines between us have become...blurred. Messy. Uneven. I don't even fucking know. All I know is that Ella Williams has fucked me up in more ways than one these past few months.

What started out as us two hating one another for years has quickly morphed into something else, something I can't wrap my mind around.

"That's funny," my sister says. "She's said similar things about you."

"Has she?"

"Yes, actually. She's told me a lot about you, and none of it matches what I know about you."

"I always knew you guys talked, but I never assumed any of it was about me."

She rolls her eyes at me. "Oh, please. When you two were at your internship, it's all I heard about."

"Really?"

"Yup. You two assholes clash heads so much *because* of how similar you are, and I know me saying that won't magically fix anything, but try to view her from a different perspective, Leo. I think it'll do wonders for you two and your relationship."

Our what? There's no fucking way she knows about Ella and my—

"If I can even call what you two have as such. Don't throw up on the couch imagining you and Ella that way."

"Trust me, Ella and I will never be anything but coworkers after I move out."

Fuck. This is the perfect time to mention the pact. I've never lied to my sister before—except about Ella. The only things I've kept from her involve her best friend and how I've fucked her a few times. I hate lying to Alissa about it, but I don't know how she would react. I doubt she'd care too much, but Ella is still her best friend.

It doesn't even matter, really. Ella and I will never talk about any of this again after I move out. It'll be like nothing ever happened.

So why does that piss you off so much?

It's just lust. That's all it'll ever be, since neither of us does feelings in situations like this. Ella doesn't see me as anything more than a guy she hates, nothing more than a fuck for her.

But why do I feel something more than anger and hatred when I look at her now? Is it just the aura of our sex that has that effect on me, or is it something else?

No. It's nothing else.

No matter how much I think about her across the hall from me at night. No matter how much I like pissing her off just to get her to talk to me.

No matter how much my heart flips when she rolls her eyes at me, when she opens her door in the mornings and her hair is all over the place and she looks more beautiful than I've ever seen her...

Woah. Where the hell did that come from? And how do I get rid of it?

"You two will be more than coworkers, that's one thing I know for sure," my sister says, a cheeky look on her face.

"What does that mean?"

"Something out there clearly wants your paths to cross. First, you two get an internship together, and years later, you work together. Something bigger than both of you is at play." Alissa pats my shoulder as she gets up. "If your egos weren't so big, I could see you both being good friends."

Friends? Yeah right.

Ella Williams is anything but my friend. As far as I know, she's another girl who got wrapped up in me, and by the end of all this, she'll wish she never did.

I'll just be another few nights for her, and she'll go back to hating me, because it's what we do.

"I'll make lunch for us, okay?"

"Sounds good."

And as I turn the film back on, I try and fail to banish all my thoughts about the girl across the hall.

28

Two Different Versions Of The Same Story

The fact that I can work from my bed in my pajamas is the best thing ever.

Today, I'm working from home because since Leo and I had sex in the office, I've been avoiding it. I talked to Imogen, and she was okay with it since I told her I was feeling a bit sick.

I'm not sick, just terrified.

Terrified of my own feelings brewing inside of my brain, heart, and vagina. Feelings that involve Leo Zimmerman. I thought I could have casual and meaningless sex with him, but for some reason, my heart has decided against that.

It's pissing me off.

Not only that, but I have to pick Lizzie up today because my dad is staying late at work. He called me yesterday and asked if I could take her to dance, and of course, I agreed. Not only am I always ready to help my family out, but since my sister and I have been split about our situation, I feel like I haven't seen her enough lately.

I thought our talk fixed it, but I'm not sure it did. I'm scared our mother is filling her head with empty promises and vacations that will never happen.

I shake the thought out of my head and get back to work. Today, I'm splitting my time at home on the work for a client at Loft Media and social media posts for an author's new release announcement. I wish I could do author services full time, but that's not in the cards for me at the moment.

About half an hour later, my phone rings—an unknown number. I answer it in case it's a client.

It's not.

"Ella," is all the person on the other line says.

I take a deep breath before I answer. "Mom."

"It's nice to hear your voice."

"It's nice to hear what you sound like. I seemed to have forgotten after all these years," I snap. Normally, I'd regret my outburst, but not to her. Not after all these years of being a ghost.

"I guess I deserved that," she sighs across the line.

"Is there something you need?" I'm not in the mood for small talk.

"I'll be picking up Lizzie today. I wanted to let you know so you don't waste your time coming out here. I know it's a bit of a drive."

I know she thinks she means well, but her passive aggressive tone pisses me off. "It's never a waste of time when I get to my sister, though that's something you've never understood."

"Ella, I understand your frustration with me, but your refusal to give me a chance is ridiculous. I've seen Lizzie multiple times, and she's giving me another chance. Why can't you?"

I move the phone from my face, pissed off she has the fucking audacity to say that to me—to one of the two daughters she left behind all those years ago. "Because I know what it's like to watch you leave."

"I made a mistake, Ella. I'm back to correct it. Why can't you let me prove myself to you? Why can't you give me another chance?"

I sit up, her tone making my body enter fight or flight mode. "I'm fresh out of those. The last one expired when you left and didn't bother to contact us until we no longer needed you. It's not fair to me, Lizzie, or Dad."

"Now, honey—"

"You can't call me that. You don't deserve to call me that. In case you forgot, *you're* the one who left us, and I was the daughter who had to pick up all the pieces. You're not my mother, not in the ways that matter. You're a stranger who happened to give birth to me."

"That's not fair."

"It is, though. I know you think I'm insane for holding this grudge against you, but you weren't fucking there when I was growing up. When Lizzie cried all through the night after she got her heart broken for the first time and wanted her mom, you weren't there. I was. When Dad lost one of his jobs, I stepped up so we could keep the house. Where were you? Where were you when I came out and realized I like girls too? Where were you when I had my first heartbreak? Or when I graduated from college? Where were you when I needed my mom? I have no idea, because you fucking left." I take a deep breath. "Have fun with Lizzie, but if you break her heart, I have no room in mine left for you."

I hang up on her because I can't keep listening to her spew lies and bullshit into my ear for another second.

When I was younger, I used to think about what would happen if my mother had come back. I used to think up fake conversations and arguments of things I would say to her. Sometimes, I'd yell at her. Other times, I would cry and explain how she hurt me.

Most of the time, it ended the same way. I was alone, staring into my mirror, my shower head, or my car.

At least I won every time.

I wish Alissa was home, because after that conversation, I need someone here. I need someone to tell me what I said wasn't too much, wasn't too mean. I need to know I'm enough as I am, even though I basically raised myself. I need to know I can be loved despite always feeling like I'm too overbearing.

But over the years, I brushed off those thoughts. Even if they stabbed into my body like a knife, I acted like I was fine. I felt like I had to—for my sister's sake.

I feel like there's a dead piece of me inside. I never feel like I'm good enough for anything or anyone. It's hard—feeling like that on the inside when on the outside, I appear so confident, so self-assured.

When I finally grew up, went to college, and left my dad and sister, all I felt was guilt. I was constantly checking in on them, as if our family was going to fall apart if I wasn't there. I felt like a horrible sister and daughter for leaving, even though I know it was what was best for me.

That never stopped the guilt, though.

And as I sit alone in my apartment, feeling so broken after one phone call with my mother, I pick my phone back up and call the one person I know understands.

She picks up on the second ring. "Hi, I know you're at work, but can you come over after your shift?"

"I'm on my way."

Half an hour later, I hear a few knocks on my door. When I open it, I'm surprised. "How did you get here so fast?"

"Well, it would've been faster, but I stopped for takeout." Paige's face brightens up my home as she sets the food on the table.

"But it's the middle of the afternoon, P. You didn't have to leave work early for me."

She takes both of my hands and leads me over to sit down. "Yes I did, Ells."

"Why?"

She simply looks at me and answers as if it's the most casual thing in the world. "Because you would do the same for me."

My eyes start to tear up. Never in my life did I think I deserved the level of friendship the girls give me. Never did I think anyone would stay around for enough time to be able to reach this amount of love we share.

I was always the friend that was doing too much, the one who was too loud, too sparkly. All throughout high school, I toned myself down to fit myself into a person other people could handle.

When I got to college, I promised myself I wouldn't do that. And if people didn't like me, then they weren't the ones for me.

But Paige and Hads love me for everything I am. They love me *because* I'm all those things, and not once have they tried to dim me. Not once have they made me feel like I was difficult to love.

Paige places a plate in front of me with all my favorite things on it—pan fried potstickers with chili oil, extra spicy Szechuan tofu, steamed vegetables, and white rice.

"We can eat in my room if you want. I need some comfort with my comfort food," I say as I grab my plate and head to my room. "Also, why did you get Chinese food when you hate it?"

Paige sits on my bed with her own plate. "It's your favorite, and I grabbed some tacos on the way too." That makes me cry. "Wait, Ella, no. I didn't mean to—"

"No, these are good tears."

"I figured by your tone of voice it's been a rough day. I thought this would cheer you up, and if you keep crying, I'm going to cry!" she sniffles. I look over at her, and she's already crying.

"I feel like a mess," I admit.

"You're not a mess, Ella. You're a human," Paige says as she bites into her taco. "And I'm another human here in case you need to talk, vent, scream, cry, or sing. I'm good with anything; just let me know what to do, and I'll do it."

I laugh through my tears. "Maybe all of the above."

"Just tell me which to start with and we're good." She smiles at me.

I bite into my food, and this is helping me feel better already. "Venting, I think."

"What happened?"

"I was supposed to pick up my sister from school and take her to dance practice. I do it whenever my dad needs me to, since she can't drive yet and he works overtime a lot." I pause to take a deep breath. "But my mom called me. She told me she was picking her up, and we got into an argument."

"Oh."

"Yeah. It was a conversation years in the making, and I don't know, it left me feeling unsettled. I feel like I'm the problem and shouldn't feel how I do. I want to give her a chance, but in my heart, I feel like I can't."

Paige puts down her plate. "Ella, your feelings are valid no matter what they are. Your mom hurt you, and she can't waltz back in here and pretend the past decade didn't happen."

A few tears fall. "I know, P. But my sister can forgive her, so why can't I?" It's the question that has been bugging me ever since my sister told me she was thinking about giving her another chance. It was so easy for her to move on and forgive our mother, but I can't—or won't.

My feelings about my mother are a rock that has grown in size over the years, and now, I can't seem to push it out of the way. It's accumulated so much hatred over the years, and no amount of erosion and apologies can make it get smaller.

Her absence was everywhere—in every empty chair, in every conversation where someone asked me about her, at my high school *and* college graduation, the ache of the empty chair where she would've sat if she was there, but she never was.

Now, she's back, and the ache is stronger and heavier than before.

"I used to think forgiveness was easy," Paige tells me.

"How so?"

She scrunches her brows, as if she's contemplating how to translate her thoughts into words. "It felt so easy as a kid—forgiving someone. It felt more natural to me than anything else because I didn't know what was happening to me wasn't normal. I used to think all of it was my fault, so when the adults in my life asked for forgiveness, I gave it to them because I trusted them. They were my parents, you know? As a kid, you think your parents are superheroes, and they make all the rules because you don't know any better."

My heart aches for all Paige has been through. Her face is so bright despite all the memories I know are flashing through her mind, but her eyes ache for the small version of her that simply wanted to be loved. I wonder if I have the same look on my face when I talk about my mom and childhood, or if I've become way too good at hiding it.

"I forgave my dad whenever he hurt me, and I forgave my mom for never noticing me—it's their first time living too, you know? But as I got older, I started to realize forgiveness was the easy part. Anyone can dole out forgiveness, but the part you don't forget is how they kept walking away—how they kept hurting you time and time again." She grabs my hand in hers. "Ells, you can forgive your mom, but you don't have to suddenly forget about all the ways she let you down by not being there for you."

"I know, but—"

She cuts me off. "You're not a bad person if you choose to not forgive her. Only you went through what you did. Don't let somebody else's willingness to forgive someone cloud all the feelings you felt. Don't let how your sister feels now make you forget about all the hurt you went through. You two lived different versions of a similar story. Your feelings are different, and that's okay."

I wipe a few tears from my eyes. "Thanks, P."

She catches me off guard when she wraps me in a hug. "I know what it's like to grow up with the weight of the world on your shoulders." She pulls back and looks me in the eye. "But the one thing *you* taught me is that I don't have to carry it all on my own."

I nod my head. I'm the worst at crying on someone else's shoulder, but I'm glad I called her today. I needed someone who understood, and Paige understands me like no other.

"Only you can decide what to do, Ells, but you're never alone. Hads and I can make another pros and cons list, Grant can hype you up in whatever decision you make, Oliver will support you, and Alissa will give you a shot of tequila when you decide what to do. We're all here for you because you've been there for us so many other times."

"You guys are my friends; of course I'm going to be there for you."

"You're also our friend, Ella. Just because you're the mom of the group doesn't mean you don't get to cry and struggle like the rest of us." Paige takes a bit of her food, a tear dropping onto the shell. I realize my potstickers probably have tears on them too.

True friendship is crying about your problems over comfort food.

"I love you so much."

She smiles at me, and it's like the sun came out after a dark, rainy day. That's what Paige does for the people she cares about. She brings light when the darkness creeps up and surrounds us. "I love you too, Ells. Now," she gets comfortable on my bed, "turn on that one reunion episode I like to quote."

I smile, already knowing which one she's talking about. Paige doesn't prefer reality television like Alissa and I do, but she knows a few episodes from some internet memes.

And for the rest of the day, we eat shitty food and laugh until she has to go home to Oliver.

It has been hours since Paige left, and all I've done is stare at my ceiling and cry.

I don't know why I can't make myself do anything. That phone call froze me in time, and now, I can't move until I cry out all my feelings. Not only is this thing with my mom stressing me out, but I'm behind on some deadlines for authors, and I *hate* being behind.

But maybe tonight, I need to feel all my feelings so they get the fuck out of my body. Maybe rotting in bed and crying is what I need to do just for tonight.

I eventually run out of tissues and have to sneak to the bathroom to get more, and of course, when I leave my room, I run into Leo walking out of our shared bathroom. I hope he can't notice my eyes or the dried tears still on my face.

I put my head down and walk past him.

His hand shoots out and grabs my arm. I don't bother looking up at him when he speaks. "Is everything alright?"

"Mhm," I lie. "Peachy."

I can tell he doesn't believe me, but he lets go of my arm. I hate that I miss the small contact.

He says nothing as he walks back to his room. *Thank God.* The last thing I need to add to my stress is whatever feelings I'm having for him to bubble up even more. I'm counting on the fact that when he's out of here, they'll go away.

I tiptoe back to bed and get halfway under the covers before I feel another presence in my room. Correction: lurking in my doorway.

"I told you I was fine, Leo," I say as I hide my sniffle. "Go away."

"Why? Because I'm the last person you would want to see when you're like this?" He's talking quietly, and I can't decipher if he's trying to be nice or what.

"Well, yes. And it's late. We have work tomorrow."

"I don't care," he says as he comes over to the side of my bed. I can't bear to look at him. I'm scared he'll take one look at me and laugh. His hand comes over to my face, and he turns it so I'm looking at him.

I know what I look like to him—weak.

"What's making you cry, love?"

"You don't care," I say. "Go back to bed, Leo." I try to flip over and ignore him until he goes away, but his hold on me doesn't budge.

"You don't have to tell me, but I'm here, Ella." He gets up from where he was kneeling and actually sits on my bed. He pokes his shoulder out at me. "If you need a shoulder, I'm here."

"I don't need you to come in here and make me feel better. Just because we've had sex a few times doesn't mean we do things like this for one another. You're not my boyfriend, Leo. I don't need you to do this."

"And if I want to?"

Does he mean that? "Well, I can't stop you."

His lips curve into a smile. "I'm stubborn, Ella."

"I know." Right here, right now, staring into Leo Zimmerman's eyes, I feel comforted. I feel safe. I feel like I'm able to need him—to want him—but only for this moment.

"Come here," is all he says, his arms wide as I lean forward, my body moving of its own accord. "You don't want to talk about it?"

I shake my head against his chest.

"Okay, then I'll just keep talking so I hopefully piss you off and the real Ella comes back. Where should I start?"

I laugh into his chest. Weirdly enough, his presence now is kind of helping. "Tell me something you've never told anyone else."

"Why would I do that?" I can practically hear his smirk from here.

"Because it'll make me feel better."

He all but pushes me off him, and the two of us laugh. This feels weird, but part of me never wants this moment between us to end. Tomorrow, we'll pretend this never happened and get back to our regularly scheduled bickering.

Before I think he's going to leave me hanging, he speaks. "I've been feeling homesick recently. But not for England—just for my parents."

Oh. I don't know what I was expecting, but it wasn't that. I assumed he would lie and tell me something fake and then leave. This feels real.

"What do you miss most about them?"

"Seeing them, I think. Over the phone isn't the same, and with my dad's condition, I worry about him. All I do all day is worry I'll pick up the phone and he won't be on the other end of it."

"I strangely relate to that," I say before I can stop it.

"Yeah?" he questions, leaning back on my bed on one arm, the other across his leg.

I nod. "My sister. All I do is worry about her."

"She's younger than you, right?"

"Yeah. She's graduating high school this year, and I feel old." This is flowing too easily, and for the first time ever, we're having an actual conversation. No bickering, no emotional walls up, nothing of the sort.

For the first time, Leo Zimmerman and I are talking like normal fucking people.

"It must be hard being away from her."

I'm about to tell him he has no idea, but he does. "It is." I grab my blankets and pull them up my body, suddenly feeling way too self-conscious, way too normal with Leo sitting on the edge of my bed.

Maybe Leo and I are more alike than I thought. Maybe that's why we always butt heads. He might be the male version of me, just without the mommy issues and great tits.

The two of us stare quietly at one another, and I don't know what it is with us and darkness, but somehow, our relationship feels more authentic when the lights are off.

"Do you feel better?" he asks me, his hand finding mine as he leans forward.

I nod, not wanting to admit out loud that he helped me tonight.

"Good," is all he says as he gets off my bed. Before he leaves, he turns around. "Let's do this again sometime."

I roll my eyes at him before he closes my door and leaves.

29

You'll Be Rewarded

I'm sitting at my desk, attempting to get work done, but I can't focus.

Why the fuck was Ella crying last night? And why the fuck did she try hiding it from me?

I don't know why it pisses me off so much. I shouldn't care. I shouldn't see her face full of sadness every time I close my eyes, but I do.

It's all I fucking see.

And I haven't been able to get anything done all fucking day because of how distracted I've been.

I lift my head up from my computer—I've been staring at it for half an hour, and nothing has changed—and see her sitting at her desk. She looks different today. Her shoulders are lower than they normally are, and she's wearing dull colors when she normally wears brighter ones. Her outfits are always office appropriate—usually a pantsuit or some variation of one—but today, the muted tones don't pop like they usually do.

When the fuck did I start paying attention to all these little things? God, she's driving me fucking crazy, and she hasn't even done anything.

I see Brody look between our offices, and before I think he's going to come into mine, he turns the other way into Ella's.

Oh, this ought to be good.

She looks up when he walks into her office, seemingly inviting himself in like he always does. I can hear muted whispers of their conversation, but I can tell by the face he made at me before he went in, he's probably going to tell her to do something.

And that usually ends with Ella telling Brody off or making some sort of comment about him. Those two have an interesting relationship; from what I've heard, they were both up for the same promotion, and Brody got it instead.

Even someone with no experience in this field could tell Ella deserved it over him, but he got it because he's friends with half the board—which he brags about. Either way, he got the promotion over her, and he's barely in the office. Nobody's in the office more than Ella; even if she works from home some days, she still bills more hours than everyone else.

When I don't see Ella giving him hell through the window in my office, I know for sure whatever she was crying about last night is still affecting her. Brody leaves her office and pokes his head into mine, looking as smug as ever.

"What's up?" I ask him.

"We should get together for a drink one of these days."

I'm not surprised by his offer. "Yeah, I'd be down."

"After Thanksgiving? Most of our big projects will be done. Maybe we can even hit the driving range together. You seem like you'd be really good at golf."

"I do alright, I guess." I'm not the most athletic person ever, but I tend to pick things up pretty quickly. I mean, how hard can it be to whack a ball with a club?

"I'll let you know." He goes to leave before he pokes his head back in. "And can you send me the report about our latest campaign when you get a chance? I want to know if our ads and shit worked for them."

"I'll have those to you by the end of the day," I tell him as I see Ella wiping her face. *Is she crying again?* "Is that all?"

"Yeah, that's all." He smacks the side of my door frame as he leaves. I'm not sure what it's going to be like hanging out with him outside of work, but I'm sure it won't be too bad. Plus, I need some more friends other than my sister and Holt. Well, and I guess Grant and Oliver. It's so fucking hard to make plans as adults. I swear, whenever I have a night open, those two are busy. I miss having a fucking social life.

And for some reason, Ella has become a part of mine. Before I can stop myself, I head over to her office, knocking so she doesn't throw something at me if I were to barge in.

"Hey," is all I can manage to get out of my mouth.

She looks up, confused as to what the hell I'm doing here. "Did you need something?"

Fight with me so I know you're okay. I clear my throat before I speak. "Are you...uh, feeling okay? After last night, I wanted to check."

She furrows her brows at me.

"Look, I've been distracted all day thinking about you crying, so tell me you're alright so I can get back to doing my fucking job."

That perks her right up. Any time I use that tone, she gets pissed.

"If you're so distracted, then stop thinking about it. How about that, Zimmerman?"

God, I've never been so happy to hear my surname. "It's your fault I'm off my game. So, are you alright?"

She stands from her desk. "I'm fucking fine. Happy?"

"Almost," I say as I close her door, not wanting anyone else to hear this. "I'd be happier if tonight when I got home, you were naked on your bed."

Surprise laces her features. "What?"

"You heard me, and if you don't listen, our pact will go down to two instead of three."

"That's not what we agreed on, dickhead."

A smirk crosses my features. *She wants this as much as I do.* "Well, I want the first time to be on my terms, Williams. So listen to me, and you'll be rewarded tonight, okay?"

"But what about—"

"Alissa's working late tonight."

She must remember her telling us she's barely going to be home this week. On Sunday night, my sister got a phone call, yelled about how stupid someone was, and ran to her room to grab her work laptop. She told us some huge company got hacked and she'll barely be home this week because of it.

What a perfect way to start our arrangement. The only crying she'll be doing tonight is crying out my name as I fuck her.

"Fine. But don't count on me leaving the office before you; maybe you'll have to be the one who's naked."

"That's fine by me, darling." I turn to leave but stop when my hand touches her door handle. "You know I don't mind being bossed around, especially by you, Ella." I lock eyes with her as I open her door. "It turns me the fuck on when you yell at me."

"Get the fuck out. I'll see you at home."

When I sit back in my chair and notice Ella's quiet smirk, I know I succeeded in making her mood more focused on arguing with me than whatever happened last night.

Mission fucking accomplished.

ELLA LEFT WORK AN hour before I did, and I was surprised she listened.

She better be naked and ready for me, because as I open the door to our flat, I can already feel my dick straining against my pants. Since I left her office earlier after bossing her around, all I've been thinking about is Ella.

I set my stuff down on the table, knowing she's hopefully in her bedroom waiting for me. The two of us will have dinner after, but all I want is to see her. She's my number one fucking priority.

When I push her door open and see her lying naked on her bed, her book in her hands, my mouth starts to water.

"Look at you being such a good girl for me," I tell her as she turns to face me.

"I figured I'd play nice to see if you could deliver."

"I've fucked your cunt three times already, Ella," I say as I round her bed, coming to the end of it. I grab her legs and drag her toward me, her book falling out of her hands. "You should know I can deliver, love."

That earns me an eye roll.

Ella looks fucking exquisite like this. I've never seen a body that drives me as crazy as hers does. I could spend all fucking night memorizing every goddamn inch of her, and somehow, I know it still won't be enough.

Her round arse is basically begging me to smack it, so I do before I flip her over, needing her eyes on me. God, these fucking thighs are driving me insane. "I'm eye-fucking these beautiful thighs of yours and, fuck, I wish they were wrapped around my head."

It has been years since I tasted her cunt, and right now, it's all I can think about, so I spread her legs wider and bury my face in her pussy. That earns me a few more noises from her, but they're too quiet.

"Scream, Ella. I want to hear the noises you make while I eat you."

My tongue takes a long lick, and I forgot how fucking sinful she tasted. I didn't realize how much I missed her sweet pussy. I regret not doing this sooner.

I spread her even wider, one of my hands underneath her arse as my tongue goes deeper. I don't know if Ella knows she's grinding her pussy against my face, but she is.

And fuck, if it isn't the hottest thing I've ever seen.

"That's it, Ella. Wrap those thighs around my head and fuck my face."

She complies with no argument, which surprises me.

Tonight is all about her, and by the time we're done here, Ella should have a hard time walking or I haven't done my job correctly.

I focus some attention on her clit, knowing the friction helps to get her off, and after a few more swirls of my tongue, her legs clench around my head, and I feel her coat my tongue. God, she tastes like Heaven. I could spend all night down here making her shake and not give a fuck about my own release.

"Get on your knees, Ella," I say to her as I discard all my clothes and grab a condom from my pocket, ripping the foil with my teeth as I roll it onto my cock. I smack her arse as she gets onto her knees, her body still coming down from the orgasm I gave her.

"Give me a second, asshole."

"Did I deliver already?" I lean down, brushing her hair behind her as I find her ear. "We're just getting started."

And then, I rub my aching cock against the remnants of her orgasm before I thrust into her in one go.

Her back arches as I get as deep as I can, and fuck, her pussy feels so good wrapped around me. "Jesus, Ella."

"Move, Leo, or do I need to take charge?" she asks me as she starts to roll her hips, her ass bouncing as she takes control.

"Fuck, just like that, love," I say as I let her fuck me. Nothing about this intimidates me; in fact, watching her take what she needs is so hot, she could make me come undone any minute. "Keep going."

Her eyes connect with mine as she turns her head and looks at me, drawing me in like a siren in the ocean. I'd willingly follow her into the darkness if she looked at me like this. She's the goddamn petrol, and I'm the match that's going to light the two of us on fire.

I don't mind getting burned, not if it feels as good as this does.

"I know you're in charge," she rolls her eyes at me, "but how do you feel about toys during sex?"

She stops, but I keep thrusting, needing to feel her every fucking second. "The more the merrier, darling."

I pull out of her so she can grab something from her bedside table, and when I see the array of options I have, I take a second to study each of them.

Oh, the things I could do with any of these. This is going to be fun.

"Don't make me wait all fucking night, Leo."

I end up choosing one of her dildos, my mind filtering through all the things I could make her feel while I fill her with my cock.

"Do you have lube?"

She grabs a bottle and throws it my way, and I grab it, squeezing some of it out onto the dildo. "Turn around and bend over."

She complies, looking back at me, her eyes carrying an unspoken question.

I take my hand and rub it around her arse. "Has anyone ever fucked you here?"

Her eyes cast down as if she's embarrassed, but I know she's not. Ella is not one to feel that emotion when talking about sex. "Yes."

I knew it. "Do you want me and your toy to make you feel good?"

She doesn't respond, so I begin teasing her tight hole.

"Tell me, Ella. Tell me you want me and your toy to take you at the same time."

Her breathing gets heavier, and I see a few drops of her cum dripping onto her bedspread as I wait for her to answer.

"I need an answer, darling. I need the words." I stick a finger into her pussy, wetting my fingers as I go back to her other hole. She shakes when I pump my fingers a few times.

"Please, Leo," she whispers as I slide my dick into her needy pussy, my fingers still pumping in her ass. "Please fill me."

God, I love hearing her beg me like this. It's music to my fucking ears.

I remove my fingers and grab the dildo, slowly sliding it into her arse as I fuck her pussy. She's clenching so fucking hard around me, I don't know how much longer I'm going to last, but Ella has to come first.

I slide it in a little more, and it's almost all the way in as she moans into the sheets.

"Fuck, fuck, this feels so good."

"Yeah, love? You like being filled like this?" I say as I up my pace on both, the toy slides in and out of her as my dick does the same. "God, you look so good taking both at the same time."

"Leo, please don't stop."

"I know what you need, Ella," I tell her, one hand on her hip to steady myself. This feels way too fucking good, and I wish I could do this to her all night. Her moans, pants, and pleas are all I can focus on, and the need to come inside her is all I can think about.

"Leo."

"Come on, Ella. Give me another one."

Her arms reach out and grab her sheets, her pussy clenching around me, and I know she's fucking close.

Her sounds are incoherent as she gives me her second orgasm of the night. All her noises are going to haunt my mind—they're fucking beautiful, and I follow soon after, seeing stars as I come. My orgasms with

Ella are always like this—overpowering. There's just something about sex with someone you hate. It makes it that much fucking better for some reason.

When I come down and pull my dick out of her, I slowly pull the dildo from her and discard it to the side as the two of us lay next to one another, neither of us saying a word as we catch our breath.

Jesus, that was fucking good, and we still get to do it two more times after tonight, since the conference room didn't count.

"I'm a fucking genius."

She turns her head toward me. "What?"

"This sex pact. It was a great idea, and you can admit that, go ahead," I say, waiting for her response.

"Over my dead body, Leo," she says as she gets up, her legs shaking so much that she can barely walk properly. *Mission fucking accomplished.* "Now, get out. We're not cuddling."

"Do you want to order food? I'm fucking starved after all that."

She nods her head as she grabs her robe. "You order. I have to clean my sheets."

I smirk as I remember the mess we made. "Your usual from the Italian place?"

"Sounds perfect," she says as she starts to strip her sheets off while I'm still on them. "Do you mind?"

"No," I say as I get up, grab my clothes, and head to my room, needing some joggers to throw on. "I'll throw on a film or something. We can watch it together while we eat."

"Fine," she says, slamming the bathroom door in my face.

And now, we're back to normal—just how it's supposed to be.

Ella

GETTING THOROUGHLY FUCKED AND ending the night with a good meal is about as good as it gets with Leo. For once, I have no complaints.

Neither of us has said much as the movie plays. Leo put on some sort of action movie, and after the orgasms I had, I don't have the energy to make any comments.

"How's your week been?"

"Leo, we live together."

He looks over at me. "So?"

"So, you've seen every single part of my week. Nothing has really happened."

"Do you still like working for Loft Media?"

"It's been my dream to work in this field, so yes. It's fine."

He cocks his head at me. "Just fine?"

"I'm fucking exhausted, Leo." Not just from tonight, but from everything lately.

"So tell me about it."

I stop myself from snapping back at why he wants to know. "You wouldn't understand," I say as I get off the couch to grab some more food. Sex makes me fucking hungry.

"Make me understand, then."

His answer surprises me. "You've only been at this job for a few months, but I've been here for a while. I've worked my ass off on every account, every campaign, every client."

"Anyone who sees you at the office knows that, Ella. It's obvious."

I set my plate on the coffee table and turn toward him. Before I can stop myself, I give him an honest answer. "No matter how much I do, it never feels like enough. I've barely moved in any direction since I got here. I was up for a promotion, but Brody got it over me, which was a bunch of bullshit."

He says nothing, so I keep talking.

"You have no idea what it feels like to be a woman in a male-dominated office. People look at you differently, you're constantly being underestimated, and earning respect from the guys at the office is basically a nonstarter. I'll never be one of them, so they don't bother listening in the first place."

"Yeah. I guess I don't know what that feels like."

"It's the fucking worst, and I can't bring it up, or I'll be treated differently. I can't fight back, or I'll be called a bitch. If I speak out of turn, I'm reprimanded. If I talk too loud, I'm arguing. It's literally impossible to do anything, and some days, I feel like I'm walking on eggshells in a place I know I belong. In a place I earned my spot at."

"I'm sorry, Ella. I didn't mean to make work harder for you."

"It's not just you, Leo. It's Brody and Brad and any of the other dude bros who think they run the fucking world because they have a penis." Plus, Leo isn't them. If he was, his dick would never come within twenty feet of my pussy, but I'd never tell him that.

"I'll try to do better going forward."

"I appreciate that, but let's not talk about this going forward." It feels like we're headed in the wrong direction of whatever this pact is, and it needs to stop now.

He nods at me before we both turn back to the movie. Neither of us says a word when we turn in for the night, heading opposite directions into our rooms.

I try not to think about everything that happened between us tonight as I lay down to sleep, but I fail miserably.

30

Were You Worried About Me?

"I NEEDED A LITTLE more from this book than it gave," Hads tells us as we sit in her living room. Book club this week is at her apartment, and Grant is on his way back from the store as we chat about this week's book.

He has really tried to step in during Amelia's absence in book club; it's sweet of him. I know we all enjoy having him around.

"I really liked the small town aspect, but same. It was missing something, I just don't know what," Paige agrees with her.

"Same. It's a solid four stars, though."

Hads nods her head. "Agreed."

"Same!" Paige says.

"Okay, I know we have shit to discuss, but I *need* to show you guys my new bookshelf Grant bought for our spare room."

I smile in excitement.

"Finally! We've been waiting patiently, Hads!" Paige says as she springs off the couch.

Hads told us she got a new shelf the other day while she and Grant were out shopping for something. She rearranged all her books but refused to send us a picture before we could see it in person.

It drove Paige and I nuts. I love seeing bookshelf photos with all her trinkets, but the refusal to show us until today was fucking rude. She got the thing on Thursday last week, and Grant built it for her that night.

It has been a week of build-up, and I'm sure it looks fantastic.

Part of their bedroom is a reading area for the two of them. Their original plan was for the spare bedroom to be their home library, but with the number of sleepovers we have, they decided to keep it as such.

"Okay, here it is," she says as she flips the light on, and in the corner of the room is a shiny, white, tall shelf filled with books. Hads likes to read all sorts of genres other than romance, so she has an entire shelf filled with classics. Another shelf is only her favorite author and the crocheted things she makes.

"Wow!" Paige's eyes burst at how beautiful it is. There's nothing better to a book lover than a shelf filled with books and decorations. I love how you can see someone's personality through the shelves they have.

For example, Paige's shelves are filled with bright ass covers of all the contemporary romance she reads, mine are filled with darker, more smutty books and sports romances. Hads has memoirs, classics, contemporary, and some young adult novels sprinkled in.

"I *love* these earmuffs you crocheted, Hads. They're fucking adorable," I say as I grab them off of her shelf. "You really picked up crocheting quickly, babe."

"Surprisingly, yes." She smiles. "I needed a new thing to keep my hands busy while Grant and I watched things at night."

"I am obsessed with this, Hads. I could sit and stare at your shelf forever," Paige says, her hand dragging across some of the spines. Hads is *not* a spine breaker. She likes keeping her books in perfect condition, but Paige and I are absolutely spine breakers. It's easier to doodle, and I hate holding the book at a forty-five degree angle when I'm reading.

One of our phones ringing in the living room cuts our tour of Hads' new bookshelf short.

"I think it's mine, but feel free to keep staring. If you want to steal anything, go for it." She smiles as she heads back to the living room.

"God, I love books. I swear, there's nothing better than escapism," Paige smiles at me. "How have things been with you, Ells?" She rests her head on my shoulder.

"I'm okay, I think. There's been a weird feeling of something resting on me since the phone call, but I'll be alright, P."

She threads her arm through mine. "Well, if you want to rant, scream, or cry, I'll be here. Just call me. I don't care how late at night it is."

"I love you." I squeeze her arm. "You know the same goes for you. I know things have been tough for you since she left."

She. Amelia. Paige's happy expression falls from her face. "I think she's really gone this time, Ella. I don't know how she could do this for so long. She has to know her silence would break our hearts."

I'm not sure what to say to that. On one hand, I agree. I think Amelia always threatening to run away was some sort of warning, but I want to believe she wouldn't just fade out of our lives.

"We'll see, P. She might surprise us all and come back."

But I don't believe that, and neither does she. This is the first time Paige has acknowledged Amelia might be gone from our lives for good. If she's hit that stage—the girl who can bring optimism to any situation—Amelia might be too far gone if she does decide to come back.

A thud from the living room causes Paige and I to perk up.

"Hads?" I ask and get no answer.

Paige and I head to where she is, and when Hads turns to face us, face pale, tears streaming down her face, her phone on the floor, my stomach drops.

"What's wrong?" Paige asks as she takes in the state of our friend.

"Hads?" I say as I grab her phone from the floor. Nobody's on the other line, but her phone is stuck on the call screen. "What's going on, babe?" I grab her hand as she stands stagnantly in her spot.

"I-It's Grant," she says through her tears. "He was in an accident."

"What?" Paige says. "What kind of accident?"

"He was t-boned on the highway coming home." She breaks out of her haze and heads to her bedroom, grabbing a bunch of things and throwing them in her purse. "He's at the hospital having emergency surgery."

"Is he okay?" I ask, scared of the answer.

"I-I don't know, but I have to go."

"We're coming too," Paige says what I'm thinking. "Ella can drive."

"Thank God, because I can't drive right now," Hads says. "I can't even find my fucking keys!"

I grab her and pull her in for a hug, Paige joining. "We got you, babe. Let us help, okay?"

She pulls back from us and nods. "Thank you."

"I'm calling Oliver to meet us there," Paige says, her phone in her ear. "Hey, Ol. Don't freak out, but I have to tell you something," and she leaves the room.

God, can't the Baker siblings get a fucking break with these fucking car accidents?

"He's okay, Hads. Surgery could be a good thing. That means he's still alive."

She turns to me, her face wet with tears. "What if—"

"Don't. We'll know more soon," I say as I zip up her bag. "Let's go get some answers, okay?"

"Okay."

"Hadleigh Baker?" someone says, and I poke Paige with my elbow as Hads gets up from her seat and heads to the doctor.

"How is he?" she asks her.

"He's in recovery now. We had to remove one of his kidneys due to extensive damage to his left side."

"A kidney?" Paige says, and I poke her again. "Sorry."

"Is that all?" I ask the doctor.

"His left leg is broken. He had a complete fracture of his tibia, so he'll be in a cast for six to eight weeks while it heals."

"But he's okay?" she asks.

"Yes, he should be fine. Anesthesia should wear off in a bit. Do you want to see him?"

"Yes," she says to the doctor. "Can they come with me?"

"Normally, I would say no, but there's nobody else in the room with him, so it should be fine if you all stay on one side." The doctor smiles at us. "Follow me."

It takes a few twists and turns before we get to where he is, and when we do, all of us see Grant laying down, eyes closed. Hads bursts into tears again.

"Thank you," I say to the doctor as she closes the door. It looks like this room isn't private, since there's another bed to the left of Grant, but there's nobody in it. "Hads, come sit."

She's leaning over onto me, and I hear Paige sniffle as I place Hads beside Grant's bed.

"He looks so weak," she says. "I miss seeing his smile. I don't like this, you guys."

"Hads, look at me, girl." She tilts her head up to meet my eyes. "He's alive, and he's fine. Grant is *okay*. You didn't lose him."

She nods her head at me as she takes a deep breath. "I need my brother, Ells." She looks at Paige. "Where is he?"

Paige sniffles but speaks. "I called him. He was out with Nick, so he was a bit far away and had to drop him off before he got here. He should be here soon. I told him what room we're in."

And right on cue, Oliver opens the door, a panicked expression on his face as he looks between us all. Paige and I both move to the side as he goes straight to his sister. Paige and I know he's as worried as Hads is. Oliver is all too familiar with car accidents, and I hope he's doing okay—his first girlfriend was killed in one their senior year of high school. Paige told me the fear has gotten better over time, but this probably dredged a whole bunch of shit up.

My heart aches for them, and for one of my best friends who's currently passed out after having surgery.

Today sucks, and after all this shit has happened, I want to put us all in some sort of protective bubble where nothing bad can hit us again. The group of us knows loss, hurt, and grief too well for how young we all are.

I'm so tired of it. I long for a day when the group of us are happy and thriving after all this shit we've been through. I know that's not realistic, but maybe it can happen for us.

"Is he okay?" Oliver asks, a tremor in his voice.

Hads nods into his shoulder. "He's okay, Ol."

"He fucking better be." He pulls back from his sister. "I'd have to kill him if he wasn't."

"Don't say that, Oliver," I tell him.

"What the hell happened?" he asks as he goes to hug Paige.

"I'm not quite sure, but one of his kidneys is gone and his leg is broken." I hand Hads some tissues.

"Fuck," is all Oliver says. I see Paige squeeze his hand, and I wish there was something I could do to help. I feel powerless as I sit here and wait for him to wake up. We won't know what really happened until he does. I assume the police will want to talk to him. I just hope it wasn't his fault, because that would be a whole other thorn in their side after Grant recovers.

"He'll be okay. Grant's an athlete. They heal faster than others do," Paige says, trying to lighten the room.

"She's right, and Grant will want to heal fast enough so he can get back on the ice for his league with Jacks in January."

"Damn right," is all we hear as Grant wakes up. "Can someone get me some water?"

I grab a cup as Hads throws her arms around him.

"Here."

He smirks at me. "Thanks, Ells."

"Never do that again," Hads tells him, pressing a kiss to his forehead.

"Well, tell the car that hit me to learn how to drive better." He smiles despite having just woken up from a heavy surgery. "God, I'm exhausted," he says as he tries to sit up.

"Here," Paige says, pressing the button to move the bed up. "So your leg stays in the same position."

"Thanks, Paigey."

Paige only smiles as a tear falls from her face.

"Guys, come on, no crying. I'm fine," Grant tells us. "Just some minor scrapes and bruises."

"You're down to one kidney and your leg is broken. There's nothing minor about that, dumbass," Oliver says to him.

"Aw, were you worried about me?"

Oliver runs a hand down his face. "Of course I was!"

Grant places his hand on his heart. "I guess you're not so stoney after all, big brother."

"Do you remember what happened?" Hads asks him.

Grant nods, taking another sip of water. "I was driving, and this car came out of nowhere. I think I passed out, but then I heard sirens and felt someone pulling me out of my car—which was totaled, by the way. I think that's what I'm most pissed off about."

"That sounds scary," Paige says

Grant's eyes soften. "It was. I definitely had a moment of panic when I was in the ambulance that I might never see you guys again, but then I passed out." He looks to Hads. "I dreamed of you."

Hads wipes some tears from her face. I reach down and grab her free hand, offering as much comfort as I can.

"You were yelling at me, saying if I didn't come back for you, you would revive me and kill me yourself."

"That sounds like her," Oliver says. "I'm surprised the ruler didn't make a surprise appearance."

Grant only nods. "Don't worry, it did. I think that's how I woke up. She was about to smack me with it." He turns to Hads, grabbing her hand and bringing it up to his mouth. "I'm okay, baby."

"I know."

"Did anyone call my mom?" he asks us, and I see all our heads shaking.

"I assumed the hospital did," I tell him.

"Can I have your phone, baby?"

Hads shuffles around for it, but I threw it in her bag when we were leaving. She was so out of it when she got the call, I organized her bag with everything she would need.

I grab it and hand it to him. "Here."

"Thanks," I hear him say as he types a few things on it. "I want to update her that I'm awake and tell her not to worry. She doesn't need to come all the way down here."

"Why not?" Paige asks him.

"I'm fine, you guys. I'll send her all the paperwork, and she can handle all the shit from the hospital. Do you guys know when I can go home?"

"No, but I'll grab a doctor," I say as I leave the room.

I take a second to gather myself, the weight of the worry and fear crashing down on me from the past few hours. I didn't want to break in front of them. I needed to be the calm, level-headed one, and I did just that. But for a few minutes, I need to cry silently in this hallway, because I was genuinely concerned we were going to show up here and Grant was going to be gone.

I'm thankful he's alright, despite losing a kidney and having a broken leg. He seems to be in normal Grant spirits, but I know those two are going to need all the help they can get in the coming weeks.

I'll be there, like I always am, because when one of us falls, the others are there to pick them up.

31

A Defense Mechanism

"I can't believe this has happened twice now," I say to my coworker across the conference room table.

My coworker also being my roommate, fuck buddy, and possible man I'm having feelings for, more than the normal feelings of disgust, annoyance, and hatred. They've morphed into something else—something I can't put my finger on.

It must be the sex clouding my brain. That's the only thing I can think of. His dick is holding me hostage or something, and now, I'm having all these weird feelings surrounding him and the pact we made.

"Blame Brody, but you did volunteer for this," Leo tells me, his chin resting in his hand as he reads something.

I slam my papers down. "I did not. Brody handed it off to me as if it wasn't his fault, and you happened to walk by."

"I guess we're both victims of the wrong place, wrong time."

"I guess so."

I'd much rather be at Hads' apartment helping her take care of Grant like I promised I would, but instead, I'm stuck here, working late, because Brody dropped the ball and failed to delegate this shit to all of us.

Grant got released over the weekend, and instead of us having book club this week, we hung out at their place and watched movies all night.

Now, Leo and I are stuck here looking over a bunch of companies interested in working with us that Brody never went over to give to Imogen at the end of the week.

It's Thursday. Tomorrow is the end of the week, and Brody is a fucking pain in my ass.

"How many good ones do you have so far?" I ask Leo.

"Out of the ten I've looked at," he shuffles through his small stack of papers, "two."

"I have three decent possibilities out of the fifteen I've looked at."

He runs a hand through his hair, and I hate that I stare at his forearms for too long. "We still have a fuck ton of them to look through, so we should get some food."

"Sushi?" I ask, my mouth already watering at the food we had last time we stayed late to work. "It's still open, you know."

He only smirks in my direction. "I'm already ordering."

I go to smile, but I stop myself. *Do Leo and I have a thing now?*

My alarm bells are going off in my head, wanting to retreat from this situation that feels too much like Leo and I are a couple. *We're not*, I remind myself. We're coworkers who happen to work late together a bit too much. That's all we are, and at the end of the night, we end up across the hall from one another like we sit all day at work—only a few feet separating us.

I slump down in my chair, and the two of us work silently until he has to grab the food. I think I got through five or six proposals before it got here, and my brain is pounding in my skull.

How is it I can read a five-hundred page romance novel in one sitting and not get a headache, but a few proposals at work have me down for the count?

He sets the food on the table and returns to the same spot as last time—right next to me. I know this time isn't going to end with sex in the office since we banned it, but that makes me feel more uneasy.

We could fight, or worse—we could actually have a nice talk.

Or better yet, we could eat in silence and not say a word, but knowing us, that won't happen.

"How's Grant doing?"

"He's okay. Smiling through the pain like always," I tell him. Grant is one of the most positive people I know, Paige too. Those two could smile through anything, and I don't know how they do it.

He was in the hospital for four days while they monitored his kidney function and made sure his body was doing alright, and when he finally left, it was on crutches.

They haven't gone to work since the crash, and I don't know how long Hads is going to be able to not work. I've offered to help in any way I can, but Grant keeps telling us he'll be fine if Hads has to go back to work.

Jacks even offered to stop working so he could be there for him, and Grant declined.

There are some stubborn fucking men in our group—Leo included. He might be the worst of all of them.

"Did he get my fruit basket?" Leo asks me, and I nod.

"Yes, he did," I laugh. "He wouldn't stop talking in an accent after he found out it was from you."

Leo chuckles, knowing first hand Grant would do that.

"How is he *really* doing? Car accidents are no joke. There's no way he's this chipper all the time."

I sigh heavily, unsure how to answer that question. "Grant uses humor to deflect from his pain, so I don't *really* know how he feels. All of us were fucking freaked when Hads got the call. It was a tough night, but he practically woke up joking."

"And how are you? Still trying to take care of everyone else before yourself?"

I scoff, knowing he's one thousand percent right. I don't want to admit he knows something about me. That's not the type of relationship we have. We bicker and argue and fuck sometimes, but he doesn't get to dive into who I am underneath the surface. He doesn't get to know that version of me.

"I don't do that," I lie.

"Come on, Ella. It's what you always do when someone you love is in trouble."

"And how do you know that?"

"I told you before that I see you, Williams." He takes a bite of his food. "The night we all went out in costumes. You dropped everything in the middle of that dance floor when you heard Paige needed help."

"I guess I didn't expect you to notice," I tell him as I take a sip of water.

"Just because you don't expect it from me doesn't mean I'm not capable of it." He looks into my eyes when he says it, and I hate that my body heats under his stare. There's just something about the way he looks at me. He almost looks like he's trying to work through a puzzle in his head, and I hold all the answers he needs.

I don't like it.

"You never answered my question," he tells me.

"I'm fine, Leo."

"You're lying to me, Ella. Why won't you tell me the truth for once?"

I put my plate back on the table. "Because we don't do this!"

"Do what?"

"Talk about our feelings! This isn't us, and it's creeping me out."

He throws his head back and laughs at me.

"Why are you laughing?"

"Only you could turn a nice conversation into some sort of argument, Ella. I know why you do it now. It's a defense mechanism."

What? "No, it's not."

"Yes, it is. Every time anyone asks you about your true feelings, you either change the subject, or with me, you go right to arguing." He stands from his chair, throwing the remains of his food in the garbage before he sits down. "Why don't you want to tell me? Are you afraid I'm going to *actually* be a prick and say something rude back to you?"

"Well, it is what you always do, isn't it?"

"No, it's not. That's what you've always assumed I would do since you've met me." Leo stands and towers over my chair. "Why have you always assumed that? Why did you judge who I was before you actually knew me?"

I shake my head at him. "You made it so easy, Leo. With your same old attitude of being better than everyone else and the fact that you've never had to work hard for anything, it wasn't difficult to get a read on who you are."

He jolts back as if I slapped him. "And that's just it, Ella," his voice is low as he whispers, "you assume I don't work hard when all I've done my entire life is work hard to prove myself. You just choose to not see that."

"You get preferential treatment because you're a man and your family has incredible connections. You got into our internship with one interview, and I had multiple rounds and other shit. What the fuck would you call that?"

"That wasn't my fault, Ella. The fuckers at our internship are to blame, but for some reason, you've always blamed me."

Shit. I guess he's right. "It always seemed easier for you. I was working a job in college while doing school full-time and the internship. I was fucking exhausted all the time, and it seemed easier to have someone to blame, and I'm sorry it was you."

"Just because I carried it well doesn't mean it's not heavy on my shoulders as I do."

I can't believe it took me this long to figure it out. I can't believe the real him was in front of me this entire time, and I was too blindsided by the fact that everything seemed easier for him than it was for me. I feel like a fucking idiot. I, of all people, should know people can carry invisible scars that don't show up on the surface.

I'm a fucking professional at that. It's how I survived growing up. It's how I kept going when things seemed bleak as a kid. I smiled through the pain and faked it until I eventually made it.

"I'm sorry," I whisper again. This is the first time we're acknowledging the bickering between us, the first time I've truly apologized for assuming all this shit about him. I know better, yet somehow, I always refused to look past all our shit and see he wasn't the problem.

"I'm sorry too, Ella." He sits back down and grabs one of my hands. "For pissing you off and pushing all your buttons. It's really fucking fun for me."

I slip my hand out of his as he laughs.

"In all seriousness, I'm sorry for hating you because you judged me so fucking quickly. I should've taken the time to show you who I really am rather than play these games with you."

"It's okay, Leo."

And as the two of us sit and stare into each other's eyes, the low light of the conference room making his sparkle, I feel my stomach somersault.

I'm well and truly fucked, because I can't seem to tear my gaze away from his, and I really want to kiss him right now. I don't want to fuck him—I want to kiss him. I want to feel his lips against mine, and I can barely think straight.

"Uh, we should get back to work," I tell him, the terror of whatever I'm feeling helping to shake me out of his fucking spell.

"Yeah, you're right," he says as he gets up, walking to the other side of the table and grabbing a proposal to read. I pick one up, but I suddenly can't focus on any of the words on the page.

The conference room isn't the only thing between us anymore, because I have feelings for Leo Zimmerman, real fucking feelings that make my skin crawl thinking about them for too long.

When did he go from someone I couldn't stand to someone I wish I had more of?

Lizzie: Mom told me you don't want to meet for dinner.

Lizzie: What happened between you guys?

Ella: She called me and it didn't go well. I'm sorry, Liz. I just can't.

Lizzie: You said you would do this for me, Ella. You're telling me you won't even give her one night?

Ella: You don't get it, sis. I'm sorry, but I can't. I don't think I can ever forgive her for walking out on us.

Lizzie: She's changed, Ella. And if you don't even want to try having her in your life, then maybe you should stop coming back here. It's not like you didn't leave us too.

Ella: You don't mean that, Lizzie. I know you don't. One day, you'll understand my side of things.

Lizzie: I'll never understand why you can't even give her a chance.

32

For What?

Thanksgiving

"Lizzie, can you start peeling the potatoes?" I ask my sister as she sits at the already set table. She nods, gets up, and goes over to the sink as I check on the turkey.

It still needs about an hour, so I turn my attention to the charcuterie board I brought and swipe a piece of salami. I'm starving; I've been cooking all day. I hear my Dad in the living room watching football.

I offered to host at my apartment since Leo and Alissa don't celebrate American Thanksgiving, but Lizzie insisted on having dinner here this year. I can cook anywhere, but it would've been easier to have them at my place since I have a bigger kitchen. It's fine, though. As long as I'm with them, it's okay.

Even when Lizzie and I were little, our dad never missed out on Thanksgiving. Even if we didn't have the standard turkey dinner and shit, he always made sure we were together as a family. I've learned over the years it's not so much about the meal or the holiday, it's about the people who sit around the same table as you—related to you or not.

This year has been tough—mentally and physically. Not only has there been a lot of huge life transitions happening, but I feel like I'm finally getting used to life and all the curveballs it throws.

Even if those curveballs are in the form of Leo fucking Zimmerman and his dick that's holding me captive.

It's not just that, though. My heart is slowly turning on me, and I hate that I've spent so much time lately thinking about Leo. I hate that I can't get him out of my head. No matter how hard I try, no matter how many books I read, all I picture when I see the main male character is him. His stupid brown eyes, his fucking curly hair, his accent.

Just as my sister finishes mashing the potatoes, I hear a knock at the door, and before I can grab it, my sister does.

"I'll get it!" she all but shrieks as she heads for the door. I know my dad mentioned something about one of his work friends coming for dinner since he didn't have anywhere else to go, but when I got here this morning, he told me he canceled.

So who the hell just walked in?

"Come in," I hear my sister say, an unusual pep in her voice.

My stomach drops, and somehow, I think it knows before I do who just walked into my childhood home.

"Wow, it smells good in here," a familiar but unfamiliar voice says. "Michael, it's good to see you."

"You too."

I don't want to move. I *can't* move. Because there's no way my mother walked in the door and is trying to make small talk with my father—the one she walked out on. Somehow, my legs move, and as I turn the corner, I see a stranger taking up space in our living room.

"What is she doing here?" She looks so unrecognizable to me right now. Her hair used to be lighter when I was younger, but now, it's a dark brown. She's a lot skinnier than I remember, and her brown eyes look at me with anger brewing beneath them.

Our expressions must match then, but that's about the only thing we will ever have in common. Thank God I get all my looks from my dad. The only thing I got from her is a crippling fear that I'm not good enough and my eye color.

"Ella..." my dad cautions me. "Today is a day to be surrounded by family, and Lizzie invited your mother. Let's not argue."

This is the first time I'm seeing her in person after all these years, and I'm the one being told to calm down? No.

Suddenly, I'm not feeling so thankful.

"She's the one who has missed out on a lifetime of Thanksgiving dinners, and I'm the one being scolded right now? Really?" I must have stepped into an alternate universe. How is he so okay with this? That's his wife! They technically never got divorced because she just up and left, and he's okay with this?

"Ella, please," is all my sister says as she steps forward and tries to comfort me.

I step back.

"So this is why you didn't want it at my apartment this year? You figured it would be better to ambush me here, in our childhood home where she walked out on us." I point the wooden spoon I'm holding at her. "Get out."

"Ella, stop," my sister says as she grabs hold of our mother's arm.

"Please just give me a chance, Ella. I'm here now—"

"But you walked out when we were kids! Am I crazy, or did you two just forget about that? Did you forget how she abandoned us to run off and do God knows what?"

"I've apologized, Ella. You just can't seem to accept it." My mother has a cold look on her face, and everyone else looks confused as to why I'm angry. Am I the only one who remembers how fucking hard it was back then? We had one income with my dad working, and that was barely enough to keep us afloat. Somedays, I was worried we were going to lose the house, and end up on the streets if we couldn't afford it anymore.

"No, I can't."

"Why not, Ella? She's here now and is willing to try—"

I laugh, my emotions overcoming me. I feel crazy right now, crazy for having to tell them how fucking difficult it was, as if they didn't live in it right next to me. "She wasn't willing to try when it fucking mattered most, Lizzie. Since we don't need her anymore, she comes back." I turn my gaze to my mother. "Did you get bored? Is that why you decided to go for round two?"

"Ella, stop!" my father yells, but my gaze never wavers.

"Do you need money from us? What is it, *Mother*? What do you need from us so badly that you're attempting this apology?"

"How dare you say that to me?" She shakes her head.

"How *dare* you try to come crawling back to us after you were the one who walked out? You want to talk? Fine! Please, since we're all here now, enlighten us as to why you think you're justified in abandoning your family!"

"I needed to leave, Ella. Maybe one day, you'll understand that."

A single tear falls from my eyes as I look at her. "Maybe one day, you'll understand I needed a mother. That *we* needed you, and you left."

"Ella, I didn't know what to do with you! You or Lizzie. I was a terrible mother! You never saw how hard it was."

The three of them are standing across from me, and for some reason, it feels like it's three against one. It is, in a way. They both seem to want to try and work this out, to try and be a family again, but since she left and never came back, our family has been split. *She* did that, not me. She was the one who fractured our family all those years ago.

Now, she comes crawling back. To make amends. To try.

It's a few fucking years too late.

"If I did it, you could have," I whisper under my breath.

"What the hell does that mean?" my mother scolds, a laugh bubbling up. "You're not a mother."

"Not in the way you're thinking, but I sure as hell raised Lizzie, and look at how wonderful she turned out. That's all thanks to me and Dad, not you."

"How's that?"

I must be going insane or something. "You weren't here! Lizzie was so young when you left, and since Dad worked two jobs to support us, to feed us, I was the only one here to raise her! I had to grow up in an instant! The moment you left, I became an adult, one who had to step up because my own mother couldn't bear to stay!"

The three of them stare at me as I unpack years of wounds and hurt that have weighed on my body since she left.

Paige was right. Lizzie and I lived two different versions of the same story. Her wounds went away a lot easier than mine did because she had me to help, to guide her, to *raise* her to be the woman she is today.

I didn't have that. I didn't have someone to do that for me. I had to figure it all out myself, and in a single second, I grew up faster than most kids, all because my mother made her choice and left.

Lizzie's wounds from our mother leaving faded so much quicker than mine did. Mine still linger. In every relationship who left me, in every friend who thought I was too much, in the back of my mind, I hear whispers of my mother.

It all comes back to her. When she left, she took so much more than herself with her. Every time I do something and think I'm not good enough, I hear her voice in the back of my head telling me I'm right.

Because if my own mother couldn't stay, then why would anyone else? If my own mother—the person who's supposed to love you unconditionally—left, then why would anyone else stay? I'm not worth it, and ever since she walked out, that's the one thing I've always been sure of.

"Are you even sorry?" I ask her, wanting to know.

She's looking at me as if I have four heads. "For what?"

For what? "For leaving. For breaking our family to pieces when you left," I say, my teeth grinding because of how pissed off I am.

I look at my father, his hand on his head, as if he's sick of us having this conversation, and then to Lizzie, her eyes filled with tears, but about what? I don't know.

But I needed answers. After all these years, I deserved them.

"I gave up my whole life to make sure Lizzie was okay. I got a job as soon as I could to lighten dad's load. I made meals, I cleaned the house, all the while helping Lizzie grow up, get good grades, and keep my own education afloat. I put myself through college while working and maintaining my scholarship. I did that!" I step a little closer to them, wanting to get my point across. "All while you were off somewhere else, living your life and forgetting the three of us ever existed."

She shakes her head. "I never forgot about you guys."

"Then why didn't you come back? Why didn't you stay, Mom?" My voice breaks at the end, and I hate how I sound right now. I'm practically begging her for answers to why she decided to leave. Right now, I'm fighting for the child in me who wanted to get angry but couldn't, for the child in me that couldn't scream or cry when something didn't go her way.

I had to be the easy kid, the one my dad didn't have to worry about, since he was worrying about everything else.

I never had a childhood. I never got to play like a carefree kid. I never had the luxury of fun because I was terrified my dad would wake up one day and leave too, deciding that the effort he was putting in wasn't good enough.

I was terrified that one day, I would wake up, and he would be gone, leaving Lizzie and me to fend for ourselves. Thankfully, that never happened, but it didn't stop the nightmares from coming. It didn't stop little me from thinking she wasn't worth being around.

I was a child when my mom left, but I wasn't clueless. I knew what it meant when my dad told me she was gone.

"All my life, I've tried to undo the damage you did when you left. All my life, I've tried to protect my sister from the pain you caused, all for you to come back and pretend like you never left." I step closer to her. "Do you know what it felt like to carry all that weight as a kid? Do you even feel bad for leaving?"

"I did what I had to do, Ella. I did what I thought was best for you three—"

I point my finger in her face. "No! No, you did what was best for you! All you've given us are excuses. You might be my mother, but we're not family. Just because you gave birth to me doesn't mean you know what it's like to raise a child, to be there for someone unconditionally."

My entire life, I've tried to create as much distance from who I am and who my mother was. If I ended up like her, I don't know if I could live with myself. But the major difference between her and me is that I stay when things get tough. I don't run the other direction like she did.

"I've tried to forgive you over the years. I've tried to look at the situation from every angle, but nothing ever made sense. I sat there as a kid trying to excuse your actions, but when I put myself in your shoes, I knew I never would have run away. That's where we differ, Mother. If I was in your shoes, running away would never be a fucking option."

"It was too much, all of it. The school, the homework, working, practices. It was all too much, and you'll never understand. If you can't forgive me, then I don't know where that leaves us." My mother puts her hand on Lizzie's shoulder, her other arm snaking through my Dad's. "If they can forgive me, you should be able to, Ella. This entire argument is because of you. So, congratulations. You successfully ruined Thanksgiving."

"Now, let's not take it there, Camila," my father says, trying to calm the situation down.

"No, I didn't," I say as I finally put the fucking spoon down and search for my purse. "I know I've said some hurtful things, but nothing is worse than leaving two kids and a husband who loved you no matter what." I take one last look at them as I open the door. "All I wanted was to be a kid. All I wanted was a mother who loved me, who felt sorry for her mistakes. It's clear you don't feel anything about what you did, so no, I can't forgive you. And I'm sorry, Lizzie, but I don't know if I will ever be able to."

Without another word, I slam the door as my dad calls my name. I get in my car and drive, tears streaming down my face the whole time, because I might've just lost my family.

Come Here, Darling

Thanksgiving

"I THOUGHT WE WERE having a roast today, sis?"

She only shakes her head as she traipses around my new place. "We are, but that's for dinner. I'm going to make some tea to go with these scones and biscuits I made."

"Fine by me," I tell her as I unpack a few of the boxes that still sit in my living room. "So, how has life been at the flat now that I'm gone? Are you two bored without me?" I don't know why I asked. It has only been a week.

"It's been quiet, actually. Quite nice." She smiles at me as she grabs a bunch of shit out of the box she brought over.

"Sis, I told you I had pots and pans. Why did you bring your own?"

"I didn't believe you when you said that, Leo."

"What am I going to do with two of the same pan then, Liss?"

She shrugs her shoulders at me. "Use one for you and one for your one-night stands."

I fake laughter as I go back to unpacking the books and shit Holt bought to make me appear more sophisticated—whatever that means. I told him I didn't need help with that, and he only laughed in my face.

Grant and Oliver bought me a brand new chess board, and the fact that it has been sitting in a box in my living room makes me mad. Something as beautiful as that shouldn't be in a box. It's one of my main display pieces in my living room, and I even bought a table and two chairs in order to display it properly.

I don't know many people who play chess, but Grant told me he would learn so he could play with me. He has a lot of time now, since he's out of work from his accident.

When my sister told me Grant had been in a car accident, I was worried. I almost grabbed my phone to call Ella and ask how he was that night, but I decided not to.

She told me he was doing okay when we worked late, but I wish I could see him for myself. I care about the lad, and I want to know he's actually alright.

"Here," Alissa says as she sets a mug down for me on the counter.

"Thanks," I say as I walk over to my kitchen. I take a sip, and it feels like I stepped back home. My favorite kind of tea is the Royal Blend tea by Fortnum and Mason, and since they don't sell that in the States, our parents sent both Alissa and I care packages with our favorite things.

My sister is insane and prefers her tea strong, so as she pours milk into her mug, she keeps the bag in it. I prefer mine a bit weaker, and all Alissa has done our entire lives is make fun of me for it. She says I'm weaker than she is, but as she squeezes her bag, I cringe.

"You're bloody insane, Liss."

"Just say you're weak, Leo, and we can be done with this conversation." She smiles at me as she stirs.

I shift the conversation all too quickly. "So what's new?"

She eyes me curiously. "Why do you care so much? You just moved out. Not much has changed. Though, I do think Ella is seeing someone."

That peaks my interest. "Oh, really?" I lean forward on my elbows. "Do tell, sis."

She sees right through my bullshit. "I know you don't care about her, but Ella has been unusually chipper lately."

Is that so? "Well, best of luck to whoever the fucker is." Me. It's me, and I don't know why the thought excites me so much. Maybe it's because of the sneaking around we've been doing, but this sex pact has definitely improved my mood recently.

My sister rolls her eyes at me. "Can you at least pretend to be happy for her? You guys didn't kill one another while living together, so if I'm not an idiot, you've become friends."

"We're not—"

"Okay, well, you don't hate each other anymore. At least, I don't think you do, so what would you call that?"

"Coworkers? Acquaintances?"

"Sure." Alissa pats my shoulder. "Whatever you say."

"Can we have dinner now? I'm fucking starved, sis."

She moves back around the counter, opening my oven and pulling out the roast as well as some potatoes and a bunch of other mixed vegetables. "Yes, and to stay true to the holiday, we have to be thankful while we eat it."

"I'm thankful you did all of the cooking, because I didn't want to."

She smiles at me. "Just grab a plate, Leo, and let's ring our parents before they go to sleep."

"On it," I smile, thankful that even an ocean away, we're able to be together, even if today is an American holiday.

A FEW HOURS OF unpacking and organizing are interrupted by frantic knocks on my door. I'm not sure who it is, but I'm guessing it's my sister, since she left a bunch of her cooking shit here.

I saunter to my front door, and when I open it, the last person I ever expected to see is in front of it.

"What are you doing here?" I refrain from any sarcastic comments because she doesn't look okay. Her eyes are red, and Alissa told me she was supposed to be with her family today like she always is.

"I'm here to have sex, Leo. Can I come in?" Ella asks, her voice raw and scratchy.

Her comment throws me off. "Uh, sure," I say as I open the door wider. She walks by me, barely sparing me a glance as she takes in my place. She and my sister helped me move in last week, and Ella made a comment about that being the first and only time she'd be in my new place.

I guess she was wrong.

Ella starts to take off her shirt, but I rush her, stopping her hands where they are.

"What?" she snaps at me.

"Are you okay?" She looks at me like my question is unwarranted. "Did something happen tonight?"

Her eyes sadden, but she brushes it off and tries to look okay, though I know she's not.

"Nothing happened. I came over to have sex, not to talk about my feelings. Are we doing this or what?"

"Ella, you don't seem okay."

She shakes my grip out of hers like I caught her on fire. "I'm fine, Leo!" Her hand brushes through her hair as she takes a deep breath. "I'm fine."

I step toward her, relieved she doesn't move back from me as my hand cups her cheek. "No, you're not. Here," I say as I grab her hand and lead her to my couch. "Sit down. I'll get you some water."

"I didn't come here to be waited on hand and foot. I came here to fuck."

I grab a bottle from my fridge and head back to where she sits, her mind running at a thousand miles per hour. I can tell because she can't look me in the eye, and she's not her usual snappy self. She looks defeated, and it's pissing me off that I don't know why.

I want to fix it for her, but I know she'd bite my hand off if I offered. Ella never needs anyone's help. She never needs anyone to fight her battles for her.

But God, I want to show her it's okay if she does occasionally.

"We're not having sex, Ella. Not when you're like this."

"Leo, this was our deal, remember?"

I nod.

"Then why won't you man up and fuck me? I showed up here practically begging, and you still won't touch me."

I take one of her hands in mine, nervous she's going to slap me with the other one, but she doesn't. "If you don't want to talk about what happened tonight, then we don't have to."

Her shoulders sag, as if there's a heavy weight attached to them. "I don't want to."

"Then let me run you a bath or something."

That makes her all flustered. "No, Leo. We don't do shit like this." She starts to get off my couch. "If we're not going to have sex, then I'll leave."

I grab her arm as she tries to get past me. "Please stay, Ella."

"Why?" she whispers, as if she didn't mean to say that.

I don't really have an answer as to why I want to do all of this for her, but it seems like the right thing to do. Something happened tonight that shook her. She has never looked so unsure of herself then she does now. I'm not even sure she meant to come over here.

She came here to fuck away whatever problem she had tonight. She wanted to use me as a distraction from whatever was going on, and normally, I'd be all for that.

But her showing up here tonight feels different, and for the first time ever, I want to prove to her I'm more than just one night. But if I tell her that, she might sprint out of here, so I say the next best thing.

"I don't want you driving in the state you're in. You could get hurt, and we don't need another person in the hospital because of a car accident."

She knows I'm referencing Grant, and as she goes through all her options in her head, she nods.

"Okay."

I snake my hand around her waist as I stand, handing her the water I grabbed her. "Drink this, sit down, and I'll get a bath ready. Does that sound okay?"

She can only nod, her eyes focused on where my hand rests against her skin. "I'm sorry if I ruined your night."

I grab her chin with my hand. "You didn't ruin anything. It's okay to admit you needed me tonight."

She rolls her eyes at me. *There she is.* "You wish, Zimmerman."

"Should I put the temperature to scalding hot? That's what you're used to down in the depths of hell, right?"

For the first time tonight, she smiles at me. "Yes, actually. That would be great, asshole."

I smirk to myself as I head to draw her a bath. My sister got me a giant welcome basket for my place, and one thing she included was this thing that makes bubbles or something. I told her I wasn't a bath guy, and she told me everyone needs a good soak every once in a while.

Since I'm not going to use it, Ella might as well. Plus, if it makes her forget a bit about tonight, my mission will be accomplished.

After making sure the water is hot, I head back out to my living room where Ella's sitting, staring out the huge glass windows that look over the city.

"It's a nice view, isn't it?"

She turns to look at me. "Yes, it is."

"Come here, darling," I say as she stares at me, those big brown eyes gleaming underneath the lights.

To my surprise, she rushes me, and I almost fall over because of how strong she runs into me. Her arms go around me, and for this moment, we're not two people who hate one another.

We're something different. This is uncharted territory for us, and I'm unsure how to navigate it, but I know that after tonight, neither of us are going to mention it again.

"I ruined everything," she says into my chest.

That makes me squeeze her a little harder. "It's okay."

She shakes her head. "It's not, but I appreciate what you're doing."

"And what am I doing?"

"Helping me through it."

"Just because we fight and bicker all the time doesn't mean I don't care about you, Ella."

I swear, I feel her eyes roll as she detaches from me, her arms going around her body as if she's feeling shy all of the sudden. Sure, the girl can walk in here and ask to fuck me no problem, but having conversations that involve emotions is where she gets shy.

"There's a towel for you in the warmer, and a robe too."

"Thank you," she says, looking like there's more about to come out of her mouth, but she spins around and heads for the bath. She stops in the doorway. "Will you join me?"

Not can I. *Will* I.

"Sure," I say as I shove my hands in my pockets and head toward her.

"Don't worry, I'm not going to jump you. I just... I don't think I can be alone right now."

And yet, she could've gone to one of her friends' places, but she drove here. She drove to me. God, tonight is fucking with my head.

This girl could ruin my life if I let her, but Ella and I would never cross that line. We would never work either, not with the constant bickering between us—we would drive each other mad. But seeing her like this makes something bloom in my chest, and if I'm only able to be like this with her for one night, I'll take it.

Because eventually, she'll move on, and so will I. Our sex pact will end, and the two of us will go back to being coworkers who argue and threaten to kill one another.

The only difference now is that I know what she looks like naked. Not just with her clothes off, but with all her defenses down, and underneath all of the confidence and eye rolls is a girl who wants to be seen. To be wanted. To be needed.

Just like me. All I've ever wanted is for someone to want me for more than one night, for longer than it takes for me to get them off. But that could never be us, because when all is said and done, Ella will warm the sheets of another person, and I'll be alone.

But as I climb into the tub and fasten myself behind her, trying not to think too much about how perfectly she fits against me, part of me thinks maybe, if I play everything right, I can have more nights like this.

I know the hope in my heart is all for nothing.

"Is this okay?" I ask her.

"Mhm," is all she says as she nestles against my chest, her curly hair sticking to my skin.

I brush her hair out of her face, my hand massaging the delicate skin around her neck and back.

It's criminal I only see her like this every once in a while. Her guard is always up at work until I break it down through our bickering. I like seeing her with no armor, with nothing between us. Because even though I like seeing her fire, I like it even more when it's on a low simmer—when it's just beginning to spark.

I feel like I'm going crazy, and every touch of her skin is causing all these emotions to stir inside me.

Gone are the feelings I'm not good enough. Gone is the guilt I feel for being away from my parents. Somehow, while Ella and I connect in a different way, I feel like everything is going to be okay.

With her in my arms, how could it fucking not be?

I lean down to her ear as her eyes flutter. "Stay the night with me." Her eyes are wide open now, surprised by my statement. It wasn't a question, and she knows it. It was more like a plea, because I don't want whatever is going on tonight to end.

"Leo..."

God, I could hear my name on her lips like that for the rest of eternity.

"Please, Ella. Just let me hold you and shield you from whatever is hurting you tonight." The next words come out roughly. "Just for tonight."

She turns her head to look me in my eyes, wanting assurance the two of us can keep whatever this is to one singular night.

"Why are you doing this for me?"

Because you're always too busy taking care of others to remember you exist too. Because someone needs to take care of you for once, and I know if I said that to you, you'd deny it, so this is the only way I can do that.

"Because I want to."

After another hour of me stealing as many touches as I can, her head starts to dip, the exhaustion or adrenaline from whatever happened tonight finally getting to her. I sit both of us up, grab her in both of my arms, and lift her out of the tub as it drains.

"I can do it myself, Leo."

I grab her a towel from the warmer. "I know you can, darling." I wrap it around her, tucking part of it in so it doesn't fall. "But it doesn't mean you have to."

To my surprise, she doesn't fight me. Ella's lips only turn up as she stands and looks at herself in the mirror. I wonder what she sees right now.

Because when I look at her like this, all I see is strength.

I head out to my room that's barely unpacked or organized and throw on some sweats, grabbing a pair of boxers and a shirt for her to wear. When I get back into the bathroom, I set it on the counter, but she's in the same position she was in when I left.

"What's got your mind all up in arms, Ella? And how can I help to soothe it?"

"You've done more than enough." She spots the clothes I brought her. "Thank you."

I grab the shirt from where I set it and start to unfold it.

"I—"

"Let me take care of you tonight. You can go back to fighting your own battles tomorrow." I shove the shirt over her head before she has a chance to say anything else, and when I get on my knees and hold the shorts out, she steps into them.

"Thank you," she whispers.

"Sorry, what was that?"

"Thank you, Leo. Don't get used to hearing that."

I shake my head at her. "I won't."

I grab her hand and lead her over to my bed. "Do you need anything before bed? Your phone? Anything in your purse?"

"No. My phone's off, and I told your sister I was staying over at my dad's." She flinches when she says the word *dad*, so I assume something happened tonight with her family. I can't imagine what. Ella has always been ride or die for the people she cares about, and I hope whatever happened tonight is fixable.

Knowing her, it will be. Ella can do anything she sets her mind to. I've seen it firsthand.

I climb onto my bed, pulling the sheets back so the two of us can get in. I open my arms for her in case she wants to come closer to me—in case she needs me.

To my surprise, she accepts, her cold body pressing against mine as if we weren't in a scalding bath for an hour and a half. As she dozes off against my chest, I try not to latch onto the possibility that this could be the start of something new for us.

Because when she wakes up tomorrow, she'll leave. And I'll get up and workout like I always do, trying to pretend like tonight never happened.

ELLA'S STILL ASLEEP, BUT I've been tossing and turning all night. I'm way too wound up, and even though I denied her an orgasm last night, I feel like this morning, I should make up for the egregious error.

It was the right call, though, and I stand by my decision to not fuck her while she was way too emotionally fragile. Now that it's morning, I don't give a fuck. She's going to leave anyway. I might as well leave both of us sated, right? What's better than starting your day off with sex?

As she stirs awake, I straddle her beautiful body before I slide the shorts I gave her off and start to tease her center. She's slick in seconds, and as her eyes open fully and connect with mine, she smiles.

I never expected that to be her facial expression after waking up in my bed. I hate that it makes my chest hurt.

"Please don't stop on my account," she mumbles, her voice still groggy.

"Put your legs up on my shoulders," I tell her, about to grab a condom from my side table before she stops me.

"I have an IUD," she tells me.

"I know, but you were the one who said—"

She rolls her eyes. "I know I was, but I'm changing my mind. People are allowed to do that, you know."

Always fucking fighting me. "Are you sure?"

She's looking right at me when she answers. "Yes, Leo."

God, I used to hate my first name, you know? I used to hate that it was just Leo—it's not short for anything. Growing up, I always wanted to change it. But hearing the way it rolls off her tongue, especially when she's whispering it like a prayer, is one of the best things I've ever heard.

"Then lay back and let me take care of you." I slide out of my clothes as she settles on the bed, all her clothes now discarded across my room.

She's fucking perfect, and I'll never get tired of seeing her like this.

I try not to think too hard that, after this, there will only be one more time between us, but it definitely annoys me.

I take my time with her, kissing my way up her exquisite thighs as I get to her pussy. I take a few languid licks, getting her ready so she can take me, edging her a little bit, because it's fun to watch her squirm under my touch.

"Leo…" she warns me, and I don't think twice before I grab her legs and lift them onto my shoulders, giving me perfect access to slide right into her.

Her pussy squeezes me *perfectly*, and as I slowly thrust in and out of her, I take my time memorizing every noise she makes, everything her body loves that I do to her. I'm not going to have her after this, but I can have the memory of her.

And that has to be enough.

"Lift that pretty head of yours, Ella. Look at how good we look together," I say as I slide in and out of her, increasing my pace as she looks at where we're joined. "Good girl, listening to me for once."

"Just don't stop, Leo."

I reach down and cup her neck, forcing her gaze to stay on where I fuck her. "I won't, darling."

God, she's a fucking dream. I swear, it could be since I barely slept last night, but the feel of her is too real to be pretend.

Ella drags her hand down to her clit, rubbing the swollen nub as I continue to fuck her, changing my pace because I know how fucking crazy it makes her. She wants to come so bad, but I'm not done with her yet.

"You're not allowed yet, Ella."

"You don't tell me what to—"

I move my hand from behind her neck to in front of it. "Want to try that again?"

She gives me a glare before shaking her head.

"Good," I say, quickening my thrusts. I'm pounding into her, but somehow, it's not enough. "Eyes on me."

She complies, and when I see her looking at me, face filled with lust and pleasure, I start to unravel. Seeing her eyes on me while I fuck her is doing things to my composure, and I suddenly have none of it as I lift her hips up and hit a deeper spot.

"Fuck!" she cries out. "Leo, please, please."

Feeling her with nothing on my dick, with nothing between us, is a different sensation than I've experienced before. I've never done this with anyone before. I never trusted any of them since it was one night, but with Ella, this feels like a huge step. Towards what, I have no fucking clue, but the way this feels is going to ruin me forever.

I'll never feel anything this good ever again, and I'd think this was some sort of prank if I didn't have the conversation with Ella about it before I slid into her.

Everything is heightened, every push into her feels like the first fucking time, and don't even get me started on how tight she feels wrapped around me.

It's unforgettable, and right now, Ella feels like the first sip of something dangerous I haven't felt in a long time.

Her screams bring me out of my thoughts of how good this feels, and as she chants my name, her release coating my cock as I pump in and out of her, I start to unravel.

"Do you like how I fill you, Ella?"

"Yes, Leo. Please, come inside me."

Fucking hell. That's all it takes, that one sentence making my balls tighten, and I follow her instructions and fill her with my cum.

A few minutes later, after our hazes subside and I see my cum leaking from her pussy, I'm ready to go again. God, I've never seen such a magnificent sight—Ella, on my bed, naked, my cum sliding out of her.

I take two fingers, slide them through our mixed releases, and shove it back inside her.

"Didn't want to stain your sheets?" she asks me.

Yeah, let's go with that. "It is a high thread count."

"I barely noticed a difference."

I roll my eyes at her, grabbing my clothes from where I threw them, watching her as she does the same thing, her legs shaking ever so slightly.

"Do you want breakfast?" I ask, knowing what her answer is going to be already.

She looks awkward, almost shy, as she answers, her hand around her neck as she looks around for her things. "I'm, uh, meeting Hads and Grant this morning."

"Got it," I say, a little disappointed, but I knew it was coming. Ella and I don't do shit like this. Just because last night happened doesn't mean anything like this will become the norm between us.

She clears her throat, as if she's going to say something, but she decides against it as she turns and runs out of my bedroom. A few seconds later, I hear my front door slam closed.

Not wanting to feel however I am after all that transpired the past two days, I head out of my room and down to the gym, needing to run out whatever stupid feelings have started to creep into my mind.

Two Moods: Horny And Depressing

Ella: Guys, I need a night out desperately.

Hads: I'm down!

Paige: Oliver is with Nick tonight, so I'm free!

Grant: Guys, are you thinking what I'm thinking?

Ella: Bookstore trip?

Hads: Yes!

Paige: Oh my, yes! I got paid yesterday! This is perfect!

Grant: Thank God. I need a new book. I've run out of things to read while I'm sitting at home.

Ella: I can pick you guys up?

Three people liked a message.

COASTING.

That's how I would describe my mental, physical, and emotional state lately. I've been coasting through work, taking care of myself and everything else. I hate it. I hate that I'm frozen where I am because of Thanksgiving.

On one hand, I feel like it's all my fault. But on the other, I said what I had to say to someone who's trying to rip my family apart.

My mother was the one who left all those years ago, and I had to step up and take care of my sister, yet she's the one able to waltz back in here like everything is fine, like she never ripped our hearts in the first place.

I know my sister and dad didn't just forget about that, so how were they able to forgive her so easily? How did I somehow end up the bad guy when I stayed and kept us afloat?

I have no clue, but I'm desperate to forget about the confusing state of my life tonight, because I cannot wait to see my friends. I swipe on some concealer to make it look like I'm not as exhausted as I feel and set that with my favorite powder. I know we're just going to the bookstore, but I have to look presentable in case there are any cute people browsing the shelves. Plus, I don't want my friends to worry about me if they saw the dark circles and general exhaustion written all over my face.

Honestly, getting ready, throwing makeup and a cute outfit on always helps me feel better. I think it's the routine of it. I know every single step of what to do. It's all muscle memory at this point, and all I've been doing lately is clinging to what I know.

Makeup and clothes is what I do well.

As I finish and put on a pair of platform boots I had to dig out of my closet, I text the group chat that I'm on my way. Paige is first, then Hads and Grant. Grant is on crutches, so he'll have to lay those down on the floor in the back so he can get comfortable. Plus, Paige always moves my passenger seat up when she's in my car, so it's perfect.

Thank fuck Alissa is out with her brother tonight, because I've also been avoiding her as best as I can since I started fucking him.

Though I'm not even sure if you could call what we're doing just fucking anymore.

I swear, she could take one look at me and know I'm hiding something from her. Thankfully, she has been working overtime lately, but we still hang out every Tuesday like normal. But work talk is banned, and so is talk of her brother while we watch reality television and eat ice cream.

Those moments are nice, but I hate lying to her. I don't think she would mind that I'm hooking up with her brother, but I don't even know how to explain it.

For one, after Thanksgiving, I somehow ended up at his apartment building. I don't even know how it really happened. I swear, I blinked, and there he was, opening up his door.

I don't know how I ended up there, but I don't regret it. Leo made me feel…wanted. He made me feel like I wasn't a psychopath for showing up and demanding him to fuck me, even though I felt like an idiot.

He made me feel like I could let my guard down and just exist, and he'll never know how much that night meant to me. I'd never tell him about my feelings—whatever they even are. I haven't had time to dissect them with everything going on, and to be fair, I'm not sure I want to.

Because I'm afraid that, deep down, after all these years, I was wrong about him from the beginning.

He's not the man I thought he was, and I made a mistake by judging him too quickly when I didn't even know him. But that doesn't erase everything that has transpired between us.

I've been looking at all our past quips from college to now with a different lens, and Leo Zimmerman may not be the asshole I thought he was.

He might've been like me—trying to keep his family together when something unthinkable happens. For me, it was my mom leaving, but for him, it was his dad's health issues.

He stayed over there while Alissa was here with me, until eventually, he got the job he has now. But he told me before that he's always worrying about his parents across the ocean.

For the first time ever, I had something in common with him. All I do all day is worry about my sister. The ache of missing her and my dad comes back when I think about her for too long lately, and I wish I could fix this fucked up situation.

But I don't know how, and I shouldn't have to be the one constantly trying to make everything better. For once, someone else should empathize with me about how I was treated as a kid and apologize for ambushing me. I was right to be angry on Thanksgiving, and I will always stand by my actions.

My heart is slowly opening to the possibility that I might have feelings for Leo—feelings other than absolute annoyance and hatred.

I'm fucking terrified.

I don't know how to navigate this. We technically still have one more time in our pact, and I don't know if I can do that without these feelings overloading all my senses. I think if he fucked me one more time, it would seal his name across my heart. I swear, his dick is holding me captive.

No matter what my feelings are, they're terrifying in whatever way they manifest. I can't have my heart falling in love with him when I know, to Leo, all of this is a means to an end.

It is, right? A means to an end?

That's what I've been struggling with. He drew me a bath. He was *nice* to me when I was having a life crisis I didn't want to be having in front of him. He didn't make fun of me or call me names; he was actually a decent guy. Anyone else might have taken advantage of the state I was in, but not Leo. He took care of me.

The part that scares me the most was that I let him.

As I pull into Paige's complex, I banish all thoughts of Leo, her smiling face greeting me as she opens the car door.

"Hi! I am so excited. I feel like book shopping and reading are two different hobbies, and I've been needing some new books to sit on my shelves!"

I smile at her. "You could not be more right, P."

Four songs later, Hads and Grant are in my car. The three of us girls have to help Grant into my car since he can't bend his leg with the full cast, but the entire time, he has a smile on his face.

"You guys have no idea how good it feels to get out of the apartment. I feel like a free bird."

And that makes us all laugh.

Five minutes later, and we're on the way to the bookstore closest to Hads' place.

"So, how is physical therapy going?" I ask him.

"Well, learning how to use the fucking things has been a pain." He kicks his crutches with his good leg. "But overall, it's okay. When I get the cast off, that's when the real work begins."

"He's basically going to have to learn how to use his leg again," Hads tells us, grabbing Grant's hand in the process. I've been checking in on her periodically because I know the crash really shook her.

My heart aches for both the Baker siblings. They're both a bit too familiar with how terrifying car crashes can be, and I know when Hads got that phone call, her heart stopped beating properly for a few minutes. I saw her face. She was as pale as a fucking ghost.

All of us were terrified as we rushed to the hospital, but I know Hads was worried that when we got there, Grant was going to be gone.

Thankfully, he wasn't. I don't know how much more loss the group can take.

"So, Ella, how is life with Leo?" Paige asks, a huge smile on her face. "Did our list help?"

My cheeks heat, because I've put this conversation off long enough, and I'm shocked this hasn't come up before now.

"Yeah, you've barely talked about it," Hads says, knowing why I haven't. "So, I'm assuming you're too shy to tell us you accepted his offer?"

"I did," I sigh heavily.

Grant screeches before Hads can put her hand over his mouth. "Tell us everything. What is sex with him like, because I figure it's like fucking some sort of Greek God?"

Hads pulls out her ruler and smacks him.

"Ow! It's just a question!"

"Why did you phrase it like that?" Paige asks, a laugh bubbling up. "But feel free to answer, Ells."

I tell them the long-winded version of what happened and how Leo and I had to work late and accidentally ended up fucking on the conference room table. For some reason, whenever Leo and his stupid mouth are around me, I can't control myself. It's how all our slip-ups have happened—my pussy thinks instead of my brain.

"He said it didn't count?" Hads asks me.

"No, I did. Because in the haze of my orgasm, I said a bunch of stupid shit. I even forgot about the security cameras, and Leo had to erase the one of us fucking in the conference room."

"Damn," Paige says as she reaches over to high-five me.

"I'm not celebrating a terrible decision. No matter how good the sex is," I admit, wanting to bash my head into the steering wheel. "I haven't told Alissa either."

"I bet she wouldn't want to know that you're fucking her brother, so that's probably for the best," Hads tells me. "I know you feel like you're lying to her, but sometimes, you have to have some things for yourself before everyone else knows about it."

Ugh, she's probably right, but all the shit that has been happening lately is fucking with my head. First, the situation with my mom, and now all these weird emotions I'm feeling about Leo. It was supposed to be sex, but somehow, it morphed into so much more for me, and I hate it.

I hate it, because I don't know how he feels, and I don't dare ask him, because I already know his answer. He's not a relationship guy, and normally, I can have casual sex.

But this time, I can't. Sex with Leo feels different—explosive and otherworldly, though I'd never say that out loud. Something about us is different, and I can't figure out if it's because we're a bit older or if the two of us have changed so much since we first met.

Or maybe it's all the *feelings* attached to us having sex. Yeah, that's probably it. Feelings tend to muddle shit up, and this is no different.

Now, I'm stuck fucking him one more time before this pact of ours is over. I don't know if my heart can survive, but it will have to when he calls it off after next time. I turn the music up to distract my thoughts.

I park in the lot of the store, and the three of us help Grant out, Hads walking next to him the entire way in. As soon as we walk into the bookstore, I feel like I can breathe a little better.

I swear, there's something so healing about being surrounded by this many books. It's a reader's dream, and it's so different from the library that surrounds me at home.

"Does anyone have any good recommendations for our next book club read? Maybe some sort of holiday book since it's almost that time of year..." I trail off as I browse the shelves.

"We can check out everything, but Grant has been going on and on about some book he saw online, but it's an indie book, so I don't know if they'll have it here," Hads tells us, and Grant's face lights up.

"Oh, we have to hear about this one, G," Paige says.

"I've been watching way too much YouTube lately since I can't go to work, and I found this girl who recommends books and does vlogs. Her sister wrote a book, and it sounds super heartbreaking. Olivia Hart is her name."

"The author or the Youtuber?" I ask him.

"The author. Her sister's name is Bree."

Paige spins around. "Wait, I know that name... Bree Hart. Why does it sound so familiar?"

"I sent you that podcast about her, Paigey. She had a stalker a few years ago, and a bunch of podcasts have talked about it, even though nobody knows what happened."

Paige's eyes sadden. "Oh, yeah. Strong fucking girl."

"Agreed," Hads says as I lock eyes with her. "Grant made me listen to it."

"Well, if we find her book, should we read it in January?" I ask, excited for another book to hopefully wreck my emotional state in the best way possible. I have two kinds of cravings when it comes to books: horny and depressing. Bonus points if a book can do both.

"I'm down," Hads says.

"Me too! I love a good sad book," Paige says.

"I'm so excited. Let's head to the fiction section and look for it," Grant says, and we all follow him. For a guy on crutches, he's still pretty fucking fast. It must be the hockey player in him. "I see it! It's the white cover."

"Thankfully, there's like ten copies here," Hads tells us.

"Take the ones from the back!" Paige says as Hads hands her one.

Hads only laughs. "I'm not an amateur, babe."

"Okay, so now that we have that out of the way, each of us should pick a book for one another that we think we would like. How does that sound?" I ask them.

"That sounds wonderful. Is this some sort of game, Ella? If so, is there a time limit?" Grant asks me, and I know he knows what I'm doing, because I sent him a video about it the other day. This guy gave his girlfriend two minutes to pick one book that he would buy for her. I'm putting a twist on this trend, though. I want us all to pick books tailored to each of us.

"Yes, but you get a few extra minutes because of the crutches," I tell him.

"Thank you."

"So, we each pick one book for each person?" Paige confirms, and I nod at her.

"Yes, but you only have three minutes. Grant gets six because it takes him twice as long."

"Oh, this is so much fun," Hads says, already looking around at where she's going to go when I start the timer.

"Ready?" I ask as I pull up the timer. The three of them nod at me. "Go!"

And the four of us are off. I head right for the dark romance table. I wanted to get Paige this book I read a few weeks ago. It was about this sex club, and I think the first book is something she would love. The third book of the series makes me absolutely feral, and I need her to start this series so we can talk about it.

For Hads, I'm heading right to the front table. There's this memoir I think she would love that one of the authors I work with told me about. It seems right up her alley, and I know she hasn't read it yet because I stalked her Goodreads account earlier.

I grab my second book and Paige flies by me toward the romance section.

"One minute, guys!"

"Shit!" I hear Hads say from behind a shelf. I'm glad there's not many people here tonight. I know a Saturday night at the bookstore isn't really a rager for most people, but the four of us aren't most people. This is an ideal Saturday night for us.

For Grant, I head to grab this new hockey romance book I read on my Kindle the other day. I think he would appreciate the amount of hockey gameplay, and the relationship aspect was just as good. It's Grant in a nutshell.

"Times up!" I say as I stop my alarm from going off. "Grant, you have three more minutes!"

"Can someone hold my books for me?" he asks, and Hads grabs the two he has in his hands before he drops them on the floor. "I only need one minute. Paige, follow me."

"Ooh! Okay!" Paige smiles and follows Grant to the book he's going to pick out for her.

Hads and I keep browsing around while they do that. "How have things been?"

Her gaze turns to me, and I notice relief in her features. "It's been okay. I'm just glad he's still in good spirits. It's tough with him not working as many hours, but the school's still paying him since he helps at practices, even if only from the bench."

"And how are you?" I ask, because this is as tough on her as it is on him.

"I'm alright. I've been talking to my brother about my feelings about it. He knows how it feels, and he's been surprisingly helpful when I worry about getting back into a car. I know I wasn't physically in the accident, but—"

"Hads, your fears are valid. It's fucking scary being in the situation you were in. Whatever you're feeling is valid. Just don't be like Peyton in season one of *One Tree Hill*." That girl was running red lights on purpose just to feel something.

She smiles at the reference. "I won't. I promise."

"Good," I say as Paige and Grant come around the corner. "All done?"

"All done." He smiles at us. "Are you guys ready to check out?"

"Yup!" Paige says as she locks arms with me. "This was fun, Ells. Thanks for the invite."

"Thanks for coming out with me. It was a much needed distraction," I tell them.

"Is everything okay?" Grant asks me, his hand somehow finding my shoulder as we stand in line.

"It is now," I say to them, not wanting to dive into the shitstorm that is my life in the middle of a bookstore. One day, I'll need them to help me decipher all my feelings about my mother, but for now, all I need is their company.

The only person who knows about what happened on Thanksgiving is Leo, and he doesn't even know the details, only that something fucked me up.

But I know no matter what, these three—and Oliver and Alissa—will be there for me when I'm ready to talk about it. Until then, their presence is all I need.

My battery feels recharged already, and it has only been a few hours.

"Do you guys want to get boba?" I ask as I grab my books from the cashier.

Three smiling faces meet my gaze.

"I take that as a yes," I laugh as Paige links her arm with mine. As the sun sets, the four of us drive with the windows down and the music way too loud.

35

Hope Is A Dangerous Thing

I AM HALFWAY TO fucking pissed. I swear I only had a few pints, but one morphed into two, which somehow transformed into six.

It has been a stressful few weeks, and besides all the crap with my dad happening, a certain coworker of mine has infiltrated my mind and won't fucking leave.

I'm starting to think sex with no strings isn't going to be possible soon, but I think that's only something I've thought about.

Ella showed up at my apartment the other day begging for sex, but I declined and took care of her for the night. Then, when we woke up the next morning, our limbs tangled around one another, I took care of her then too.

She's fucking my head up, and the only way I know how to get rid of her is to drink until the only thing I can see is darkness or the world spinning. At this point, I'll take either.

It's not that I have feelings for her—we both agreed this was a means to an end, and it will be.

It's going to be really fucking hard to watch her date and know she's fucking other people. I'll still be around since we still work together, and the fact that she's best friends with my sister. I'll have to hear from Alissa how happy she is when she finds someone who's perfect for her.

It pisses me the fuck off that it won't be me.

Thus, the reason I agreed to Brody's proposal for a drink. He's not nearly at the same level as me, but he's getting there. Brad is here though, and he's as trashed as I am.

"So, is Leo Zimmerman going to try and pick up a lady tonight, or is he too busy drinking his feelings away?" Brody asks, his arm slung around my shoulder.

"No women for me tonight, lad."

"And why is that? Every person in here keeps staring at you. There's not enough for the rest of us." Brad tries to smack my arm, but he misses and almost spills his beer. "Shit."

"I'm seeing someone, but it's just physical."

It's just sex but for some reason, it feels like more. Something happened recently that caused the switch for me, but as hard as I try, I don't think I'm capable of casual anymore.

Ella coming over to my place—her coming to *me*—when she had a rough day made me think I'm capable of more than one night for her. That maybe I could be the person she runs to when things start to feel like too much.

But hope is a dangerous thing—especially when it comes to us. We may have reconciled in the past few weeks, but that doesn't mean anything. We still argue and bicker. We still play games with one another, and I like that. I like what our relationship has come to.

I want more, but I know I can't have it. We only have one more slip-up for our fucking pact, and I'm willing to never fuck Ella again if it means she keeps running toward me instead of away for once.

"Just sex, huh? Is that a personal preference, or can most girls not handle more than one night with you?" Brody laughs as he sips his beer, and I take a long swig to try and combat what his stupid statement made me feel.

"It was a mutual agreement, mate. No strings attached."

"And you like her?" Brad asks me.

I shake my head. "She's a fucking firecracker, but all it will ever be is sex." *No matter how fucking confused I am about it right now.*

"A firecracker, huh?"

"Yup," I say, finishing my pint. I think that was my seventh? I honestly haven't a single fucking clue. All I know is that I haven't pictured my firecracker in my mind since I finished it. The beer is starting to settle, and all I can feel is the hum of the music in my bones, and I love it.

God, she's so pretty though. I hate that I like how she points her finger in my face all the time. I hate that her hair wraps perfectly around my fist. I hate it all so much, and it's all I can think about.

She is all I can think about.

I guess that beer didn't really help.

"Well, maybe after you're done with her, I can take a stab. I could use an arrangement like yours, but mine would be never-ending."

"Over my dead body, Brad. Plus, Ella would never go near your dick with a six meter pole."

"Ella?" Brody asks me, his arm retreating from my side.

"What?" I ask him.

"You're fucking Ella? Ella Williams? The bitch from our office?"

Did that really come out of my mouth? "No, no, I'm not. And don't call her that." I try to play it off, but the two of them have weird looks on their faces.

"Wait a minute, it all makes sense now," Brody says, putting his glass down. "You guys were always staying late at the office, the bickering; it was all a ruse because you're fucking her."

"Are you guys in a relationship or something?" Brad asks me.

"No. Ella and I aren't anything as far as you two are concerned. Forget you even heard anything, because there's nothing going on with us," I say in an effort to change the subject. Maybe if I say it one more time, they'll believe me.

"Whatever you say, dude. I hope the sex was good. She seems like she would be a good fuck."

Not wanting to punch this fucker in the mouth after the bomb I just dropped, I fake a phone call and get the hell out of here.

I go to call a car but decide to walk instead, the weight of what I said sobering me up so fucking quickly.

I don't think they would say anything, and I feel like I covered my tracks well, right? God, I can't even remember exactly what I told them. All I know is that I hope those two were fucked up enough to forget any trace of the conversations we had. I sure as hell want to go back in time and stop myself from blurting that out—especially in front of those pricks.

Brody is technically above me and Ella at work, and that worries me. I don't think he'd do anything, but now he has something to hold over our heads. I wouldn't put it past him to use that piece of information to get something he wants or needs in the future.

I'm such a fucking idiot.

This could be a disaster if it comes back to bite us, and it will be all my fault. Not only did I proposition her in the first place, but I was the one who outed it to the people we work with. And Ella would be pissed at me if this got out.

It is partially her fault, though. If I could get her out of my mind, then this might not have happened. If she wasn't attached to me like a fucking tick, maybe I could move on, fuck someone else, and call it a fucking day.

But I can't. Even after this is over, I don't know if I'll be able to.

Would she stand by me after all this shit? Would she believe me if I told her what I did tonight? Would she fix it? Knowing her, she would. She's good at that, fixing everyone else's problems for them, but I never wanted her to fix mine.

Though this is *our* problem, not just hers.

I should just tell her. I should go to her place and tell her what happened.

But then I could lose her. I could lose the one shred of Ella I have still—our sex pact. She would break it off, I'm sure of it, and then she'd probably punch me in the face for what I did—for how careless I was with my fucking mouth.

This is my mistake, and I have to be the one to fix it, no matter what it costs me.

36

Ominous As Shit

THERE'S SOMETHING IN THE air today. I can't pinpoint what, but since I got up, I've had this weird feeling sitting in my gut.

Maybe it's the fact that I haven't talked to my family in a while, or maybe it's because I have feelings for Leo, but all I feel is unsettled as I pull into the parking garage. I didn't even listen to music on the way here because of how I'm feeling.

I'm bummed my family hasn't reached out to me yet. I know I was the one who walked out, but they were the ones who invited my mother without telling me. I was the one who got ambushed, so as far as I'm concerned, they should reach out to me first.

But I've been fixing things my whole life. Not just with my family, but in general. I'm a fixer, and when I can't do anything about that, I spiral a bit.

It drives me fucking insane that there's a rift in my family I can't fix—or don't want to yet. They hurt me. My mother hurt me, and after all I said to their faces, I know I probably hurt them.

I've been holding all of that in for years, and now that it has been said, I can breathe better. I didn't realize how much weight it held over me until I purged it all from my system.

What doesn't help is that I miss them. Before all this shit happened, we had a nice routine going, and we talked every single day. Now, it feels like way too long since I've heard their voices.

I wish I could turn the part of me off that's always looking out for them, but I can't. It has been ingrained in me since I was a kid, and after so many years of always being the one to take care of others, I'm exhausted.

It's tiring always being that person. One of these days, maybe I'll allow myself to need someone like everyone seems to need me.

I sigh heavily as I finally get out of my car, hearing my name called almost immediately. When I turn and see Rae's beautiful face heading toward me, I already feel like this morning is looking up.

"I brought you a coffee!" she smiles, stretching her hand out to me.

I almost burst into tears. "You're a lifesaver."

In my fog this morning, I forgot mine on the counter.

"It's Monday, Ells. I figured coffee can't hurt. Why not start the week off right?" She smiles at me.

"I wish I had your optimism, Rae." The two of us step into the elevator and when we get up to our floor, I can already feel this day looking up from whatever spiral I almost entered this morning.

But as Rae and I head to our offices, I can't help but feel like everyone is staring at me. I feel crazy, but I feel their gazes hit my back as I turn the hallway to go to my office. I shake it off. I think I'm being paranoid. This week needs to be over already and it just started.

"I'll see you at our meeting later?"

I stop in front of my door, confused because I don't remember one being scheduled today.

"For our client, the chain restaurant?"

"Right." It clicks as she mentions that. "Sorry, I forgot. It's been a hectic few weeks."

"It's okay, babe. If you ever need to talk, I can shut my door, and we can pretend we're on a conference call."

I smile at her, thankful she's here. If I didn't have her, I think I'd go crazy. "I might take you up on that," I say as I swing my door open, only to find Leo already sitting in my office with all the lights off. "What are you doing here?"

"Ella, look, we need to—"

I set my stuff down on my desk. "Leo, you look like a fucking psychopath. Why were you sitting in the dark?"

"Because I have to tell you something, and I wanted to get to you first thing in the morning before anyone else did."

That sounds ominous as shit. "Okay, I thought we were good? Is this some sort of ruse to get me to a secondary location and kill me, because Paige said—"

He shuts me up with his hand over my mouth, and I feel my back hit the wall. "Ella, just please let me explain."

I shake my head out of his hold when I hear another voice clear their throat. Leo and I look over at the same time and see Brad leaning against the frame of my door that's now open. I shove Leo away from me, and when I notice Brad smirking like the son of a bitch he is, I know something's wrong.

"Brody wants to see you," he says, looking right at me before his gaze shifts to Leo. "And you too, buddy."

I almost roll my eyes at the *buddy* term. Of course, Leo has befriended these assholes.

"I just need to talk to Ella," Leo says, not having moved from in front of me.

"It can wait," I say, not wanting to leave Princess Brody waiting. He's our superior, after all. Though, he couldn't even bother to come get us—he had to send his lackey to do it.

The men in this office wouldn't survive if they didn't have one another. Poor fucking bastards.

"Ella, *please*," Leo grits out. "It's important."

"After, okay?" I say, moving out from the wall and following Brad through the hallway. For some reason, he walks us both all the way to Brody's office, and the rock in my gut gets heavier as I sit down and notice Leo's leg won't stop bouncing.

I doubt what he had to tell me was that important, though I've never seen him so serious before. Normally, he has the same smirk and asshole expression on his face—one that screams he knows he's the hottest guy in every room. But this one looked genuinely worried, and I don't know what to do with that information.

Leo hasn't said anything, and Brody just sits across from us with a smirk, so I break the weird silence. "You wanted to see us?"

"Indeed I did."

"What does this pertain to? If it's about the project we're working on, then—"

"No, it's not that, Ella. In fact, it's more interesting." He leans back in his chair and throws his arms behind his head.

All my alarm bells are going off, and as I turn and see Leo with his head down, I get more nervous. *What the hell is going on?*

"Well, I heard you two have been involved recently, and we can't have that, can we?"

Involved? How the fuck did he find out? "I'm sorry, what?"

"I know about your little arrangement, Ella. You can drop the act."

I have no idea how to react right now, and Leo not saying a fucking word isn't helping. Isn't he going to say something? He's the one who's all buddy-buddy with Brody, so he could easily get us out of this.

"And you called us in here to discuss a personal matter that doesn't pertain to you? Wow, that's a new level of meddling, even for you, Brody."

"This company has a zero tolerance policy for dating within the company."

"We're not dating. We're not anything, so can we leave?" Leo asks, his leg still bouncing. *I bet he's itching for a cigarette right now.*

"Well, Leo, I know you had nothing to do with it. It seems Ella is more conniving and manipulative than we thought, right?" Brody leans forward in his chair and smiles at Leo. *What the fuck?*

"I'm sorry, what did you say?"

"It's become clear to me that Leo here had nothing to do with this little deal you two made. Ella, I knew you were desperate, but if you wanted to sleep with someone to get a promotion, your chances would have been better with me."

I almost throw up in my mouth. "Excuse me?" I can barely form words. Where the fuck does Brody get off accusing me of this?

"Watch it, mate." Leo leans forward in his chair. "It's not just her involved in this. It does take two to tango, if you know what I mean."

Brody only keeps looking at me, ignoring Leo. "What were you wearing to entice him, Ella? Or did you just get under his skin so much that he had to shut you up?"

"I don't have to listen to this," I say as I get up, but as I go to grab the door handle, he speaks again.

"It sure would be a shame if Imogen found out about this—or the board members."

I turn around and march over to his desk. "Are you threatening me?"

He only shrugs his shoulders.

"Then you'd have to tell them about me too. I propositioned Ella, not the other way around."

At least he's sticking up for me. I'd have to cut his dick off if he just sat there silently. "What do you want, Brody?"

"I want you to know that I know all about this. Ever since Leo let it slip at the bar the other night, I've been thinking about what to do, and this is as sweet as I thought it would be. It's going to be so much fun, holding this over your head, Ella, especially, since all you talk about all day is how terrible I am at my job and I don't deserve the promotion I got. So, going forward, I hope I have your complete cooperation."

I barely heard what he said after Leo's name came out of his mouth. We both agreed to keep this between us, and he fucking ruined it. Brody only found out because Leo hung out with him outside of work and blabbed his stupid British mouth.

"Get fucked, Brody. I'll tell Imogen myself if that's what it comes to. I won't have you blackmailing me when everyone knows I should be in your seat and not you. The only reason you got promoted is because you're a man. And you've never known what it feels like to work hard and achieve something." I turn to face Leo, but he can't even meet my eyes.

I guess there's my answer about what he wanted to talk about this morning.

I leave the office, slamming the door behind me as I head back to mine, anger and annoyance swimming through my veins. I swear, if someone even looks at me the wrong way today, I might kill them.

I go to close my office door, but Leo's foot stops it.

"Get the fuck out," I say, not wanting to listen to anything he has to say to me.

I trusted him to keep this a secret, and now this stupid pact we made is coming back to bite us in the ass. Well, not us. Me. It's always the woman that gets blamed for shit like this, and I'm so fucking exhausted. Of course Brody is taking Leo's side. Of course I'm getting blamed.

The thing that hurts the most is I thought I could trust Leo, and look where that got me. I feel like I'm the girl back in college struggling through her internship where nobody even spared a glance in her direction. I feel like that same small girl who wanted to have the same chances Leo had.

"Ella, let me explain."

"No," I say as I slam my laptop closed. "Get the fuck out, Zimmerman."

"Ella—"

I shut my door and punch his chest. "You said nobody would find out! You came to *me* and asked to hook up because you needed a distraction, and I was fine with it! We had rules, Leo, and you were the one who broke them! I could lose my job if Brody blabs his fucking mouth!"

He runs a hand through his hair, his arms straining against his shirt. "I didn't mean for it to slip out, but I was drunk, and—"

I start to laugh. "That's no excuse." I jam my finger into his chest. "I thought I could trust you. I thought we were—" My voice breaks on the last word before I cut myself off, and I have to will myself not to cry because of how mad I am.

I'm glad I'm a yeller when I cry. I'm glad I still have a voice through my tears because I've always cried alone in my room where nobody could see it, but right now, all I want to do is yell and scream.

Knowing I'm in my office, I can't. But I sure can do it with Leo since we're in the corner of the floor.

"You can trust me! I can convince Brody to keep his mouth shut and—"

I put my hand over his mouth. "I'm sure he'll fail to mention your involvement, but my name will be the first thing that falls from his fucking lips."

"I can fix it, Ella." Leo says when I pace around my office.

"No, you can't. You're the one who ruined it in the first place!"

I thought I could trust him. I thought he had changed, and for a split second, I thought we could turn this pact into something long-lasting and serious. All of that went out the window as soon as Brody said Leo's name in the office minutes ago.

I thought I was falling into him more and more every time I saw the man underneath who I thought he was. I thought all those late night talks, all the times he comforted me meant he changed—that he wasn't who I thought he was.

I could have loved Leo.

It turns out, I was wrong, and that guy was still underneath all the walls I built around him. Leo Zimmerman is still the same annoying, untrustworthy, pain in my ass he always has been. I should have known a few rounds of sex and some vulnerable chats wouldn't change who he really is.

"Ella," my name rolls off his lips like some sort of prayer. "Please let me fix this. Don't shut me out."

"I should have seen this coming. God, I'm such a fucking idiot." I slump down in my chair and start packing up my things.

"Where are you going?" he asks, suddenly appearing in front of my chair. He's kneeling on my fucking floor, and I want to kick him in the shins.

"Home. I can't bear to look at your fucking face through my window all day. I can work from there."

"Ella—"

"Stop, Leo! Stop pretending like you give a fuck about me! The game is over. Our pact is done, so you can go back to being the normal asshole I know you are."

His face is stone cold. "Ella, I wasn't pretending."

"Stop lying to me and get out."

His hand grabs my chin and forces me to look at him. "You have every right to be pissed at me, but don't shut me out when I come to talk to you about this in a few days. Because we will talk, Ella, and we're going to lay all of this shit out on the table."

"Great, I'll see you around. I have some free time in about fifty years, is that okay?"

He releases my face and drops his head into my lap. "Promise me you'll answer when I call."

I can feel the small piece of my heart remaining start to break. I can't trust him. I can't fall for him, even though I already have. I have to let him go, but part of me doesn't want to. Part of me actually wants to hear him out, but I also want to kick him so hard in the balls that he doubles over.

"Whatever we had between us is over." He lifts his head to look in my eyes. "As far as I'm concerned, there's nothing else to talk about."

And then, I get up and walk out of my office. By the time I get to my car, I've sent Imogen a message about working at home for the rest of the week since it isn't too busy, and she said that was fine. She's out of the office this morning, and I'm glad she didn't witness any of the shit that happened first-hand.

I'm sure half of the office heard me yell at Leo, and I don't even care. Leo Zimmerman and I are no longer on speaking terms, and even though it's what I had to do, the ache in my heart still sits on my chest.

When I get into my car, the tears start to fall.

In the past few weeks, I've lost my family, whatever Leo was to me, and if I'm not careful, my friends might finally catch up and see I'm not worth it.

Even I don't feel like I'm worth it lately, and as I drive home, it feels hard to keep trying to stay afloat like I always am. All I've wanted from the people around me is what I give them, but I'm so tired of waiting for the right people to treat me how I deserve.

I'm fucking exhausted, and I've finally hit my breaking point after all these years.

I'M THE DUMBEST MOTHERFUCKER on the planet.

I should have told her sooner. I had all day yesterday to go over to her place and prepare us for what just happened.

God, the look on her fucking face. Everything she said was like a stab to a different part of my heart.

"I thought I could trust you."

Those words are what killed me. She *can* trust me, but my slip-up to Brody was completely my fault. I was too fucking drunk, and I can't even blame her for acting how she did.

I'm surprised she didn't slap me or something, but Ella had some sort of tunnel vision going on—I could see it in her eyes.

I have to fix this. I *have* to, because hearing her say all that shit and seeing the tears fall from her face? Yeah, I never want to be the one to cause that ever again.

Once upon a time, I was becoming the guy she ran toward when things in her life were getting tough, and I thought we were turning the corner and opening a locked door we've never gone through.

I'm the only one to blame for keeping the lock on that door.

Never again will I cause Ella pain.

Never fucking again.

37

My Fatal Flaw

> **Hads:** Ella, are you okay?

> **Paige:** Are we still on for book club at your place tomorrow?

> **Hads:** If you don't answer, we're coming over there.

> **Paige:** It has been a while since we've heard from you and we're worried!

Grant: Ells, we need to know you're okay.

Grant: Please.

Oliver: If you're dead, I'm killing you.

Paige: Oliver! Don't say that

IT HAS BEEN TWO days of letting my anger brew and sit in my body. I've barely moved from my desk chair since I got home on Monday. Now, it's Wednesday, and I've gone radio silent on everything.

Not that anybody has really tried calling me anyway. Alissa's even worried about me. She keeps bringing me meals because I can't bear to leave my room. I've gone through a thousand different emotions in the past two days, and all I want to do is stop feeling all of this. I want to shut my emotions off and just exist, because that seems a whole lot easier than feeling all of this at once.

My family is broken. Leo betrayed my trust. Amelia has been radio silent for months.

Sooner or later, I think the rest of my friends will leave too. They texted me yesterday, and I still haven't answered them. I feel guilty about that, but I can't get out of the headspace I'm in where I'm a bother.

I feel like a giant placeholder in everyone's lives, and at the same time, I've fallen out of the lives of everyone who's important to me.

I slam my laptop closed since it's after five, and as I do, I swear I hear my door slam open. Alissa isn't supposed to be home for another few hours since she's working late. She left me a note on the counter this morning, along with three fully prepared and wrapped meals in the fridge. All I have to do is heat them up.

I cried about that this morning. She hasn't asked about what's going on with me, and part of me wants to blab and tell her everything.

But the other part of me is too afraid to say it all out loud—to admit I had feelings for her brother and he let me down. Why tell her anyway? It's not like anything is going to happen between us now. Unlike Leo, I'm capable of keeping a fucking secret.

"Ella?" a familiar voice shouts in my living room.

I grab a cardigan and open my door. When four familiar faces meet mine, I know I can't hide from them anymore.

A few more tears start to fall as I look at them.

They came for me. They didn't run away, they still aren't running now, and I know it's not because they need something from me.

"Ells?" Paige whispers as she comes closer, wiping a few of my tears.

"I'm really happy to see you guys," I tell them all.

Grant crutches over to me, throwing them onto my couch as he reaches me and wraps his arms around me. "We're so glad you're okay."

I feel three more sets of arms wrap around me—a fourth barely touching me, and I know that's Oliver—and I break. I can't hold it in any longer. I'm so fucking tired of presenting myself as this impenetrable person when, in reality, I'm barely holding it together.

And in the arms of four people I love, of four people I know love me for who I am, I sob.

When I pull back and look at them through my tears, I center myself. "Grant, get your crutches back. You're supposed to be healing."

"Ella, just let us worry about you for once. Fuck my leg. I want to know what's going on with you."

"If you want to talk about it, of course." Paige smiles at me.

"Or we could go for a drive?" Hads suggests, and that actually does sound nice. I definitely need to get out of my apartment for a bit. I've been inside the four walls of my room for too long, and I think a change of scenery could do me some good.

"That sounds good," I say, my voice raw from how much crying I've done lately. I hate it. I hate feeling weak and emotional, but I need to feel all of this and cry it out, or it's going to fester.

I don't even know what I'm crying over sometimes—the tears just fall as I think about all of it.

"I'll drive," Paige says, a smile on her face as she adjusts her tote bag on her arm.

"No offense, P, but I'll drive," Oliver says as he takes the keys from her. "You three girls are in the back. Pretty boy can sit in the front with me."

"Okay," is all I can say as Hads grabs my water bottle, fills it up for me, and the five of us head out to the parking lot, all filing into Oliver's car.

Grant turns the music on, and it plays quietly as Oliver starts to drive. Paige is in the middle of Hads and me in the back, and the two of them stare at me for a few seconds before I unload all the past few weeks onto them. I spare no details as I recount Leo and I's agreement, how I might be falling for him, Brody's ambush at work, and everything that has been going on with my mom. By the time I'm done, they're all sporting the same expression.

Well, Oliver looks the same as he always does.

"So, that's it."

Grant turns around way too fast for someone who's injured. "That's it? Ella, what the fuck?"

"What?"

"You just dropped like twenty bombs on us in the span of half an hour, and you're acting like it's nothing!" Hads tells me.

"And?"

Paige grabs my hand, squeezing it softly. "You might be a superhero, because I don't know how you've been carrying all of this for the past few months on your shoulders."

"It didn't seem difficult. It's what I've always done, but lately, I've been tired. Exhausted. I don't think I can handle one more bad thing happening." I might *actually* hit rock bottom if anything else were to happen. "I'm not good at sharing my feelings, and I've always dealt with things myself."

"You don't have to anymore, Ells," Hads says, her hand coming around to my shoulder. "You have us."

"No, I know—"

Grant cuts me off. "Ells, I know we've always joked about you being the mom friend of the group, but that doesn't mean you always have to put everyone before yourself."

"Guys, I—"

Oliver, of all people, cuts me off. "What you've been going through is some serious shit, Ella. Just because you're always taking care of us doesn't mean when you're going through some shit, we don't want to hear about it, because we do."

I know that. Deep down, I do, but it's still hard for me to rely on people, especially when I'm always afraid that in a few weeks or months, they'll leave like my mom did. "It's my fatal flaw. I care way too much about everyone else and not enough about myself."

"We know, Ella." Paige smiles at me. "But we love you anyway. We just want you to know if you need a shoulder to lean on, someone to rant with, or advice, we're here."

"And we're not going anywhere," Hads says, a flicker of disappointment on her face because one of us did leave and not come back.

"Damn right." Grant reaches back and puts his hand on my knee. "Ella, we want to take care of you as much as you take care of us all the time. You just have to let us in."

Tears start to fall from my eyes. It's all I've ever wanted to hear, deep down. That I'm not too much. That I'm worth the extra effort of people wanting to do what I do for them. My whole life, I've been searching for someone who would do that for me, and now, I've found four people who want to.

Not because I asked them to, but because they love me.

"Thank you," I say as Paige wipes my tears. "Can I start now?"

"Go for it, babe," Hads says.

"That's what we're here for," Oliver says as he turns his signal on. He's the last person I thought would want to listen to all my shit, but he's full of surprises. Paige must really be doing a number on him.

"Okay, one thing at a time," I say as I take a deep breath. "What the hell do I do about my mom?"

"P," Grant says, throwing the conversion to her.

"Well, it sounds like you finally got to tell her everything you've wanted to for years. How did it feel?"

"Freeing." That's the first and only word that came to mind. I know whatever I said isn't going to change her mind and undo all the shit she put us through, but I feel better knowing she understands how her actions hurt me.

"And do you want to have a relationship with her going forward?"

That's the question I've been struggling with the past week, because I have no idea. I can only shrug my shoulders.

"It sounds like she didn't apologize for the past," Oliver says.

"She didn't, and I hated how my dad and sister ambushed me with her on Thanksgiving, of all days." It was supposed to be a normal holiday like it has been my whole life, but of course, that day of all days was when they decided to do it. "I don't think I need her anymore."

That's what happens when you grow up: you stop needing or relying on your parents and you become an adult who can stand on your own two feet. I've had my dad there for me, but have I? He was working so much, he barely raised me. It's pretty much been Lizzie and I since I could remember, I basically raised myself.

Did I ever really need them? Yes. It would have been nice to experience my childhood and live without all those responsibilities hanging over my head, but I also don't need her now. I don't need my mother, even though I've always secretly hoped she'd come back my whole life.

"What do I do about my family? They haven't spoken to me since I stormed out on Thanksgiving."

"They might just be giving you space, Ells," Hads says.

"You basically poured your heart out to them on Thanksgiving, and assuming you've never said any of that before, they probably didn't know," Grant reminds me.

"Yeah, there's no way they would have. I kept all my feelings buried in front of them." Like I always do.

"So, they're both probably seeing things from a new perspective, and they might need time like you do." Hads brings up a good point.

"What about Leo and this situation at work?" Oliver asks me, and my heart bottoms out of my chest.

"I have no clue what to do about him. We had a time limit with the pact, and I doubt he would want to continue it just because I'm having confusing feelings."

"Are they really that confusing?" Paige asks me, her gaze moving to Grant and back.

"Yeah, I mean, we all saw this coming. I thought he would fall first, not you." Grant winks at me.

"Don't listen to those two," Oliver tells me. "Listen to your feelings, Ella. Only you know what you want."

"I don't know what I want, but I know I feel safe with him. I ran to him after the huge Thanksgiving blow up."

"What?" Paige screams. "You didn't tell us that!"

"I didn't know where else to go, and if I was alone, I might have spiraled so far that I'd never come out. My car basically drove itself to his place."

"Oh, you're gone for that man, Ells. Might as well give in now," Grant says.

Hads smacks his arm. "Take some time to really think about it. It could just be the sex clouding your brain."

"Yeah, it might. Plus, I don't know if I can trust him after everything that happened at work. I might have weird feelings for him, but can I trust him? My gut says no."

"Talk to him about it. Maybe let him explain," Oliver says as he parks the car in my lot.

I guess I never did give him a chance to tell me what happened, but would that change anything? I don't know if it could, but it's something I have to figure out. "You guys are right."

"Of course we are. And as for this work situation, if you think you're outgrowing it, it might be time to move on, and that's okay too." Hads smiles. "Just think about it. We love you, Ells. Don't ever doubt that again, okay?"

I nod at them. "I won't."

"Good, because you can't get rid of us that easily. You're stuck with us for life—until we're all old and sitting on our porches talking about books," Paige says, her eyes getting glassy at the picture she just painted.

My phone buzzes as she says that, and when I see my dad's contact pop up, a smile comes to my face.

> **Dad: I know you're probably still upset with us, and you have every right to be.**

> **Dad: But Lizzie hasn't come out of her room in two days, and I'm not sure what to do.**

"I'll see you guys soon," I say as I hug them all the best I can before I hop out of the car. As I watch them drive away, the girls waving at me from the back seat, a few more tears fall from my eyes.

If my memory was to be erased tomorrow, I know for a fact I could never forget them. Those girls and the bond we have is infinite, and we fit together like a key going into a lock.

I take a deep breath as I answer my dad, already getting in my car.

Ella: I'm on my way.

AN HOUR LATER, I softly open the door to the place I used to call home, and my dad perks up from the couch as I come in. Thank goodness I'm working from home for the rest of the week. It's late, and by the time I get back, it's going to be even later.

"Hi," I say.

"Hey, bug."

"Is she upstairs?" I ask, unsure of what else to say.

He nods at me, and as I start up the stairs, I hear him say something else.

"I'm sorry."

I know he's talking about more than just Thanksgiving, and as I turn around to face him, his face full of regret, I let a few tears fall. "It's okay."

"It's not." He shakes his head. "But I'm proud of you, Ella."

"We'll talk later, okay?"

He nods at me, returning to whatever he was watching as I walk up the stairs, headed straight for my sister's room. I knock on the door and hear her mumble something.

"It's me, Lizzie."

I hear a few footsteps before the door swings open, and I barely have time to say anything before she wraps her arms around me.

"I'm sorry," she mumbles as I squeeze her. I can hear her voice tight with emotions, and my first instinct is to make it better, but maybe all she needs from me right now is a hug.

Trying to rewire my brain to stop having my first thought being to fix something is going to be hard, but I need to let the people I love figure things out for themselves sometimes.

"Do you want to sit?" I ask as she leans back from me.

"Yes." She grabs my hand and leads me to her small twin bed, the two of us sitting cross legged across from one another like we used to when we were kids.

I don't say a word as I wait for her to start the conversation. She might need me to listen to her, and I don't know what happened in the past week with our mom to make her upset. Or maybe it was because of what I said? I don't know, but my stomach is flipping as I wait.

"I'm sorry about Thanksgiving. It was all my fault, and I guess I didn't think it would go the way it did. Looking back, I realize I was a little naive."

"It's okay, Liz. I'm sorry for my outburst."

"Don't apologize, Ells." A few tears fall from her eyes. "I never realized how hard it was for you. I only really focused on my own pain, but hearing you say all that to Mom opened my eyes to what you went through too. You had more pressure on you, but you always made sure I was okay as a kid. So, thank you. Thank you for all you did and all you continue to do for me and Dad."

"You don't need to thank me, Lizzie. You're my sister." I grab her hand. "I would do anything for you."

It's quiet for a few moments before I hear her sniffle and speak softly. "Mom has been flaking on our last few get-togethers."

My heart breaks as I hear her say that. "I'm sorry, Liz." I know my sister wanted to have more of a relationship with her than I did, but I guess I wished our mother changed enough to give it a shot with her. It kind of feels like my fault. My outburst was warranted, but it might've made her second guess even trying to have a relationship with Lizzie.

Tears fall onto my sister's shirt, and I grab the tissue box from her side table, handing her a few. "I thought she changed."

"Look at me, sis," I say, and she does. "She might've changed, but sometimes, people do things that don't make sense. It's not on you, Lizzie. Her leaving and flaking isn't on you; it's on her."

"I wish I was as protective of my heart as you are. Maybe then, I would realize some people don't deserve the chances I give them."

"I love how open you are to seeing the good in people, Liz. You shouldn't change that about yourself just because of her." I squeeze her hands. "You just need to be a little more protective of who you give your heart to. Don't let what she did break your faith in people."

"I would love to have her in my life, but I don't know if I can handle being hurt over and over again."

My heart breaks when she says that. I'm not sure there's a normal piece of it left with how many blows it has taken over the past few weeks, but whatever was left just shattered. "It's hard, Lizzie. It's difficult putting your all into someone like her. Maybe you need to start slower with her and let her prove she's going to stick around. Baby steps, you know?"

She nods at me. "Yeah, I think you're right. Maybe I tried to jump into the deep end without having any floaties on."

I laugh at her metaphor. "That's a good way to describe it."

She sighs heavily, and I can still see the weight of all this on her shoulders.

"Just don't let this break you, Liz. It took me a really long time to learn that the decisions she made don't have to define who I am and how I love going forward. It's hard to come to terms with that, and it's a fight every single day to remind myself what she did won't define who I am."

"How do you do it? How do you make it seem so easy?"

I shake my head. "It's not. I've been faking it until I make it, which isn't the best, so don't do that. But we have to wake up every day and fight to not let her actions determine who we are. I'm not her, Lizzie, and neither are you. We're only parts of our parents, and our experiences in life make us who we are. We're a culmination of so many different things. We're not only who we're born from."

She nods at me, her face twisted as the words sink in.

"It's not because of you, Lizzie. I need you to remember that."

"I will, Ella. Thank you." She leans forward, and I wrap her in my arms, tears falling from my eyes as we hug. It feels good to be home.

"Now, let's say we go downstairs and watch a movie with Dad?"

Her smile brightens her face. "Don't you have to work tomorrow?"

"I'm working from home, but for tonight, I want to hang with you guys. I've missed you."

"We've missed you too," Lizzie says as she grabs my hand and drags me down the stairs.

As I surround myself with my family, all is well again. Even if I'm still unsure about everything with Leo, I'm glad my family is still intact for nights like this.

Home has always been the most important thing to me, and that will never change.

38

Just A Distraction

December 2nd

It's Monday morning, and I've barely slept since last week.

Ella's been working from home since the big blowup with Brody, and my leg shakes underneath my desk as I wait to see if she's coming in today. I hate that she hasn't answered any of my messages. I hate that I keep looking up from my computer to see if she's in her office, but I'm worried about her.

I even asked my sister how she was, but Alissa wouldn't give me much of anything because she thought I was joking when I asked her about Ella. Then, she told me to stay away from her because she's going through something and I would only add fuel to the fire.

So all I've been doing the past few days is try to not think about Ella and the situation we're in, but it hasn't worked. I've tried to distract myself by throwing myself into the projects here, by working out until I can't breathe, but it hasn't helped.

I don't even know why I'm so up in arms over this, but I need her to know I'm sorry. I didn't want this to happen, and it pisses me off that Brody is holding this over her head. Only hers, because the guy is a fucking arsehole.

When I see movement in my peripheral vision, my head shoots up, and I see a familiar figure walk into her office and settle at her desk.

I should give her some time. Maybe I'll wait and see if she comes to me first. I don't want to look too pushy.

I type random shit on my computer before my legs move of their own volition toward her office. I don't bother knocking, since her door is open, and when she sees me walk in, she doesn't make a face. That's good, right?

"H-Hi. Hey." I sound like a blubbering idiot.

"Hi, Leo."

She didn't say my last name, so that's good, I think. "How are you?" What a stupid fucking question.

"I'm okay." She sets her water bottle down on her desk. "Did you need something?"

"Get a drink with me after work." It was supposed to be a question, but it comes out like a statement. No wonder I piss her off.

She takes a few seconds to ponder my offer. "Okay."

"Really?"

She and I are both surprised by my answer. "Yeah. Just let me know when you're leaving, and we can head there together."

"Okay," I say as I leave her office. "I'm glad you're back."

Her gaze meets mine as her computer turns on. "Thanks."

I head back to my office and try to get some shit done, but I fail, because I'm way too excited to see Ella after work in an environment we can't get fired from.

I OPEN THE DOOR for Ella as we head into a small restaurant around the corner from the office. I've only been here once before—the last time being with Brody and Brad. I'm sticking with one drink this time. I'd hate to see what would slip out of my mouth around Ella, and I'm not sure I want to find out.

I pull her chair out for her, and the two of us sit across from one another as we place our orders. Ella gets a small appetizer, as do I. I'm not too hungry, and all I want to do is talk with her. That's the whole reason I invited her out. I needed a neutral place to have a chat.

"So, how has work been since I've been gone?" she asks, breaking the silence.

"Quiet."

"Really? I bet with asshole one and asshole two, you've been riding high on getting the publishing contract." She takes a sip of her drink. "I assume you got it?"

"Not exactly. Brody said it was mine if I wanted it."

She raises her brow at me. "I'd say yes, Leo. There's no way he's giving it to me without strings attached."

I shake my head. "I didn't earn it. We should ask Imogen to decide instead of him."

"It's fine. Take it. You *did* earn it."

"No, I—"

"Did you ask me out here just to talk about work? We could have done that at the office." She sips her martini as our appetizers come. "Thank you."

"No, I didn't."

"Then stop talking about work. It's not everything, you know."

I scoff at that. "You're the biggest workaholic I know."

"I'm a perfectionist, but lately, I've realized there's more to life than working your ass off all the time, especially when it's not worth it."

"What do you mean?"

She leans forward, her elbows on the table as her arms cross. "There's more to life than work, and I know me saying that sounds insane, but it's true. I thought my standings at work dictated my whole life, and ever since we left college, I've been struggling to find a balance between it all."

That sounds eerily familiar. I took a bit of time off in between this job and graduating to help take care of my father, but I still worried every second about not being able to find a job over here. It's hammered into you your entire four years at university—your first job post-graduation is the most important thing you'll do. It's all I obsessed over at our internship and in our classes.

I guess as I look back with all I know now, it really doesn't matter that much.

I miss having a life that didn't revolve around work. I miss being able to leave work at the office, but I find it keeps seeping out while I'm at home. It's probably part of the reason I've been stressed out ever since I got back here—besides all the shit with my dad, of course.

"You have to take time to find out who you are in the world, not just at the office. It's become abundantly clear to me recently I've been putting too much focus on things that drain me." She takes another sip of her drink. "Brody being an asshole opened my mind more than I care to admit."

I take a bite of my food. "You're right. Is that why you want me to say yes to the publishing company as a client? To focus more on your life?"

She shrugs her shoulders. "Maybe. Or maybe I've outgrown the job I do now. I haven't really decided yet."

I never thought I'd see the day Ella Williams would be saying all this. The girl was a fucking force to be reckoned with at our internship. Before her, I'd never seen anyone so passionate about anything, let alone what we were doing.

Now that I know her a little better, I know that's who she is as a person. In everything she does, Ella gives her all. I don't think she knows a setting below one hundred and ten percent.

I want to ask her about us, about the pact we made, but I have no idea where to start or what to say, so the two of us eat and drink in silence.

If I ask her, she might get up and leave. We were only supposed to have sex one more time before she called it off. Maybe she thinks that twice with me—technically four, if you count the other two—is enough. Nobody else has ever lasted this long, and it still shocks me she agreed to fuck me more than once on purpose.

I feel like a broken record, but maybe it's because I am—broken, that is. Maybe I'm not wired for the love my parents share. It's not lost on me that I've never even attempted it, but if I tried, I doubt it would work.

I'm a one and done kind of guy. One and done is all people will ever want from me, which is probably why I throw myself into my work—I've never had a relationship to distract me from it.

But do you want that?

I'm unsure of what I really want out of life. I think Ella's right. I need to figure out who I am outside the office. I need to figure out who I want to be in the world, not the persona I've been showing everyone since I was in college.

One night stands were fine back then because I didn't need any distractions from my studies, but I don't think I ever really focused on what would happen after I left.

It didn't seem important, but now that I'm adrift out in the world all on my own, I have to decide who I want to be. I don't want to be the guy who overworks himself and never has any friends because he's too busy at the office. I want to be there for my family, for my friends, for the person I fall in love with when the time comes.

If I close my eyes, I imagine it could be Ella.

But with our history and how complicated things are between us, I shake that out of my head. I'm a distraction to her, and after tonight, we'll go back to normal.

Just like it was meant to be.

"So…" She trails off, twisting the stem of her glass between her fingers.

"Do you want to ask me something, Williams?" I can tell she does. She has this look on her face, like she's trying to look straight into my brain, like she's trying to see what I'm thinking.

"About our pact," she says.

Part of me is nervous. I don't know what she's going to say. "What about it?"

"Do you think we should continue it? I know I ended it at the office, but that was a spur of the moment thing."

It feels like that question has a double meaning, but I'm unsure of what else she's trying to say. "Well, neither of us wants to lose our jobs if Brody decides to blab, right?

She nods, her face tight, as if she wasn't expecting me to say that.

"And it was just a casual thing between us," I confirm with her.

Another nod. "Exactly, so we'll have no problem going back to how it was before. That's what we both want, right?"

Her face studies mine as she waits for my answer. I don't know what to say. I feel like I'm on the spot, and part of me wants to sprint out of this conversation as fast as I can.

Because the truth is, I don't have a clue what I want, especially where it concerns her. The past few weeks have fucked my mind up, and I'm afraid to say something that will make her run.

Plus, I doubt Ella has even considered being in my life after this. All we've talked about is going back to being coworkers; that is, if she's not thinking about leaving Loft Media. I wouldn't blame her if she did, especially since Brody would keep lording this over her head.

"Yes, that is what we agreed upon when we started," I tell her, swirling my drink around in my glass, unwilling to look at her face.

She's silent for a few moments, so I look up, and her mask slips back into place. She looks composed, like she always does in most of our conversations. "Good."

"Yes, great."

The bill slides onto our table and neither of us moves to grab it, the two of us suspended in time, as if the words from our conversation wrapped around one another and won't let us go.

I grab it before she can. "It's on me."

"Are you sure?"

"I asked you to come out, Ella."

"I know, but this isn't a date, so—"

I reach over and grab her hand. "Just accept the free dinner. It's my fault you're in the mess with Brody. If I had kept my mouth shut—"

She cuts me off this time. "Leo, it's okay. Actually, it's helped me realize a lot of things, so I guess I have you to thank."

"My pleasure," I say as I raise my glass.

She grabs her coat, throwing it on as she rises from her chair. "I'll see you tomorrow?"

I only nod as I sip my drink.

"Have a good night, Leo."

She walks away, and I'm stuck watching her leave, wishing I had an idea of how I really feel about her.

It shouldn't be this hard, watching her leave. We weren't exclusive. We were fuck buddies—distractions from the shit we didn't want to think about, and that was all.

But each step she takes feels like a stab in my chest, and as she swings the door open and doesn't spare a single glance back, I realize I made a mistake.

And as I go to run after her, throwing some bills down on the table, my phone rings.

I pick it up, not knowing who's on the other end of the line.

"Hello?"

"Leo, something's happened."

39

If You Need Me, I'm There

I FEEL LIKE MY heart just got stomped on.

Of *course*, Leo doesn't want anything serious. I shouldn't have even asked him about the pact and what it meant for us going forward. I knew what the outcome was going to be, but I still asked because a small part of me thought he might have changed his mind.

He didn't, and now, I feel like an idiot.

Leo has always been an answering machine that's full. He will always be the guy with options upon options because of how he looks, who he is, and what he wants. *Casual.* I can't wait to overhear about all his conquests at work since we're done. I'm sure he'll have one tonight since I'm not having sex with him anymore.

I'm trying to make myself feel better by thinking about all of this, but it's not working.

I knew Leo was never a guarantee. I knew this stupid pact wouldn't end how I wanted it to, even though I agreed to do it; falling for him was never an option for me.

But my heart and head got different memos, and I fell for Leo so quickly, I didn't even know it was happening. It feels like overnight, he became someone important to me, and even though that's scary to think about, it feels right. In my soul, we make sense.

Normally, I don't allow myself to depend on others, but I think with him, I could.

I can't even remember what my days were like before him. Leo Zimmerman is burned into my life like a goddamn forest fire that no amount of water could put out. I'd willingly walk into his flames, if he would only let me.

The only things I've ever wanted in life were comfort and success. I wanted to have the ability to stop worrying about money and my family, and right now, I don't have those worries. I make enough to support myself, and even the work I do for authors keeps expanding as more of them discover my services.

If I was brave, I would quit my job and do that full-time, but I can't. I have the financial stability I've always craved, and I don't want to let that go until I'm sure I have enough saved to pull the plug.

My life feels like a bunch of different moving parts, and I know I can't make any big decisions right now. I'm not heartbroken per se, but I am disappointed I misread Leo and my situation.

I step into my apartment, sliding out of my coat and boots since December just started and it's fucking cold out. It hasn't snowed yet, and I'm thankful for that. Driving in the snow is the worst, especially heading toward work where all the traffic is.

"Liss? Sorry I'm late. I got stuck doing something for my boss, and I—" I stop when I see Alissa running around the kitchen, clothes in her arms as if she grabbed them out of the dryer and forgot a basket. "Liss?"

She doesn't spin to greet me. I know she's not ignoring me; I think she's in hyperfocus mode, and not in a good way. She's got tunnel vision, and I jump right into action as I follow her into her room.

Her suitcases are spread out on her bed, and she's haphazardly throwing clothes into them with no rhyme or reason. If we were together, I'd ask if she was leaving me, but I've never seen her so out of sorts.

I softly knock on her door so I don't scare her. "Alissa, what's going on?"

She turns to face me, tears streaming down her face as her arms brace herself against her dresser. She's shaking—like full body shaking.

"I-It's my Dad."

I rush her, knowing she might need some help staying on her feet. "What happened?" I ask as I throw my arms around her.

"He's in the hospital. He had a stroke," she sobs into my shoulder. "He might not make it this time."

Oh, fuck. I hug her a little tighter before I pull back. "What can I do to help?" I don't even wait for her to answer before I start packing her suitcases in a neater manner. Her brain is spiraling, and I know with news like this, all she can focus on is getting back to England.

So, I do what I know best—I make it easier for her.

"Do you have a flight yet?"

"N-No, all I did was call Leo. He's picking me up."

"Okay, well, get a flight for you guys and I'll handle this, okay?" I look over at her, and it looks like she's frozen in time. "One step at a time, Liss. Can you do that for me?"

She nods as she heads to the kitchen, her laptop still on the counter.

I grab some outfits I know she has worn before and throw them in. I find her passport and all the important documents she needs for the airport and place them on her dresser in a neat pile. Then, I pack the essentials and her favorite perfume. She didn't tell me how long she was going to be gone, so I pack enough for at least two weeks.

I throw her important stuff in her carry-on, and when I hear a few knocks on our door, I rush to open it, not wanting Alissa to worry. She told me Leo was coming to get her, but I can't imagine he got here that fast. I left him at the restaurant with most of his drink left, so I assume he went to his place when she called him.

When I open the door and see him standing in front of me, still in the same clothes he wore to work, hair a mess, eyes red and puffy, all I want to do is make his pain go away.

I can't, but I try anyway.

I throw my arms around him and try to take some of the weight off his shoulders. This was his biggest fear: his dad dying when he's not there to help.

If I was him, I'd be going crazy. I bet he is; he's just really good at hiding it.

But you can't hide from someone who does the exact same thing, and I know nothing I do or say will help him.

His arms wrap around me, and I feel him cry into my shoulder. Gone is the man from a few hours ago who was so sure of himself, so confident.

In his place is a helpless man who doesn't want to fly back home only for his father to have passed and he wasn't there to say goodbye.

My heart aches for the Zimmerman family. I know I can only help them so much, but I wish I could do more.

Leo and I detach, and I let him fully into our place. "Alissa is in the kitchen."

He nods before following me in, shutting the door behind him. His sister looks up when we enter; she takes one look at her brother and starts to cry. He passes by me and goes right to Alissa, and I stand here feeling helpless.

Two people I care about are going through something I can't fix. I can't make it better, and it's killing me.

The sounds of their tears are all I can hear, that and sniffling, as I try to busy my hands with something.

"I haven't even booked tickets yet," Alissa says into her brother's chest. "Leo, I can't believe this is happening. Do you think he's—"

"Don't go there," I tell them. "You'll drive yourself crazy. Just trust they're doing everything they can. And when you get there, you'll know more."

"She's right, Liss," Leo says, his voice tight with emotion. "Let me get the tickets."

"What else can I do to help?" I ask them. "I can water the plants while you're gone, and Leo, if you need anything done at your place, I can—"

"Come with us," Alissa says to me, and I swear I misheard her.

"I can't, Liss. I—"

"Babe, please. I could use a familiar face who isn't one of my family members. I need you to keep me grounded if something goes wrong."

I can't believe what I'm hearing. "What about the apartment?"

"Can one of the girls water my plants?"

"I can ask them, but—"

"You should come, Ella," Leo says, catching me even more off guard. "We're both going to need someone like you around."

"Guys, this is your family. I don't want to intrude."

Alissa grabs my hands. "You won't be." She wraps her arms around me. "I need you, Ells."

"Okay. If you need me, I'm there." I have to tell work and my family—both of them. I'm sure the girls are going to have a million questions, but I'll answer them at some point. "Liss, you're all packed, but double check and make sure I didn't miss anything. Give me five minutes, and I'll be ready."

"I'm buying tickets," Leo says, his sister's computer in his hands. "There are a few seats left on the flight leaving at ten tonight."

"Try to grab three in the same row," Alissa says.

"I am."

Ten minutes later, the three of us are in an Uber on the way to the airport, the tension in the car thick as they wait for an update. Nothing comes by the time we get through security and are sitting at our gate. By the time we're on the plane, we still have no idea what we're walking into when we get off this flight.

Leo sits between his sister and me, his hand shaking so hard, it makes me grab it, trying to ease some of his stress if I can. To my surprise, he doesn't let go.

For the rest of the flight, none of us say a single word, and Leo's hand stays firmly in mine.

40

The Monkey Bars

As I SIT IN the hospital room and watch my dad breathe via a machine, I struggle not to fall apart where I sit.

My sister is next to me, her hand on my shoulder as she listens to the doctor tell us what happened. We landed about an hour ago, the flight ten long hours of all the unknowns shooting through my head. It's about what I expected, but the gut punch at seeing the man I looked up to all my life lying in a bed, not being able to breathe on his own, is something I'll never get out of my head.

I can't unsee it. I can't undo what happened, and I can't help.

I can't do anything but wait and see, and I'm not good at that. I'm good at helping, following orders, making a plan. I'm great at figuring out how to fix things.

I can't fix this, and it's driving me fucking crazy.

The doctor leaves, but the tension in the room remains. My mum sits across from me, holding my father's hand.

God, this sucks.

And sitting in the chair farthest from all of us is the girl who won't leave my fucking mind.

The girl who held my hand and soothed my worries on the flight.

The girl who dropped everything to be here for my sister and me.

If my mind wasn't such a mess, I'd start to think our relationship—whatever it is—is more than sex.

But I can't think about that right now, not with my family like this, and I know she understands that. She left me at the restaurant after I saw the look on her face when she asked me what I wanted. The truth remains: I don't know. I've never been sure about anything, and I've never been a relationship guy.

With Ella, I could be. With Ella, I would try my hardest.

Someone once told me when Ella is all in with you, you'll know it.

I think flying across the country at the drop of a hat when we asked her to is all in, but I'd never get my hopes up.

All I need to focus on now is my family. She knows that, and I know that, but it still doesn't dull the ache in my chest.

"So he had a stroke?" my sister asks my mum.

"Yes. He had gotten out of bed to go to the bathroom and he woke me up," she sniffles, composing herself. "We were talking about the two of you, and his speech started to slur. I checked on him, and I couldn't understand what he was saying, so I called an ambulance, and they rushed him here."

I reach over and grab her free hand. I can't imagine how fucking scared she was. My worst fear came true, and I can't do anything to fix it.

"I'm sorry you had to go through this alone."

"My sweet Leo." She squeezes my hand. "I was prepared for this. Since your father denied the surgery, I knew what could happen. It was scary, that's all."

"Yes, but—"

"Stop blaming yourself. He knew what could happen, and he declined the surgery anyway. It's not your fault, Leo. You either, Alissa, so get those thoughts out of your head now."

I try to, but I can't. Not when a machine is making his chest rise and fall. Not when he's in a medically-induced coma after surgery—they thinned out the walls of his heart during it.

Apparently, the stroke was caused by his heart not being able to pump because the walls were so thick. His condition was so bad, his heartbeat was irregular, which formed a clot that traveled to his brain, and if Mum hadn't acted as fast as she did, my father would be dead.

They performed surgery and fixed it as much as they could, but since the surgery was so long and tough, they put him in a medically-induced coma to rest and heal. So now, we're playing the waiting game. It's up to him when he wants to wake up, and that could be days or weeks from now—or never.

Nobody has any answers for us, and it sucks.

"Do you guys need anything? Food? Water? I can run and grab something," Ella speaks up, her voice higher than normal—sweeter than normal.

"I'm okay for now, Ells," my sister tells her.

My mum only smiles at her. "Water would be nice."

This is their first time meeting in person. Alissa introduced her on the phone when the two of them moved in together, but I know this isn't how they wanted to meet, not with my father in a hospital bed after having surgery.

She looks at me, her eyes full of empathy.

I hate that I've dragged her into this, but I didn't really drag her, did I? She came willingly; that's who she is as a person. She's kind, caring. One of the best people I've had the privilege to know, and she dropped everything to help us.

She's fucking extraordinary.

"Water's fine," I say, my voice rough. I'm not a crier per se, but all I've done is shed tears since I got the call about my dad. He's my role model, the person who taught me what it means to be a man.

He's a stubborn son of a bitch, but he's still my dad. All the good things about who I am come from him and how he raised me.

"I'll be back in a few minutes," she says, her gaze still on me before she leaves the room.

Alissa squeezes my shoulder as the door shuts. "If you want to talk to her, you can. Dad will be alright with us here."

"It's okay, sis. I need to be here."

"Your father won't be awake for a while, Leo," my mum tells me. "He'll be okay for a few minutes if you leave."

I look at him where he lays before I get up and try to find where Ella went. I notice a sign for vending machines, so I check there first. When I see a familiar, curly-haired girl staring at them, I sigh with relief.

It's crazy how she does that—calms all my nerves. I never realized it until her hand found mine on the plane. In an instant, all my worries soothed. For the entire flight, I was anxious, but I knew if I let her go, it would have been worse. So, I didn't, and that's when thoughts of her started clouding my head instead of the worries.

Now, I'm a giant mess of emotions. All I want is for my father to wake up and to hold Ella in my arms until he does.

I can't do that, though. I have to fix my family before everything else, but I'm struggling to find that balance. All I want to do is fall into her arms and let her comfort me. Never have I felt this way about a woman, and all I crave is her. Not just her body, but every single part of her. I want her laughs, her cries, her fears, her dreams. Anything she wants to give me, I want to take, and I want to give the same to her.

I can't stop the words from flowing out of my mouth. "Did you pick something, or are you going to hope the machine does it for you?"

She turns to greet me, a single tear running down her face that she quickly wipes away. "Sorry if I was gone too long. I—"

I take a step toward her. "It's okay, Ella. I didn't mean..." I trail off, unsure of what to say. Things between us feel so awkward, and I don't know if I should bring it up.

"How are you feeling?" she asks me, pressing a few buttons before the machine starts to work.

"Terrible." Why lie? She knows how shitty I feel. There's no point in skating around the truth. "I can't fix it."

She grabs the waters and snacks before setting them on the floor. "No, you can't." She steps into my personal space. "But you're here for them. That's all that matters, Leo."

I look down at her, those brown eyes shining under the fluorescents, making me feel safe and free to admit any worries I have. I know she won't judge me for it. She would probably just hold me until the pain went away. "I'm scared, Ella. More scared than I've ever been in my whole life."

She reaches for me, her arms wrapping around me like a safety blanket in a storm—like she has the key to all my worries, all my troubles, unlocking them in this small room. "It's okay to be scared, Leo."

"What if he never wakes up?" I say as I rest my chin on her head. "What if I never get to speak to him again?"

She only squeezes me tighter. "It's going to be okay."

"But what if—"

She untangles from me, her eyes peering into mine once again. "Have you ever used the monkey bars on a playground?"

The sudden change of topic confuses me. "I have..."

"Well, I've always thought life was like the monkey bars. In order to get to the other side, you have to grab each bar and swing across them."

I cock my head at her, still confused.

"You grab the first one, and you feel confident. You think it's easy at first. But then, your arms start to feel heavy as you hold your body up and try to keep holding on. I think life is a lot like that. It all feels so simple as a child, but as you swing into each new phase of life, it gets harder and harder to get a grasp on the things you love."

"I've never thought of it that way," I say, her arms still around me. "But what does it have to do with this situation?"

"In order to get to the other side, you have to let go of one bar and grab the next one. Letting go is okay. Letting go is the point of the monkey bars, Leo. All you have to do to get through this is to let go of all the shit keeping you in this guilt and grab the next bar."

"The next bar could either be my dad waking up, or—"

"He'll wake up. And when he does, you'll be by his side. Eventually, you'll get to the other side of the monkey bars."

I slide my hand through her hair. "How can you be so sure?"

"I'm not sure of anything, Leo. But I believe it. Sometimes, all you can do is believe. Sometimes, all you have is hope."

"But what if that isn't enough?" I was never one to believe in hope. I never let myself; it always ends with misery—at least for me.

"Then you let go, grab the next bar, and decide if you have enough strength to get across."

I let her words sit in my mind for a second. "Thank you for coming, Ella."

"I would do anything for you and your family, Leo. Whatever you need the next few days, I'm here." With that, she leaves, heading back to the room as if she didn't say what she did. I'm speechless.

I thought I could fuck Ella out of my system. It turns out, though, she's the one who created it. Every eye roll, every time she talked back to me, every annoyed glare cemented her into my skin, and she became everything I could want—everything I *need*. Behind all those glares and comments is someone soft, someone who wants to be seen, loved, and heard.

Never has Ella wavered on who she is, and I respect her so much for that.

Never mind the fact she dropped everything to be here for me and my family; even without doing that, she's still the best person I know.

And I want her. I want all of her.

Ella Williams is mine, and I'll stop at nothing to prove I can be hers too—if only she'd let me in enough to allow me to prove that.

The two of us could be something great together, and at some point, I'm going to grab the next bar, and we'll start a beautiful life together.

I have hope for us. I want it to be us.

When I walk back into the room and don't see her, I get nervous. "Where did she go?"

My mum and sister look up at me, the snacks and water she grabbed on the tables beside them both.

"I told her to head to the house and take one of the spare rooms. She looked tired; we'll meet her there later after visiting hours."

"I'm staying here with your father in case he wakes up tonight," my mum says to us. "He might not, but I can't leave."

"We know," Alissa tells her.

I sit back down beside my father and hope he wakes up so I can tell him all about the girl who stole my heart and how I don't want it back.

41

Overstimulated In Another Country

As I sit at a bar—pub—by myself, all my messages to Amelia unanswered, I start to think about how insane it is that I'm in an entirely different country. I've been here for a week. I've been away from my friends, family, and job for a whole week, and I haven't gone completely insane yet.

Yet being the keyword.

Of course I didn't hesitate to come after Alissa asked. I'd do anything for her and her family—anything to lessen the load during this tough time. That's actually why I'm in this pub alone. I left the hospital because their Dad woke up; I didn't want to intrude on their family time. Plus, I felt awkward being in that room. It felt like I didn't belong. I felt like an outsider, even though they both asked me to come back with them.

There's something so strange about being alone in a foreign place. I can't quite describe the feeling, but I thought since I was over here, I'd try and get in touch with Amelia. I should have known just because we're on the same continent that she wouldn't magically answer me.

> **Ella: I'm in London if you happen to be around. It's a long story, but if you have time and aren't dead somewhere, I'd love to have a talk.**

> **Ella: I doubt you'll answer this, but I can't say I didn't try, right?**

It still stings, though. I think the worst part is that our relationship felt like *more* to me. It never felt like it could fizzle out. I never thought Amelia would do this. I know she always joked about it, but I thought that was all it was—jokes.

Turns out, it was a warning instead, and none of us were smart enough to lock onto every signal she sent us.

I could try and say I saw this coming, but that would be idiotic. Hindsight has been punching us all in the face, and I don't know how to help my friends through this weird time where Amelia is concerned.

Especially Paige. I know she's hurting, and according to Oliver, she hasn't been sleeping well. I can't fucking help her because all three of us are without any answers.

Amelia disappeared from our lives. It was gradual at first, but with all the messages going unanswered, all the calls, everything being how it is now, it feels final—like we should stop trying.

After I leave, I probably will. It hurts, being ignored by someone you trusted, by someone I thought was my friend.

I don't know if we'll ever have an answer as to why she left. I don't think we did anything—if we did, I can't think what—so this must be an Amelia problem.

I've done all I can do at this point. I've texted her and asked if she needed someone to listen while she goes through whatever she's dealing with, but again, I got no response.

If the universe felt like playing a game with me, I'd run into her on the street while over here, but I doubt that will happen. Ames would probably run the other direction if she saw me.

My phone buzzes and brings me out of my spiral about Amelia.

> **Alissa: He can leave the hospital in a few days! The doctors want to make sure his heart is okay before he can leave.**

> **Ella: That's great, Liss.**

> **Alissa: If you want to go home, I can buy you a return ticket. I know you've missed work. Leo and I are going to have some much needed family time.**

> **Ella: I can buy my own ticket, Liss.**

> **Alissa: Too late. Leo offered to pay for it anyway, so you can shout at him and not me. Please pop by and see us before you go back.**

> **Ella: I will.**

Alissa: Thanks again, Ells. I really needed you this week, and I owe you big time. I love you.

Ella: You owe me nothing. You would have done the same for me. I love you too. I'm glad everything is okay.

I throw my phone in my bag, smiling because their dad is doing better. I was worried for a second he would never wake up. All I've felt the past few days is worry—worry I'm overstepping while I'm over here, worry about my family and friends back home, and more worry I'm not doing the best I can with everything going on.

Don't even get me started on my feelings about Leo. They've taken a back seat this weekend, but the ache is still everywhere, and I don't know how to remove it. If I could cut it out and shove it somewhere else, I would.

God, why aren't feelings for someone like wrinkles? Why can't I shove some Botox into them and forget about it?

Before I spiral about it, I grab my phone again and dial my favorite people. It's close to dinner time here, so it should be around lunch time for them. They both pick up immediately.

"I miss you. Please come back soon!" Paige smiles through the phone.

"She's coming back, P—unlike someone else we know," Hads rolls her eyes. "But we do miss you."

"Is that Ella?" I hear Grant shout in the background. He comes into frame, his brown hair all over the place. "How is England, mate?"

I laugh. Oh, how I miss them. I grab my headphones and put them on so people can't hear this conversation, especially if Grant keeps doing his accent. "England is okay. Rainy, but I'm hanging in there."

"How are the Zimmermans?" Paige asks as Oliver comes into the frame.

"Love, I just got out of the shower," Oliver quickly backs out of view.

"Ew! Paige, seriously?" Hads all but gags.

"He went for a run!" Paige quips back. "Ella, answer my question."

"They're okay. He's awake now, so I'll be heading back soon."

"With or without Leo and Alissa?" Oliver asks, still out of frame.

"Without. They're staying for a bit longer so they can make sure their Dad is alright."

"That's good he's awake," Hads says, Grant nodding with her. "How are you, Ells?"

"I'm okay," I say, lying through my teeth. I'm overstimulated in another country with all the things running through my mind. "I'm excited to be home."

"Hads and I have been watering the plants. They're all still alive, in case you and Alissa were wondering." Grant smiles at me.

"Thanks, guys. I really appreciate all the help while I'm over here."

"We would do anything for you, Ells," Paige smiles, and I fight the urge to cry.

"So, how are things going with Leo? Have you guys talked?" Grant asks me.

"Grant, that's a stupid fucking question. Of course they haven't. His father is in the hospital," Oliver chirps as he enters the camera, now fully clothed.

"As much as I hate to say it, Oliver is right," I confirm. "It's not the right time."

"Do you think you'll ever talk about it?" Hads asks, and I can only shrug.

"I have no idea. I asked him at dinner before all this, and he didn't really give me an answer as to what he wants. I don't think I'll bring it up again." I can't get rejected again. It's fucking humiliating. Plus, Leo has always said from the beginning he's not the type of guy who does relationships.

I thought I could show him he's worth more to me than one night, but I guess I haven't done that, so of course he wouldn't want me for longer.

"But what if he brings it up?" Paige asks, a hint of something in her tone.

"Then I'll cross that bridge when I get to it." I can't idle on this topic, or I'll go crazy. All I need to worry about right now is getting home and getting back to work.

Though I've started to be uncomfortable at work; I don't feel like I can be myself because of this entire thing with Brody hanging over my head.

My life feels like one giant mess I can't clean up. I'm really thankful my sister, Dad, and I worked everything out before I left. If I had that on my plate too, I think my body would explode from stress.

"How long until your flight?" Oliver asks me.

"It's in the morning. I should probably head back and start packing." I don't have much, but I always like being at the airport early, especially since I have to go through customs.

"Well, we can stay on the phone and talk until you get back safely," Hads says as she and Grant settle onto their couch.

I smile to myself, thankful for my friends during this weird period in my life. "Perfect. Now, you guys can update me on you. I feel like all I do lately is talk about myself."

"Yeah, and you should do it more, Ells," Grant tells me. "We love hearing about your life."

"And I love hearing about yours, so hit me with every small detail about the last week, and don't leave anything out," I say to them as the breeze blows across my face on my walk back.

I can't wait to go home, but for some reason, leaving England tomorrow feels like a chapter closing on Leo and me.

I guess it's time to grab the next monkey bar and move on. I knew it couldn't last forever, but I sure wished it would have ended differently than this.

Leo: Thank you for coming. I hope your flight goes smoothly.

Ella: Thanks.

Leo: Is the seat okay?

Ella: No.

Leo: Really?

Ella: Of course it's okay. It's first class, Leo. I could have flown economy.

Leo: Well, I didn't want you to be uncomfortable on the way back. It's a long flight.

Ella: Thanks, I guess.

Leo: Why didn't you say goodbye before you left?

Ella: You're spending time with your family. I didn't want to intrude. You guys have done enough for me.

Leo: You're not an intrusion, Ella. Far from it.

Leo: Can I see you when I get back?

Ella: I'll see you at work, Leo. But our pact is over, so there isn't much to talk about.

Leo: You know that's not true.

Ella: I don't know anything other than you should spend time with your family. I should be the least of your worries, Zimmerman.

Leo: You're right. Text Alissa when you land so I know you're safe. Is someone picking you up from the airport?

Ella: My friends are. I'll be fine, Leo.

Leo: Okay. Thank you, again.

Ella: Stop thanking me, weirdo.

42

Does That Mean I Won?

Two Weeks Later

Leaving England has proven difficult. I knew it would be, that it would be as bad as last time, if not worse, and it was.

Alissa and I almost missed our flight because we couldn't bear to go, but my parents insisted everything would be fine. We flew back the day after Christmas, and we've talked to our parents every day since to check in. Thankfully, there's a plan in place to minimize the risk of another stroke. I think the family conversation we had helped. We told him how scared we all were, and when he woke up, he was surprised to see us in England, as if we wouldn't have dropped everything to see him.

But he finally agreed to the plan. He's on the road to recovery with a physical therapist, and since we left, our parents have called every single day with updates. It's nice still feeling like a family even from two different continents.

Alissa and I also got tested for my dad's condition while we were at the hospital since it's a genetic condition. Neither of us was positive, thank fuck. It feels good knowing, but I was definitely terrified to get the results back.

I could have used a hand to hold, but the only one I wanted in mine was back in the States.

Which is where I am now. I'm back in my flat, trying to fucking sleep, but I can't, and it's all her fucking fault.

I've seen her at work the two days I've been back, and all we've done is speak in passing. It's like every single time I want to talk to her about something more, she shuts me down. I get it; we're in a professional setting, and Brody is always lurking around every corner, but she even turned down offers to talk outside of work.

She always has some sort of excuse ready.

Ella is officially avoiding me, and if I had to describe a feeling it's comparable to, it would be like being shot in the face.

I miss her fight. I miss watching her eyes narrow at me when I piss her off. I miss watching the wheels in her head turn with whatever comeback she has for me.

Now, it's like we're strangers who only coexist in the office. I have to pretend I don't know all the little things I know about her. I have to pretend I don't know all her orders from the places we used to eat. I have to pretend I don't know her matcha order from the place she loves—an iced matcha with two pumps of vanilla and oat milk. I have to forget she sleeps with her favorite books on the stand next to her bed so they're always close. I have to forget the way she furrows her brows when she starts to get pissed off at me, the way she giggles over her favorite fucking romance books.

I have to pretend like I don't know what her lips feel like on mine.

I miss the way her cheeks used to flush when I called her by her name—or the nickname that slips out every once in a while. I have to pretend my guarded heart I used to keep under lock and key wasn't completely demolished by Ella, and that I never want that wall back up.

I have to fucking talk to her. I need to tell her all this shit, or I might explode.

She even infuriates me when she won't talk to me, and that's how I know she's the only one for me. The girl won't leave my bloody mind, despite my many efforts to rid her from it.

Now, I never want her gone. I want her by my side, in my bed, and even after I claim her as mine, I want us to argue and fight. I want it all with her; I've never been so sure of anything in my life.

Most of all, I want to know she feels the same way I do, right now. I think she does, but I won't be sure of it until I talk to her.

I swing my legs out of bed, grab some actual clothes and throw them on, uncaring if they match or look good, before I grab my keys and hop in my car.

It's almost midnight, so the roads are empty, and as I'm about to pull into their complex, I dial her number.

I'm afraid I'm going to get her voicemail until her voice filters through my phone.

"Leo?"

God, the way she says my name should be illegal. "I'm glad you're awake." I park my car in their lot and head to their place. I know my sister is home, so we'll have to be quiet about this, but I can't go another night without knowing how Ella feels about me.

We've been dancing around one another for too long, and I'm tired of it.

"Um, why?"

"I need you to open your door," I say as I jog up the stairs.

"It's almost midnight, Leo. I'm about to go to sleep."

"I'm not going to knock and risk my sister answering it. Get your sexy arse out of bed and open your door." Just as I reach her flat, the door swings open, and I'm met with the most beautiful girl I've ever seen, wearing her usual matching pajama set she has in a thousand different colors.

"What the hell are you doing here?"

WHEN I SEE LEO standing in my doorway with a smirk on his face, I feel like I fell into a parallel universe.

What the hell is he doing here at midnight?

"Could this not have waited until tomorrow? Or better yet, Monday at work?" I ask him as he leans against my door frame.

"Can I come in?"

"Why?"

"Ella, I need you to invite me in."

I roll my eyes at him, but I hate that I'm happy to see him. He looks good, despite his shirt being on backward. "Come on in," I tell him, confused as to why he needed an invitation when normally he just barges in.

Before I can spin around and ask what the hell he's doing here, he grabs my hand and leads me back to my bedroom, softly shutting the door.

"Leo, what's going on?" I hate that I love how his hand feels in mine. I've missed his touch, as much as I hate admitting that. Tonight might be getting my hopes up, and I thought I killed all those after I left England, but I guess they decided to stick around.

He's pacing around my room, and as I'm about to ask him again, he speaks. "You're driving me crazy, Ella. This time, I might actually go insane."

"And you're telling me, why?"

"Because it's all your fault." He faces me and grabs both my hands. "I can't get you out of my fucking head, Ella. You're all I can think about, and I'm tired of pretending you don't cloud all my thoughts every second of every day since that conversation in the restaurant."

"That was like a month ago, Leo. I thought we had moved past it," I say, my heart in my ass as he speaks.

"That's just it, though. There's no moving past you, at least not for me. I can't move past, through, or beyond you, and I don't want to, Ella. I want to be *with* you, and I know you feel this too. I know I betrayed your trust, and I'll do anything to gain it back, because this torment I feel over you? I know it's not enough to slide back into your good graces, but fuck, I want more than anything to be yours. I want to call you mine, and I need to know how you feel, because it can't just be me feeling this."

"Leo, what—"

He drops his hands from mine as if they're on fire. "I know I didn't answer when you asked me what I wanted. Truthfully, it took you walking away from me to figure it out."

"And what do you want, Leo?"

"You, Ella. I want you."

His confession makes my body freeze. This isn't what I was expecting to happen when his name flashed across my phone.

"No, you don't," is all I manage to say.

"Yes, I do. I want to know how you feel, Ella. Please tell me you want me how I want you."

"And how do you want me?"

"Forever, Ella. I want to fight with you forever if I'm able."

"No, you don't." I don't believe this. I cannot believe he would show up here and say all these things.

The other part of me—the stupid part—wants him to keep talking, wants him to keep begging for me to say how I feel.

"I don't know what I want in every aspect of my life, but the only thing I'm sure of is that I want you."

"Well, I don't want you," I lie. I can't handle this. It feels like too much. I must be dreaming, because there's no way in hell this is actually happening.

He scoffs as he comes over to me, his hands finding my waist as he pulls me closer. "You're lying, Ella. I can see it all over your face. You forget how good I am at reading every single part of you, even the parts you hide from everyone else."

I shake my head. "Leo—"

"Am I truly that bad? Truly so awful that you would lie and pretend like you don't feel this pull too?" His hands snakes up to my throat, and my head lifts to welcome it. Stupid fucking force of habit. "Even your body remembers how much it loves me, darling."

"Stop, Leo. My feelings aren't some fucking joke you can throw around whenever you choose." I loosen from his hold.

"This isn't a joke, Ella! Nothing about what I'm feeling is a joke, and I'm over here hanging by a goddamn thread waiting to hear how you feel about me." He kneels in front of me. "You're all that's been on my mind night and day since you walked out of the restaurant. My heart is in your hands. Please, free me from this grasp you have on me if you don't feel the same way."

My hands rest on his shoulders, his body keeping me upright as his words filter through my ears. "You drive me crazy, Leo. With your stupid fucking smirk, your perfect hair I want to run my hands through, all of it. You've been a thorn in my side since I took that shot from whatever girl you were trying to send it to."

"I'm the luckiest bastard in the world that the bartender gave it to you instead."

"Don't say that," I tell him.

"It's the fucking truth, Ella! Now, you need to tell me the truth: do you love me? Yes or no?"

"Leo—"

"It's a simple question, Ella. Yes or no!"

It bursts out of me before I can stop it. "Yes! I do!" He stands back up, the two of us now chest to chest. "I love you, you ass! And it pisses me off because I swore for so long I would never end up in this situation with you, yet here we are!"

"Give me all of it, Ella. Lay it all out," he coaxes me, his smile spreading from ear to ear.

"I used to hate needing people. I used to think I could go through life all on my own without needing help, and then you decided to come along. For some reason, these past few months, I've started to run toward you, rely on you, and it pisses me off you were able to break down my walls so effortlessly. I thought I was stronger, but somewhere along the way, you became my person instead of the pain in the ass I always thought you were."

"Keep going."

"At some point, I started to see the real you, not the version I had created in my head, and in his place was someone who reminded me of myself. Someone who wanted to be loved without asking. Someone who wanted to take care of me because, my whole life, all I've done is take care of everyone else."

"And I'm that person for you, Ella?"

I smile at him, my body feeling lighter after my admission. "Yes, you are. I can't believe I'm admitting this, but I love you, Leo. So fucking much, it scares the crap out of me."

He cups my face. "It scares the hell out of me too, darling. But nothing could have stopped me from falling for you like I did, and I'm so fucking thankful you feel the same way."

My smile takes over my face as I settle into his embrace. I feel safe here. Loved. Wanted. Not just for who I am, but for who he sees me to be. "If you don't kiss me in the next two seconds—"

"Always so fucking bossy, Ella," he says as he captures my lips with his. This kiss is unlike any other ones we've had. It's consuming. It's loving. It's *perfect*, and he deepens it as if he never wants to let go.

I don't want him to. I want to get lost in him for the rest of my life; if I told myself that a few months ago, I'd have laughed.

But now, I'm sure wherever the future takes us, Leo will be by my side for all of it.

"You broke one of our rules, you know," he says between kisses.

I smack his arm. "So did you!"

"Well, you broke it first by falling for me, so does that mean I won?"

I roll my eyes at him. "I wasn't aware we were competing." I grab his head and bring his mouth back to mine.

"You're right, darling. You win," he says as he grabs my shirt and starts to undo it. "How about I make it up to you with a few orgasms?"

"Well, it is the *least* you could do," I say as I smile, and for the rest of the night, Leo and I get lost in one another as we whisper sweet nothings through soft kisses.

It's the best night ever, and all my worries fly out the window when I wake up to his arms around me, my head on his chest as I feel him breathing steadily.

And just like that, the two of us have reconciled. We're on a new path forward—one filled with love, laughter, and lots of mind-blowing sex, just like it's supposed to be.

43

Quite A Show

WHEN MY EYES FLUTTER open the next morning and Leo's body is still next to mine, I smile. It's a real smile; I'm happy, truly happy, for the first time in a long time, despite the past few months feeling like they would never end.

I shift to grab my phone like I always do when I wake up, only for Leo's arms to wrap around my waist and pull me back into him.

I don't stop the giggle that comes out; I can't. I'm too damn happy he's here with me.

"Where do you think you're going?" He nips at my ear. "Trying to sneak off and leave me already?"

"I would *never* do that."

"You little liar," Leo chuckles. "After we had sex for the first time, you bolted so fast, I woke up without you."

I roll my eyes, but he can't see it. "I bet you missed me."

"I didn't back then, but I would now."

I turn my head to face his. "You would?"

"Did you forget all the shit I said last night already? Oh, darling, we must work on that memory of yours. If I'm that forgettable—"

I lightly smack his arm. "You're not, Leo. This new dynamic is going to take some getting used to."

"I know, love, but it's going to be fine," he tells me. "Do you need your phone to tell your friends about us? You know as well as I do none of them are going to be surprised. I, for one, would love to hear what Grant thinks—"

I put my hand over his mouth. "I think we need to worry about your sister first. She might not be up, so if you want to sneak out now, you can."

"Shit, you're right," he says as he gets out of bed, throwing his clothes on. "I can come over later, and we can tell her together."

I smile. *Together.* "That sounds good."

I grab my pajamas from the floor and throw them back on before Leo and I huddle behind my door. He presses a kiss to my lips before he steps out, quietly padding across the small hallway between his old room and mine before a voice permeates my ears.

"You two put on quite a show last night, I must say." Alissa sips from her mug as she looks between us, a huge smile on her face. "It felt like I had my own version of reality television in my flat!"

"Shit," is all Leo can say.

"Hi, Liss," I say, feeling like I've been caught doing something I shouldn't have.

"It's about damn time you two got together. I swear, Grant, Paige, and I have been waiting for this to happen since Halloween."

"What? I thought you were drunk on Halloween?"

Alissa cocks her head at me. "Not this year. The one at Grand Mountain. You two trying to kill one another is practically foreplay. It was bound to happen." She shifts her gaze to her brother. "And don't think I didn't notice how you looked at her in London."

"So, you're not mad?" Leo questions his sister.

"Why would I be mad?"

"Because I'm shagging your best friend and roommate?"

She sets her mug down on the table. "Just don't hurt her, or I'll have to punch you." She stands from the couch before heading to the kitchen. "Do you guys want some food? Tea?"

I don't know why I expected Alissa to react similarly to Hads when she found out about Oliver and Paige, but that situation was far more tense than Leo and me. At least there's no dead bodies.

"Sure, Liss," I say as I sit on one of our stools. "I could use some coffee."

Leo takes over and starts making my coffee for me, just how I like it, and I smile, loving that he knows how I take it. I really underestimated him before, and I hate that it took me so long to see the kind of guy he really is.

Perfect—for me, at least. Attentive as fuck and sweet. Leo Zimmerman is a sweet guy.

"Here, darling," Leo says as he slides the mug I always use in the mornings toward me.

"What are you guys going to do about work? Unless you no longer work together. It's been a hectic few weeks," Liss says as she grabs some stuff from the fridge to make avocado toast for the three of us.

"I haven't really thought that far ahead," I say, my voice defeated. "I haven't been liking work lately with the whole Brody situation."

Leo's eyes narrow at me. "I could try to find another job—or beat the shit out the guy so he doesn't say anything."

I smile at him willing to do all that for me. "No, babe, it's okay. I think..." I trail off, the thought in my head but unsure if I want to say it out loud.

"Why don't you work with authors full-time, Ells? I know you love it, and it would all be on your terms. You'd be your own boss. Doesn't that sound perfect?" Alissa asks me.

I sigh heavily. "I've been thinking about it, but it doesn't bring in that much money yet. It's enough to cover rent and such, but I worry about all the other expenses. What if—"

Leo's hands wrap around my waist as I feel him come behind me. "You're insanely talented, Ella. Any author out there would be lucky to work with you."

"You guys are disgusting, but he's right," Alissa says as she mashes an avocado. "You have lots of connections already, Ella. Imagine what you could do working on it full-time." She throws me a wink.

"I guess I could do it, but is it right to leave Loft Media after all the years I've put in? Could I do that?" It terrifies me to jump into the unknown, unsure if it will actually work. If it doesn't, I would be out of money, a job, and I don't know what would happen. That's terrifying.

But I would love my job again instead of hating going into work every single day...

"You can do whatever is best for you, Ella. That's all that matters," Alissa says as she plates our breakfast for us.

"But what about rent? And what if my car breaks down and I can't pay for it? Or what if my dad needs help with—"

Leo spins me around on the stool. "Darling, breathe for me."

"Okay," I say as I take a few deep breaths. "Sorry."

"Don't apologize, Ells. It's scary, but I believe in you. The work you put out is good, and you know the trends from working in marketing your entire adult life."

I look up at Leo leaning against the kitchen island. "And what will you do?"

"I'm going to stay and ruin the fucker." He smiles. "Brody is a terrible person, and I'm sure I can fuck with him a little without getting fired."

"If anyone can, it's you, brother." She smirks at him. "I did grow up with you, and you're a menace when you want to be."

"Oh, I'm well aware of that," I smile.

"Will you two hush up and listen to me for a second?" Leo drags a hand through his hair. "Ella, you're insanely talented, and if you need some help with your rent, I can cover it."

"But—"

"I know you hate taking money from people, but it's only a last resort because, knowing you, you have enough money saved—you've probably been thinking about doing this for forever. Am I right?"

I say nothing because he already knows he's right. I've always had a safety net of money saved up that I haven't touched. I started it when I was young, as my *just in case* fund, and thankfully, I've never needed to touch it.

But maybe I could use it to sustain me until business picks up.

No, not maybe. This *is* what I've always wanted to do, and I'm going to do it.

"Okay. I'll turn my two weeks in on Monday." Oddly enough, I'm going to miss this job, but it hasn't been bringing me anything but stress lately. I'm not happy there; I'm comfortable.

But now, heading into this new chapter, I feel better already.

I'm paving the path I've wanted to walk down since I was young, and I don't feel guilty about it. I only feel excitement about what's to come.

"You're going to be amazing, Ells." Alissa smiles at me before biting her toast.

Leo leans down to hug me from behind again. I never expected him to be this touchy in a relationship, but I like it. "I'm so proud of you, Ella."

I smile, loving this man who nuzzles his head into my neck before kissing the top of my forehead and sitting next to me.

And for the rest of the morning, I hang out, laugh, and smile with my best friend and my boyfriend as we chat and live our lives together.

Best morning ever.

44

You're Learning Already

"Darling, will you breathe? It's going to be fine. It's just your family." I try to grab her hand, but she's wiping her palms on her skirt.

"Says you, Leo. You're the one who lit a stress cigarette earlier." I can only nod, because she's right. I'm nervous to meet her family for the first time, but from what I know about them, I'm sure it will be a fine night. Ella hates when I smoke, so she grabbed it from me and stomped on it before we got into my car.

Her mum isn't around anymore—at least not as much as she was a few months ago—and I'm glad all that has been sorted. I know how much it weighed on Ella, and I'm glad to see the happiness back on her face.

I'm glad to see her glowing like she used to, and I can't believe this beautiful, powerhouse of a woman is mine to kiss whenever I want. I grab her hand as I turn onto her street, pressing a kiss to her knuckles to try and calm her nerves.

She's calming mine just by being next to me.

I park the car and swing around to open her door for her.

"Leo, I can do it myself," she says, grabbing the dessert she made for tonight.

"I know you can, but it doesn't mean you have to." This girl will never *not* argue with me, and I *love* it. I crave it. "I love how independent you are, but you can let me help you sometimes. I *am* your boyfriend."

She only rolls her eyes at me. "If you must, then I can't stop you." I follow her to the door, my hand behind her back the entire time in case she slips. It's a bit icy out; December in Virginia is a bitch and a half weather-wise.

Ella opens the door to her house and, instantly, I'm hit with a warm familiarity. This place *feels* like a home, not just a house.

It reminds me of my home back in England, and I make a mental note to call our parents tomorrow before the new year. We talk every day now, but I still miss them. It was another adjustment, being so far apart again. I'll never get used to it.

And they keep asking me about Ella. We had a call with them a few days ago, when I formally introduced her as my girlfriend, and it wasn't as bad as I thought it would be. They welcomed her with open arms, especially after she dropped everything and came to England with us when Dad wasn't doing well.

They've loved her ever since, and she finally got to meet my father. They clicked instantly, and I went to sleep that night with a huge smile on my face and her tucked into the side of me.

"Dad? Lizzie?"

"In the kitchen, Ells!" I hear a voice say.

I follow her, taking off my shoes and leaving them at the door. When we get into the kitchen, Ella immediately steps into action and starts stirring things. I'm unsure of what to do, so I stand in the doorway and try not to look like I'm freaking out.

I've never met a girlfriend's family before. In fact, I've never really *dated* anyone, at least not as seriously as this current situation.

Her sister wraps her arms around her, a huge smile on her face, before Ella hugs her dad and then turns back to me.

"This is Leo, my boyfriend," Ella says with a smile, and I reach my hand out for her father to shake.

"It's nice to meet you guys. Ella doesn't stop talking about you both."

Her dad smiles at me, shaking my hand before her sister holds hers out to me too.

"I'm Lizzie, but you can call me Elizabeth." Her stern expression makes my mouth turn up.

"Nice to meet you, Elizabeth."

"Lizzie, don't."

Her eyes narrow at me. "I'm just making sure he knows his place."

Yup, they're definitely sisters. "Believe me, Ella reminds me every single day."

Ella rolls her eyes as she takes in the kitchen. "What can I help with?"

"Take over for me if you can." Her father looks toward me before he speaks again. "Can we have a talk away from the girls?"

"Dad…" Ella warns.

"It's fine, darling," I tell her. "I'll follow you, sir."

"Good man," he says as he walks past me into the living room. He sits on the couch, and I sit across from him in a chair.

Neither of us speaks for a few minutes, and I shift in my seat, uncomfortable because I don't know what he wants to chat about and nervous for what he's going to say.

Ella told me a lot about her childhood; we laid everything out on the table one night when we stayed up chatting. She told me all about what happened at Thanksgiving and why she came to my flat.

I know all she has had her entire life is her father and her sister, and I'm really scared he won't like me. Mostly everyone does when they meet me, but Ella's father? I wouldn't be surprised if he didn't like me.

"Do you realize how big of a night this is?" he asks me, his voice serious and tense.

"Yes, sir, I do."

"No, I don't think you do, son, so I'm going to tell you." He leans forward as he speaks. "My daughter can be stubborn, and I guess she gets that from me. She doesn't let people in very often, but when she does, it's special. Do you realize how special it is that you're here right now? That she let you in enough to bring you here?"

"I know how special your daughter is, sir. She might be a tough nut to crack, but I do know how huge this is. I've known her for a long time."

He only nods at me.

"You've raised a wonderful daughter, sir."

"That's nice of you to say." He pauses to put his arm on my shoulder. "Ella has one of the biggest hearts I know, and she's kept it to herself for most of her life, always worrying about everyone else. All she's done is look out for her sister and me, especially when her mom left."

"All I want to do is take care of her—if she lets me." Which she has over the past week. She's slowly becoming more dependent on me; I never want her to lose her independence, because it makes her who she is, but I want her to know I'll always be here for her.

"Good, because if you fuck this special thing up, I might have to hurt you."

I smile to myself. "I'm sure her sister will also be first in line, sir."

He can only laugh. "Good man. You're learning already."

"Dad?" I hear Ella yell from the kitchen. "Tell me Leo's still alive out there, please."

The two of us laugh as we rejoin them in the kitchen, and Ella sighs with relief. *Did she really think he would send me running?*

"Now, how can I help?" I ask as I roll my sleeves up. Ella smiles at me before putting me to work.

I can't wait for more nights like this with her by my side.

I never thought the two of us would end up here, but I wouldn't change anything about our story. We've seen the messiest parts of one another, yet we still found each other amidst it all.

I guess hope really isn't that dangerous of a thing if it's what got me to Ella. All I feel about our collective future is hope that it'll be messy, fun, and everything the two of us deserve.

45

A Metaphor Of Sorts

New Years Eve

I'm scrambling to get everything set up perfectly before I hear a knock on my door.

Shit, they can't be here already, can they?

"One second!" I yell to whoever is behind the door.

"Babe, open up."

Ella. "Oh, thank fuck," I say as I slide across the floor and open the door to my flat. Ella's beautiful face is my saving grace right now. "I don't know how you make it all look perfect."

"Why are you freaking out?"

"Because this is my first time hosting something with our friends!"

She gives me a weird look. "You know it's only *at* your place, right? I literally bought all the decorations and shit."

"Yes, but it's at *my* place! I want it to be perfect."

Ella only sets her bags down on my table, walks over to me, puts a cigarette in my mouth, and takes out a lighter. "Just calm down and let me do what I do best, okay?"

The cigarette hangs from my mouth as I smirk at my beautiful girlfriend. "I thought you hated when I smoked?"

"I do, but one isn't going to kill you, and you need to relax and get out of my way."

I cock my brow at her. "There are other things we could do to relax," I say as I wrap my arms around her and pull her hair.

"As much as I would love to," she lights my cigarette for me, "we do not have time for that. They'll be here in an hour."

"Then put me to work, darling," I say as I take a drag.

Half an hour later, Ella has transformed my once drab flat into a sea of streamers, balloons, a bunch of champagne, and about every snack food you could ever want.

Even though it's just her friends and my sister coming over to ring in the new year, Ella has pulled out all the stops.

I truly don't know how she does it.

"You might be the best party host I've ever seen," I tell her as we sit and snack.

"Yes, well, I'm an expert, not an amateur like you."

"I am *not* an amateur. I'm just a bit rusty."

"Rusty?" She cocks her head at me, a challenge on her face. *Jesus, she's fucking beautiful when she's annoyed at me.* "All you did was hang one streamer and set off two party poppers!"

"And I did it well, didn't I?" I laugh as she grabs a pillow to hit me, only to stop when someone knocks on my door. "I'll grab that, darling."

"We might as well go together," she says as she gets up. "What kind of host would I be if I didn't greet my guests at the door?"

The two of us saunter over to the door, and I already have a guess who's behind the door.

"Oh my goodness, aren't you two just the cutest!" Paige exclaims as the door swings open. Oliver is being typical Oliver and standing behind her with his usual facial expression.

Paige throws her arms around Ella and they hug while Oliver and I shake hands.

"Come on in, you guys," I say as I step into my place.

"God, I'll never get over that accent," I hear Paige whisper.

"Me neither, babe," Ella whispers back.

These girls might be a little crazy, but I love their relationship. You can tell it's special, and I know Ella spent the entirety of book club last week talking more about us than the book.

I don't mind at all, though. I'm just glad there's finally an *us* to talk about.

The girls head to the living room as Oliver pulls me aside in the kitchen.

"What's up, mate?" *Is he about to kill me right now?* I've heard rumors...

"I'm pre-apologizing for when Grant gets here."

I wait for him to say he's joking around, but he doesn't elaborate. "Why?"

"He's probably going to ask if you want to take a blood oath as the newest member of the boyfriends of book club."

"I'm sorry, the what?"

"I'll let him explain, but this is your formal warning," Oliver says as more knocks hit my door.

"I'll grab it, Ella," I say as she and Paige continue to chat on the couch. I swing the door open to find Hads, Grant, and my sister.

"I ran into them in the car park," Alissa tells me, a big smile on her face.

"Man, isn't language so cool?" Grant says as he smiles and walks into my place. Hads stops me and holds out something.

"It's banana bread, a new recipe I tried. Where should I put it?"

Before I can answer, my sister does. "Follow me, Hads. I'll show you."

"Thanks, sis," I say as I close my door. Everyone is officially here, and my palms have started sweating—I want tonight to be perfect. I know these guys are my friends too, but that doesn't stop my nerves.

I want tonight to be perfect; not just for me, but for Ella. For *us*.

"Psst," I hear someone say as I walk back into my flat. "Over here."

Grant shifts behind the bathroom just off my living room, and I turn to see Oliver shaking his head, already annoyed at whatever's going on.

"Both of you, come here." Grant pokes his head back out before Oliver and I make our way into the bathroom. He shuts the door and locks us all in here, turning the lights off as he turns his flashlight on. "Have either of you done this before?"

"You are spending way too much time with Paige lately, Grant. It's starting to show."

"Oliver! I told you we were going to do this when it wasn't just us two! And now it's not," Grant says as he pulls out a pocket knife. "Who's first?"

"Is this really necessary?" I ask, a bit in fear for my life in my voice.

"What a great question, Leo." Grant smiles at me.

"It's not," Oliver deadpans.

"Oliver! Why are you always trying to ruin my fun?"

He cocks his head at Grant. "Because I'm terrified of Ella if we happen to hurt her perfect boyfriend."

"Perfect, huh?" I smile to myself. "Did you actually hear her say that?"

Oliver shakes his head. "Sorry, dude."

"Damn," I say under my breath. I would have loved to have gotten that on tape or something.

"So, are we doing this or not?" Grant asks us, his face way too excited for someone asking us to take some sort of blood oath. "We have to do it before—"

A few knocks on the door make him pause. "Guys, what are you doing in there?" Hads asks.

"You don't think they're measuring, do you?" Paige asks, and I start to laugh.

"I wouldn't be surprised, if I'm being honest," Ella says. "Can you guys put your dicks away and come join the party?"

Grant sighs heavily before he turns the light back on and opens the door. "Why did you have to ruin the initiation ceremony, baby? I told you to give me fifteen minutes when we got here!"

Hads rolls her eyes. "I never said I agreed to your plan, Grant. Actually, I believe what I said was that this was insane."

"Thank you!" Oliver says as he walks out of the bathroom. "Love, stop talking to Grant about blood oaths."

"I only mentioned it a few times!" she exclaims, a huge smile on her face as Oliver presses a short kiss to her forehead.

Ella comes over to me, nestling her body in mine as she checks my hands for signs of a cut. "Grant didn't slash you, did he?"

"No, my perfect face is just fine," I smirk.

"Whatever, weirdo. Can you grab the slips for charades?"

I press a kiss to her lips before I head to the kitchen and grab what she needs. I also bring some snacks into the living room in case anybody wants them.

"We have an odd number, so someone might have to—"

"I'm fine sitting out," Alissa says, a glass of wine already in her hand. "It's been a long day."

"Okay, perfect," I tell everyone. "Ella, do you want to pick first?"

As Ella and I pick our teams, I can already feel the competitive energy pick up in my place.

Team Ella consists of Grant and Paige.

I've got the other siblings, Hads and Oliver.

I'm already worried Ella is going to win, but I'm not going down without a fight.

"Okay, it's a movie," I say, on the edge of the couch. I *have* to win, and my team has been helping me a lot, but Leo's team is close to us in points. I thought for sure Oliver wouldn't be of any help, but he has been doing surprisingly well.

It's too bad I have to crush them.

"Four syllables," Paige says next to me.

Grant is playing in front of us, and if we win this, we win the game. He starts to fiddle with his hair, making it seem like wind or something. I honestly have no idea. It looks like he's throwing dice, as if he's at a casino.

"*Oceans 11*?"

He shakes his head at my guess and changes the way his body moves, but I'm still confused.

"It's *Ratatouille!*" Paige shouts, and Grant nods his head.

"Yes!"

"Ah!" I get up and hug him, Paige joining a few seconds later. "We won!"

"Sorry, Leo," Grant says, and I smack him.

"It's alright, mate. Ella isn't the type to let me win anyway," he smirks before sipping his drink.

"Exactly." I smile as I check the time. "Oh, shit. We have like ten minutes until the clock strikes midnight. I'm going to go grab the champagne."

I saunter toward Leo's kitchen, grabbing the champagne from the ice pail and shaking off the condensation as two arms wrap around me from behind.

"I'll grab the glasses if you pour," Leo says into my ear.

I smile to myself. "Okay." He heads to his cabinets and grabs a few, setting them gently on the counter. "Don't forget Oliver and Paige aren't having any, so can you grab the sparkling juice?"

"I know, darling," he says, looking at me as I start to pop it, careful to not let it fly anywhere.

As I pour the glasses for each of us, I'm all too aware of Leo's eyes on me the entire time. I've always been able to do that—tell when he's looking at me. Even when I hated him, I was always aware of his eyes.

"Can I help you or are you going to stare at me all night?"

He sighs heavily. "Can't I just look at my gorgeous, sexy girlfriend without being berated for it?"

"You should know nothing with me ever comes easily."

"Well—"

I pin his eyes with a stare. "Don't even, Zimmerman."

He throws both of his hands up in defeat. "Woah, not the surname, Ella. I thought we were past that."

I throw him a wink as I fill the glass.

"Here I was, thinking we could have a nice conversation before we ring in our first new year together."

"Well, that can still happen," I say as I look at him across the table. "What did you want to talk about?"

He says nothing before he slides a small key toward me.

"What's this?"

"A key."

I roll my eyes. "Well, duh. But why are you giving it to me?"

He slides around the table and joins me by my side. "I'm not giving it to you, Ella."

"I'm so confused right now," I say as I face him, holding the key up. "Elaborate, or I'm shoving this somewhere you'll never be able to get it out from."

He only laughs at me. "It's a metaphor of sorts." He reaches out and takes it from me. "It's the key to my flat. Now, it's yours."

"Leo, I told you—"

"I know you love living with my sister, Ells," he tucks a stray piece of my curly hair behind my ear, "but when you're ready, you'll always have a place here waiting for you."

"Hence the metaphor, I see."

"Exactly, darling. I didn't want to pressure you because this is still very new and I could piss you off in eighty different ways tonight alone."

"True." I smirk at him.

"However, I wanted to extend the option for when you're ready. Like I said, this is all on your own terms, but I'd love to have you in my bed every single night. I'd love nothing more than you putting your own spin on this place decor wise."

I take a long look around his apartment I once called a bachelor pad when I helped Alissa move him into this place. "It could use a woman's touch."

He presses a kiss to my forehead. "Not a woman's touch, Ella. Yours. That's the only one I want in the place I call home." Then, he reaches behind me, grabs the champagne flutes, and heads into the living room, leaving me speechless in his kitchen.

I love living with Alissa, and eventually, I do want to live with Leo and create our own corner of the world. But I can only do so much at a time. Adding an entire move on to my already full plate would be too much.

And just because I'm capable of handling so many different things at once doesn't mean I *have* to. It's been a slow and steady process, but I know, eventually, I'll get better at relying on other people to help me when I need it.

Before I head back into the living room and ring in the new year with my favorite people, I send a group message to my *other* favorite people.

> **Ella: Happy almost New Year! I miss you two.**

> **Dad: Happy New Year, Bug. Here's to brighter days and clearer skies for 2025.**

> **Lizzie: Happy New Year! I love you, sis.**

> **Dad: Thanks for bringing Leo around yesterday. It was nice meeting him.**

> **Lizzie: He's even cuter than you described...**

> **Ella: Thank you for not scaring him off.**

> **Dad: That was meant for you, Liz.**

Lizzie: I was perfectly nice!

Ella: Sure, sis. Be safe at your party tonight. If you need me to pick you up, I can.

Lizzie: I'm sleeping over, Ells. But thank you.

Dad: Have a good night, girls.

Lizzie: I love you, Dad.

Ella: I love you guys.

My mom hasn't reached out in a while, and it's safe to assume she isn't around anymore, which is for the better. My sister and I haven't needed her since she walked out the first time.

As I throw my phone into the pocket of my skirt, I head to join my chosen family waiting for the clock to strike midnight, the group of us huddled around Leo's television.

"Here, darling," Leo says as he hands me my drink, and just as the clock is about to hit two minutes, Paige clinks her drink and clears her throat. We all turn our attention to her as she steps in front of us.

"I wanted to make a toast," she says, her voice already tight with emotion. There's always something so sad about a new year. In a way, I never thought this year would go how it did, but I wouldn't change any of it for the world.

This year brought growth, scary moments, new adventures, risks, loss, and, best of all, love. I can almost *feel* the love blanketing this room. With these people, I feel safe, feel like myself. They'll love me no matter what.

Because that's what friends do. They stay when you want to run. They love you even when you feel like you can't love yourself. Whenever I feel like too much, I know they'll smack some sense into me and remind me how much they love me.

Paige's voice surprises me with what she says next. "To new beginnings," she starts, and Grant cheers. "And to Ella, because without her, none of us would be here."

I feel my eyes start to fill with tears as everyone repeats what she said and takes a drink. "What?"

"Well, it's true, isn't it?" Paige smiles at me. "Our book club would be nonexistent if you didn't talk to me that day in the library."

Two tears fall as I think back to the day I walked up to Paige in the library. "I've never thought of it like that."

"Well, we have," Hads says. "If you hadn't done that, I don't know if we would have ended up here."

I smile as I hug the two of them, a little champagne spilling from my flute. "We absolutely would have found one another if that didn't happen."

"I second that," Grant says with a smile.

"Me too," Oliver says.

"Because what would life be like without the book club?" Leo smirks as he wraps his arms around me, the ten-second countdown beginning.

As the clock strikes midnight and we cheer in the new year, Leo's lips against mine, I say a silent prayer to whoever is listening to let this moment last forever.

I'll never tell him, but Leo's right. What *would* life be like without the book club?

I sure as hell never want to find out.

Epilogue

A Serial Killer

September 2025

"CAN YOU BELIEVE YOU'RE getting married this week, Paige?" I ask as I plop down on her bed, the four of us girls gathered on her king-sized bed together.

Her face lights up, the happiness radiating off her body in waves at the thought of marrying Oliver. I couldn't be happier for one of my best friends, and it's insane to think she's the first one of us to get married.

Hads and Grant would have been, but they've taken the long engagement route. I'm sure they'll set a date at some point, but for now, they're enjoying the new nicknames they call one another.

Even Ames is here. She finally showed up and managed to get her shit together. I told her when we started all this bachelorette stuff that if she ruined this week for Paige, I'd kill her. To my surprise, she's on her way to mending the trust she broke, apologizing and proving to the three of us she can show up for us.

Let's hope she doesn't ghost us like she did last time.

I'd like to believe she won't, since she's actually trying, but she still has a long way to go before she gains my trust back. But for Paige's sake, I'm being as nice as I can.

"It almost feels like a dream," Paige tells us. "I don't think I ever want to wake up if it is."

Hads grabs her hand. "It's not a dream, babe. I still can't believe you're marrying my brother."

"You guys will be *actual* sisters now." Ames smiles. "Poor Grant has to deal with Oliver being his brother, though."

Hads only rolls her eyes as she throws her arms around P. "Nobody is more excited than me that Paigey is joining my family."

I get off the bed and grab a few snacks, throwing them in the middle of the small circle we've made on Paige's bed. It reminds me of all the times back in college when we used to sit on the floor of someone's apartment or dorm in this same way.

God, that feels like forever ago, and I have half a mind to curse out whoever is making time go so fucking fast.

Paige is getting married. *Married.*

And Leo and I haven't killed one another yet—in fact, we're still as strong as ever. We still argue and bicker how we used to, but at the end of each night, we end up in bed together. That's the only difference. Now, we fight *with* one another, not against each other.

I couldn't be happier.

Ever since I made the jump into my new career, life has been booming for me. I never thought what I do now—work with authors and shout about their books—would be something I could make work.

I never should have doubted myself—because I can do anything I set my mind to—but the fact that I'm actually happy working every single day is the *best* feeling ever. Leo is still at my old job, in Brody's position, since he got caught stealing money under the table from clients. Brody was fired, and Leo took over his role and had to clean up the mess he left behind.

And he did it wonderfully. Business is booming again, and the two of us are happy with what we've chosen to do with our lives. Leo even has a pansexual pride flag on his desk at work. He bought one because, apparently, he still wants a piece of me in the office.

It's the cutest thing someone has ever done for me.

Speaking of Leo, he's currently with the boys celebrating Oliver in...some way. I have no idea what Grant has planned, but I can almost guarantee Oliver is going to hate most of it. The dude just wants to make Paige his wife, and I know he's suffering through all these activities for her.

He'd do anything for the girl, and that's how I know the two of them will live a long and beautiful life together.

"So, I know this trip is supposed to be about me, but I think we should make a toast to the book club," Paige says. "We should have a little drink before dinner."

"Yeah, that's a good idea," I say, walking to the main area of the hotel room, only to find the champagne *not* on ice. I poke my head back into the room. "How about we drink while we get ready? That should give it time to get cold."

"Shit, did I forget to grab ice?" Hads asks me.

"It's fine, babe," I tell her. "I'll run and grab some. You three stay put and throw some music on or something. I'll be right back, and then we're all getting dressed and looking hot to meet the boys at dinner, okay?"

"It feels like college all over again," Ames says, her voice low. "Except now, you're getting married."

Paige grabs her hand, squeezing it. "It'll be okay, Ames. We have plenty of time to catch up."

"We have our entire lives together, you psychos. Stop making me want to cry," Hads jokes, and I laugh.

"I'll be two seconds," I say as I grab the ice bucket from the counter and grab my key to leave.

"Ella!" someone shouts, and I run back to the bedroom.

"What? Are you guys okay?"

Paige eyes me curiously. "Room key?" she questions, and I can't believe I almost forgot to show it to her before I left. It's something we always do when we stay places so we don't get locked out of our room. You can never be too careful.

I lift it up, showing all three of them before she nods at me. "Good."

"You know we can just open the door for her," Ames says.

"I know, but it's better to be safe than sorry. What if there was a serial killer staying on this floor?" Paige asks, entirely serious.

Hads only sighs as she runs a hand down her face. "That would only happen to you of all people, Paige."

"I'm not an idiot. I would obviously throw a bunch of ice at this person and book it the fuck out of there," I say as I leave the room and head to the ice machine near the lobby.

I could have gone to the one on our floor, but I want to grab something sweet for all the girls. There's truly nothing better in life than eating a sweet treat, drinking, and listening to music while you get ready with all your friends.

The elevator dings, and I grab the things I need before I fill the ice bucket for our champagne. Then, I head back to the elevator, finding some guy standing in front of it, though he hasn't pressed the button.

I sigh heavily before I press it, holding all my shit in my hands as I do, and when the candy I bought falls from my arms, the robot next to me finally moves to help.

"Shit, I'm so sorry. I'm kind of in a weird fog—"

A familiar face meets mine, and he has to recognize me, because his entire face drops in surprise.

"Henry?"

He looks exactly the same as he did back in college, just older. He has the same wire-framed glasses and build. His face looks exactly like it did when Amelia left him standing in the airport after breaking his heart.

"Hey, Ella." He rubs his hands on his shorts, clearly nervous. "I'm sorry I didn't press the button. I feel...weird."

"What are you doing here?" I ask, curious as to how he ended up where Paige and Oliver's wedding is taking place.

"Oliver invited me," he says, the elevator opening, his arm in front of him, as if he's telling me to go ahead. "Ladies first."

"Thanks," I say, confused as to what the fuck he's doing here. I might have to have a chat with Oliver, because what the fuck was he thinking? He knew Amelia was going to be here, didn't he?

What the actual fuck is going on?

"What floor?" he asks me, the button for ten already pushed.

"Ten."

He only nods at me. "Oh."

The ride to our floor is quiet, neither of us wanting to ask the questions on our minds. I'm sure he wants to ask me about Amelia, and I desperately want to ask him what the hell he's doing here, but neither of us says a word.

If anything, I need to talk to Oliver and Paige first. It's their wedding, and I would never tell them who to invite, but something else is going on here. This can't be a coincidence.

When we get off, Henry turns the opposite direction, and I practically book it back to the room, swinging the door open before I shove the champagne in the ice and burst into the bedroom.

They must notice something off on my face, because Hads comes over to me, but the only person I can look at is Amelia.

"Did something happen?" Hads asks me.

"Please tell me someone isn't dead again," Paige says. "I'd hate for this to be a theme."

My eyes are still on Ames. "Ella, what's wrong?" she asks me, and in a minute, I might be asking her the same thing.

"I-I just ran into someone in the lobby."

"Did the boys finally get here?" Hads asks me.

I nod. "Yes, but that's not who I'm talking about."

"Did you see an author or something? Oh my gosh, is Olivia Hart here? Or maybe it's that one hockey author we love?" Paige squeals as she continues to name our favorite authors.

"Why would any of them be in Virginia Beach, P?" Hads questions.

"I don't know! A girl can dream." She smiles.

"It was Henry."

All voices mute as soon as I say that, and I swear, I see Amelia's face go through eight different emotions before landing on one we've all seen before—fear.

"What?" she whispers. "H-Henry is here? Like, h-here, in this hotel?"

"Yes," I tell her, and before anyone can say anything else, she gets up. Just when I think she's going to throw up or something, she locks herself in the bathroom.

The three of us stay where we are, frozen in the memory of what happened when they fell apart that day at the airport, the day she ran away and we had no idea what was to come.

But then, we go over to the door. Paige leans against it while Hads and I stand next to her on either side.

"Ames? Are you okay?" Paige asks her.

"Did you know he was going to be here?" I ask her.

Her face turns red before she shakes her head. "No, I didn't."

"This has Oliver written all over it," Hads says. "He's always been a sneaky motherfucker, even as a kid."

"Amelia, you never did tell us what actually happened with you two," Paige says through the door.

"Now is as good of a time as any if you have to see him all week," I coax, trying to get her to talk to us instead of running away. "We're here for you."

We can all hear her pacing around the bathroom, but I don't think she's crying. This feels more like a freak out than anything else.

"Do you want me to get the prosecco?" Paige asks, and a few seconds later, the door swings back open.

Her face is red, her hair a mess, as if her hands were running through it. She's not breathing normally either.

"We're all going to need a drink."

"Why?" Hads asks.

"Because I'm going to tell you what happened."

And then she walks by all of us before jumping onto the bed face first and covering herself in a blanket.

This week is only getting started, and we've already been thrown for a loop.

Please let this wedding go smoothly, I say to whoever is listening, knowing they probably won't answer.

Because with Amelia and Henry facing one another again, who knows what could happen? All I know is, I'm going to try my hardest to make this week before Paige's wedding the best week of her life.

Fingers crossed I can actually make it fucking happen.

Extended Epilogue

Rivals To Lovers

April 2026

"WAIT, YOU GUYS ARE doing what?" Grant asks us, his face full of bewilderment as he looks between Ella and me.

"We're eloping," Ella says, kind of lying, since she has been planning this out since we all agreed to come to Vegas this April. It was mainly to celebrate Ella's birthday earlier in the month, but it's also a trip for all of us. Today is the last day, and when Ella came up with the itinerary for this week, she purposefully left the last day blank.

For our wedding.

The group of us plan a huge trip once a year, when all our schedules lineup the best, and this year, we chose Vegas.

The only thing we didn't tell our friends was that we planned on getting married while we're here. It's not a typical Vegas elopement with an Elvis impersonator and all that shit you see in movies, but an *actual* wedding.

The main reason we're doing this is because we've been to our fair share of weddings together, since most of us are now married. Paige and Oliver got married first, then Hads and Grant. Grant's friend Jack also got married, Amelia and Henry soon to follow. After the fourth or fifth wedding, Ella and I realized we didn't want this huge and flashy reception.

We just wanted to be one another's as soon as we could. Thus, the elopement.

We're not even worried about our families being here for this, since we planned ahead. When Alissa and I visit England in June, we're going to have a small ceremony and reception with them as well—Ella's father and sister included. I haven't told Ella yet, but I bought them tickets to come with us.

It's going to be perfect. Not only do we get to celebrate with our families for the first time ever, but we also get to get married in front of all our friends.

I spared no expense for Ella to have the wedding of her dreams, and every single dollar I spent was worth it.

The girls throw their arms around her as Oliver, Grant, and Henry come over to me, patting me on the back with smiles on their faces. Even Oliver has a smile. God, that son of a bitch has softened out immensely because of Paige.

"Can you guys help me get ready?" Ella asks them, her eyes misty as they continue to hug her.

"Of course we can!" Paige shouts before she throws her arms around me. "I'm so happy for you guys."

Grant hugs her as soon as she unwraps herself from me. "We totally called this, Paigey."

"I know!"

Hads smiles at the two of them. "I hate to break it to you, husband, but Paige was actually first."

I only cock my head at them. I distinctly remember both Paige and Grant shoving Ella and I together way back when.

"Don't you guys remember?" Hads asks the girls, and they all shake their heads. "We were at that party at the beginning of my sophomore year. Grant had just stopped flirting with me, and when I came back over to ask where Ella was—"

Amelia's eyes light up, as if she remembers. "Oh, yeah! She was arguing with Zimmerman about who knows what, and Paige told us she shipped them together."

I tilt my head at my soon-to-be-wife, remembering that night *very* well. She cornered me at the hockey house and spewed a bunch of bullshit. I think she just wanted to chat with me. This girl has had the hots for me since we first met—no matter how much she denies it.

"I don't remember that," Paige says. "But I am a genius, aren't I?" She looks at Oliver.

"You're the smartest, love," he says as he kisses her forehead.

"You don't remember because you were drunk after one drink," Hads smiles at her.

"Oh, that makes sense," she nods. "Ella, what time is this all happening?"

With that, Ella reaches into her purse and pulls out new itineraries for everyone. "It's our last night, and this is how we're making it count! So, everyone be ready by three!"

"Got it!" Paige says as she all but drags Ella into our bedroom while the guys and I remain in the main area of our hotel room. The eight of us all have adjoining rooms—our door leading into Hads and Grant's room. Amelia, Henry, Paige, and Oliver have their own connected room across the hall.

"I'll order some room service. Are you guys hungry?" I ask the guys as they all stare at me. "What?"

"Why don't you let us take care of that?" Grant says, taking the phone from me.

"Why?"

"Dude, it's your wedding day," Oliver pats my shoulder.

Henry sits next to me. "Let us take care of this, and you can relax and think about your wife in the other room."

Ella's going to look beautiful no matter what, I'm sure of it. She did forbid me from looking at her dress, but I'm sure it's going to be gorgeous. Ella has this annoying habit of looking astonishing in anything she wears. She'll say it's the clothes, but I say it's because of the girl wearing them.

"All I have to do is put my suit on and fix my hair," I tell them. "It's not too much, guys. I promise."

"Well, then you have to actually get married," Henry points out.

"That's the easy part." All three of them look at me like I'm insane. "What?"

"You'll absolutely have a freak out at some point today," Grant tells me.

"No, I won't."

"That's the exact same thing Oliver said." Grant smiles as he jams his elbow into Oliver's side. "And then he worried about the color tie he was wearing all fucking day. It was hilarious."

"Grant, you were the one who almost shaved your head before you walked down the aisle," Henry points out.

Oh, shit. I remember that. *Am I going to freak out*? I've known about this for months, and all I've felt is excitement, but these fuckers are making me second guess myself.

"It didn't look good enough! You know what? Save it, Hayes. When you get married, I guarantee you'll have some sort of stupid meltdown like we all did."

"Hey! I'm not a part of that statistic yet," I remind them.

"Just wait," Grant and Oliver both tell me.

About an hour later, as the four of us are sitting and watching a show, the food arrives, and the girls walk out of the room—half of their hair not done and only part of their makeup applied.

"You guys look..."

I cut Oliver off. "Beautiful. He was going to say beautiful."

"Well, duh," Hads says. "But you," she points at me, "can't see Ella until the ceremony. So, turn around."

"Is this really necessary?" I ask them.

"Just do it," Grant tells me, turning me around himself. "Come on out, Ells."

I hear her feet pad across the floor and, a few seconds later, I feel her press a kiss to my back before she retreats again. When the girls are gone, I turn back around to the three men staring at me. Grant looks enchanted at me—bit weird, but normal for him—and Henry and Oliver have normal expressions on their faces.

"Why don't you shower and then we can eat?" Henry says.

"Sounds good, mates," I say, and as I walk toward the other bathroom in the suite, I hear them whispering.

"He's totally going to flip out. We should place bets on what it'll be about now," Grant says. I don't stick around to hear what they say before I hop into the shower and prepare myself to marry the love of my life.

A Few Hours Later

As we all stand in the beautiful red rock canyon, the sun just starting to set in the sky, I can't help but feel a bit nervous.

Those fuckers have officially gotten into my head, and I can't help but turn to them as we wait for the ceremony to start. The girls are around the corner, waiting for the music to play.

I know elopements are usually spur-of-the-moment, but nothing about this is screaming elopement. This entire day was planned out by us over these past few months, but now, it all feels wrong. My suit feels itchy, and all I want to do is grab Ella and make her my fucking wife. I'm restless, and I can't bear another second of Ella not being my wife.

"Dude, are you good?" Oliver asks me, and I shake my head.

"She didn't run away, did she? Is she still around the corner?"

"Here's the freakout." Grant smiles. "Hads just texted me that she's scared as hell you won't be here when she turns the corner. God, you two are perfect for one another."

"I just want to see my wife," I tell them.

"Slow your roll there, dude. She's not your wife yet," Oliver says as I pin him with a glare.

"Can we just get this going?" I ask as Grant looks at the photographer. She signals for the music to start playing, and I suddenly feel better when I see the girls walking toward me a few moments later in what Ella picked out for them.

She didn't want to tip anyone off about our elopement, so we got all their measurements and picked out dresses they would all like. I did the same for the guys with suits. They offered to pay me back, but if they saw the price tags, they would take that kind sentiment back.

Plus, everyone needs at least one nice, expensive suit they can wear for things like this. I was basically doing them all a favor.

Then, the music switches to a song Ella and I both love—the instrumental version, of course—and I swear, my heart stops beating for a moment as I see her turn the corner and start to walk toward me.

She looks absolutely alluring, and I swear I have a hard time looking at her without thinking of the life we're going to create as husband and wife.

This girl holds the key to my heart, our future, and everything in between, and I cannot believe I get to call her mine.

Her dress is fucking gorgeous. It's a midi-dress, corseted in typical Ella fashion, sheer on top. The sleeves drape over her shoulders, her veil falling over her curly hair as she walks toward me, looking more beautiful than I could ever describe.

By the time she reaches me, I feel like I'm going to cry. I'm not an emotional person, but something about the scene in front of me, something about her, is making me emotional.

"Hi, darling," I say to her, and she smiles.

"Hi, Leo. Are you ready for this?"

"As ready as you are." I smile as I grab her hands in mine, needing to touch her. She grounds me in every moment when I feel overwhelmed, and today's no different.

The officiant goes through all the usual shit before he asks us to say our vows, and I go before Ella, since I know she loves having the last word—she has always been like that.

I grab mine from Grant before I clear my throat. "My darling Ella," I say as I try to make my voice less shaky. *Why the fuck am I so nervous?*

"I don't think I could love you more than I do now. I'm going to spend every second of our marriage proving to you that the easiest thing I've done in my life is love you."

A single tear falls from her eyes, and I already feel myself getting emotional as well.

"I know you worry about who you are sometimes, so I've decided to gather my own promises to you to go along with the usual ones—'til death do us part and all of that." I take a deep breath before speaking again. "I promise you'll never be too much for me. I promise you could never sparkle too much around me. In fact, I promise to pull more of that shine out of you when we're married. But I want you to think back to this moment when you feel like you're being too much."

She sniffles in front of me, tears falling from her beautiful eyes.

"You will always just be the right amount of everything for me, Ella. I'll spend every second of the rest of our lives reminding you that you are the most beautifully smart and amazing woman. If people say I'm a good man, it will be because of you. I love you, and I hope I piss you off for the rest of eternity and well after we're both gone."

I hand my papers back to Grant, tears on his cheeks, before I look back at my forever.

Paige hands her a few papers, wiping her tears and making sure her makeup is still intact. Ella takes a deep breath before she speaks. "Leo, I'm going to keep this short, because you know I always have a lot to say. When I sat down to figure out what to say to you in this moment, though, I could only think of one thing I wanted to tell you."

"And what is that?" I ask, a huge smile on my face.

"That you positively annoy the shit out of me most of the time." Everyone around us laughs. "There's nobody else I want to annoy me for the rest of my life. There's absolutely nobody else on this planet I want to ask for help when I need it."

The laughter has now turned to sniffles.

"And there's nobody else I want to run to when things get too tough. You may have started as someone I never envisioned being in my life, but you're ending as my husband. Leave it to us to make our relationship more complicated than it needed to be."

More laughter.

"I love you so much. I love you so much some days, I fear it might swallow me whole, but I know you'll pull me out if that happens, or you'd jump in and let it swallow both of us."

She folds her small paper and hands it to Paige, who pockets it.

Then, the officiant pronounces us husband and wife, and I kiss Ella with all the love that has been in my body since the day I saw her. All my emotions—the good, the bad, and the wonderful—leave my body, and when I pull back, I hear and see nothing but my wife.

My wife. God, that sounds fucking fantastic.

All I can see is her in front of me, the entire world ceasing to exist as I cup her face and kiss her again.

"I love you so much, Ella.""And to think, I swore I'd never reconcile with you way back when."

I smile at her, a laugh slipping from my mouth. "Rivals to lovers suits us, doesn't it?"

"It absolutely does, husband."

Acknowledgements

Being an author would not be my reality if I didn't have these amazing people around me.

Lexi and Hannah—my own version of the Grand Mountain book club. I'm so grateful that two years later you're both still here helping me tell these stories that are so near and dear to our hearts. Lexi, Ella is for you. I am so grateful you both exists and it has been an honor being able to *finally* bring her story to these pages. It took so much longer than I wanted, but I hope it was worth it. Thank you for everything you do behind the scenes to make each book perfect. Hannah, your covers just get better and better. I am so thankful for your creative, beautiful brain that somehow understands mine even with some of the incoherent messages I send you. I'm forever in awe of your designs. I can't wait to make a thousand more covers and doodles with you. I love you both so much. Only one more to go in Grand Mountain!

My alpha reader—Amy. THANK YOU! There are not enough words for me to explain how much I enjoyed your help making Alissa and Leo more British. Thank you for reminding me about correct terminology and giving me some insights on the language you use. I appreciate it so much. Leo and Alissa are for you, my girl.

My beta readers—Holly, Sarah, Soph, & Joana. Thank you all for making this story truly shine and for answering every insane comment I left for you guys on the doc. You guys were so helpful and I love any and all of the feedback you give me to ensure my characters and stories shine. Thank you all for your help.

Janisha Boswell—You already know I couldn't do this thing without you. For every chaotic voice note, for every text saying I want to quit, to every message about how terrible my first drafts are, you have kept me going. From across the pond, I love you. Somehow we're both authors and I struggle to find the words to what your friendship and sisterhood means to me.

My editor—Alexa, at The Fiction Fix. Thank you for always making my stories shine! Your excitement for future novels always makes me laugh, and I always love working with you.

Josh—For being the most supportive and loving guy I could ever ask for. Thank you for feeding me, reminding me to drink water, and for always boosting me up when I feel low. And thanks for reading the smut in my books early to make sure it's perfect. You are the reason I can write such swoon-worthy book boyfriends.

My readers—Thank you for bearing with me. I know this novel was supposed to come out way sooner, but somehow you all still stuck around while I veered slightly off course, so thank you. For sticking by me, for annotating my books, for sharing them on your accounts, and for talking about my stories. You'll never know what it means to me whenever I see my books on your posts next to authors I myself admire. I will always and forever fangirl over you guys.

To me in July of 2023 who never thought she could write this book—Look at you go, girl. I guess all it took was unemployment to write these two fiery, crazy characters who have office jobs. I'm proud of you for pushing through, and for not giving up when you wanted to so many times.

Also by Emily Tudor

The Hart Sisters
The Road Not Taken
The Road Less Traveled By

The Grand Mountain Series
Replaying the Game (Hads and Grant)
Redefining the Rules (Jacks and Claire)
Reconsidering the Facts (Paige and Oliver)
Reconciling With the Rival
Rewriting the Story (Coming soon...)

About the Author

Emily Tudor creates characters and stories about platonic and romantic love for anyone and everyone. She lives in the state of New York and loves listening to music and creating stories. She loves Marvel movies, the song *mirrorball* by Taylor Swift and buying too many books when she already has many to be read at home.

You can find her on Instagram at:
@authoremilytudor
www.authoremilytudor.com

* 9 7 9 8 9 8 9 6 6 3 4 2 2 *